# FOREVER SILENT

## MITRA LANGSETH

# ABOUT THE AUTHOR

Mitra Langseth was born and raised in Iran. She immigrated to the United States as an adult, where she taught herself to speak, read, and write in English.

# CHAPTER ONE

She sat staring at the powerful mountains filled with so many secrets. She always thought, "If they could only talk". This place was her little sanctuary, where she found peace and could sit back to fantasize. There was no one there to judge her for dreaming. The Rocky Mountains were her allies. She cherished her moments there, and trusted the rocks to never repeat her secrets. In this, her forbidden little hiding place, she was only a child, but had dreams of which she could never speak. Somehow she always lost time, forgetting who she was and dreaming about who she wanted to be. It was getting late, she had to finish washing the rest of the clothes in the little pond and hurry back to the village. She threw her clothes in the basket and began running toward the village. Her heart was pounding. "What am I going to tell mother for being late?" Her mind was searching for ideas, and her feet ran as fast as they could carry her, but then she was there before she could think of something. One look in her mother's face, and she knew that she was in trouble. Her mother grabbed her long braided black hair and yanked it with force. The young child gasped in pain that brought tears to her eyes. "This is the last time you are going to wash clothes outside the village. I can never trust you, Soraya."

At times she thought her mother didn't have a heart, even though she believed her punishments were justified.

"You better go wash your face and start helping me with dinner, we have guests coming over tonight."

She was reluctant to ask who was coming over but decided to find out anyway. "Who is coming for dinner?"

Her mother looked at her still in anger, and whispered, "Mullah and his family."

"What for?"

"They are coming over to talk about you marrying their son."

There was a pleasure in her voice as she said those words, knowing it would be the last thing Soraya wanted to hear. Her daughter had no desire to get married. She always thought her daughter was a strange child and couldn't wait to finally get her out of her hair once and for all.

Soraya burst into tears, not wanting to hear those words. She already felt captive, and now someone was going to throw away the key forever.

"I will never have a chance to leave this place. They will force me into a marriage and soon I will have kids and be converted to my mother."

She hated the thought of re-living her mother's life, but she didn't have time to feel sorry for herself, she grabbed the broom and began sweeping the old torn rug in their little cottage, thinking of her life with a man she hardly knew. It was all part of her life, but there was nothing she could do to change it. She knew that only too well.

Soraya lived in a small village in the Damavand mountains in northern Tehran. She was the oldest child. Her father had a small farm, but somehow he could never get ahead struggling all his life to make a living for his family. She was allowed to finish sixth grade at the small school right outside the village before her parents decided to put an end to that. She went to school longer than all the other girls in the village because of all her pleading with her father. It was now time for her to get married or work as a servant in the city for some wealthy family. Those were her only options. The villagers didn't give their daughters many choices, getting married was obviously the better choice. As far as her parents were concerned, they had their share of raising her. But Soraya had different dreams, being a servant or getting married were far from what she had in mind.

Her younger sister, Zahra, embraced her, "I wish I was in your place, I know that unless you get married, it can't be my turn."

Soraya looked at her younger sister and felt sorry for her innocence. This was all she knew of life: getting married, having babies and running a household for a man who thinks of her as a possession. He would see her as a wife who could give him children, hopefully sons; clean his house; wash his clothes; and satisfy his every desire. There was so much more to life than her younger sister ever imagined. By the time she finished her chores, her father came home, looking old and tired. He lived a hard life, and she felt sorry for him. He was a quiet man and never spoke his thoughts and dreams. He told her to sit by him and listen, and she did. For some reason, she knew he wanted more out of life for her, but this was all he could offer. Just like Soraya, he often dreamed of a different life. He had a special place in his heart for his first born, and as he stroked her hair in a gentle way, he looked down. Like all the other men in the village, he had to give her up to a different family so she could start a family of her own.

"Time has come that I can't take care of you any longer. Mullah's family is willing to pay a good price for you to be their son's bride, and this will help all of us."

He touched her hair again and saw tears in her eyes, those beautiful brown eyes that he admired all his life. He was ashamed to look at her, but knew she would never disobey him. They had a quiet understanding between them. Knowing his daughter's wishes were far from what he had in mind for her, he wished to offer her more. But life in that small village was like a dead end, and he knew this was not a beginning for her; it was the beginning of an end.

She wiped her eyes and held her father's hard working hands in hers and kissed them. As more tears continued to seep down her cheeks, he held her tight for a short moment.

The guests arrived shortly thereafter, and the men sat down talking about their future ties together. She brought tea on a small tray and held it in front of each guest. She looked into the eyes of her future husband. They were kind and warm looking back at her.

She felt warm and tingly all over and whispered "tea", admiring his strong tan hands. Somehow they reminded her of her father's hands gently caressing her beautiful hair. Her heart pounding she stood there red faced before she ran outside. She still heard laughter inside, which meant things were going well. They were deciding her fate, and she had nothing to say about it. She wished to be a bird flying to a faraway place so that no one could reach her. Knowing life was so different in other parts of the world. It would be almost unheard of for a young girl to get married with no say over her own life. But her life was rare, and she knew that. In spite of her desire to start again in a different direction, it seemed that nothing would change for her.

She heard some commotion, the guests were about to leave. Soraya ran behind the cottage, so no one could see her.

She looked at the man she was about to marry, so young and handsome. In a way, she was lucky; some of the girls her age married men as old as their fathers or even older. She had to be grateful to marry someone so young and from one of the wealthiest families in their village.

Her mother came looking for her with a smile. It was all set. The wedding would take place after the holy month of Ramadan. The woman was overjoyed as she said those words. This meant there would be more food on the table and from that moment on, things would be better. After all, there were four other daughters. Every time one got married, more money and gifts would come to the family. Soraya was not to ask questions or say anything, just do as she was told. That was the reality of her life in that small little village hidden in the mountains. That night after everyone went to bed, she took the holy book of Quran and went outside. As she held the holy book, she began to pray. There she sat, under the stars, talking to her God and praying.

"Dear God, please help me cope with all this." She was mad at herself for being different from all the other girls in the village. She thought it would be easier if she was just like everyone else. This was a sad day for her. "Dear God, hold my hand and walk me through the right path. If this man is the one who will give me happiness, then I am your servant, and I will do as you wish. I put my life in your hands and trust you. Show me the way, and I will follow. I am just a child and need your guidance and love." With that she closed the holy book and kissed it. She thought of going to her hideaway once more before all of the wedding preparations began and with those thoughts, she went to bed.

It was a beautiful crisp morning. She opened her eyes and wished everything that happened the night before was just a dream. She rubbed her eyes and realized it was all a reality. Soon she was to get married.

4

Her mother had made tea and warmed up some bread with a few slices of cheese. She was in a particularly good mood.

"You will be married soon and make me a grandmother, and I will be so proud."

"Mother, you are too young to be a grandmother."

Her mother looked at her in irritation. "Stop talking like that! I will be thirty-two years old soon, and there is nothing left for me to do."

"This is just the beginning of your life, you have your whole life ahead of you, Mother."

"You know something, Soraya? I am glad you are getting married, I don't like this kind of talk out of your mouth, and I think it is all that reading you did in school. It's a shame that I ever allowed you to go to school. What do you know about life? Giving me lectures, telling me how long I have to live? Only God knows that; and as far as I am concerned, I've had my share and am very thankful to live this long. Now eat your breakfast, because your future husband was concerned that you are too thin. We have to fatten you up before your wedding night."

Wedding night? Soraya closed her eyes for an instant. She remembered some of the young girls in the village talking about that. After the wedding celebration, the bride and the groom go to their private room. They have to make love immediately because the parents from both sides wait right outside the room for the groom to come out with a bloody handkerchief. That is the proof that his bride was a virgin, and no one leaves unless they see that. The father of the bride goes home very proud, knowing that he did his job raising a virgin girl until her wedding night. This was the end of his obligation toward his daughter; she is now someone else's responsibility. Soraya was in deep thoughts and almost embarrassed by her own illusion. She got up and cleaned the breakfast dishes and decided to sneak out of the village, knowing her mother was too busy to notice her absence. She took off going to her little hideaway. She sat next to the pond, looking in. She could see herself in the water. What she saw never impressed her much. She never thought of herself as pretty. She was strikingly beautiful with silky black hair, rosy plump lips, high cheek bone, big mysterious brown eyes and soft tan skin. She had on a long floral dress which belonged to her mother once. She had the face of an angel. Soraya was lost in her thoughts when she felt an arm on her shoulder. She turned around startled, and saw the face of a strange man trying to cover her mouth. A second man appeared only seconds later "Oh my God, what is happening? Who are these people? The first man took a knife out and told her to be quiet. "One word out of your mouth, and you will be dead."

She had no idea what they wanted from her staring at them, in horror. Who were they? Thoughts were racing through her head when one of the men reached under her dress and began touching her legs with an offensive grin. Once he had reached her panties, he tore them off with one yank. She was like a wounded bird, horrified at what was happening to her.

Soraya started pleading with them to let her go, but it was useless and she knew it. A sudden sense of fear ran through her. Soon he took his pants down, and with the other man holding her down, he forced himself between her legs. She screamed and tried to free herself, but they were much stronger than her. Soraya was overpowered and completely defenseless. She could feel the hard ground beneath her almost crushing her fragile bones. Her eyes locked into his but he quickly looked down at the neckline of her dress and his hands cupped her breast and squeezed it. The pain took her breath away. His body on fire, sweat dripping down his face. She saw the tightening of his facial muscles and the animal howling sound that followed it shortly after. At the time in her mind she was being punished. Her mother warned her about coming out here, but she didn't listen to her. By now she knew that her virginity was gone. She was now stained, damaged merchandise. Soon the second man was on top of her as she bit her lips as hard as she could to stop all other pain she endured. Blood poured from her lips as it streamed with her tears. She used every inch of strength she had to pull herself up and spit in his face but only met his forceful punch. She fell back defeated and broken as her body went limp. This man already so aroused had no mercy on her as his pounding began. She turned her face to the side to avoid his foul stench and stared from the corner of her eyes at a tree in the distance. The leaves freely moving about by the breeze as she closed her eyes and prayed to be freed of this nightmare and began to drift away. The clouds above her were moving at a steady pace, the sky blue and everything seemed the same but she knew her life had taken a drastic turn.

Soon he was also done with her but it seemed like an eternity. They both got dressed looking around making sure no one had seen their treacherous action. "One word out of your mouth, and you will be dead" one of them said with a nasty grin on his face.

She pulled her knees up to her stomach and laid there in a fetal position. Everything began spinning around, and seconds later, she passed out.

She finally opened her eyes, just like she had the day before, but this time, things were so different. In a few short moments, she remembered everything. Her life will never be the same again. Never to get married to anyone in the village. They will look at her as someone not worthy of anything. Soraya had lost her family's honor.

She was in a lot of pain and wished to be dead. Her body ached from all the beatings. She tried to sit up, but became so dizzy that she fell back down. Feeling so dirty she wanted to crawl out of her skin. She took off her dress and climbed in the water to wash the filth and blood off her body. The same blood that was once the sign of her purity was now the indication of her disgrace. As the blood washed away, so was the proof of her virginity. It was dissolving in the water like it never existed. Her skin so raw to the touch. The temperature of the water so cold but almost welcoming to numb her flesh. She scrubbed as hard as she could stand it to wash away all signs of the two who felt her and touched her, knowing her wounds were much deeper than that.

She thought about her father and how this would destroy him to the point that he would never be able to look anyone in the face again. After all, where she was from, the only thing a woman could offer her community was her virginity and babies. If you were not a virgin, no one would want you. At sixteen, she was robbed of her whole future and she began crying quietly, wondering what to do.

"How am I going to tell my family I was raped? That I was held down by the throat and raped?"

She broke down in tears and physical exhaustion as she walked toward the village, looking back at the mountains once more, knowing she had lost her faith and trust.

She walked in the cottage as her mother began screaming at her for not telling her where she went that morning when she suddenly stopped. "Oh my God, what happened to you?", looking at her bruised face, her torn clothes, not knowing what to think. "Talk to me, tell the truth!"

Her father walked in as did all her siblings. They all looked at her as if they had seen a ghost.

"Zahra, take the kids outside," her father ordered.

Fear had taken over him, and he walked slowly toward her and took her hands in his.

"Talk to us, Soraya. Tell us what happened to you?"

She was still numb from what had taken place earlier; she looked down for a moment, and then began telling them everything that had happened with no emotion. Her mother was in shock, but it didn't take her long before she ran toward Soraya and grabbed her shoulders, shaking her as hard as she could.

"How could you do this to us?"

"You will pay for this the rest of your life! God will punish you," as she collapsed to her knees sobbing in distress.

Soraya looked at her listless and whispered, "God has already punished me. I have been to hell and back."

Her father came to her rescue, pulling his wife away, looking at his daughter. There was nothing he could do that hadn't already been done to her. His innocent daughter was gone forever. It was almost as though she had no more soul left in her, just flesh. He helped her get up and held her in his arms for dear life, tears rolling down his face. In a way, he wanted to baby her one last time, hold her in his arms and protect her from any more harm. He wasn't mad at her, but he knew he had lost her forever. The end had come for them, so he had to let her go.

There was a chill in the air. Her mother sat in the corner of the room, still sobbing. To her, Soraya was dead. They had never heard of a child being raped before, not having an idea how to deal with it. To them it was truly a punishment from God, for whatever reason. She envied her husband for being able to hold Soraya in his arms. Filled with uncertain emotions, thinking that if she held her and comforted her abused body, she may never let her go. The only answer to this tragedy was to send Soraya far away, where no one would know what happened to her. Her daughter would have to be gone before dawn the next day. She had the rest of the family, and their reputation, to think of. Soraya was the one to be sacrificed in order to save the rest.

Her father held her in his arms, rocking her back and forth.

How could he tell her, on top of what she had already lost that she would soon lose everyone she's known in her short life? How could he let her live with that grief and not even be there for her?

"Those bastards, how could they do this to my child? The one I have always loved the most."

His heart ached for her. He saw something in her eyes that told him the light inside of her has been dimmed. He gently laid her down, holding her head in his arms. Her eyes soon closed and she was fast asleep, safe and protected in her father's loving arms. He didn't move all night just sitting beside her, staring at his child, wondering what path her life would take.

Soraya woke up the next morning, her body so stiff that she could hardly move. She looked up and saw her father still sitting next to her, looking a hundred years older, and as soon as he saw her open her eyes, he gave a faded smile. Taking his hands in hers she smiled and gently kissed them. In her mind those hands were the healers of her body and soul, and her trust in life.

Soraya had a good idea what was about to happen to her and didn't want to make things any more difficult, so she got up and told her father she was ready to face her fate whatever that may be.

Her father woke his wife up and told her they were about to leave. She walked over to her daughter, taking off her gold necklace, and she put it around Soraya's neck. Holding her daughter for a few seconds and told her to be careful. She was not able to look her in the eyes or to show her true emotions.

Soraya looked at her mother as her eyes overflowed with tears, feeling sorry for her. Her mother was hurting but didn't know how to show it. She whispered good bye and walked out of the cottage with her father, not knowing when she would see any of them again or if she would. This day began like all other days as one looked at the surrounding but within Soraya there was a turmoil. She looked out into the distance as they began the long walk to the bus station, but in reality she only saw a few feet in front of her. No one would ever hurt her in that nature again. Soraya watched everything that was coming her way in a different light.

# CHAPTER TWO

It was a beautiful fall night as Oliver Reed drove home thinking about his life with Kate in this far away country, thousands of miles away from his home. He worked for an American company which exported computers to many other countries worldwide. He and Kate had moved to Tehran three years earlier, as the relocation involved a tremendous raise which they decided they could not turn down.

Once they relocated to Tehran, they realized it was different from what they had imagined. It was surprisingly better than they had expected. Oliver had a friend who lived in Saudi-Arabia and always complained about how bored he was; but, Tehran was a big, modern city where women didn't even have to cover up, like they did in Saudi. This was, of course, a relief to Kate. Tehran had everything from night clubs to fancy restaurants, from movie theaters to little side walk stands; and, the beautiful mountains surrounded it all. It had a perfect four seasons. Summers were a little too hot, but to their surprise, they even saw snow every winter.

There were many American families who lived there for different reasons. Some were married to Iranian spouses, and many of them were there because of their jobs like Oliver and Kate. They didn't mind living there at all, and had gotten to know many people with whom they got together on occasion. The length of their stay in Tehran was unknown. They didn't have any immediate plans to leave, not unless they decided to start a family. Oliver and Kate decided that when that time came, they would rather bear their children on their own soil.

Iranian culture and food became familiar to them sooner than they expected. Kate would get frustrated when she couldn't find American ingredients in the local shops and had to go to the specialty shops and pay higher prices. She somehow managed and didn't complain too much, but lately she was after Oliver to get a maid who could help her with the housework and everyday shopping. Kate often found it difficult to manage work as well as the household chores. Plus, help was so inexpensive that she thought it was crazy not to have it.

Kate was an English teacher at the Iranian-American society, a place for upper class people. English was her major in college anyway, and this gave her a chance to get out of the house.

Oliver arrived home and could see Kate through the windows, on the phone.

"I wish she would close the drapes at night," he told himself as he parked the car in the parking area of their apartment building and walked upstairs.

She was still on the phone when he entered.

"Hi honey, I am home, he said jokingly.

Kate waved to him and went on talking on the phone.

"I have to talk to Oliver first, but don't give her away, not until I get back to you," she went on for a couple more minutes. "Thanks Mina, I will talk to you soon."

"Who was that on the phone?" Oliver asked.

"It was Mina, the lady I work with."

"Did I hear you saying you have to talk to me?"

Kate walked over to him and wrapped her arms around him, "Have I told you lately how much I love you?"

He smiled, "Okay Kate, what's going on?"

"You are terrible, I just told you that I love you, and you want to know if there is a reason behind it?"

Oliver laughed and kissed her on the tip of her nose, "It's because I know you too well, my love. Okay, shoot."

"But you have to hear me out first," she took a deep breath, "My friend Mina has found someone who is badly in need of a job."

"What kind of a job?" Oliver asked.

"Housekeeping. The only problem is, she has to live with whoever hires her."

"You mean a live-in maid? Please honey, it will take away our privacy."

"I know that, but listen to me Oliver. She is a young girl who is very smart and can read and write, which is one of the qualities I am looking for. You know most of the lower class who work in homes can't do that. Plus, she sounds perfect."

"I don't know Kate; I am not crazy about having someone living with us."

"Oliver, she is only sixteen and doesn't have a place to live."

"Sixteen?" Oliver shouted. "Kate, she is just a child."

"You know, this is their rules. If we don't hire her, she will work somewhere else."

"Let someone else hire her then. I don't feel exactly right hiring a kid to do my house work."

"Oliver, in this country, some of the servants are as young as twelve or thirteen. We didn't make up those circumstances, it is part of their culture. She would be thankful that we gave her the opportunity."

"We haven't made any decision on that yet, and what do you know about her?"

"Just what Mina has told me. The girl's father is a friend of Mina's gardener. He needs to find her a place to live, because he has to go back to work in a couple of days and can't wait too long. Oliver, we can't run a reference check on her, for heaven sakes. You know the rules here; it is all word of mouth. And if it doesn't work out, we will let her go."

Oliver scratched his head for a moment, "Okay Kate, two weeks. I will give it two weeks, and if it doesn't work out for any reason, we let her go."

Kate ran toward him in excitement and gave him a hug, "Thank you sweetheart."

"Two weeks Kate, not any longer."

She went to the phone and called Mina to give her the okay.

Kate woke up the next morning and realized it was already seven. Mina was coming over at seven-thirty. She took a quick shower and was getting dressed when she heard the doorbell. It was Mina, with an older man and a young girl.

"Good morning, did we wake you up?"

"No," Kate smiled, "Come in, I was just getting ready. Would you like some tea or coffee?"

"Only if you have some made."

"By the way Kate, this is Akbar Noor and his daughter, Soraya."

"Nice to meet you, I am Kate," she spoke Farsi, enough to get by. "Please sit down."

They walked in and Mina and Akbar sat on the couch and Soraya sat next to her father on the floor. She looked so frightened to Kate.

"Soraya, you can sit on the couch," Kate said.

She smiled, "Thank you, this is fine."

Her father looked at Kate and began talking to her.

"I just want her to stay with someone who will be kind to her. She is a hard worker, and you can let her keep whatever she makes. There is no need for you to send any of her money to us. Soraya has never been out of the village, so this is all new to her. Please be patient and give her time to adjust."

"Soraya has finished sixth grade and will be a great help to you. She is very honest, and you don't have to worry about anything with her. I won't be a bother to you either; but, I will check on her from time to time."

He went on giving Kate some more information, but he never looked up . It pained him to talk about his daughter as if she was a slave. Everyone could tell that there was a special love in his voice for her.

Kate and Mina left the room a few minutes later to give them some privacy to say good bye, at the same time, Mina needed to go over some last minute instruction.

Her father turned to her, as tears stung his eyes immediately. This was all so crazy. He was leaving his beloved daughter with total strangers from some other country of which he knew nothing about. All he knew was that they were Americans. But it didn't matter. All that mattered was that he had to leave her all alone, in a way, abandon her. He knelt down on the floor next to her, and his hands reached hers. Unable to even talk, choked up and not wanting his daughter to see him like that, he let go of her hand and began sobbing. She held him and cried too.

"I will be fine, father. Don't worry about me, for some day I will see you again; and, things won't seem so bad. I will never forget about you, and that is a promise."

He wiped his eyes.

"If you have to get in touch with me for any reason, tell Mina. She knows how to find me."

He kissed her on the forehead, gave her some money, and walked out of the room, not knowing when he would see her again.

Kate closed the door and walked back in the room to find Soraya crying. She felt so sad for her, but didn't know what to do to ease her pain.

"Do you want something to eat or drink?"

Soraya shook her head, "No thank you; I am sorry."

"Let me show you to your room. Take a shower, you might feel better; and, then I can show you everything else."

Soraya nodded.

"Are you okay, is there anything I can do for you?"

"I'm fine. You don't have to worry yourself about me."

"I want you to get situated and to unpack." As soon as she spoke, she realized that Soraya had brought hardly anything with her.

"Well, I can gather up some things for you. But first, I want you to feel at home. I know this is hard for you. I'd like to help you as much as you can help me. We can be friends."

With that, Kate got up and asked Soraya to follow her.

"We have some work to do before Oliver gets home."

She wanted Soraya to clean up before Oliver met her, or he would never accept her. Kate was nervous, not knowing if she had done the right thing; but, she had to make the best of it.

Soraya followed Kate to a small room.

"This is your room. Hope you'll be comfortable here."

It was bigger than what her entire family lived in. She looked around and didn't know what to say.

"But you don't have to give me a room. I can sleep on the floor, or anywhere you want me to. I don't want to be any trouble to you."

Kate smiled, "You are not any trouble, and you don't have to sleep on the floor. You have your own room so that you can have some privacy. Now, let me show you where the shower is, and I will give you what you need."

Kate realized she had probably never seen a shower in a home before. She knew that in the villages, people went to public baths every couple of weeks. She was starting to have her doubts about the decision she had made.

"What did I get myself into? Is she going to help me or am I going to baby-sit her?"

She ran the bath water and told Soraya to get undressed. Soraya looked at her in shock.

"It's okay, we are all the same; you don't have to be bashful." She handed her a bottle of shampoo.

"Wash your hair with this; it works better than soap."

She gave her everything she needed and walked out.

Soraya closed the door and leaned against it for a few seconds, wondering why she had to take a shower right away.

Kate gathered some clothes and knocked on the door a few minutes later.

"May I come in?" she asked, as she slowly opened the door.

She was shocked at what she saw. There were bruises all over Soraya's body.

"Oh my God, who did this to you?"

Soraya tried to cover up and reached for the towel. She closed her eyes and turned away.

"Please don't make me tell you. I can't talk about it because I am not allowed to say anything."

Kate had seen bruises on her face, too. Her heart went out to the young girl. For the first time, she realized how beautiful Soraya was, long black hair, and those angelic eyes. Even bruises couldn't cover her beauty.

"It's okay. You don't have to tell me anything if you don't want to. Here are some clothes for you. Get dressed, and come out when you are ready."

Soraya put her clothes on as fast as she could, pulling her hair back in a braid.

"You look great and I am glad you took a shower. Do you want something to eat now?"

She shook her head and looked down, not used to compliments.

Kate patiently showed her everything throughout the house and told her of all her duties. It took several hours before she finished showing her everything. She hoped Oliver wouldn't get home earlier than usual.

Soraya observed everything, as best she could, and tried to do her best to remember what Kate had told her. Everything seemed so different from the village. There were appliances that she had never seen before, like a vacuum cleaner and a refrigerator.

Later, they took a walk to the market so that she would learn where to purchase all of their food. In a way, it was all so fun and interesting to her. But, it was a full day for both of them, and they were exhausted when it was all done.

Kate somehow realized that this young girl was carrying a dark secret. There was a sadness in her eyes which spoke volume and, Kate had, of course, seen the signs on her body and in those sad eyes. Kate wondered what she was hiding.

They ate lunch, and Soraya automatically did the dishes without being told and then asked if there was anything else that she could do.

"No," Kate said, "I think you have done enough for your first day. Why don't you go to your room and rest for a while? I will call you if I need anything."

Soraya went to her room and closed the door. She grabbed her little pack that carried all of her belongings, put it on the floor, and rested her head on it. This was the first time she had been alone in a while, and she remembered the nightmare as tears burned her eyes once again.

"I can't think about my past, they don't belong to me any longer." It was as though that part of her life had ended. It was a part of her past, like the horror of her brutal rape; the curse that would stay with her for the rest of her life. She thought about her father, how he sat next to her and sobbed. Thinking of him made her sad. She truly loved and missed him and wished he was there to comfort her, just like he had done on the night of her rape. Soraya closed her eyes and fell fast asleep.

There was a knock on the door and then another one.

"May I come in?"

Soraya opened her eyes and for a moment couldn't remember where she was. Kate slowly opened the door and found her lying on the floor.

"Why are you sleeping on the floor?"

Soraya looked at her, puzzled, looking around and then jumped to her feet.

"I am sorry I must have fallen sleep."

Kate smiled, "You don't have to apologize. I am glad you got some rest. By the way, Oliver will be home soon, and we are going to eat dinner shortly. I thought you might want to wake up and get ready for dinner."

"Yes, of course. Is there anything I can help you with?"

"Sure, you can help me set the table."

Soraya was helping Kate set the table when they heard the door.

"Hi honey! We're in the kitchen."

Oliver walked in and kissed Kate on the lips. Soraya looked away embarrassed, having never before seen two people embrace in that fashion.

"Oliver, this is Soraya, our new friend and helper. This is my husband, Oliver."

He walked toward her and raised his arm to shake her hand, but she didn't know what to do. She decided to copy him and raised her hand too.

"It is nice to meet you. I like your name; it's pretty."

She blushed, but looked up and smiled.

"Thank you, no one has ever told me my name is pretty."

"Well, I am honored to be the first one."

He liked her right away.

"Tell me, what part of the country are you from?"

"A small village in the Damavand mountains, but I couldn't tell you where that is from here; this is my first trip to the city."

Despite the bruises on her face, he realized how beautiful she was.

"What a beautiful child," he told himself. And he felt sorry for her, but didn't know why? He decided to avoid asking her questions which might make her feel uneasy.

"Do you have any brothers or sisters?"

"Yes, I have four sisters and two brothers. They all live in the village with my parents."

Kate jumped in to change the subject, knowing that Soraya felt uneasy talking about her family.

"How was your day, honey?"

"Very busy, as usual. How was yours?"

Kate smiled, "Busy and challenging."

Soraya looked at them in confusion, not understanding a word they said to each other.

Kate noticed her perplexed look and said," do you know where America is?"

She just shook her head and whispered, "no Mam."

"That's where Oliver and I are from, and we speak a different language. What you just heard is called English."

She nodded in amusement.

"I have never heard of a place called America. You two are very nice. Americans are nice if they are all like you."

Kate smiled, "Thank you."

"Can you teach me English some day?"

"Sure, if you like. I teach English at a language school."

"You are a teacher?" She asked, her eyes widening.

"Yes, I am a teacher."

"That's what I'd like to be some day. I wanted to stay in school to continue my education; but my parents, mostly my mother, decided to take me out of school."

They could see annoyance in her face as she spoke, and felt rather guilty for hiring her as a maid. They never would have done such a thing in their own country.

They sat down for dinner. Soraya had a difficult time keeping up with all the unusual customs. Everything was so new to her, even using a fork.

"Would you like to use a spoon instead?" Kate asked softly, not wanting to offend her.

"I think I'd better," she said quietly.

She didn't have much of an appetite and played with her food for a while. She finally decided to ask if she could be excused to start on the dishes.

"You didn't eat much, aren't you hungry?"

"I am sorry. The food was very good, but I am just not very hungry. I hope you don't mind."

"It's okay. You can start on the dishes, and we will help you in a few minutes."

"Please sit, and let me do it. I really don't need any help. You have already done enough for me."

"We haven't done anything but give you a job, Soraya."

"That's plenty for me, and I appreciate that." And with that she got up and started cleaning.

Kate and Oliver both were surprised at how mature and serene she was. Most sixteen years old they knew were still just kids, having fun.

By the time they were done eating, she had finished most of the cleaning in the kitchen.

"Would you like some tea?"

"We would love some. Thank you," Kate answered.

They were in the living room talking when she walked in with a tray. She sat the tray down on the table, gave them each a cup, then started walking back toward the kitchen.

"Aren't you having some tea?"

"Yes, mine is in the kitchen."

"Why don't you come sit with us?"

She looked down for a moment, "I would rather not be a bother to you."

"Soraya, get your tea and come sit with us. We would like to talk to you for a while."

She came back with her tea and sat on the floor with her legs tucked under her.

"You can sit on the couch with us. This is your home, too," Oliver said. "We don't expect you to work all day and night. Kate just needs someone to help her with the everyday cleaning and shopping, and you will have hardly any work to do after two or three in the afternoon. You can go for walks, watch T.V., read, or do whatever you like, as long as we know where you are and who you are with."

"You don't have to wait on us all day," Kate looked at her kindly, picking up where Oliver left off. "We would like to be your friends and maybe part of your new family. We know it must have been hard for you to leave your family."

Soraya looked up with tears in her eyes. "Except for my family, no one has ever been this nice to me before."

"You miss them don't you?" I do but specially my father. He is a good man and I will always miss him, no matter where I live."

Oliver decided to change the subject, knowing it bothered her to talk about her family. "Would everyone like to watch T.V. for a while?"

Soraya knew what a television was, but had never actually seen one before. She watched with great interest, but she didn't know how those people got into the square box. If only her siblings could see her now, sitting in this fancy apartment, dressed like city people, talking to Americans, and watching television! They would never believe it. She realized she never even had a chance to say goodbye to them and wondered what they thought. Their big sister had suddenly vanished out of their lives.

"What is my father going to tell Mullah and his family?"

She knew that whatever that was, it would be hard on him.

Her parents would offer them Zahra instead. She would miss Zahra so much, her only friend. At times, she had confided in her about some of her trance; but, those were nothing but memories now, and she couldn't think about them too much. These thoughts were all so painful to her. It was getting late so she decided to go to bed.

"Well, what do you think, Oliver? Is she going to work out?"

He ran his hands through his hair, as he had a habit of doing, and said, "She is a nice girl, but very reserved. It seems to me that she has some secrets in her life. "Maybe I'm wrong, but she has a sad look in her eyes that makes me feel we should give her a chance. What do you think? You had more time with her. Did she say anything to you?"

Kate just shook her head, "I feel the same way. She is very smart and picked up on everything right away. It was almost like being a village girl wasn't what she was meant to be. I wonder why they sent her away."

Oliver was tired, "I don't know, babe; but, I am tired. Let's go to bed."

Soraya sat on her bed. "What if I fall off during the night?" But then she decided it was worth trying.

She got undressed and stood in front of the mirror looking at herself. She had cuts and bruises all over her body and realized why Kate was so shocked when she saw her. It looked awful. These wounds would heal someday; but, would she ever be healed of what happened to her? There would never be a man who could touch her again. In a way, she hated them all, with the exception of her father.

She put on a long shirt that Kate had given her and went to bed, thinking about her father.

"Dear God, give me strength to get through these hard times. Help my father deal with this tragedy. I hope someday my mother can find it in her heart to forgive me for my sins. If only I had listened to her, none of this would have happened. I deserve everything that has happened to me, but my parents are innocent. Please don't punish them for my sins."

Soon her mind drifted off to other things, and she couldn't help but find herself by the pond again. She looked into the water, and the entire pond turned red with blood.

"Oh my God, what is happening?" She was awakened with a jolt. Her heart pounding as she tried to catch her breath.

Soraya tossed and turned and couldn't fall sleep. She decided to lay on the floor and felt much more comfortable. Before she knew it, she fell back to sleep.

It was still dark out when she awoke again, knowing it must be about five in the morning. She got up to make some tea and wait for Kate and Oliver. Kate came in the kitchen and was surprised to find Soraya up and ready.

"Good morning. How long have you been up?"

"Since five I think. That is the time I usually get up. Can I get you some Tea?"

"I would love some, thank you. Have you eaten anything yet?"

She shook her head, "Not yet."

"Why don't you have some breakfast with us?"

"Are you sure that's okay?"

"Of course it is." Kate told her what to get for her to start making breakfast. They were busy at work when Oliver walked in the kitchen.

"Would you like some tea?" Soraya asked.

"Sure, but I can get it myself. Sit and eat your breakfast," he replied as he poured himself a cup of tea. "Listen, Soraya, don't act too formal with us. Relax. Feeding me breakfast is not one of your duties."

They all sat eating breakfast together, and Soraya felt a little more relaxed and ate with more appetite this time.

Kate and Oliver went to their room to get ready for work while Soraya washed the breakfast dishes and waited for Kate to tell her what to do next. As she waited, she looked at some of their family pictures and was amazed at how different they looked, with their fair skin and blue eyes. She looked around at her new home, so different from what she was used to.

"Maybe I can have a place like this someday."

"I wonder what my family is doing right now, and if my brothers and sisters are mad at me for leaving without saying good bye? And my father," she remembered him sitting right where she was, sobbing. He was so different from anyone else she knew. If he hadn't been born in that village, he would have been somebody today, and she was sure of that.

"But he is my father, and the best father anyone could ever have. I wish I had a chance to tell him how wonderful he is, and that I knew all along that we shared the same dreams. Most of all, I wish I had told him how much I love him."

"Someday I will take him away from everything and give him the life he deserves."

We will go on walks together where we are both safe and no one can ever harm us."

24

Kate broke her train of thought, "I will be back early this afternoon." And she gave her a list of things to do.

Soraya got busy with her work and was eager to please them. She didn't want to be sent away to a different family. She knew that this was her ticket out of every bad thing that had happened to her in the past. She wouldn't be a maid for the rest of her life.

A few weeks went by, and Soraya learned everything remarkably fast. Kate and Oliver were impressed with her. She was intelligent and eager to learn everything. This young child had already begun to gain respect for herself. They couldn't have been happier with her. Kate's life was much easier now that Soraya took care of everything. She wouldn't let Kate do anything, and all she asked Kate in return were books.

Soraya couldn't get enough to read. She'd read everything from newspapers to books, magazines, and so on. She read absolutely everything she could get her hands on, and thus buried herself in her work and books. Soraya usually got done with all her work in the early afternoon, and there wasn't much of anything to do but read or sometimes watch television.

Something had been on her mind for a while now, and she finally got enough courage to talk to Oliver and Kate. They both sat looking at her wondering what she was about to tell them. She didn't know how to begin.

"I was wondering if you two would allow me to go to night school? I wouldn't ask you this if you had any work for me at night. I would like to start taking some night classes. With the money I earn, I can pay for my classes. That is, if you let me."

Kate and Oliver looked at each other with surprise. Oliver decided to reply being caught off guard.

"We couldn't be happier for you. I am glad you made a decision to go back to school. You are too smart to do what you are doing for the rest of your life, and we will help you in any way we can."

Kate gave her a hug and told her how proud she was of her. Soraya's eyes growing misty and she couldn't believe her ears. This was a new beginning for her. Her life was about to change, and she was going to make the best of it and go on with her life.

What was clear to her was that none of this would have been possible without this nice couple from a place called America.

"Thank you for everything you have done for me and all the support you have given me. I think maybe God has forgiven me for my sins and given me a second chance in life."

"Soraya, you have to remember that no matter what you think you have done, it couldn't be all that bad. You are just a child and can't punish yourself and let whatever it is destroy your life."

Soraya whispered, "If you only knew how many lives I have destroyed."

Kate looked at Oliver and they both got a chill. They wondered what this little innocent young girl could have done that was so dreadful?

"If you ever decide to talk about it, we will be here for you. Don't forget that. You can always rely on us."

That night Oliver laid in bed thinking of Soraya, wondering what this mysterious secret was that she carried. He knew it had something to do with her being there. He had a lot of mixed feelings; yet, he wanted to let her know that it would all be okay. There was so much he didn't know about her, yet he felt an obligation toward her.

Kate had similar thoughts. This young girl had a mysterious spell on them, and she didn't know how to express those feelings. Curiosity was getting the best of her, but she knew not to push the girl too much.

"She has to open up to us on her own, and whenever she is ready," she thought to herself.

Soraya started school right away and buried herself in her school work. She studied every free moment she had.

Soraya wasn't the same care free young girl anymore. Physically, she didn't have the same energy, but she never let Oliver and Kate find out. Nothing was going to stop her from achieving her goals. She worked and studied and began to lose a lot of weight, not having much of an appetite.

Kate began teaching her English in their spare time, and Soraya amazed her by how fast she was learning. At the same time, they got to know one another and developed a special bond between them. They were all away from their families, and that brought them together even more. Kate and Oliver were a little concerned about how pale and thin she looked. At times they even felt guilty, seeing her work so hard. But Soraya wouldn't hear of them lifting a finger. Nothing was going to jeopardize her situation there, not even a little weight loss or the way she felt lately.

One evening, Oliver and Kate were having their dinner when Soraya walked in, looking like a ghost.

"Hi, you are home early! Are you feeling well?"

Soraya shook her head and ran toward the bathroom. Kate followed her, asking "Are you sick?"

"I felt sick to my stomach all day. It must be something I ate."

Kate looked at her with concern.

"Soraya, you haven't looked well for a long time. Maybe you should see a doctor."

"No, I will be fine. It's probably something I caught from one of the kids at school."

"You should go to bed and stay there until you feel better." Kate helped her to bed and brought her a glass of water.

"You have been pushing yourself too much lately."

"I am okay, I just need to rest for a while," she said drowsily, and she closed her eyes and soon fell sleep.

Kate closed the bedroom door and walked back to the kitchen.

"How is she," Oliver asked, still sitting in the kitchen and eating his food.

"She is sleeping for now, but I am worried about her. She doesn't look too well. If she doesn't feel better by tomorrow, I will take her to see a doctor."

Kate woke up to a sound and looked over and saw Oliver sleeping next to her. She sat up and listened more intently. It sounded like

27

someone was moaning. She got up and opened the bedroom door and found Soraya sitting by the bathroom door. She was trying to get herself to the bathroom and could hardly do it.

"Oliver," she screamed, "wake up, Soraya is sick!"

Oliver jumped up, put his robe on, and ran toward the hallway. Soraya looked pale and very sick.

"That's it, you have to go to the doctor."

She was too sick to argue.

He knew an American doctor whose office wasn't too far away from their home. Oliver helped Soraya up and walked her to the room, asking Kate to help her get dressed.

They drove to the doctor's office shortly after. Oliver had met the doctor a few months earlier at a company party.

"Hello Oliver, what brings you out here so early in the morning?"

Oliver explained the situation as fast as he could and asked if the doctor could examine her. Soraya followed the doctor into his office, and he ordered several tests on her immediately.

The couple sat in the waiting room and looked at each other, not knowing what to say or do.

The doctor came out of the room and found them both waiting.

"I should have the results soon, and I will call you as soon as I can. Meanwhile, she should rest and drink plenty of fluid. It's probably nothing to worry about."

They all went home, and Kate told Soraya to stay in bed.

"Everyone is entitled to a few sick days, and you are not any exception. Relax. Get some rest, it's doctor's orders.

Soraya was worried. She didn't want to be a burden. She needed her job there more than ever, now that she was going to school.

Oliver and Kate both left for work and Soraya gathered all her books. She decided to study for a while. Suddenly she felt stronger. She studied for a while, but then her eyes began to get heavy, and she fell sleep on top of her books.

She was sitting by the pond and day dreaming like nothing had changed. The mountains looked as beautiful as ever. When looked up she, saw his face. He was standing on the other side of the pond laughing at her.

"You son of a bitch, come near me, and I will kill you this time with my bare hands," she yelled.

Then she saw the other man appear on the other side, also laughing at her. Soraya began to run away, but couldn't get far.

"Oh my God, not again!" She started screaming, "Get away from me! Don't touch me! No! No! No!"

Kate was shaking her, trying to wake her up.

"Soraya, wake up. You are just dreaming."

She opened her eyes and looked horrified for a moment. It was just a dream.

"Thank God it was a dream," she whispered hugging Kate as tight as she could and crying.

"It will never go away. It will always come back to haunt me," she continued as she held on to Kate for dear life.

"I want to help you; but first, you have to tell me what's bothering you. We know you have secrets in your life that you don't want to talk about, but you have to trust us."

"No one can help me. I have to live with my sins and hope that someday I will be forgiven."

Kate held her tight and wondered what this deep secret was that was devastating her peace. Soraya wiped her eyes and apologized to Kate once again and tried to change the subject.

"I just need a couple of days to get better, and I promise you that I won't be a bother to you anymore."

"You are not a bother to us at all. I have told you that before. We like to see you happy and healthy, and that is our biggest concern. Remember, we are here for you if you ever decide to talk about what's bothering you."

Soraya was weak but felt better. She ate some food with more appetite and felt even stronger. She hoped that she was on her way to a speedy recovery.

The phone rang, and Oliver reached over to answer it.

"Oh hello Doctor. Yes, the results of her tests," he said and listened for a few minutes without any response, "Are you sure? Thank you doctor, we will get back to you as soon as possible."

"Who was that?" Kate asked.

"It was Doctor Benson."

Kate immediately knew that something was wrong.

"What did he say? Is she going to be okay?"

Oliver looked up in dismay and said, "She is pregnant."

Everything began to make sense to them now. She had been having morning sickness and did not even know it. Having lived in Iran for several years, they were aware of their culture. It was shameful, and above all, a sin to get pregnant before marriage.

"We have to talk to her. I wonder who the father is."

Kate called Soraya into the kitchen and told her to sit.

"That was the doctor on the phone."

"What did he say?" Soraya asked, knowing there was something wrong.

"He told us that you are pregnant," Kate said, still in shock.

Soraya looked horrified at what she heard.

"I am pregnant? Oh dear God, no."

Tears were rolling down her face.

"I am still being punished by God. This nightmare is not over yet. What am I going to do?" she lamented as she hid her face in her hands.

Oliver came closer to kneel down beside her, "Do you know who the father is?"

She shook her head, still crying. Oliver looked a little confused.

"Soraya, you have to be honest with us. No more secrets. You have to tell us everything if you want our help."

She looked up, not knowing where to start, so ashamed.

"Listen sweetheart," Oliver started, trying to make Soraya feel more at ease, "Not being a virgin and having a baby is not something to be ashamed of. At least not in our eyes. We look at things differently. Please don't be embarrassed. Just tell us what happened to you, so we can help you."

Soraya began telling them her story, even though she had promised herself that she would never tell anyone. It pained her to talk about it, and they could see the struggle in her face. She told them everything from the beginning to the day she walked into their lives.

Kate and Oliver were shocked at what they heard. They both sat frozen, not knowing what to say or do for this wounded child. Kate walked over to her and held her tight, and they both cried. She felt so sorry for this young girl. She looked broken and in so much pain.

"What am I going to do now?"

"Do you want to keep the baby?"

"What other choice do I have?"

"Would you consider abortion?"

Soraya looked up. "That means terminating the pregnancy," and her eyes widened. "Kate, that is the biggest sins of all. Not listening to my mother is what got me here; I can't even think or consider abortion. I have to bring this baby into the world, and maybe then give him up for adoption. It's my only way out."

"Are you sure that's what you want to do?" Oliver asked.

"I have no other choice. But I don't expect you to keep me here. No one knows me here in the city. I can tell everyone that my husband was killed in an accident, and that I didn't know about the pregnancy until after my departure from the village."

Neither Kate or Oliver wanted to make any promises to her as far as her staying there, unless they talked it over first.

"I will start looking for another place to live as soon as I can," she said and walked out of the room.

"Oliver, I just hate to let her go. She doesn't have anybody else. She is only sixteen and has already been through so much. Her family has abandoned her for a rape that was out of her control. Now she is pregnant. Life hasn't been too kind to her. She is not going to keep the baby anyway, so why not let her stay here? She can help out the same as she has been, and if it gets to be too much, she can stop school until after the baby's born."

"What if she changes her mind after the baby is born?" Oliver asked, "What if she decides to keep the baby?"

Kate looked puzzled for a moment.

"Well, we will deal with it then. I just hate to kick her out now. It wouldn't be right, and it's not fair."

Oliver was filled with emotions. He wanted to be fair to Soraya, yet he wanted to do the right thing for them also. He was afraid of getting involved.

"What about all the expenses of delivery; who is going to pay for that?"

"There are home nurses who deliver babies all the time at a very low cost. She can deliver the baby right here in the house. It would raise fewer questions anyway."

Oliver didn't have the heart to send her away.

"I guess you have everything worked out. I just hope everything goes as smoothly as you think, and we don't run into a lot of problems." He looked at her for a moment, "Why do I let you talk me into things?"

Soraya sat on her bed, holding her knees, thinking of what she had just learned. It could destroy all her dreams. Her life was on a new course now and the future looked dimmer than it ever had.

I can't risk having people know about my past.

"I have enough money to buy a bus ticket and go to a faraway place where no one knows me. I could just get lost in the crowds," she thought to herself. Such thoughts were racing through her mind when she heard a knock on the door. Kate and Oliver walked in. She sat there waiting for them to tell her their decision.

Oliver cleared his throat and began talking, "When Kate and I decided to have someone come and help us with the house chores, we had no idea what was in store for us. When we both met you, we decided you were perfect for our needs. Things have changed since then. You are not in the same situation as before, and neither are we. We never thought that we would get so attached to you, that you would become a part of our family. Kate and I would like to help you, mostly because we care about you, not just because it is the right thing to do. We respect your decision and will stand by you. We would like to help you if you'll let us. By leaving, you will only increase the chances of more turmoil coming your way. You have been through enough and we would like you to stay here and work things out in a safe place."

Kate picked up where Oliver left off, "We don't want you to leave. Please, stay here and let us help you, because we both care about you very much."

Soraya was still in shock about the pregnancy and couldn't believe what they had just offered her.

"Are you telling me that I can stay here and have the baby?"

"Yes we are," Kate answered.

Soraya looked down for a second, not knowing what to say.

"This is very generous of you. I have come to bond with both of you also; but, at the same time, I can't take advantage of your generosity. You've been so kind, and I will never forget everything you have done for me, but I think is best if I find a different place to live. I hope you both understand and realize how hard it is for me to live here and look you in the eye every day when you know that I am carrying an illegitimate child. It's the way I was raised; I truly believe this child is a punishment from God."

Kate looked shocked at what she heard.

"Soraya, you are wrong. This baby is innocent. If you truly believe in God, you wouldn't think he would use an innocent baby to punish you or anyone else. You have to understand that you didn't do anything wrong. You were raped. If anyone deserves a punishment, it is the ones who did this to you in the first place. We don't pity you. Everything we do for you is out of love and respect, and nothing more. I wish you could believe that and go on with your life."

Soraya listened to everything that Kate was telling her and smiled.

"I don't know how to thank you for everything. At this moment, no matter what I say, it will only be words. So I am not even going to try. I hope someday I can pay you back."

They left her alone to rest, and she sat there, trying to figure out how far she was in her pregnancy. It had been almost four months since she moved in with them, and it was easy to figure out the exact time of conception. She now knew the reason behind her sickness; so she decided not to sit around and mope about it anymore. She was confident that she could pull it all off. After all, she had seen her mother take care of a houseful of children and also do the housework

"This is nothing compared to what she had to do. I can keep up with my job here and still go to school."

It almost seemed as though the harder things got, the more determined she became in beating the odds. She put her hand on her stomach and looked down at it. She had no feelings toward this child that was growing inside of her. It was a reminder of many heartaches and of a horrifying memory of the child's father, whoever he was.

"I am sorry, little one, but I could never love you like a mother should. I can only carry you to term and then you will have to survive as I do, without your mother or father around you to give you their love and support. Maybe a nice family will adopt and love you. I know you are innocent, as I was; but, you have to know that I just can't let you stop me from planning my own future. For once, I will take charge of my life; and, no one is going to stop me, not even you, little baby."

As the weeks went by, everything fell back to normal. Soraya began to feel much better. She saw the doctor once more and decided not to see him again until she was six months into her pregnancy. She paid her own way and wouldn't accept anything extra from Kate and Oliver.

Everything was going well, and Kate even noticed that Soraya had gained a few pounds. She looked more beautiful every day. She didn't look like the typical maid in Iran. Kate gave her some of her old clothes, and everything she put on looked very becoming on her. Soraya looked much older than her age. Being pregnant made her blossom even more.

Kate was getting anxious to go home for Christmas, but she was worried about Soraya. She felt uncomfortable about leaving her alone for a whole month. But Soraya insisted that they shouldn't change any of their plans on her account. They were truly proud of her. The subject of their departure came up often, and every time they said the same things.

"Maybe you should stay with someone while we are gone."

But Soraya would not hear of it.

"I don't want to stay with anybody. It would be uncomfortable for me. You are only going to be gone a month anyway. Besides, I 've talked to Mrs. Solayman. She told me it would be okay to stay with her if I needed to."

Mrs. Solaymai was an older widow who lived in the same building. At times, Soraya helped her with her grocery shopping and other chores and was really fond of Soraya. From time to time she gave Soraya a little money for all her work.

Kate decided to pay a visit to Mrs. Solayman in order to make sure it would be fine with her if for any reason Soraya needed to stay with her while they were gone. She was a kind old woman and Kate understood why Soraya liked her so much. Of course she was a bit curious about the relationship between Soraya and the Reeds. However Kate explained to her that Soraya had lost her husband and came to the city to work, then found out that she was pregnant.

"Is she going to keep the baby?"

"We don't know that yet. It is her decision, and whatever she decides, we will support her."

Mrs. Solayman was satisfied with Kate's explanation and left it at that. Kate also felt better having had a little talk with her. Knowing there was someone close by to watch over Soraya in case of an emergency.

They had just celebrated Soraya's seventeenth birthday, and it was the first time that she was ever recognized on her birthday.

She was so mature for her age, that at times, they forgot that she would still be considered a kid in their own country.

Kate was very fond of her; and as timed passed they became good friends. They could talk about anything, and Kate found herself to be very protective of her. She noticed how men looked at her. Even Oliver had made a comment about how beautiful she was. Kate had no doubt in her mind that this young woman would someday be somebody. She learned and spoke English faster than anyone Kate had ever taught before. She even insisted on speaking only English at the house with Kate and Oliver.

Kate and Soraya went shopping almost daily. Kate bought beautiful hand crafted souvenirs for everyone in their family. There were so many people to buy for, and Kate didn't want to leave anyone out. They all enjoyed the beautiful gifts Kate and Oliver gave them each year and looked forward to the next year's presents.

Kate enjoyed having Soraya with her. It was a different experience for her, and they both enjoyed each other's company. They came home with armfuls of packages.

Kate bought Soraya a new outfit. She had never owned a brand new dress before, everything she owned were hand-me-downs. The dress was her Christmas present from Kate and Oliver, and Soraya couldn't wait to wear it once the baby was born.

Her life had changed so much, and she couldn't wait to have the baby so she could get everything settled and go on with her life.

She got to know some young girls at school, and they were surprised to find out that she was pregnant. She kept to herself most of the time and didn't like answering a lot of their inquisitive questions. She told them the same story that Kate had told Mrs. Solayman. Young girls getting married at an early age was nothing out of the ordinary there, so they had no reason not to believe her.

It was getting closer to Kate and Oliver's departure. Soraya was going to miss them, but still was happy for them. She knew how much they looked forward to their trip each year.

She kept busy every day and studied hard at night. Her teacher paid close attention to her progress and was amazed at how well she did. He often wondered why she had dropped out of school for so long. And one night after class, he asked her to stay.

"Soraya, I want to talk to you about your grade. I am not sure if you are aware of the different programs we have to offer. But I wanted to make sure you understand them, so you can make some choices."

She listened to him carefully, not knowing what he was trying to say.

"You can easily pass this grade's test and move up to a higher class. It is just a waste of time to hold you back when I am confident you are capable of passing the test and moving on."

"Are you saying that I can move up faster than the other kids and finish before they do?" Soraya asked with surprise.

"Yes, that is exactly what I am telling you. I need to talk to the school board to get you the tests you need. Then I will give you some time to study for them. You can take the tests in a few weeks, if you think you are ready. That is not all, you can take the next exam at your own pace and move up. I just don't think you need to be held with the other students. You can do this until you take your big exam, which gives you your high school diploma."

He looked at her kindly for a moment, "What do you think? You think you can handle it?"

Soraya was ecstatic over the news. She didn't know what to say.

"This is the best news I have heard in my entire life! It couldn't have happened at a better time. You see, the family that I live with is leaving for a month, so I have nothing to do but study. Then I can take my test as soon as possible." "I don't want you to push yourself too much."

"I won't. I promise," she said as she giggled. "And thank you so much for noticing my work."

Soraya left the school almost walking on clouds. She couldn't wait to go home and tell Kate and Oliver her news. The bus ride seemed to take forever, and she was getting impatient. She practically flew out the door and ran as fast as she could. Almost out of breath when she opened the door and ran in. Oliver and Kate looked at her and thought something was wrong.

"Are you okay?" Kate looked worried.

She had to catch her breath before she could say, "I am great! You won't believe what I am about to tell you!" And she went on to tell them her news.

Oliver and Kate walked toward her with open arms, embracing and acknowledging her news with as much enthusiasm as they could. They both knew how important this was to her. They both were glad to share this moment with her.

"I am so proud of you, Soraya! I guess we have a genius in the family." Kate said with tears in her eyes.

They looked at her, knowing this young woman had chosen her path and nothing was going to stop her. She had made it against all odds, and they couldn't have been happier for you.

"You better settle down, young lady, or you will have that baby jump out sooner than you think."

Soraya sat, still beaming with joy, and apologized for frightening both of them. "I am so happy."

All I want to do is to get on a bus and go to my village and tell my father not to worry about me anymore. I'd tell him that I am going to be okay. He has no idea how my life has changed. I know there is not a day gone by that he hasn't thought about me and wondered how I am doing."

"Why don't you do that," Kate asked?

Soraya just laughed, "Are you kidding? That would destroy him. He wouldn't take it too well, not to mention my mother's reaction." She suddenly looked distant, "but maybe someday I will."

"He must be a very special man," Oliver said.

Her eyes lit up.

"He is. He is the only man that I will ever love," she declared looking up with a funny grin, "and you too, Oliver."

The next few weeks everything happened so fast. Before they knew it, it was time for them to leave for the U.S. Soraya in the midst of her exams, and Kate was busy with last minute shopping.

The last night before their departure, they all sat around the table for dinner. Kate still didn't feel all that great about leaving Soraya alone, but at the same time knew that she would do just fine and could handle anything.

They had a nice quiet dinner together and mostly talked about their trip and how excited they were to see everyone. They were truly like a family now. Soraya hardly heard from her own family anymore, though she often thought about them, especially her father. At Thirty-seven, Oliver was old enough to be her father, but she would never allow herself to think of anyone taking the place of her father. There was a special place in her heart that no one could take. She did trust and love Oliver, but in a different way which she couldn't explain. He was almost like a good friend. He was gentle and kind, like her father, but she avoided comparing the two. Her father was only ten years older than Oliver, but he had a hard life and you could see it in his face. He had put in years of hard work without many accomplishments. That was what Soraya feared the most: To fallow their path in life.

The cab was picking them up at four the next morning, but Soraya didn't want to say good bye to them that night. She wanted to get up in the morning to see them leave. Kate wanted her to stay in bed and not even bother getting up; but Soraya, as usual, insisted, and there was no arguing with her. They said good night and went to bed. Everything was already packed, and all they had to do was shower and get dressed in the morning. Soraya went to bed and set the clock for three in the morning and before she knew it, the alarm went off. She couldn't believe it was already time to get up. It seemed like she had just gone to bed. Kate and Oliver were up, too, getting ready. Soraya began making them breakfast, knowing they had a long road ahead of them.

Oliver walked in the kitchen and could smell the coffee and eggs cooking. He peeked in the kitchen and saw her hard at work.

"What are you doing?"

"Just making you two some breakfast before you leave. Where is Kate?"

"She is almost done," he replied as he poured himself a cup of coffee.

Soraya put his plate in front of him.

Kate walked in a few minutes later, and said "Oh, smells so good. What are you cooking?"

Soraya set her plate on the table, too.

"I know it will take twenty-four hours to get there, and I thought you probably need at least a good breakfast."

They ate their food; but everyone looked kind of sad, thinking of how they had to say good-bye soon.

"The taxi will be here in ten minutes," Oliver said, walking over to Soraya. "I want you to be a good girl and take care of yourself. Call us if there is any problem."

The door bell rang before he finished his last word. The driver came in and helped with the luggage. Kate walked toward Soraya with open arms.

"You call us, even if you are just lonesome, you hear?" She said, as tears welled up in her eyes.

Soraya was crying, too, and had a hard time answering her back. They were holding each other tight when Oliver walked in and told Kate to get in the car. Kate walked out, still crying.

Oliver came to Soraya and put his hands on her shoulders.

"You be good. Put this envelope away in some place safe. There is some money in there in case you need it. We will call you and check with you as soon as we get there."

Soraya was still crying.

"Listen to me," Oliver said, lifting her chin, "Don't cry". I don't want to leave you like this." He pulled her in his strong arms and held her close. He felt the small bulge in her stomach and for the first time and it gave him an unspeakable joy.

"Take care of this little one until we get back. Remember, we love you very much; and I promise you that you never have to worry about being alone again. This is the last time, and it is only because it's been planned for a long time. Now go wash your face and go back to bed. You can leave the dishes for later."

Soraya nodded and smiled. "I love you both, too," she whispered.

Oliver walked to the door and turned to looked at her one last time.

"Good-bye miss Noor."

"Good-bye, Mr. Reed."

He shut the door and left. Soraya ran toward the window and looked out to see Oliver wave at her before he got in the cab.

She turned around and looked at the empty apartment. She couldn't stand the emptiness, and she threw herself on the couch and cried as hard as she could. The intensity of her emotions was more than she could handle. They would be coming back soon. It was only going to be for a few weeks.

Somehow it was more than just their departure that made her so sad. Maybe it had to do with the fact that she had lost so many people in her life. She never had a chance to say good-bye to any of them. Maybe it was how tragic her life had been. For the first time, she didn't have to pretend any longer. She was all alone and free to cry about everything that had happened to her, even for her child who she would have to give up at some point.

She laid on the couch for a long time, feeling empty but free. Her eyes got tired and soon she fell sleep. For the first time, she didn't dream about anything. She just fell into a deep, deep sleep.

# CHAPTER THREE

Oliver and Kate sat in the back seat of the taxi, not saying a word. Kate was sad to leave Soraya. This strange country with its mysterious cultures and long history was such a part of her life now, that for the first time, she felt like she was leaving her home. Was it because of Soraya?

She stared at the morning night and could hear the stray dogs barking. They always came at night and left with the day-light. Where do they go? No one knew. Maybe this was part of the mysterious magic of this old country that had grown within her so deeply. Now she was sad to leave it even for a short time. She kept on staring.

Oliver was also uncertain of his feelings. He looked out the window, and saw Soraya's face everywhere. Those beautiful, tearful, black eyes were haunting him no matter where he looked.

The driver had the radio on and Oliver could hear the morning prayer.

"Alaho Akbar, Ashhado Ana Laelahe Elalah, Ashhado Ana Mohammaden Rasoolelah."

The Muslim prayer, which gave him a chill throughout his body. He didn't know its meaning, but it always gave him a chill. The sacred prayer sounded familiar to him. He liked listening to it, the holy sound of Muslim prayer.

Why did she have this hold on him, he wondered. He felt a part of his heart and soul was left back at the apartment. Oliver looked over at Kate and took her hand in his. It felt like ice. He kissed the tip of her fingers, smiling at her, unable to say anything. Before they knew it, the taxi had pulled over to the curb and stopped. Everything happened so fast and they suddenly found themselves on the PAN AM flight, ready for take-0ff.

"Why don't you try to get some sleep?" Oliver asked Kate.

She put her head back and shut her eyes. Oliver looked out the window and felt a single tear roll down his cheek from the corner of his eye. He couldn't remember the last time he had cried.

"What is happening to me? I feel so empty," he said, seeing her eyes again. Those tear filled eyes that was asking him to stay.

"Oliver, don't leave. I need you. I am all alone. Don't do this to me!" She was now screaming, "Oliver!"

He opened his eyes to the screaming sound of the plane.

His eyes shot open, breathing heavy. Sweat beads ran down his face and he was drenched in cold sweat. He looked over and saw Kate sleeping peacefully.

"This is ridiculous," he told himself, "It was just a dream. She is fine, probably sleeping."

Soraya woke up feeling stiff and couldn't believe she had fallen asleep on the couch. She saw the envelope that Oliver gave her, still in her hand, all wrinkled, and decided to open it. She found some money in it and also a letter that she began to read.

By the time you read this letter, Kate and I will be in the skies somewhere over the ocean going home. Somehow home has a different meaning since you have come into our life; I hope you take care of yourself while we are gone. We wouldn't forgive ourselves if something happened to you while we were gone. Don't push yourself too much. I know you will do just fine and will pass your exams with flying colors. Kate and I respect your determination to achieve your goals. You have found yourself a spot in the corner of our hearts forever. Now, I want you to get up and wash your face and eat a healthy breakfast and get busy. Time will pass quicker than you think, and we will be back before you know it. You have become such a member of our small family that it's even hard for us to comprehend. I am sure there is a good reason as why you are in our life.

Soraya smiled and read the letter over again and decided to do exactly as he asked.

The next couple of weeks went by fast. She studied hard and took all her exams, passing with high scores. Soraya was thrilled and couldn't wait to talk to Kate and Oliver and give them the news. They had told her to call them anytime she needed to talk, and this was as good a time as any. She dialed the number, and the phone rang a few times. Someone answered and she recognized Kate's voice immediately.

"Hello Kate."

"Hi sweetheart, how are you doing. Is everything okay?"

"I am just fine, and yes everything is perfect. I called to tell you that I passed my tests."

Kate let out a scream.

"Congratulations! I knew you could do it. I am so proud of you. Listen, Oliver wants to say hello, and I don't mean to cut you short; but I have a doctor's appointment and have to leave in a couple of minutes. I will call you later."

"Kate, are you okay?"

"I am just fine. Everything is great. I do my annual checkup here every year. Nothing to worry about. Here is Oliver. I have to go, but like I said, I will call you later. Take care of yourself."

She talked to Oliver for a few minutes, and he assured her everything was okay. She put the phone down, feeling sad for no apparent reason. Soraya felt so emotional and knew it had to do with her pregnancy, wondering what to do once the baby arrived. Kate wanted her to wait and not make a decision until after the baby was born. Getting emotionally involved with the baby was not what she wanted to do, and she kept reminding herself of that.

"This baby will be a constant reminder of my worst memories," she said looking down and feeling her belly. "I hope you never have to find out the truth about how you were conceived. It won't be fair to you to live with me and witness the pain and misery that I go through to forget the day you were seeded in my body. I will have to live with my decision for the rest of my life, but I am not willing to share that life with you."

Meanwhile, Kate and Oliver sat at the doctor's office trying to digest what they just heard.

"I can't believe it's a tumor. How did that happen, Doctor? What did I do wrong?" Kate asked bursting into tears. Thoughts were racing through her head thinking if she closed her eyes it would only be a dream. This is not how she envisioned her life to be. She could no longer hear the doctor or Oliver as they talked about the tumor and the method of treatment.

Oliver held her close and tried to comfort her, but how could he? This was as much as a shock to him. Within seconds their life had turned upside down.

"Kate, there have been many successful treatments for people in your condition. I know people who died of old age, who had had a brain tumor their entire life. The tumor didn't kill them. You have to believe in that and deal with this in the right frame of mind."

"What is the next step?" Oliver asked.

"We have to find out the exact location and the size of the tumor. I can't give a specific diagnosis until then. I have ordered all the necessary tests. We have to wait and see. Meanwhile, I don't want you to consider yourself as good as dead, because I won't let that happen to you," the doctor replied, forcing a smile looking at Kate knowing he was only talking to Oliver.

"Come on sweetheart, let's go and schedule all your tests."

She got up and followed Oliver, still in a state of shock. Oliver wasn't feeling any better, but he had to be strong for her sake.

They went back to Kate's parents when it was all done.

"I don't know how to tell my parents," Kate said with tears in her eyes.

Oliver took her in his arms and looked away so she wouldn't see his tears flowing.

"Darling, you can't worry about anyone but yourself right now. Let me handle everyone else.

Her mother was sitting at the kitchen table going through some Christmas mail.

"Hi Mom."

"Hi honey, how did everything go?" She asked as she looked up. "What's the matter, dear? Have you been crying?"

Kate looked down, and Oliver walked toward his mother-in-law and knelt down by her chair.

"We have some disturbing news," he started as he held her hand in his.

"What's wrong," her voice was shaking now.

Oliver cleared his throat and continued, "the doctor diagnosed a brain tumor. I am sorry."

"Oh my God, no!" she cried. "I don't believe it."

She was trembling, and Oliver just held her, trying to calm her down so as not to upset Kate anymore.

"We shouldn't lose hope. The doctor is optimistic; and until we find out differently, that's how we should all act. They are going to take an x-ray tomorrow. We will find out a lot more then; so let's not lose hope. He thinks it must be in the beginning stages, otherwise it would have caused some side effects."

Kate's mother listened as Oliver told her everything the doctor had told them.

"Listen Sweetheart, no matter what it is, or how bad it sounds, we are going to be beside you. We will fight this together. You don't have to go through this alone, darling."

Kate held her mother and cried quietly. Her mother held on to her only daughter tight, not wanting to let her go from her side.

This was a very sad day for all of them. They never even dreamt of something like this happening. Kate had always been such a healthy woman. Oliver suggested that she take a nap, and he walked her to their room. He sat next to her on the edge of the bed.

"Are you okay?"

"That's the whole point. I don't feel any differently. Why isn't the tumor making me sick? Because that would be easier to handle."

"The doctor said it is in the beginning stages, and thank God for that. We are going to beat this together, and we can't lose hope. I need you to be strong, so please don't bury yourself already. We have our whole life ahead of us. I am not going to give up easily, and I need you to do the same."

Kate listened to her husband and was thankful to have him beside her at a time like this. He kissed her on the lips and decided to let her rest for a while.

"I will check on you later, darling," he assured her, and he closed the door.

In a matter of hours, his entire life was shattered before his eyes. He couldn't even imagine a life without Kate. He didn't even want to think about it that way, but couldn't help it. Oliver left the house and decided to go for a walk to a small lake near the house, where they used to spend many hours planning their future together. They had known each other almost all their lives. They began dating when they were in junior high and had been together ever since. He could still see Kate's face when he asked her to marry him on this very spot where he stood, tears of joy in her eyes. She had kissed him and asked how long she had to wait to be Mrs. Oliver Reed.

"Not until we both graduate from college," he had said.

She thought that was too long, but was willing to wait. They got married right after they graduated from college, and been blessed with a good life until this news.

He thought of all the times they had discussed starting their family together. He always told her it was best to wait until they were back in their own country, but what if Kate couldn't have the children she had always wanted? Oliver had talked her out of it so many times, and now it could be too late. He would never forgive himself if that was the case.

"What if she dies and doesn't survive this tumor?"

He buried his face in his hands, praying it would all work out, not believing this was happening to them.

Suddenly he thought of Soraya; with everything happening so fast, it seemed like she didn't even exist. What would happen to her? There were so many things to work out that it didn't even seem logical to think about her.

"I have to only think of Kate right now, no one but Kate."

Later, they drove to the clinic, and everyone was quiet in the car. No one wanted to speak too soon, fearing things wouldn't turn out the way they hoped. The nurse escorted Kate to the other room, and their waiting game began.

It seemed like hours before the doctor called them all in to give them the first results. Kate sat next to Oliver, holding his hand and biting her lips. Oliver wasn't in any better shape, but acted calm for her sake. The doctor turned around in his chair and looked Kate in the eyes. He began explaining by first showing her the location of the tumor.

"The good news is, it is not malignant and is only as big as a green pea. There have been many successful recoveries with this kind of tumor through medication; so, that is what we are going to start with. Surgery is our last option, and we don't need to worry about that at this point. You will be on medication for three months before we will take another x-ray to see how you have responded to the medication. This will tell us if the medication has shrunk the tumor or not."

"Kate, if this works, you can have a long normal life like the rest of us, except you will be on medication for the rest of your life. You might never need surgery, which is what I am hoping for. This is all good news. The bad news is you can't get pregnant with this kind of medication. The meds will affect your female organs and will not enable you to get pregnant. Eventually, you might have to have a hysterectomy, to prevent future complications. However, that is not in the near future." He then stopped and looked at Kate, "do you have any questions?"

Kate was at a loss for words, and Oliver jumped in to ask some questions regarding the medication and any kind of side effects it might have.

"We won't know that unless she starts taking it; and if she does show some signs, we will have other options. I recommend you get a second opinion. Sometimes that helps people in making a decision sooner, and therefore start with their treatment sooner."

Oliver couldn't help being happy with what he heard. At least they now knew it was treatable. Kate was also relieved. Of course her parents were all so thankful, knowing they were not going to lose their only daughter.

Kate suddenly turned to the doctor.

"What if the medication works and the tumor shrinks to nothing? Do you stop the drugs then?"

"From time- to-time, yes, we will stop the medication, just to see how the tumor does on its own."

"Can I get pregnant when I am off the medication?"

"Kate, this is a long-term treatment. If you get pregnant, chances are the baby won't be healthy. In most cases, patients aren't able to get pregnant. I am sorry."

She looked down, tears welling up in her eyes.

"Honey, we can talk about all that later. For now, I am so thankful that you will be okay, and that is all that matters."

They left the doctor's office kind of relieved. The news was a blessing to all of them. So they decided to celebrate the good news.

She was to start the medication right away and was already told not to leave the country for at least a month. They had to make sure there would not be any kind of complications, and they would have to see the doctor in three months for another x-ray.

She was thankful the results came out well, and that she was not going to die of the tumor.

"At least," she told herself, "not anytime soon, anyway."

They drove home together, and this time there was laughter in the car. Everyone was in good spirits. It still was a shock to them all, knowing Kate had a brain tumor; but, she was going to stay in their lives and that was the important fact. They had a long road ahead of them, and they all realize that. The part that pleased everyone was that Kate was taking the long road with them and not alone. Her mother insisted on a second opinion before she started her meds and everyone agreed with her.

By the time they got home, Kate was exhausted. She had hardly slept the night before and decided to take a nap before dinner. Her mother went upstairs with her, wanting to give her some motherly comfort.

"Honey, I know how much it hurts you, but you always have the option of adopting a child. You have so much love to give that it doesn't matter if it is yours or not. You will love him just as much, and he will love you the same. For now, I want to see you back to health, and I don't think it is a good idea for you to go back to Iran with Oliver. You should stay here with us for at least the first three months to see how the medication is working. I really don't think you should go until then."

"I don't know, Mom. I really have to think about it first and see what Oliver wants me to do. My big worry right now is Soraya. She is due in five weeks."

"Oh darling, you can't worry about her now. Think of yourself first. If it was up to me, I would never let you go back there. Oliver should wrap things up and move back home. You two have been away long enough. Your dad and I are getting old, and we hate having you so far away all the time. I think that as long as the good lord had mercy on us and hopefully given you back to us we should be thankful. It's time for you to move back home where you belong." Kate didn't expect her mother to understand their situation.

"Don't worry mom, everything will work out okay. I don't want you to worry." Kate crawled into her bed and thought about everything that she had to do the next few weeks. One thing was certain, she was not going to miss Soraya's delivery, no matter what everyone said.

Oliver and Kate's father were having a similar conversation downstairs. Oliver thought Kate should stay home until the doctor was more confident about her condition. He just wished he could stay there with her. It was hard for her parents to understand their relationship with Soraya and in reality they didn't quite understand it either.

Oliver called the airlines to cancel her plane reservation. He also set up an appointment for a second opinion. There were a lot of things he needed to take care of before his departure and was busy at work when Kate came downstairs a couple of hours later.

"Hi sweetheart, how are you feeling?"

"I am fine. What are you doing?"

"Just taking care of some loose ends. I made an appointment for you to get a second opinion. I explained our situation, so they squeezed you in for tomorrow."

"Oliver, you are not planning on leaving me here, are you?"

"Not for long, darling. Just until you are on the medication for at least a month, and we can be sure there is no complication afterward."

"What about Soraya? I have to be there for her."

"Kate, you have to get well first."

"I am just fine. We will have the second opinion tomorrow, and I will stay on the medication for a week, and then I will leave with you. If I am going to show any negative reaction, it would show right away. Please Oliver, I need to be there when she has the baby."

"You can't be thinking of Soraya right now. She wouldn't want you back there in this condition."

Kate was desperate.

"Okay, then I will start the medication immediately and stay here for three weeks. If there is no problem, I will fly back to Tehran right away. It would be about two weeks before her due date, and then I will come back for my quarterly exam. Either I leave with you or stay an extra three weeks."

She was upset and Oliver could see it clearly. He didn't want to upset her anymore. She was too stubborn once her mind was made up. He decided not to argue with her for now and hoped maybe she would change her mind later. They both decided not to tell Soraya anything until he got back.

"We better get ready for dinner and the fight with your parents next. You know how they are going to react?"

"They won't like it, but they have to respect and understand our wishes."

"More like your wishes, darling, not mine," Oliver replied with a smile.

The news didn't go over too well with her parents; but just like Oliver, they knew better than to argue with her. They just hoped she would change her mind later.

They got the same result from the second doctor, the next day; so Kate started the medication immediately. She didn't feel too good for the first week, but that was to be expected. Oliver was to leave in two days and had a hard time leaving Kate behind, especially with her condition; but, he didn't have any other choice.

They spent as much of the last two days together as they could, taking long walks and having intimate moments together. This was the first time they were to be separated for a long length of time. Neither one looked forward to it.

Oliver held his wife close, saying, "I want you to take care of yourself when I am gone. You need to get plenty of rest. The doctor said it is the best thing for you while you are on the medication. I promise you, everything will be okay."

He lifted her chin and kissed her passionately.

"It's going to be hard getting up in the morning and not having you by my side Mrs. Reed. I hope you know how much I love you."

She looked pale these days, and he was concerned about her. He held her tight, not wanting to ever let her go.

Kate kept busy all day packing for Oliver. It was a sad day for her, and she couldn't wait for the day that she could join him again. She felt like a prisoner being locked up and having no control. Oliver took care of the last minute things before his departure. They had decided to have a quiet dinner together. They both got all dressed up and went to a romantic little Italian restaurant. Kate looked especially radiant that night, and Oliver couldn't take his eyes off of her. It was a romantic and beautiful dinner, and they both enjoyed it fully

"I can't stand being away from you for almost a month, Oliver. It is almost like this is not home without you. It doesn't matter where I live, as long as we are together."

He kissed her gently. "I feel the same way, darling; but for now, we have to do what is best for you, even if it means being apart from each other."

On the way home, Kate brought up Soraya again.

"I feel so guilty. What if I miss her delivery? She is going to need me with her."

Oliver just smiled at her and put his finger on her lips, asking her to stop worrying about Soraya.

Everyone was sleeping and they went to their room and closed the door. They felt like a couple of teenagers sneaking around. He lit a candle and walked over to her and unzipped her dress and her dress fell to the floor.

"Have I told you, lately, how beautiful you are?"

She only smiled and looked at him with loving eyes. He undressed his wife and placed her on the edge of the bed, feeling her soft pale skin and kissing her all over. He took her breath away and she trembled with need and they soon lost themselves in each other's arms, making all their desires come true. It was a magical night full of passion for both of them. Neither one got a good night sleep as the pale morning light streamed in through the drapes. There was a sadness that consumed them both.

The next day, Kate drove Oliver to the airport. She held on to him so tight, thinking somehow she was losing him but not knowing why. For some reason, they both thought about Soraya, and how they left her by the apartment door crying as their eyes filled with tears. Oliver clenched his jaw trying to control his emotions for Kate's sake and kissed her passionately one more time before leaving her by the curb.

# CHAPTER FOUR

Soraya knew Kate and Oliver would be back that day, but didn't know exactly what time. She was thrilled to have them back home again. It seemed like they had been gone forever, and she was starting to miss them terribly.

She was eight months pregnant now and didn't move very fast. Everything was a real effort. It took her all day to get the house in perfect condition. She also decided to make one of their favorite dishes, just in case they came home for dinner. The bus wasn't going fast enough for her, and all the stops were making her crazy. It finally arrived at her stop, and she got off the bus and almost ran the last few blocks just to find the house dark and quiet. They weren't home yet and it disappointed her to find the house the same way as she had left it that afternoon.

She set the table and decided to take a hot shower and just sit there and wait for them. She kept looking at the clock hanging in the living room. It was eleven o'clock, and there was still no sign of them. Holding on to her pillow she finally gave up to the exhaustion and closed her eyes and fell asleep almost instantly.

Oliver walked in quietly, thinking she was probably sleeping in her room. He saw the table and the food on top of the stove. He found her curled up on the couch, holding her pillow like a little girl. Quietly, he walked over to her and knelt down by her.

"Hey you, sleepy head, wake up."

She slowly opened her eyes and saw Oliver.

"Thank God, you guys are home!"

And she almost jumped to her feet looking for Kate.

Oliver noticed how much bigger she had gotten the last few weeks.

"What do we have here? This baby has definitely grown!" Oliver exclaimed, and they finally flew into each other's arms.

"Where is Kate? Is she in the bathroom?"

Oliver scratched his head and told her to sit.

"We need to talk."

Her heart dropped as she held on the arm of the couch and slowly sat down.

"Kate had to stay back home for some medical reasons. There is nothing to worry about anymore, but it scared all of us when we first got the news. She has a brain tumor, but it is treatable. In fact, she has started the treatment already. That's why she couldn't come back with me: the doctor wants to make sure there won't be any kind of complications with the medication."

Soraya looked horrified at the thought of Kate having a brain tumor. Oliver could see the terror in her face and was not happy about delivering such and emotional news.

"She is going to be okay or I wouldn't have left her there. Everything is under control. She is hoping you won't have the baby until she gets back, and that is the only thing that is bothering her right now, not being here with us."

"What caused her to have a tumor? Maybe you shouldn't have left her; she needs you now more than ever."

"I know that, but I had to get back to work, and the doctor assured all of us that everything would be okay. Plus, she is with her family."

"When is she coming back?"

"Three weeks from now. So you have to hang on until she gets back. She wants nothing more than to be here with you when you have that baby."

"Soraya, we didn't want to tell you over the phone. I know you are disappointed she is not here right now, but you have to understand; we couldn't take the chance of telling you over the phone. Not when you are eight months pregnant."

"Is she going to be okay, Oliver?"

"She will be fine. We don't know what the future will bring, but for now her doctor is very optimistic; and that's how we should be."

They were busy discussing Kate when the phone rang. Oliver answered, knowing it must be Kate.

"Hi honey, how are you?"

"I'm fine, how about yourself?"

"Just tired. It was a long trip as usual. I got home just a little while ago."

"How is Soraya?"

"Big and sassy and very concerned about you. I think you should talk to her yourself. I will call you in a couple of days."

"Hi Kate."

"Hi, how are you doing? Oliver said you are getting big."

"I'm fine, but I don't understand everything that is happening with you."

Kate went on explaining her situation the best she could, and told her not to worry too much. She made her promise she wouldn't have the baby until she got back, and they both laughed.

Soraya felt a little relieved hearing Kate's voice.

"Are you hungry, Oliver? I made some dinner."

"I know you did, but more than anything, I am tired. Can we eat it tomorrow?"

Soraya just smiled, "I'm sorry, I know how tired you must feel. I'll warm it up for dinner tomorrow."

Oliver walked over and gave her a peck on the forehead and went to bed.

That night she laid in bed awake most of the night wondering if Kate would be alright. It was a very emotional night for her; and she spent a good part of it praying for Kate, hoping she would make it through these difficult times.

The following day she woke up totally unaware of the time or the day. She sat in her bed and stared at the small clock near her bed. Soon she realized it was morning and also Friday, which is considered the weekend in Iran. She followed the aroma of coffee all the way to the kitchen and found Oliver sitting at the kitchen table reading the paper.

"Good morning. Sorry I am so late getting up. I had a hard time going to sleep last night."

"It's okay. I am glad you could sleep in a little. Sorry I had to go to bed so fast last night. I was exhausted and fell asleep on top of the covers, with my clothes still on. Sit down and talk to me. Tell me what you have been doing the last month."

She sat after making herself a cup of tea.

"Oh just going to school, studying, and getting lots of sleep."

"I know you are worried about Kate. We all are, but you have to remember to be positive. She needs our support and strength, and that is the best thing we can give her right now."

Soraya nodded in agreement, still in awe of Kates illness and her heart ached for her. She began making breakfast as they talked easily about school, weather and the gossips in the building that she had heard from Mrs. Solayman. She suddenly cried out from a sharp pain pierced through her as she fell to her knees. Oliver looked at her startled, and ran to her aid.

"What's the matter?"

She took a deep breath and then let it out.

"I have no idea what that was. It was a sharp pain and then it was gone. Thank God, it didn't last long."

"Have you had this kind of pain before?"

"No, not like this one."

"You don't think you will have the baby anytime soon, do you?"

She smiled at him.

"I don't know, I have never done this before. On second thought, I think it's best if I sit right here and let you make breakfast."

They spent most of the morning talking about his trip, and the Christmas parties he and Kate went to. Soraya listened to him describing this other world to her and tried to visualize what it would be like to live there. To live free and not be criticized for wanting to go to school and not be forced into a marriage at a young age.

The next day everything went back to normal. Oliver went to work early the next morning, and Soraya kept busy with her everyday routine. Oliver picked her up from school most every night from that night on, seeing how even walking had become a chore for her.

The following couple weeks went by fast; and Oliver spent most of his free time at home with Soraya, trying to get to know her better. He truly enjoyed her company. In this, her youth, he found a maturity that he had never seen in other kids her age.

He decided to get her out of the house one night and thought dinner would be appropriate. The waiter at the restaurant made a remark about her being his wife, and they both laughed.

It was a Thursday night; the beginning of their weekend. She got very tired right after dinner which was not unusual for her those days. They drove home with her half sleep, but he was glad he had taken her out.

It was a cold night, and she felt the chill more than usual, deciding to go to bed and get some rest. She was glad the next day was Friday, and she could sleep in. It was another restless night which was not unusual these days. Even the baby was restless, and she couldn't figure it out. She began reading her book and tried to ignore all the odd things that were happening to her that night.

She felt a pressure on her lower abdomen and soon it turned into a mild pain. It was about two in the morning and the lack of sleep was beginning to annoy her.

"Am I having this baby tonight?"

Soon the pain was more pronounced, and she decided to take her child delivery book off the shelf and read it. The book covered all aspects of labor and delivery, but it was hard for her to concentrate. She was starting to get anxious and twitchy.

"This is probably false labor," she thought, having read about it in the book.

The pain was not regular for a long time, so she figured it couldn't be the real thing or it would start at a more regular pace.

"I am not going to wake Oliver up unless I know it is the real thing." Even though nothing made sense to her anymore, she continued to read to busy herself wishing Kate was there with her. It would be so much easier.

The clock showed 3am and the pain came at a more regular pace and it got more intense. She was trying to avoid waking up Oliver but knew at that rate she needed to wake him sooner than later.

"I can't have this child tonight. Kate isn't here." Without warning an intense pain broke her train of thoughts and soon after her water broke.

"Oh dear God, I am having this baby tonight!"

She quickly got out of the bed and took the sheets off not wanting Oliver to see it. The pain was far worse than she ever imagined kneeling down and bit her lips, at the same time holding to the sheets as tightly as she could. She could barely make her way to the closet, but tried as quickly as possible before the next one came on. This one came only five minutes after the last one.

"Okay, calm down. You have to get out of these wet clothes, put on your robe, and wake up Oliver."

Swiftly, she took her clothes off and changed. She was reaching for the door when she felt another contraction. This one took her breath away. There was no doubt in her mind that she was about to have the baby. She sat there on the floor until it went away. This was all happening too fast. According to her book, it was supposed to take hours before she should reach this point. What she didn't realize was that a few hours had passed while she talked herself out of the idea.

Soraya was finally able to get up and open the bedroom door to walk to Oliver's room. She knocked on his door, noticing that the pain got worse with each contraction. She knocked on the door a little harder the second time and called his name.

"Oliver, please come out. I need your help."

Revealing her need embarrassed her to no limit, but she didn't have any other choice.

She heard Oliver's voice calling, "I'll be right out."

Oliver jumped out of bed, putting on his robe as quickly as he could. He opened the door and found Soraya hunched over by his bedroom door.

"What's wrong?"

"I think the baby is coming," she said.

He couldn't believe his ears.

"Oh boy. Okay, let me see. I will call the nurse. No, I'll call the doctor."

"Oliver, just call the nurse," and with that said the pain spun through her and brought her to her knees. He looked at her in shock.

"How long have you been having these pains?"

He looked at the clock to see what time it was.

"Are you sure this is the real thing?"

She nodded, "My water broke about twenty minutes ago."

"Oh lord, why did you wait so long? Okay, there is no time for that. Where is the number?"

"By the phone in the kitchen," she said, and she let out another scream.

Oliver sat there on the floor holding her until the pain passed and decided to help her to bed and then call the nurse.

It took a long time before someone answered on the other end of the line. Once the nurse answered, he explained everything as fast as he could. She gave him the necessary instructions and told him it would be about forty-five minutes before she could get there.

"I don't understand why you waited so long to call for God's sake." She exclaimed He just told her to hurry up and heard Soraya scream again. He gathered a bunch of towels and ran to the bedroom only to find her curled up from the pain.

"Oh my God, I need to push, but I don't know if I am dilated.

Oliver looked at her, helpless.

"I have never done this before. I don't know what to do. The nurse won't be here for another forty minutes."

She had another contraction. He held her and told her to breathe, remembering what he saw in a movie once.

"That's it, just breathe through it, baby. You can do it," he assured her and found himself breathing with her.

She couldn't take it anymore and started crying.

"I can't do it anymore. Oh my God, here comes another one. I need to push!"

Oliver was lost for words. He had no idea how to comfort her.

"Do you think it is time for you to push?"

"I don't know, I just don't know," she broke into a sob.

There was no time to waste any longer. Oliver covered her with some sheets and looked between her legs and the color rose to her cheeks of embarrassment.

Oliver held her hand, whispering, "Don't worry, sweetheart; it's okay."

He looked down at her and screamed, "Oh my God, I can see the baby's head!"

She let out another cry and screamed, "I need to push!"

"Go ahead and push," Oliver encouraged her.

So she pushed as hard as she could. All the muscles in her face tightened, and she thought her eyes were going to pop out. He held her hand tight and told her she was doing great.

"Just breathe. I am here for you. I won't let anything happen to you."

He switched back to his previous position as soon as she had another contraction.

"That's it, sweetheart, push one more time. You are doing just fine," he reassured her, and his eyes widened.

"One more time Soraya; it's coming; the baby is coming! Push. Push! Here it comes." Soraya screamed and pushed as hard as she could.

"This is God's miracle," Oliver said, when he heard the baby's cry.

Oliver took the baby, laughing and crying at the same time. He laid the baby on the bed by her feet and came toward her. It was a moving moment for both of them. She was crying, and he just held her close and kissed her on the forehead. Their tears crossed together and before he knew it his lips met hers, and his arms wrapped around her. She didn't reject him and allowed him to kiss her. He held her in his arms for a few short seconds before he heard the doorbell. He quickly pulled away, and ran toward the door. The nurse pushed through the door in a hurry searching for Soraya.

"The baby came a few minutes ago." Pointing to the direction of the bedroom.

The nurse ran toward the bedroom."

Get me some warm water," she ordered Oliver.

Oliver did as he was told and took the water to the room and knocked. She took the water from him and told him to wait outside. He sat on the couch, shocked at what he had just witnessed. It truly was a miracle. He was also confused at what happened after the baby's birth.

The nurse came out half an hour later.

"Everything is fine and she is doing well. A doctor should see her as soon as possible, just to make sure everything is okay."

Oliver thanked her, paid her some money, and sent her on her way. It was early morning hours as Oliver stood outside her room trying to find the courage to knock. He slowly opened the door and saw her looking down at her baby boy with such unconditional love, it took his breath away. Oliver walked in and looked at the baby.

"He is beautiful."

He took her hand in his, didn't know if he should be ashamed or joyful. All he knew was that he had just shard the most unbelievable experience of his life with her.

She looked up and gazed into his eyes.

"Are you okay?"

"I'm fine, just a little tired."

He didn't know where to start explaining what had taken place earlier.

"The birth of the baby was the most beautiful thing I've ever witnessed. What happened between us was just out of love and excitement on both of our parts. It is not something that I regret, but at the same time it is not to happen again. We both love Kate too much to let this happen in the future. It was an emotional moment for both of us and for a split second we lost ourselves. I hope you understand what I am trying to tell you."

"I do. And I also want to thank you for everything you did today. I couldn't have done this without you."

He squeezed her hand in his but felt such a rush that for a moment thought she could see it in his eyes that the speech he just gave her didn't come from his heart.

The baby started to cry, and she asked Oliver to give him to her.

"He needs to get fed."

He placed the baby in her arms and walked to the bedroom window looking out giving her privacy. She took her breast out and held the baby close to her as Oliver wondering what all this meant. It was so strange. He couldn't describe his feelings even to himself. It was almost like she now belonged to him and so did this child that he just helped enter the world.

These emotions were all wrong, and he knew it; but in a strange way he needed to protect this young woman and the boy from any harm. He needed to love her no matter how wrong it was. She was to remain in his life forever. He had no way out and didn't want one. The silence in the room was deafning.

"What are you going to name him?"

She smiled, "I am going to call him Ali. It almost sounds like your name."

She looked down at the baby again, smiling. He was asleep again, and Oliver took him from her to hold him for a while.

"Hello little one. Welcome to the world. You are beautiful, just like your mommy."

And he put his face close to the baby's, and kissed him and knew he could never let him go. In a way, he felt that the baby belonged to him. He helped bring him to this world and was going to help him grow up and become a man someday. This was the closest he could come to calling a child his, and he was not about to part with him, no matter what the cost was.

Soraya closed her eyes and fell asleep. Oliver carried the baby to the living room.

Kate had bought the baby some clothes when they were in the States. He put them on the little child and sat on the couch, rocking him to sleep. He was deep in thought, amazed at how fast everything had happened since the day before. He was almost old enough to be her father; yet his feelings were different from a father toward a daughter. He loved her with all his heart and also loved Kate. How could this be possible? Was he hurting to become a father so much that anyone who gave him a child would be loved in his heart?

"These feelings are all wrong," he told himself and he looked down at the baby, "but you are all right. You will be our connection in this triangle. Kate will take one look at you and never let you go. I know what goes on in her heart. She will love you like her own. Why couldn't Kate and I adopt you, instead of some strangers?"

It was Friday and he didn't have to work that day. He wanted to stay there all day and take care of the baby. It was time to call Kate and give her the news.

She answered the phone on the other end.

"Hi honey."

"Hi," she replied and knew immediately that something was not right. "Is everything okay?"

Oliver stopped for a second before continuing. "Everything is just fine, but I have some news for you. Soraya had a baby boy this morning."

She screamed on the other end of the phone. "Oh my God, I wanted to be there so bad!"

Oliver went on telling her all about the birth.

"He is absolutely beautiful, Kate."

"Oh, Oliver, you helped deliver the baby."

A stab of envy ran through her, knowing she would never be able to share a moment like that with the man she loved.

"It was incredible. I wish you could be here," he told her, and in a way he truly believed that. Maybe nothing would have happened if Kate had been there.

"Listen Love, we need to talk. I know it is too soon to talk about all this, but there is not going to be a lot of time once you get here. I want you to think about maybe adopting this child. You will absolutely love him once you see him."

Kate remained quiet for a short time.

"I've been thinking a lot myself. With my situation, this is the closest we will come to having a child and being able to call him ours. But I don't know how Soraya would feel about this."

Thoughts were racing through his head. He felt this child belonged to him and the thought of someone else taking him away tore at his heart. It would not happen but he needed to think of the woman who just gave birth to him and not act selfishly.

"I don't know, but we have to talk to her together when you get back."

Kate was too excited to stay away and unlike Oliver she didn't have any time to think about it but in her heart of hearts she thought this was meant to be and maybe this little baby belonged to her. She didn't know to weep at the thought of missing the birth or overjoyed at the possibility of adopting this child.

"I am going to try and see if I can make an earlier reservation. Everything is fine with the medication, and there is no reason why I can't come sooner."

Oliver thought for a moment.

"Well, let me know if you can get an earlier flight."

They said good bye; and he put the phone down, wondering if he did the right thing, talking to Kate about adopting Ali without discussing it with Soraya first.

He went to the kitchen and made some breakfast for her. He put it on a tray and walked to her room. For the first time he realized that she gave birth to the baby in his bedroom on his and Kate's bed. She was still sleeping so he put the tray down and sat beside her, looking at her. She looked so innocent and peaceful laying there. She moved her head and slowly opened her eyes. She saw Oliver next to her looking at her.

"How long have you been sitting there?"

"Just a few minutes."

"Where is the baby?"

"He is in the living room sleeping. How are you feeling?

"Still tired and sore, but I will make it, no doubt."

"I talked to Kate and gave her the news. She was hysterical and, of course, sends her love. She also said she might come a few days earlier if she can get a reservation."

Soraya looked away and closed her eyes.

"What's the matter?" he asked, seeing tears in her eyes.

"I don't know. Maybe it is guilt or shame at what we did."

He looked down.

"I feel the same way. I've never felt like this in my entire life. It's almost as if I am not in control of my own mind, and I just don't understand it. I want to take you in my arms and make love to you and never let you go. I know it's wrong, but can't help the way I feel."

She felt the same way and didn't like herself for it.

"You can't make love to me, but how about just holding me."

He held her in his arms and smelled her thick black hair and buried his face in it. His lips were thirsty for hers. They lost themselves in each other's arms once again.

Oliver stopped and tried to get a hold of his emotions.

"The last thing I want to do is to hurt you, not after everything you've been through. I am married to Kate and I just don't know what to do so neither one of you is hurt."

She looked at him with fire in her eyes.

"Then we should stop. This is not right, and we both know it. Nothing is worth hurting Kate. We have to stop and go on with our lives like nothing ever happened."

"We can stop our actions, but can we just stop our feelings too?" Oliver asked.

"I don't know, but we have to try. There is no future for us. You are married to a wonderful woman. And I have to get on with my life, now that this baby is born. Maybe someday I can experience the kind of love that you have shown me today for real, with someone who is free to love me."

Oliver knew she was right but had a hard time thinking about another man even touching her let alone loving her. He brought the baby back in the bedroom and laid him down next to her, and she fed him once again. The two of them fell asleep shortly after. Oliver laid on the edge of the bed, closed his eyes, and dozed off also. He took care of the baby for the remainder of the day and enjoyed every minute of it. He was in love with this child. He had always thought Kate would give him such a child, but instead, it was Soraya who gave him that joy. He called the doctor and also requested a nurse to be sent to the house for the next couple of days. Soraya was not to do anything for the next few days; so Oliver decided to sleep in her bed that night and let Soraya and the baby sleep in his room.

He lay awake in her room most of the night, smelling her pillow and thinking of her.

"I have got to get her out of my head. This is just crazy. How come I never felt this way before? Is it possible that I was unaware of my feelings?"

He had to get over these emotions before Kate came back. She would know and it would destroy her.

"I can't do that to her. She is my wife, my best friend and also my lover, and that's how it should be. I can't risk losing Kate."

His mind soon drifted off to Soraya. She had a magic that was hard to explain.

"Her eyes melted him to the bone, her innocence, her beauty and intelligence. How can I let her slip away from me? I can't take this any longer."

He had noticed how most men looked at her and knew it wouldn't be long before they would stand by their door step wanting her. He couldn't bear the thought of someone else having her.

"She doesn't belong to me," he argued to himself, "she has a mind of her own and someday will go her own way."

Oliver knew the answer to his questions, but it was hard for him to deny his feelings. He hoped he would have the strength to do the right thing and not let anything come between him and Kate. Not even Soraya, with all her magic and mystery, should do that.

It was a long night, and he woke up the next morning feeling like he had hardly slept. He checked on her first thing and found her feeding the baby.

"Hi beautiful, how did you two sleep last night?"

"Good morning. He woke up a couple of times for feedings, but went right back to sleep. Oliver, we need to talk about the baby. I've been thinking, and the longer we keep him here, the harder it will be for me to let him go. I haven't changed my mind, and I don't intend to do so either. But the longer he stays here with me, the harder it's going to be."

Oliver listened to her carefully.

"I think you should wait until Kate gets back, and we will all sit and talk and make some decisions. For now, I have a nurse coming here to help you for a few days, until you can get back on your feet. Don't try to do anything. The more you rest, the sooner you will be back to normal."

She looked down and whispered, "thank you."

"I have to get ready for work. Can I get you anything before I leave?"

She stared at him at once and sensed a coolness about him.

"I know this is hard on you. It's hard on me, too. And I will leave if you want me to. Making you feel uncomfortable is not my intention. I will do anything to make it easy on you."

Oliver sat on the edge of the bed.

"I don't want you to leave. I don't want you out of my sight for the rest of my life. It's just that we can't let our emotions control our logic. It would destroy me to let you go. Don't ask me how these feelings suddenly crept up on me. I don't have the answer to that. All I know is that we have to be fair to Kate, and we can't get close anymore. I will see you tonight," and with that he walked out of the room.

She was crushed even though she knew he did the right thing. It was over before it had hardly started, and she was mad at Oliver for leading her on.

He got in the car and rest his head on the steering wheel.

"I hurt her. I knew it would hurt her. Why didn't I stop it before it came to this? She is just a child who has never been loved before. I should have never let my feelings get the best of me, and now I've broken her heart. I can never forgive myself. Somehow, I have to make it up to her without getting close to her the way I have been. It has to stop, and this time for Soraya's sake and no one else's."

Back inside the house, the phone rang and Soraya answered it.

"Hello mama."

She was glad to hear Kate 's voice.

"Hello, Kate. How are you feeling?"

"I am fine. How about yourself?"

"I am doing just fine, and so is the baby."

"That's great. Sorry I couldn't make it back before you had the baby."

"Kate, I miss you."

And she meant that with all her heart.

"Same here, and that's why I called. I am leaving first thing in the morning, and I should be there tomorrow night your time."

They talked some more before Soraya put the phone down. She was all nervous and shook up and looked around like a confused child.

"First thing I have to do is get back to my own room."

The nurse helped her get situated in her room, and she felt much better there. She decided Oliver was right, and she had to let things rest and pretend it never happened. She spent the rest of the day reading, feeding the baby, and sleeping. The doctor paid her a visit, giving her and the baby a clean bill of health. But he did tell her to rest for at least a week.

The nurse left right before Oliver got home. He walked in and found the house quiet. He had bought Soraya a big bouquet of flowers and knocked on his bedroom door. He slowly opened the door and found the room empty. His heart sank.

"Soraya?"

"I am in my room, Oliver."

He took a deep breath and walked into her room.

"What are you doing here?"

"I thought it was best if I went back to my own room."

"These are for you," he said, holding out the flowers.

"They are beautiful, Oliver. It reminded her of the wild flowers she used to pick by the pond. Thank you."

"Why didn't you call me today?" he asked.

"I got kind of busy with the nurse and the doctor; and the baby took all of my time today."

"I am sorry for the way I left today."

"Don't be. You did the right thing, and I admire your honesty. You were right. We should have never let things get out of control, and it is not too late to stop now. By the way, Kate called and she is coming home tomorrow night."

He looked at her carefully.

"Are you okay with that?"

She didn't feel at ease answering him and didn't like the fact that he would even ask her.

"Of course I'm okay with that. Why shouldn't I be? This is her house, and you are her husband. I may be many things, but I am not stupid. In a way this is your child, too, yours and Kate's. Isn't that true, Oliver? Haven't you and Kate talked about maybe adopting Ali? So what right do I have not to be okay with everything? It's okay, I am used to that."

"Slow down. You have every right to anything that belongs to you, including this child. I don't want you to punish yourself for everything that has happened in the past. You know how I feel about you, and it bothers me, knowing you are so hurt right now. This is Kate's house; and yes, I am her husband. But this is your child, and you have to decide what you want for him."

"Soraya, you have to be honest with yourself. I have a feeling that it is not the child that has you all bothered. There is more to this than you are letting anyone know. If I was a loser, I would want nothing more than to go to bed with you, make love to you right now, and never let you go. But I can't do that. You and Kate are both very important to me. How can I do the right thing and not hurt either one of you? Please don't hate me for my choices. And don't be angry with me. I can't love you the way I think you deserve to be loved. I am only doing this for both of you, and it is killing me. But I have no other choice."

She looked away feeling so empty.

"I am sorry, Oliver. I shouldn't have said anything, not after everything you have done for me. Please forgive me."

"I don't know why I feel this way about you. In a way, I will always love you, and I want you to remember that. It would be so hard for me to leave this country knowing that I am leaving you behind. For some reason, you have grown within me so deeply that I could never free myself of your love. It's like magic, and that magic is you, my love. I will always love you, no matter what the future brings."

She listened to him and loved him even more for the man he was.

Oliver picked Kate up at the airport the next night. She looked well, but tired, and was so glad to be with him again. When they got home he put her suitcases down by the front door, and she threw her bag on the floor and turned around to kiss him passionately. Soraya stood there without them seeing her and watched them together. For all the right reasons, her heart ached.

"This is going to be a lot harder than I thought," she thought.

Oliver saw her from the corner of his eye and didn't know how to react. He saw her go back to her room. A few minutes later, she made another appearance and called out their names.

"Hey you two."

Kate turned around and ran toward her and they threw their arms around one another, as Oliver stood back and watched the women he loved so much.

"Where is he? I am dying to see him!" Kate said.

Soraya smiled and took Kate to her room where she sat and looked at the sleeping baby.

"He is absolutely beautiful. He is perfect. Can I hold him?"

Soraya nodded and smiled at her child. He opened his eyes as Kate Lifted him off the bed.

"Hi, Sweetheart. You are precious."

She wrapped her arms around him and got as close as she could to him.

"You are truly a miracle. Soraya, he is beautiful. I think he looks just like you."

"I think it is too soon to tell, but I hope he does."

"So tell me, how do you feel?" Kate asked her.

"Still a little sore and tired, but I will be back to normal in no time."

"The doctor said you should really take it easy for at least a week," Oliver added.

"That's right, and I am going to wait on you for a change," Kate said with a smile.

"I think you two are making too big of a deal out of this whole situation. My mother had babies and went back to her normal routine in just a few short days."

They all walked into the living room with Kate still holding the baby. They talked about all sort of things, just like they used to. It seemed like nothing had changed, but they all knew that wasn't true.

Kate had bought Soraya and the baby some new clothes and Soraya thanked her and told her she shouldn't have, not with everything she had had to go through.

Soraya needed to discuss the baby with both of them as soon as possible and decided to bring it up as long as Kate didn't feel too tired.

"I think we should talk about the baby and discuss what we are planning to do with him. I hate to put it in those words, but I am just at a loss and don't know how else to start."

They both looked at each other and couldn't believe she was discussing it already. It was a very difficult situation, and they had discussed it on the way home from the airport. They had decided to wait until she brought it up, knowing that if she allowed it, they would adopt him in a heartbeat.

"I can't keep the baby for too much longer. I need to make some decisions soon."

She knew they wanted the baby, and she was going to let them keep him if that's what they chose to do, but she needed to hear it from them first.

Kate walked over to where Soraya was sitting and knelt down by her.

"Soraya, I feel close enough to you that I don't need to beat around the bush. You know with my illness I will never be able to have a child.

We would be honored if you allowed us to adopt Ali instead of some strangers. We know this won't be easy on you, and it is a lot to ask; but at the same time, we hate to let him go. At least you would never have to worry about who is raising him, or if he is happy and loved. We will raise him and love him as our own. I hope you know that. The rest is up to you. Like I said, we know it is a very hard decision for you, and we will respect and support whatever decision you make."

Soraya took a moment to digest everything Kate had just told her. Her breath caught in her throat, trying not to cry.

"I need to stop breast feeding him as soon as possible, and he needs to move to your room, as he belongs to you. I will help with him as if he were your child and not mine."

She looked down so they wouldn't see the tears in her eyes.

"You may change his name if you choose, and I want everything to be done legally. You have a lawyer draw up all the necessary papers; and also get him an American passport as soon as possible, just in case you have to leave the country on an emergency. I don't want you to leave him behind for any length of time or with anyone else.

Oliver's heart went out to her, knowing how hard this was on her. He wished he could hold her and tell her that everything was going to be okay. His heart ached and he couldn't even look her in the eyes. It didn't seem fair to ask her to live with her child.

He thought to himself, "It is selfish of us, asking her to do the impossible. How can she shut off all her feelings toward her child and pretend he wasn't born to her? Oh dear God, this is not fair. I can see the pain in her eyes, and in the end, this will destroy her."

He knew she would never turn them down because of everything that they had done for her in the past. But after all, she was this child's mother, and how can any mother be put in that kind of situation and not want her child back at some point? He couldn't keep quiet any longer and decided to speak up.

"Kate, we can't do this to her. Think about it, both of you. This baby will live in the same house and under the same roof, yet we are asking her to give up, not only her rights, but her natural feelings toward this child. I don't feel right doing this."

"I have no feelings toward this child like a mother should. He was not conceived out of love, but force and hate, and I could never love him like my child. He will always be a reminder of what happened to me no matter who he lives with. It won't be hard on me, of course, I want nothing but the best for him. I understand that none of this was his fault and he is just an innocent victim of a brutal crime. You two are the best. I couldn't find a kinder and more decent loving couple than you two anywhere. I hope you both enjoy him and give him what he deserves out of this life. I hope you love him as yours and I have no doubt that you will. That is what I want for him."

She said all this staying calm, and somehow unfeeling toward the baby, in order for Kate and Oliver to accept and adopt him. She loved him more than life itself, but couldn't let it be known to anyone. This was something she had to do for him. She just wished maybe someday this child would understand why she did what she had to do. No one knew what the future would bring, and she might never see him once they decided to leave Iran. Just the same, she had to do the right thing. Kate and Oliver were the right choice for her son.

"I will be honored if you two adopt him, and don't worry about me. This is what I want for him, and the rest is up to you."

Kate had tears in her eyes as she walked over to her and held her, but Soraya remained calm and showed no emotion. It took all the strength she had to give them her blessing, allowing Kate and Oliver to take over her son's future. There was nothing left for her to give or do.

"I admire you for your courage and strength. It would destroy me to give up my son, and I understand you are only doing it for him and not for yourself. It is the most unselfish act that I have ever witnessed in my life, and someday he will hear about his courageous mother. He will love and respect you for the kind of person you are. I promise you that."

Oliver could read through her, knowing she had just put on an act in order to convince them of her decision. But there was nothing more he could do without getting Kate suspicious.

Kate told her she was going to take care of everything the next day. She would take him to the doctor to get him on some kind of formula.

"We would like to keep the same name for him," Kate told her; and that pleased Soraya.

That night they all went to bed with their own thoughts. Oliver was still concerned about Soraya, knowing how hard this was all going to be on her, and not believing anything she had just said. Kate was thinking about how she was going to be as a full-time mother starting the following day. And Soraya went to bed with her son for the last time, knowing that tomorrow he would look to a different face for love and comfort.

She lay her son on her bed, a single tear rolling down from the corner of her eye.

"This is our last night together like this. As of tomorrow, you will have a new mommy, who will love you very much. I will be close to watch over you, and I know God will always be with you, no matter what religion you grow up with. He will always protect you and watch over you wherever you are. I am only giving you up out of love and nothing else. I never dreamed of loving you this much, and I surely am glad. You have brought to life a kind of love that I never thought was possible. You are God's true miracle."

She held her baby close and rocked him back and forth, remembering the night her father sat up all night holding her before he let her walk out of his life to face the cruel world all alone. For the first time she realized how hard that was on him, to let go of his first born. Fresh tears were rolling down her face as she wondered if her father cried that night while she slept in his arms, grieving for what he was about to lose.

"My darling boy, you will always be on my mind, no matter where you are or who raises you. I will always wonder what you are doing, or if you are happy, and I will forever love you."

The next day, Kate took the baby to the doctor and got him formula. She spent the rest of the day shopping for him. They had set the nursery in the room next to theirs which had been Oliver's office, and Kate began her journey as a new mom. Soraya stayed in her own room pretending to be asleep. Kate left Soraya alone most of the day, knowing how hard it all was on her. She figured it was Soraya's way of dealing with it. She understood and felt sorry for her. Wishing she could do something to make the young woman's pain fade away but time was the only thing that would heal her wounds and nothing else.

The next few days, everyone did their part to make things easier on one another. Soraya eventually went to the doctor and got a shot to dry her breast milk and, for the first time, felt the detachment from the baby.

Oliver took care of all the necessary paper work regarding the adoption, and much to his surprise, it was less complicated than he thought. It took a few weeks before Oliver finally got him a birth certificate under the name of Ali Oliver Reed, and they even got him an American passport as Soraya had requested. Soraya was glad it was all done and that he now legally belonged to Kate and Oliver. She kept to herself most of the time but kept up with her duties, and hardly said a word to Oliver, which bothered him to no limit. They had all started a new life. She started school again and was glad to be out of the house and on her own more often. It was a difficult change for all of them, but they all did their best to get used to the situation.

Oliver came home one day to find Soraya alone in the house. He never had a chance to talk with her privately since Kate's return.

"Hi. Where is Kate?"

"She is out shopping. What are you doing home?"

"I was a little tired and decided to leave early. How are you doing?"

"I am doing fine," she replied, trying to look down and avoid any eye contact with him.

"I miss you."

She looked away and pleaded, "Please Oliver, this is hard already. Don't make matters any worse."

"You have built a wall around yourself and don't let anyone inside. I am worried about you."

"This is best for everyone concerned," she said firmly.

He walked closer.

"Look at me. You are not alone in this. Please don't shut me out."

"Sorry you feel that way. I am doing my best to deal with everything and also be just to myself."

"You have hardly said a word to me in days. And the baby, you don't even look at him. It's obvious how badly you are hurting."

"It's best this way. I can't let my feelings get the best of me, and this is my way of dealing with the situation. All my life everything has been decided for me: how much education I need, whom to get married to, how and when to give up my virginity, when to have a baby, and who will get to raise my child. For once, I am making a decision in my life and it feels good. It may not be to everyone's satisfaction, but it's mine, and I am for once willing to sacrifice everything, even if it is wrong. Just so I can call it mine. I have paid a very big price for things that have been out of my control.

This time I am in control and it feels good, Oliver. My feelings toward you haven't hanged, but you see, I am not even allowed to love the right way. I fall in love with a man who has a wife, and his wife has done more for me in less than a year than my own mother did my entire life. You think life is fair; and maybe a lot of people do, but not me. Don't get me wrong, I will forever be thankful to you and Kate for everything you have done for me, but you have to understand what I am going through."

He cut her off, "Damn it, I do! That's why I am having this conversation with you. I want to help you. Don't close the door on me. That's exactly what you are doing."

"You can't help me, Oliver."

"Try me. Let me in; let me be your friend; talk to me."

She looked at him in anger and shouted, "Okay! You want to know what goes on inside of me? I want you to leave Kate; choose me instead; take me away and love me forever. Help me raise my child and marry me."

She broke down in a sob. Oliver looked shocked at what he had heard and didn't know how to respond.

"You see Oliver, what I am going through is heartache. It is a broken heart that needs to be healed. You can't help me. You have your family to think about, and I have to heal my heart and soul."

He looked down, his heart ached for her, and he knew she was right. All he wanted to do was to take her in his arms and protect her from any more harm.

"I am sorry and I am at a loss for words."

"Don't be sorry. You have given me the gift of love. But for now, I need to get on with my life and put my feelings aside. I need to take the right steps and, for once, fight for my rights. All you can do is let me do it my way."

Oliver walked over and took her in his arms and held her close. She inhaled his scent and closed her eyes and enjoyed the moment, knowing that it wasn't going to last long.......

Soraya kept very busy between school and helping Kate at the house the following few weeks. She set high goals for herself, and no one was going to stop her. Kate had noticed the changes in her and knew it had partly to do with the baby. But when it came to Ali, she was as possessive as she could be. There was nothing she wouldn't do in order to keep him all to herself, even if it came down to risking her relationship with Soraya. Hoping it would never come to that, but did not completely ruling it out.

Her quarterly check-up was coming up and she was taking Ali with her. He had become her life. She loved him more than anything else in the world and couldn't wait to go home this time to show him off to her family. Soraya helped her in any way she could to get ready for the trip. She helped with the baby as often as she could. The night before her departure, they had a similar night to the one before Christmas, but so much had changed this time. Soraya held Ali in her arm talking to him in silence, not wanting anyone to see her true emotions.

"Be safe, my darling; and remember, I love you so much, my sweet boy."

Oliver took them to the airport the next day and had a hard time parting with them. He held the baby in his arms.

"You watch over mommy, you hear. And don't forget about your daddy."

Their lives had changed so much in such a short time that it was beyond his wildest imagination. This was another sad good-bye for all of them. He stood there and watched the plane take off.

He decided to go back home and check on Soraya before going back to work, knowing this was just as hard on her. The house was quiet and he found her in her room with puffy eyes, which gave him the indication that she had been crying.

"I am sorry to barge in on you like this, but I thought you may like some company."

She wiped her eyes, there was no denying it.

"I know Kate and Ali will return this time, but my tears are for when you will all leave someday, and I may never see any of you again."

"Soraya, you don't have to worry about that. When the time comes you will have the choice to come with us. I promise you that."

She looked like a lost child, not knowing where to find her loved ones, but his promise brought a little smile to her face.

"I have a good idea; why don't I call work and tell them not to expect me today. Then we can go for a ride and forget about everything. What do you say?"

She wasn't in the mood, but decided it would do her some good, knowing this was hard on him, too. He drove up Pahlavi street, which is one of the most beautiful drives in Tehran, all the way up to Tagrish where he parked the car. They got out of the car and decided to go for a walk. It was a beautiful, sunny day and they were both glad to take the day off.

"What is that big gate with all the soldiers guarding it?" Soraya asked.

"That's the Shah's mansion. That is where he lives. Haven't you ever been here before?"

She shook her head in amazement. "This is where he lives with his queen? It is beautiful, even though we can't see much. It is like magic, knowing there is a king and queen living in that palace.

"Do you believe in magic?"

She smiled. "I don't know. I like to believe magical things still exist, but they just don't seem to happen to ordinary people."

Oliver saw an unusual kind of sadness in her eyes.

"Did you know the Shah's second wife was named Soraya?"

"I didn't know that until I moved to the cities. One of the girls at school told me and was surprised that I didn't know it. It is very unusual for village girls to be called anything but religious names. Maybe my dad thought I was his little princess."

"You never talk about your family. Is it hard for you to talk about them?"

"In a way it is. My father, he is so different from all the other men in the village. He is a nice, kind man, and not being able to see him is one of the hardest things that I have ever done. I often wonder what they are all doing."

"Can you ever go back and visit them?"

"It is too soon. Maybe someday I can go back and take him away from all the heartache. When the time comes, I need to be somebody that he could truly be proud of. My departure was mixed with all kinds of shame."

They stopped at the corner food stand, and Soraya asked him if he had ever eaten barbecued liver before."

He shook his head, "I don't like liver."

"You have to try it. It is wonderful."

He wasn't very excited about eating liver, but decided to try it. They both stood there watching the man cook it on the grill just like Kabobs. He then put the meat inside an Iranian bread which looked like a flour tortilla.

"It looks good," Oliver said.

"Have a bite. Just one bite and if you don't like it, I will eat the rest."

"Okay, one bite.

And he decided it wasn't too bad. Then Soraya took a bite, with a twinkle in her eyes.

"Oh this is so good, I love it."

He was glad to see her smile. He hadn't seen her this happy for a long time.

They spent the day walking and driving around. It was starting to get dark outside when they went to a small restaurant and had a nice dinner together and talked some more. After dinner, Oliver drove up more toward the northern mountains and stopped the car on top of a dirt road near a cliff. Soraya couldn't believe her eyes; it was fantastic.

"How did you know about this place?"

"Most everyone knows about it. They call this point Tehran's nights."

"The name surely fits it perfectly."

They sat there looking at the view and listening to the soft music that was playing on the car radio. She turned and saw him staring at her.

"Has anyone ever told you how beautiful you are?"

She blushed, not used to compliments, and then smiled.

"Yes, you have."

"I must be very smart, because I think you are the most beautiful woman I have ever seen."

"You are making me blush, Mr. Reed."

"Well, it's true. I have noticed how men look at you, and you can't tell me you haven't noticed that yourself."

She smiled up at Oliver and enjoyed hearing compliments from him.

"Did you have a nice day?"

"I had a wonderful day and thank you."

"In that case we should go back home; it's getting late."

They didn't talk much on the way back. It had been a relaxing day for both of them and, for now, they preferred not to say anything, but to just think about other things.

She thought about her life in the village. It seemed like ages ago. Like a dream that took place a long, long time ago. She had new dreams and people whom she loved very much. So much had changed and she hardly ever thought about the day she got raped. Like a bad dream, she tried not to think about it, but block it out of her mind. It was all part of her past and that's where she liked to keep it, far away from her present life.

She thanked Oliver again for the nice day they had together and told him she needed to do some studying. She went to her room and closed the door. It was hard for her to concentrate. Studying was even starting to frustrate her a bit, and so finally closed her book, walked over to her dressing table, and sat there in front of the mirror, looking at herself.

"Am I as beautiful as he said?"

She began combing her hair and staring in the mirror, not even seeing herself. Her mind was elsewhere.

Kate had given her a pale pink lipstick that she had not worn yet. She opened the top and rubbed it over her lips.

"It's amazing how a little lipstick can change your look," she told herself, liking what she saw in the mirror.

She could hear Oliver going to his room and closing the door. Her heart was pounding.

"Why can't I get him out of my mind?"

All she thought about was being in his strong arms and him holding her. She felt captive of her thoughts. Everything was out of her control as she opened the door, walked over to his room, and stood behind the closed door, not knowing what to do momentarily. She knocked on his door and waited.

Oliver got up and opened his door. There she stood looking more radiant than ever, taking his breath away.

"Are you okay?"

"I am fine," she said leaning on the doorway.

"You never wear your hair down. It is beautiful."

And he felt her soft silky hair.

"Oliver, do you remember I told you from now on I will make my own decisions, whether they are right or wrong, as long as they are mine?"

He thought for a second, not knowing what she was trying to say.

"Yes."

She smiled with eyes that were almost not seeing anything except him.

"I want to be with you right now, and it is my decision. You don't have to feel bad or guilty. This is what I want, to be with you, more than anything in this world. She felt dizzy almost shocked with love, wanting him with every fiber of her being.

He pulled her in his arms.

"What am I going to do with you Miss Noor?"

"Just love me for now, and show me what it is to be loved."

"You know what you are asking me to do?"

"Yes, I do. And I've never been so sure about anything in my life."

I can't do this. It is against the law. It's the wrong thing for me to do, and it is unfair to Kate. Plus, you are only seventeen."

"There is not such a law in this country. If so, where the hell was the law when I got raped? Plus I am almost eighteen.

She stared into his eyes.

"Will you kiss me, Oliver?"

Thoughts were racing through his mind, and he said, "I love you so much, and I want you more than anything. But it's the wrong thing for me to do, taking advantage of your youth and innocence."

"It's been done to me before against my will. This time it is my own decision. I want you to be the one who takes me, loves me, and shows me what it is like to be truly loved."

84

And with that she dropped her robe and stood before him with nothing on. He couldn't resist looking at her beautiful body. Staring into her eyes, he picked her up and carried her to her room. There he lay her down on the bed gently feeling her soft skin. Every joint in his body was aching for her as she lay in bed melting away with his touches.

"You are beautiful."

He got close to her and pressed his lips on hers and kissed her with all his passion.

"I want you so much. His fingers searching for and discovering her soft skin, took her round breast. She was breathless as he kissed her and parted and kissed her again and again. He gently placed himself between her legs and their bodies became one gazing in her eyes and forgetting everything else around him. With every movement of his body proving his love for her. He was in awe of her grace, beauty and innocence. This time she was loved like she had never been loved before. They were both left breathless when he finally stopped and starred into her eyes.

"I do believe in magic, my love. And you are everything I ever dreamed of and more. I love you."

He held her close and smelled her hair.

They wrapped their bodies around each other and lay enjoying the soundless night. Everything was so peaceful as they made love all through the night over and over again.

"Where did the night go?" She asked him as they both looked at the morning light shine through the shade.

"The night belonged to us and we took it away." There was no regret on either side; it felt right to both of them, like they truly belonged to each other.

"I hate to end this wonderful night, but I have to get ready for work. And you, little princess, can go in the kitchen and make us some breakfast, or else I will have to nibble on you again."

She smiled, filled with love and more desire, but decided to leave the room to do as he asked before they got started again.

Oliver quickly showered and cleaned up for work after which he found Soraya in the kitchen. He pulled her close to him and kissed her on the lips.

"Good morning, my love. How did you sleep last night?" "I think I dreamt all night."

"Good dreams, I hope."

She smiled and responded, "Wonderful dreams. The kind of dreams that you only have in your sleep."

Oliver kissed her once again before leaving the house that morning; and finally he left her sitting at the kitchen table, day dreaming about everything that happened the previous night. She had no desire to do anything else.

Oliver left the house and wondered where this forbidden love would take him. Also, concerned about her getting pregnant, he decided to stop at the drug store to buy some birth control pills. Knowing birth control pills are like most over the counter drugs, you can buy them at any drug store in Iran.

Oliver waited for her until she got done with school. She ran toward the car and got in. They talked about school and work and neither one said anything about the night before, like it had never happened. Back at the house, he opened the door, she walked in as he followed her and put his brief case down. Soraya went to her room to put her books away and bumped into him as she left her room.

"Well, hello beautiful."

She smiled. He grabbed her waist and pulled her close to him.

"I thought about you all day; it was hard getting anything done; I had a hard time concentrating. We have to have a little talk."

She followed him into the living room, fearing what she was about to hear.

He took a small bag out of his pocket and asked her to open it.

"Do you know what these pills are?"

"No. What are they?"

"They are birth control pills. You have to use these; otherwise you might get pregnant again."

She looked horrified and cried, "Oh my God, what about last night?"

Oliver smiled, "Don't worry. I was very careful; so everything should be okay. But you might need these in the future."

She read the instructions carefully as Oliver sat at the kitchen table, doing some paper work. He walked out of the kitchen and found her studying.

"I need to go to bed. I am just exhausted."

Soraya looked up and nodded, "I am going to study a little longer and go to bed, too."

He kissed her gently, went to his own room and closed the door, as did Soraya a little while later. They both fell fast asleep in their own rooms.

Soraya woke up the next morning and couldn't believe it was almost nine in the morning. She slowly opened the door and found the house quiet. Oliver had already gone to work and she missed not seeing him that morning. It almost brought tears to her eyes. Nothing mattered to her anymore except her love for Oliver. All she wanted was him and nothing more. She was sad knowing this would not last long and that as soon as Kate got back everything would go back to normal. What was she to do then? She decided not to think about it at the time. Instead she went grocery shopping and made Oliver dinner before she left for school.

That night Oliver came home later than usual and noticed the food she had made for him and decided to wait for her.

Soraya got off the bus by the big park several blocks away from her normal stop. She decided to go for a walk. It was a beautiful park with a children's play area all lit up, and it was almost full. There was an empty bench near the playground where she sat watching all the children at play. Her childhood was so different from that of these kids. She was never allowed to play. All she ever did was work and take care of her little siblings, and those were the only memories she had of her childhood.

Her thoughts drifted off to Kate, Oliver and Ali, and also her father. These were the people she loved the most in the world, and none of them belonged to her. It was a lonely thought, and she felt more alone than ever before in her life. No one belonged to her, and she didn't belong to anyone else.

She got up and walked alone telling herself, "this is how the rest of my life is going to be: all alone and no place to call home."

Oliver began worrying about her.

"I wonder where she is. She's never been late before without calling."

It was almost ten and there was no sign of her.

"I should have gone to school and picked her up."

And then he wondered if she ever made it to school that afternoon. It was shortly after ten when he finally decided to go and look for her. He picked up his car keys and opened the door only to find her on the other side with her keys in her hand ready to put them in the lock. He pulled her in and closed the door.

"Are you okay?" he asked, startling her for a moment.

"I am fine. You never told me how late you were going to work, so I decided to go for a walk in the park."

Oliver looked furious.

"You should have called, Soraya. Please don't ever do this to me again.

She was shocked at his harsh reaction and didn't know what to say or do.

"I am sorry. I didn't mean to worry you."

"I am glad you are okay, but next time call me and let me know you are going to be late."

"I will," she whispered, still shocked at his tone.

She went to her room to put her books away and just sat on her bed wondering what the hell just happened.

Oliver waited in the kitchen for a few minutes, but there was no sign of her. He decided to knock on her door and apologize for screaming at her.

"Are you mad at me?"

"No, she replied.

"I am sorry for getting upset with you. I thought something had happened to you."

"I know. It's okay."

"Should we kiss and make up?"

Not waiting for her to answer he pulled her close and held her for a short time and gently kissed her.

"Are you hungry?"

She nodded, but couldn't stay mad at him any longer and smiled. Even their little quarrel was thrilling to her.

"Let's go in the kitchen and see what we can find to eat."

They sat down and ate the dinner she had made earlier.

"So tell me, what is going on at school these days?"

"Well, I can go to a higher grade if I pass my test which will be in a few weeks. I could probably get my high school diploma by the end of this year and take the big test. Depending on how I do, maybe I could start at the University of Tehran, which is all paid for. That's only if I get very high scores."

He was truly proud of all her accomplishments and had no doubt in his mind that she was going to get accepted with high scores. They finished dinner, and he helped her clean up and asked if she was going to study that night.

"I don't think so," she answered, wondering why he asked her that.

"Good, because I missed you. Come here and sit by me."

She sat next to him on the couch. He held her hand and kissed the top of her fingers.

She wrapped her arms around him, and their lips met once again. Soon he unbuttoned her blouse and took her clothes off one by one admiring her bare body, which made her blush and look away. His lips met her bare shoulders and showered her with kisses. He lifted her chin and told her, "You have nothing to be embarrassed about. You are beautiful, and I can't resist looking at you. Besides, I feel you belong to me."

Their bodies soon wrapped around each other, and as they were making love the phone rang. They both stopped, breathless. Oliver reached for the phone without thinking and heard Kate's voice on the other end. He jumped to his feet.

"Hi, honey! How are you and the baby? That's great."

"You sound like you are out of breath, Oliver."

"I had to run down and get some papers out of my car right before you called."

"You should start exercising," she said, laughing at her own remark.

"Yah, I will."

"I can't hear you. What did you say?"

"Nothing, honey. I didn't say anything."

"Oliver, are you okay? What's going on?"

"Nothing, babe. I am just fine. How about yourself?"

He could hardly hear anything she said. It was a very stressful conversation for him, and he hoped she wouldn't suspect anything. They talked for a few more minutes. He finally put the phone down as did Kate, half-way across the world, wondering what was going on with her husband.

Soraya put on his shirt during his conversation with Kate.

"Is everything okay with Kate and Ali?"

"I think so."

He thought for a moment and added, "I don't think she believed a word I said."

"Don't you think you are being paranoid right now?"

"Maybe. She must never find out about us. Never, it would destroy her."

"I understand. And I want you to know that if at any time you decide to end our relationship, I will respect your wishes, but it has to come from you. Right now, I don't feel any guilt. As far as I know, it was a fair exchange."

Oliver interrupted her, "Stop talking like that, Soraya. It sounds like vengeance. This could have happened between us even if there was no baby. I don't want you to try and justify it because of the baby; he has nothing to do with our relationship."

Soraya didn't look at it that way. In a very strange way, she had changed during the last few weeks. She didn't care about anyone but herself and Oliver. She was going to get what she wanted out of life, no matter what the cost was. Oliver was what she was after the most, and Kate wasn't her concern anymore.

Talking to Kate got him upset and filled him with mixed emotions again. Soraya could see that in his face, yet she was not about to push him too much. He sat there on the couch, still undressed holding his head. She decided to give him some room to sort things out.

Soraya got in the shower and stood there for a long time letting the water pour all over her body. She tried not to think about what had just happened. She could hardly see anything in the small bathroom when she finally got out and reached for her towel. Instead of getting her towel, Oliver was there and took her hand in his and pulled her close to him. He looked her in the eyes.

"What am I going to do, Soraya?"

"That has to be your decision."

"And you?"

"What about me?"

"Is this enough for you, to sneak around behind Kate's back and make love to me whenever she is not around?"

She smiled, "I want the skies. I want everything with you: the whole fairy tale, but I have nothing to say about your decision."

"So it is all up to me?"

"Yes. You have to decide, and I will respect your decision, whatever it is."

"Are you willing to be my lover while Kate is my wife?"

"If that's what you choose, yes. I will do everything in my power to keep what we have going, as long as it is your wish too. All I want from you is to be honest with me and tell me if you ever change your mind. I don't need your pity; I need your love."

"That won't be fair to you or Kate."

"She doesn't have to know; and I want you however I can get you, even if it means sneaking around. It has to be from your heart; that's all."

She hoped he would never know the desperation she felt in her heart to keep him close to her. Oliver was caught in a trap and didn't see a way out. He couldn't give up either woman but knew it was wrong. He couldn't imagine life without Kate and the baby. At the same time, he couldn't bear the thought of giving up Soraya.

The next few weeks went by quickly. Oliver and Soraya spent romantic and passionate nights together. Just the same, both knew when Kate came back, it would all have to stop.

Soraya took her test and passed with the highest scores. She surprised her teacher and the school principal. She had one more test left that she could take at school to get to the twelve grades. The last test was going to be given by the city board of education, and that was her last step before entering the University of Tehran. The University is all paid for by the government for qualifying students. Soraya was hoping to be one of the lucky ones to get accepted at the University. In her mind, that would be the way out of a dead end life. She had talked to Oliver about her plans for the future several times, and he didn't like the fact that she might be moving out once she started college. One of her teachers had told her she could earn a good living by tutoring kids in school once she started college. She had told Oliver that. He didn't want to stop her from improving herself or her life, but he didn't want to lose her either. As far as he was concerned, moving out was the beginning of an end in their relationship. That was something he wasn't ready to risk.

Soraya's schedule was very hectic. She tried to get as much studying done as she could before Kate's return in two days.

Oliver wasn't himself these days, knowing it would be hard to look Kate in the face with everything that had happened in her absence. He knew Soraya was too busy to feel anything for anyone except them. Their last night together was very touching for both of them; they had to put everything aside and pretend like nothing had ever happened.

"What would you like to do tonight?"

Soraya looked at him with a long face.

"I don't know. Just be close to you one more night, sleep in your arms, and wake up next to you. I am glad for all my school work keeping me occupied so I won't go mad every night when you lay next to Kate."

"I know this is going to be hard for you. I wish there was something I could do to make it easier."

"I want our love to be cherished and not get lost in the shuffle. Don't forget what we had together these past few weeks. I want to go on believing you meant everything you told me, even if it never happens again, or if you decide to end it once and for all."

He wrapped his arms around her.

"Sometimes I wish I could just walk away from everything that happened between us and never look back. But you see, my love, it is not that easy anymore. I look at you and want you more. I love you more every day. There is no walking away from it or wanting to stop because it's out of my hands. You are here to stay, in the corner of my heart, for as long as I live. To me, that is where you belong, and that's where I want you to be."

She liked nothing more than listening to his words when it concerned them and their love. Just like she asked, they spent the night in each other's arms and went to sleep.

The next day she left the house in the afternoon, knowing when she walked back in that house, Oliver wouldn't belong to her any longer. He would be all Kate's, and there was nothing she could do about that. She knew Kate's test results had come out very well. The tumor had shrunk to half its original size, which meant the medication had worked. Soraya was truly glad for her.

She had a hard time paying attention to what her teacher said that night and couldn't wait to get out of there. The thought of seeing Ali brought a smile to her face. She couldn't wait to get home and hold him in her arms. Motherhood was calling and her heart was pounding with joy of seeing her Son. Her heart filled with envy toward Kate, she had everything Soraya wanted and yearned for. For now she wanted the warmth of Ali's small body in her arms. She wanted to smell him and fill her heart with the love she felt for him. She couldn't feel or see beyond that.

# CHAPTER FIVE

Soraya's heart was pounding as she slowly opened the door and heard Oliver and Kate in the living room. She glanced over and saw Kate sitting on his lap, where they had made love just a few weeks ago. Ali was laying on a blanket on the floor. One look at him, and she forgot about everything else.

"Hi you two."

They both turned around, and Kate ran toward her, hugging one another like good friends.

"Kate, you look wonderful. I am so glad about the results of your test. It was great news."

Kate laughed out loud.

"I feel great. How are you doing?"

Soraya almost didn't hear her as she turned and looked at Ali looking at them with a big smile on his face.

"Look at him. He has grown so much. I can't believe how big he is."

She picked him up.

"Hi, little guy. Do you remember me?"

She held him close to her and kissed him all over.

"I missed you so much!"

The baby gave a big smile that took her breath away. She turned to Kate.

"He looks so good and healthy."

Kate had never seen her with so much affection toward the baby before, and it caught her off guard. Yet she understood the month separation must have been hard; so didn't let it bother her too much.

Soraya took the baby in the kitchen and hid him from the wondering eyes of Kate and Oliver. She kissed and smelled his soft skin, holding him ever so close. Ali looked around and began to cry.

"It's okay. Mommy just missed you so much when you were gone."

It was the first time she ever called herself "mommy", recognizing him as her child. It was a happy moment for her; there was no denying it.

She walked back in the living room to find the couple kissing. She closed her eyes and trembled. This was going to be a lot harder than she thought.

"Get used to it. This is the way it's going to be from now on."

For some reason she was mad at Oliver, but didn't know why.

Kate finally stopped and turned to Soraya with a smile on her face. She felt happy to be home and in her husband's arms. She told them all about her trip and how much everyone loved Ali.

"I was told he is by far the most gorgeous baby they have ever seen; and of course, I happen to agree with them. My mother bought him so many things that I had to buy an extra suitcase to bring everything back."

Soraya smiled, "You have to show me everything later."

"You can help me unpack tomorrow and see all the new clothes and toys; but right now, I'd like to take a hot bath and go to bed.

"And this baby is yours tonight, my love," she said glancing at Oliver.

Kate left the room, and they heard the bath water running. Soraya couldn't look at Oliver as he came toward her and gazed into her eyes.

"I know this is hard for you, but there is nothing I can do at the moment to ease your pain. All I can say is, I am sorry and I love you."

He had hardly finished his last word when Kate called him from the bathroom. He handed Soraya the baby and left the room.

"Come in the bath with me, Oliver."

"What about the baby?"

"Soraya will watch him for half an hour. She is a big girl and understands we haven't seen each other for a month. Just go tell her to watch the baby for a while."

"I am not going to tell her that."

"Why not?"

"Oh Kate, I don't know. I guess she just will figure it out on her own.

He knew she would figure it out and that tore at his heart as he took his clothes off and climbed in the bath with Kate.

Soraya knew what was happening. She couldn't stand the thought of it; so she decided to take the baby to her room and turn the radio on so she couldn't hear anything. As she held the baby close to her chest, Oliver was making love to his wife; and the thought nearly crushed her. She laid on the floor playing with the baby, trying to get her mind off of what was happening in the other room just down the hall. It was nice to spend some time with Ali without anyone around. She fed him and changed his diaper and finally rocked him to sleep, things that she had missed doing for so long.

It seemed like hours before she heard a knock on her door. Oliver appeared, not even able to look at her this time.

"Thanks for putting him to sleep."

She just nodded, "It's okay."

He came in and picked up the baby and whispered, "Good night."

There she sat, all alone, in her room, knowing she had no part in that family. She stayed in her room the next day until after Oliver left for work. He was glad not to face her, too. It was a hard night for both of them, thinking about the previous nights and how their love had to be on hold perhaps forever.

Kate was feeding the baby when Soraya came out.

"Good morning."

"Hi. Did you sleep well last night?"

"I stayed up late studying."

"I am so happy for you. I think it is wonderful what you already have done with your life in such a short time. Oliver told me you were thinking of getting your own place once you start at the university. Just so you know, we would love to have you living with us. It's good for all of us, and you could help us out whenever you are able. It doesn't have to be morning or afternoons; it could be whenever it works for you.

"Thank you, Kate. I really appreciate everything you have done, but right now it is too soon to decide. Why don't we wait and see how everything goes; then, we can all decide what's best for all of us."

"So tell me, how was everything here?"

"The same as always. Nothing ever changes around here."

"Does Oliver seem okay to you?"

"I guess so. Why?"

"I don't know. He just seems so distant."

"He has been working a lot and bringing a lot of paper work home with him every night. Besides that, I don't know."

Kate just nodded.

They sat and talked most of the morning and unpacked all Kate's suitcases. She showed Soraya all the new things she had bought for the baby. Soraya had never seen such beautiful baby clothes. She was glad for her son. Kate bought her some new clothes, too. In a way, it made her feel embarrassed for everything that had been done behind this woman's back.

"Where am I going to wear all of these clothes?"

"Maybe to college next fall. You never know."

Kate smiled at her as she spoke, truly hoping nothing but the best for this young woman. Soraya could see the sincere look in her face.

She went to school that afternoon with a lot on her mind, and Kate was glad to have the house to herself. When Oliver got home he was more relaxed than the night before.

The next few weeks, Oliver hardly saw Soraya. She studied until late hours every night and slept in a little longer. It wasn't something that she planned, but at the same time, it made it easier on everyone else involved. Kate didn't really care what time Soraya got up, as long as she kept up with the list of things that was left for her to do. Soraya didn't have much of an appetite anymore, with lack of sleep and the pressure of her school work; she began to lose weight. Kate was worried about her and encouraged her to take better care of herself; but at the same time, she enjoyed her private nights with Oliver.

Oliver missed Soraya in every way, but she didn't give him many chances to even talk. The thought of holding her in his arms had become more of a fantasy than anything. There was never a time that he could find her alone to at least tell her nothing had changed in his heart. If anything, he loved her more than ever. It was a Friday morning, and Oliver decided to make a big breakfast for everyone, hoping to catch Soraya or at least have her near.

She was to take her test the following week and was planning on going to the park, spreading her books all around her, and studying all day. Her life consisted of school and studying and a few short hours of sleep. Kate and Oliver were eating breakfast when she walked into the kitchen.

"Good morning."

"Hi," Kate said and looked up. "Boy, do you look tired. Sit and have some breakfast with us."

She smiled with very tired eyes and replied, "thanks, but I am not hungry right now."

"Are you going somewhere?"

"I am going to the park to study. Tomorrow is my first test. I hope you don't mind."

Oliver was disappointed.

"Don't you think you should eat something before you leave?"

"I will take a sandwich with me and eat it later."

She walked over to the counter and started making herself a sandwich. She left shortly after, while Oliver sat there feeling so deserted. He hardly said a word after that.

"Are you okay?" Kate asked, wondering why he was suddenly so quiet.

"Yeah, I am fine, honey."

Kate knew him too well and could tell something was bothering him, but she couldn't put her finger on it. He was having a lot of mood swings lately, and she didn't understand why.

"Do you mind if I go to the office and get some papers to do some work at home? It won't take long."

"I was looking forward to spending some time with you and the baby as a family as long as you had the day off."

"I will do my work while you are making dinner. There are some papers that I forgot."

"As long as you don't sit there and work all night."

He gave her a smile.

"I promise."

He got dressed and drove straight to the park. He had no intention of going to the office. All he wanted was to have a moment with Soraya alone.

It was a big park made like a maze, and he had no idea where to look for her. He decided to park the car and walk around. His search didn't last long before he found her sitting under a big tree with her books all around her. His heart was pounding and he felt a little nervous as he approached her.

"Would you like some company?"

She looked up, startled.

"What are you doing here?"

"Isn't it obvious? I am here to see you. I am under the impression that you are either avoiding me or punishing me."

"Neither. Why would you say that?"

"You don't stay around much, and run away any chance you get."

It's easier for everyone this way."

"Not easier for me. I miss you more than you know."

He looked around to make sure no one was watching him, and he quickly kissed her on the lips.

"I would like to make love to you right here and now."

She pulled away.

"You are crazy. Stop that! People are watching us."

"No one knows us."

"These students come here all the time to study, and they know me. They have seen me here before."

"Good, then they will know that you are mine and will stay away from you."

Soraya smiled. She liked hearing him call her his. It gave her a sense of security and of belonging to someone, especially Oliver.

"I think you should leave before Kate starts looking for you and wondering where you are."

"On one condition," he said, smiling back at her.

"What's that?"

"That you don't hide in your room when you get home, but have dinner with us, at least for a couple of hours."

"I will sit and have dinner with you, but then I have to go to my room and finish my work. This is my last night before all my tests start next week."

He nodded, "I understand."

He leaned toward her and whispered in her ear, "I love you."

She looked back at him with eyes that repeated what he had just told her.

Oliver got up and walked away. She looked at him until he disappeared behind the trees. Somehow she felt so much better having spent some time with him alone once again and knowing he still loved her. The sky suddenly seemed bluer and the sun shined so much brighter. She returned to her books and never noticed all the young men in the park and how they all looked at her, trying to find a way to talk to her.

Usually she was so buried in her books that they wouldn't allow themselves to interrupt her, fearful of what she might say. They all searched for the right moment, but they knew she was a hard one to win. She was different from all the other young girls that came to the park with the excuse of studying, but who spent all their time looking for the right man. As far as she was concerned, there was only one man who existed on this earth, and that was Oliver Reed, the American man with blue eyes and light brown hair, the one who stole her heart. No one else could ever have it again. There weren't too many men that she trusted. She preferred to let them wonder about who she was and where she had come from.

It was almost five and the park was getting crowded, so she decided to go home and keep her promise to Oliver. She found Kate in the kitchen and Oliver doing some work. This was a good night for her to bring up the possibility of her moving out on her own. But, Oliver couldn't bear the thought of not having her close by.

"Soraya, you know how unaccepted it is in this country for a young girl to live on her own. There will be gossip and all kinds of difficulty in your life. I don't think you should think of moving out. We like having you here with us. You are a big help to Kate and also a friend."

He was trying to be logical so Kate wouldn't suspect anything. Soraya on the other hand thought she would be able to see him more privately, but it was Ali who she had a hard time giving up. She wanted to be a part of his everyday life as long as she could. Kate didn't want to see Soraya leave either. With her schedule, she was hardly around, and Kate had all the privacy she needed with Oliver. Plus, all Soraya's help during the day was a necessity. The most important thing of all was that she just didn't trust anyone else to watch over Ali when she had to be somewhere else. At times she felt a little threatened, but she never let herself forget the kind of sacrifice Soraya had made by giving up her child to the family she lived with. Kate knew it was an everyday torture for her to watch him grow up before her eyes, not having any kind of right to him. And as long as Soraya was willing to deal with the situation and understand her position in Ali's life, Kate felt comfortable and was willing to have Soraya stay there. A lot had changed. Kate had never realized how much or how fast Ali would change her life.

Soraya took her last test which left her totally exhausted. She was running out of energy. It was a beautiful spring day and she felt a big load off of her shoulders when she was finished. She decided to go to the park without studying for the first time. She laid on the grass and looked at the bright blue sky, feeling so free with no more deadlines, no more pressures. For now, all she had to do was wait for the result.

For the first time she looked around and noticed all the young people hanging out. Life was so unpredictable. There was no way of telling what challenges would come your way. She knew someday winning Oliver would be her biggest challenge of all. She wished he was there to share this moment with her. She had ignored him for so long now, but it had been her way of dealing with the pain of knowing that he would never belong to her.

Soraya envied Kate so much. She had everything that Soraya wanted in life. At such a young age, she had given up so much. There were others whom she had to consider, though, and closed the door on all her own feelings and emotions. Sadness had filled her chest and tears filled her eyes. She did not know if she would ever have a chance in life to love and be loved without losing that person to someone else.

The fresh air and sunshine made her even more tired; so she took a hot shower once she got back home and went to bed without seeing anyone. Kate slowly opened the door once and found her sound asleep. She quietly closed it and did not see her again that night.

Oliver was glad it was all over. He had been in a bad mood lately, and Kate was concerned about him, not knowing what was bothering him.

It was Friday morning before they saw Soraya for the first time.

"Good morning, sleepy head. How are you feeling?" Oliver asked, glad to see her.

"I think, I'm still alive. Can you believe I slept for seventeen hours? I am sure glad it's over."

Oliver looked at her without Kate seeing and murmured, "So am I."

"How about some breakfast," Kate asked?

"Sounds great. I am starved;" She said, and helped herself to some eggs and bread.

"How did you do on your test?"

"I don't know. Hopefully, well enough for college."

"When will you find out?"

"In a couple of weeks, I hope; but for now, it is all behind me, and I don't want to even think about it. Whatever happens is okay. I have done my best. For now, we have to wait and see what the results will be."

Kate got up and picked up the baby.

"Well, I think we are going for a little walk. Anyone interested in joining us?"

"I pass. Hope you don't mind; but I will help you get the stroller downstairs."

Oliver couldn't wait to have a private moment with Soraya, and when he came back in, she was in her room.

He opened the door and leaned against it starring at her.

Soraya almost threw herself in his arms.

"I missed you so much."

He lifted her chin and kissed her hard. He couldn't get enough of her and walked her gently toward her bed.

"What if Kate comes back?'

"She won't be back for a while."

He opened her robe and reached under and felt her soft skin once again. He wanted her so badly that it drove him crazy. Wishing he had all the time in the world to sit there and admire her perfect body, to smell her scent and feel her flesh.

He made love to her without hesitation and realized no one had ever made him this insane before. He slowly pulled away from her, leaving her breathless, knowing Kate would be back any moment.

"I am sorry, love. I just had to have you."

He kissed her again.

"I will make it up to you soon."

He quickly got out of the room before Kate's return and left Soraya uncertain of her feelings.

She wondered how much more could she take. There was so much more she wanted from him. This sneaking around behind Kate's back wasn't enough for her anymore. This was more than she could bear. She sat there on her bed, holding her knees, deep in her own thoughts. They took her away to her past, and she thought about her father. She missed him so very much, and she would give anything to see him again to let him know how far she had come since they last parted. She needed him to be proud of her. And she needed his blessing and his forgiveness. She needed him to hold her in his arms once again, so she could go on to face another chapter in her life, a new chapter. Even though she could never tell him about her son or Oliver, there was so much more she could share with him. She could put his mind at ease, so he could go on living the rest of his life without worrying about what happened to his daughter. That's what she wanted then more than anything else. He was the only man in her life that she could call hers, and no one could cheat her out of that title: Her father.

This life had given her so many people to love and then taken them away from her one by one. Now she was faced with a new love in her life, Oliver, the man she loved more than anything. Did she have a right to fight for him, or should she give him back like everyone else, to let him go and walk away from her?

"Do I love him enough to free him? But for how long should I allow my loved ones slip away from me? There was one thing that she was certain of: she had to arrange to see her father once again. She needed the comfort of his arms and unconditional love, at least one more time before she got lost in a world that would not allow her to be who she really was.

She decided to get in touch Mina to make arrangements for her father to come down to the city. She had enough money to send for him and pay for his trip out. Nothing mattered to her more than seeing her father once again, and she was ready to do anything to make that possible.

The next two weeks were like a whole lifetime. She had no school to go to anymore and was waiting to hear about her test results. She got ahold of Mina and asked her to arrange for her father to come, giving her some money to get to her father and to give him the message. There were a nerve-racking couple of weeks, but all was coming to a head.

She had a knot in her stomach from the moment she got up to go to school for the results of her exams. For the first time she was anxious. Oliver and Kate could see how tense she was, and Oliver offered to drive her to school.

"I will go in with you and I promise you, everything is going to be just fine. Don't worry."

She got ready, and before leaving, held the holy book of Quran and prayed. She then walked out the door with Oliver a few minutes later.

"I am so nervous."

"Just hang in there, sweetheart. Everything will work out."

Soon he parked the car and looked at her. "Are you ready?"

"Yes and no."

"Let's go. I will be right there with you."

They walked in and she stopped right outside the principal's office. She did not have the strength to knock on the door. Oliver didn't allow her to wait any longer and knocked on the door and slowly walked in. Her knees wanted to buckle.

"Please sit down."

Oliver introduced himself to the principal.

The principal turned to Soraya and smiled.

"I had every confidence in you the day we offered that you take the test. This is a very proud moment for me, also. You not only passed, but achieved the highest scores this year. The university of Tehran will be proud to have a student such as you. Your tests were so perfect and complete that some of the authorities had to go over them twice, making sure their eyes were not playing tricks on them. The average score of all your test is twenty; and as you know, you can't get any higher than that. Congratulations, my dear. I wish you the very best. I know you are a prize to your family and friends. Good luck, and call me in the next few days when everything sinks in. I can give you some tips on how to go about getting registered for school."

She shed tears of joy and just sat there crying, unable to do anything. She finally got up and held her principal's hand in hers, and then she kissed it.

"You were a God's send and I could have never done it without you. I don't know how to thank you."

"You already did. To have a graduate with your scores in my school is a shining star for me. You, my dear, are that star. God be with you."

Oliver was at a loss for words. This was more than he had ever imagined. He looked at Soraya with pure admiration.

"You truly are a jewel, my dear."

Soraya held her diploma in her hand and was flying high. She had never dreamed of anything so fine. She had done it, and there was no stopping her now. The two of them walked out of the building and jumped into each other's arms, laughing and screaming without a care about all the strange looks they were getting.

"You did it, my love. You did it!"

Soraya was crying one moment and laughing the next. She held onto her diploma with great pride. Oliver was glad to be with her and to share this moment.

Kate was waiting for them, not knowing what to expect. Soraya flew out of the car before Oliver had a chance to come to a complete stop. She ran toward the door and yanked it open and screamed with joy.

"I passed!"

Kate stood there with wide eyes and embraced Soraya in her arms.

"I passed, Kate; and I can start college this fall, full scholarship."

"Oh my God, I can't believe it." Oliver walked in and shared the happy moment.

"This calls for a celebration."

Oliver went on telling Kate everything the principal had said, and Kate just shook her head in joy.

"Soraya, you deserve everything that happened to you today. Oliver and I are very proud to be a part of your life and to be able to share this day with you."

Kate then handed her an envelope of money that they had both put aside for her.

"This is a small gift from us to you. We want you to spend it on yourself and enjoy it."

Soraya opened the envelope and counted the money. There was a thousand dollars. She had never seen that much money before.

"This is a lot of money. I can't take this. You don't owe me anything."

Oliver walked over to her and said, "Listen, Soraya, we want you to have it. You have given us our son, the greatest gift of all. This is just a way for us to say thank you and to let you know how proud we are."

All she could do was to smile and thank both of them for their generosity.

This was a turning point in Soraya's life. No one could look at her as a naive little village girl who was lost in the big world.

Kate suddenly remembered something and exclaimed, "Oh, Soraya, I forgot to tell you. Mina called and said that your father will be here in a week, and that she will call you back with the exact time of his arrival."

It was a wonderful day; and, for the first time, she saw a flicker of hope.

"Did you know he was coming out here?"

"Actually, I asked Mina to send for him to come out for a short visit."

"That's great. I am glad you decided to see him again," Oliver said.

"Sorry I never discussed it with you. I really didn't know if he would come and didn't want to get my hopes up."

"I think it is good for you to see your dad. He will be so proud of you, Soraya."

She smiled, "I couldn't wish for a better time for him to come out here. I have already asked the building janitor and he told me my father could stay at the small room by the parking area for a few days. It's furnished and no one ever uses it.

"He could stay with us," Kate said.

"That is not necessary. He would really feel out of place. Also, I could spend time with him without invading your privacy. I hope you don't mind."

Her mind drifted off to her father's visit, and she couldn't have been more pleased.

In the next few days she took care of all her college papers and cleaned the room for her father. She put out clean sheets and bedding for him. Everything was just the way he was used to, and she made sure of that. He had to feel at home. There was nothing more to do except count the days until his arrival.

There was so much she wanted to tell him. So much that was unsaid. She wanted to share her joy with him and most of all to take that walk with him. She would hold on to his arm and tell him how much she loved him and respected him for who he was and what he had meant to her all her life.

She wanted him to see the woman that she had become and let him know that he didn't need to work so hard anymore. She was going to take care of him any way she could.

"Oh my dear, old Father, there is so much I need to share with you. I hope you understand and give me your blessing. That will be all I need to go on with my life, to face the odds and feel the untouchable and dream of the unbelievable. You, my father, need to give me your blessing, and I will do the rest."

She woke up early on the morning he was to arrive and finished most of her work before Kate and Oliver even got up. She was too excited to sleep and woke up every hour to look at the clock, knowing it was too early yet. Her father was to arrive at noon. It was a beautiful morning, and she was in a particularly great mood.

Oliver and Soraya had hardly any time to talk in private the last week. He wanted her to have as much time and space as she needed to be with her father. He enjoyed watching her happy and that was enough for him at the time. He offered to give her a ride to the bus stop; but she turned him down and told him she would rather go alone. She left the house in plenty of time to get there and sat on a bench and waited for the bus. It was twenty minutes late, but she finally saw it pull into the parking area. Her whole body was trembling as she stood there waiting for the passengers to get off the bus. It took a few minutes before they started getting off one by one. She anxiously waited to see his face. She tried to look in the crowded bus to see him before he got off, but was not successful. It was a waiting game, and she waited longer. There were still a lot of people in the bus, and suddenly she saw a familiar face, but it wasn't him. Soon all the passengers were just about out, but there was still no sign of him. She walked toward the bus as the last passenger got off, but her father was nowhere to be seen. With tears in her eyes, she stepped in and looked inside. She gave the bus driver a description of her father, but he told her that no such person was ever on that bus. She got off the bus, heart broken.

"Where is he? Maybe he missed his bus and is taking the next one."

She decided to go inside to inquire about the next bus and was told there wouldn't be one until the next day, same time. The weight of the world was on her shoulders as she left the bus station.

"Maybe Mina knows something."

Soraya decided to go home and call her. She got out of the taxi and looked at the room across the parking lot, with tears in her eyes.

She whispered, "You were supposed to be there now. Where are you?"

She was surprised to find Oliver at home that time of the day.

"Hi, I have to call Mina. My father wasn't on that bus; I think he probably missed the bus."

Oliver and Kate stood in front of her looking shocked. Oliver walked closer to her and took Soraya's hand.

"Come here, Sweetheart."

"I have to call Mina."

"You don't need to. We just heard from her."

"What did she say" Does she know what happened to him?"

Oliver looked down for a moment and said, "I don't know how to tell you this."

She looked at him with wide eyes.

"What's going on?"

He cleared his throat to continue, "Soraya, your father had a heart attack and passed away last night. I am so sorry."

She pulled her hands away from him and looked at him in a strange way.

"You are telling me he is dead?"

Kate went to her crying.

"We are so sorry for your loss."

She just stood there, staring. Oliver tried to comfort her, but she pulled away. His heart went out to her, knowing how special her father was to her.

Kate couldn't stop crying.

"Soraya, I was told that he asked for you before he died. He wants you to go to your village for his funeral. That was his last wish."

"He will get his last wish," she whispered. "I will leave on the next bus."

Soraya walked to her room and quietly closed the door. Kate and Oliver just sat in the living room not knowing what to do. Oliver wanted to hold her in his arms and comfort her tell her its ok to cry. He wanted to let her know she was not alone. But he knew she had to be alone for a while to work things out her own way.

Soraya sat on her bed. There were no tears to shed, no crying or screaming. All she did was to sit there frozen.

"He is gone and it is my fault. It was too much for him to bear, and his heart finally gave in."

She got up and packed a small bag and walked out of the room, feeling so empty, not knowing what to do or which direction to turn. She called the bus station to find out the time that the next bus would be leaving. It was less than an hour.

"I have to leave now. The bus leaves shortly."

Soraya glanced over to Ali's room and walked over to the doorway. The baby was playing in his crib and looked up, smiling at her.

"Hello, my sweet boy. I came to say good bye. I will be gone for a while and wanted to tell you that your grandfather died without knowing about you. He never got to see your sweet face. I never had a chance to take that walk with him."

She gently kissed him and walked out of the room and picked up her bag. Kate looked at her desperately.

"Is there anything we can do for you?"

She just shook her head.

"I am sorry to leave like this."

And she left the room. Kate stood watching her leave, with tears in her eyes. She wished that Soraya could cry for her father. It wasn't a good sign, not being able to cry and keeping it bottled up inside.

Oliver followed Soraya to the car. They hardly said a word, knowing nothing was going to give her any kind of comfort. He parked the car at the station and turned to her.

"Please talk to me before you leave."

"Oliver, don't. Not right now. Go home to your family. I have to do the same and go to mine."

"Take care of yourself and call if you can."

He saw her nodding her head as she got out of the car.

"Be careful."

The bus took off shortly after. She sat in her seat, thinking of the last time she had seen her father. She felt so alone with so much on her mind. The bus stopped a couple of times, but she never got off for anything. It was almost like she couldn't see or hear anything. She felt totally shut off from the outside world, and that's where she wanted to be. Where it was safe and no one could invade her private world or harm it in any way. Once she got to her destination, she rented a car with a driver to take her to the village. It was an hour drive and was starting to get dark out. She couldn't see the beautiful mountains when the car stopped right outside the village.

"I can drive further if you like."

She looked around.

"No, this is where I want to get out."

She made arrangement with the driver to pick her up the following week and take her to the station.

She paid him and got out of the car. It was a cool night and the smell of the fresh air felt good. She began to walk slowly toward the village, remembering the last time she took that same walk. It was the day her nightmarish journey began.

Everything was so quiet, but soon she heard noises as she got closer to the village. They were coming from her house, and she remembered them all too well. Anytime someone died, all the villagers gathered at the house and kept the family company. She slowly walked toward the house and saw her sister, Zahra, sitting on the front porch. Zahra was looking at her trying to figure out who this shadow was walking toward her house. She did not recognize Soraya as she didn't look like the village girls anymore. She just stared and finally stood up, narrowing her eyes.

Soraya didn't want to keep her in suspense, so called, "It's me, Soraya."

Zahra looked at her in surprise, like she had just seen a ghost. It wasn't long, however, before she ran toward her sister and hugged her tightly.

Zahra was crying, "I thought I would never see you again. Oh dear God, thank you."

She cried uncontrollably and laughed the next moment, but never let go of her big sister.

"It's okay. I am here now. I will explain everything to you later. Where is mother?"

Zahra wiped the tears.

"She is inside."

They both walked in and the whole room went silent. No one could believe their eyes. Her siblings ran toward her, and she sat on the floor holding all of them and kissing them like they belonged to her. She looked up and saw her mother all dressed in black and looking older than she had remembered. People began leaving the room one by one, and soon everyone was gone except for her family.

"Hello, Mother."

Her mother looked at her and shook her head, tears running down her face.

"He was never the same after you left. Nothing was the same for him. He would sit on that porch and stare at the mountains, thinking you would someday walk back into his life. In the end, he didn't even care if everyone found out; he wanted you back in his life so much and didn't care. He never blamed you for what happened, and he told me that himself. He was just never the same Soraya, never."

Soraya let go of her little brothers and sisters and walked over to her mother and sat by her on the floor. There were tears in her mother's eyes, but Soraya couldn't cry.

"It's okay, Mother. Everything is going to be okay. I promise you that."

"The week before he died he was in a good mood. He smiled and laughed and acted almost silly. Then he told me he was going to the city for a few days. I knew he was going to see you, but he never said anything. He was so happy, that silly old man."

Tears filled her eyes again. It pained her to talk about her loss.

"The heart attack struck him the day before he was to leave. By the time we got a doctor to come out from the city, he was dead."

"Did he say anything before he died?"

She stared into Soraya's face and then looked down.

"Did he say anything? Oh yes, he did. You were all he talked about. He didn't want a doctor; he wanted you. His words were that if he could see you once again, then he didn't care if he lived or died. You were his last wish, his only wish. He made me promise to forgive you for your sins. That's when he told me again that it wasn't your fault."

She looked Soraya in the eyes again.

"For whatever it is worth, I had forgiven you; I did that the day you left."

Soraya didn't express any sentiment at what her mother had just confessed to her.

"When is the funeral?"

"We will bury him tomorrow. He wanted us to wait until you came. He said you would be here."

Soraya felt the warm tears on her cheeks.

"He knew," she whispered, and for the first time she burst into tears "Oh Mother, he knew."

They sat on the torn rugs in their cottage and cried, holding each other for a long time. Her mother made some tea and gave her a hot cup. Soraya saw him everywhere she looked. His memory was there; and she felt his presence, looking down at all of them and smiling. She was home and somehow felt he knew. Maybe he could rest in peace now.

"I should have come a long time ago. I shouldn't have waited so long."

He had sat there on the porch waiting for her to come back. She couldn't bear the thought of him sitting and waiting. It broke her heart. Now she had lost him forever and she would never see his gentle face again.

Just a few days earlier she thought maybe life had changed for her, but she now realized this was the beginning of all her heartaches. She had given and sacrificed so much already. She wondered how much more she could give. There was nothing more to give; it was all gone. There they sat, all her young siblings, as she looked at them.

"Who is going to take care of them? How can they survive without my father?"

There was so much they had to work out before she left for the city. For the first time, the reality hit her; and she looked at her mother, wondering how it was at all possible for her to take care of all those kids.

In a way, her mother was glad Soraya was there. She always had a confidence that used to be a threat to her mother, but now she needed her daughter's strength and influence. She was glad to have her near.

"Did he leave you any money?"

"Very little. We won't make it more than a couple of weeks. There is always the farm, but I can't run the farm, not with all these kids."

"Can you sell it?"

"Yes, but that money would be gone fast too. What then?"

"Mother, I have some money that would get you through at least six months. If you also sell the farm, it would be okay for a while. That would give me enough time to save up more money. I will take care of you as much as I can. Don't worry about anything right now."

Her mother looked at her in disbelief.

"What are you doing in the city?"

"It's a long story; but I know I can handle it. That is one thing I can do for my father, to take care of his family and not let them go hungry."

Her mother couldn't believe how grown up she was. And she was thankful for her return. Even if it was for a short time, she was able to put her life in her daughter's hands and let her take over. Somehow, she trusted her. She wasn't the same child who left the village a while ago, and she realized that. What she didn't know was that Soraya was capable of a lot more than she ever thought. She got up and put all the kids to bed. Soraya and Zahra sat out on the porch looking out. There was so much Zahra needed to know, so much that was untold, and Soraya didn't know where to begin.

"Why did you leave?"

In her, faded smile there was more pain than joy.

"Don't ask me why yet. I will tell you someday, but not now. It's not the right time. I hope you understand."

"Why can't you come back and live here?"

"Oh Zahra, my life has changed so much. I can't even begin to tell you, but for now more than ever, I need to be where I am if I am to help mother. Zahra was filled with questions, but knew better than to ask. One thing hadn't changed and that was her sister's secrets. She had always been a private person and she still had the same mysterious ways about her.

"What about you? What is going on in your life since my departure?"

"I am engaged to be married soon."

"To whom?" Soraya asked.

"To the same man you were engaged to," she replied, and she looked down.

"How do you feel about that?"

"I feel good. He is a nice man, and mother doesn't have to worry about me."

"You don't sound very happy about it."

Zahra looked into her sister's eyes, her own filled with tears.

"Because I know he still loves you. You are the one he wanted. You were his first choice."

"Did he tell you that?"

"No, but he didn't have to. I can tell."

"Do you want to marry him?"

"Soraya, I am different from you. I want to stay here, get married, have kids, and live my life here. I don't have the same aspirations as you, and I couldn't ask for a nicer man to be married to. My only wish is for him to love me for who I am, not because I am your sister."

"How could he not love you? You are beautiful, kind, and smart. Just give him time. He'll come around, but that's only if you love him and want to marry him. Let me tell you something, Zahra, life doesn't turn its wheels for you. You have to be in control and do what you believe in to make things happen. It is all up to you and no one else."

Their mother stepped out, hoping Soraya wouldn't tell her sister the truth about why she left the village. She still believed certain things should be buried and never talked about, but she couldn't say anything. She turned to Soraya and gave her a ring.

"Your father left this ring for you. He wanted you to have it and made me promise you would get it someday. You might as well have it now."

He had always worn that ring and never took it off. Now it belonged to her, and it meant so much to her to have it. She held it tight in her hand.

"We all better go to bed. Tomorrow will be a long day."

"You two go on. I am going to sit here for a while."

Again, she looked out at the mountains.

A few minutes later her mother walked out with a blanket in her hand.

"It gets cold out here." She handed Soraya the blanket. She wrapped it around her and just sat there, as her mother watched her sitting where her father used to sit, looking in the same direction he did. They were so much alike, and now she sat in his seat, taking over where he left off. It was a shame she never got too close to Soraya and never got to know who she really was. She had always wanted more than they could offer her in this small village, and now she had more. But was she happy?

"I hope for his sake, she is. That is all that mattered to him, her happiness. He was willing to risk everything, if I allowed him."

Soraya sat looking at the dark night. The mountain breeze felt so good on her skin. She closed her eyes and hoped she could fall asleep right there and let the magic of the night take over.

Someone touched her on the shoulder, as she turned she saw her father. He was smiling at her and said, "Welcome home, my child."

"Oh father, I am so sorry I didn't come sooner."

He took her hand, saying "Come with me."

"Where are we going?"

He looked at her and smiled again.

"We are going for a walk, and you can tell me everything."

"I dreamed about this day. You just don't know how badly I wished for the day we could take this walk."

"I know, My Child. Now here is your chance."

They walked through the forest into the most incredible valley.

"I want you to know how much I love you. I never had a chance to tell you that before I left. We have the same dreams, and maybe someday I can live out our dreams. Most of all, Father, I want you to know about my son, Ali. Just like you, I had to give up my child, and for the first time I realized what you went through the day we said our good-byes. Your love has always been with me, and because of your love, I have made it against all odds." Tears were now running down her face.

"What am I to do without you now?"

"You have to continue your journey. You have places to go, and I want to see you on top, the highest you can get. For the first time in my life, I am free to go wherever I want. No one is here to stop me; and be sure, my child, my place is with you. I will always be with you, and you have my blessing in everything you do. Choose the way, and go to the top. You have to be loved and should choose the one. You have to be strong, and you should know the level of your strength. You have to be the leader, and you choose the followers. And all the ways that you choose, my child, remember, I am right beside you, walking with you."

She rested her head on his shoulder and held on to his arm and they walked through the forest in peace and harmony. Soraya opened her eyes and saw her mother.

"You slept on the porch all night, just like he used to do."

Soraya looked around and heard the sound of the roosters waking everyone up. She smiled.

"I haven't slept this well for a long time. I took my walk with him. He knows everything and still loves me for who I am."

Now it was time to bury his body; his soul was with her, and she truly believed that.

It was a very long and hard day for everyone. They buried the man they all loved so much, knowing life would never be the same for any of them. There were a lot of people that came in and out of the house that day, and Soraya couldn't wait for them to leave. She wanted to spend every moment with her family before leaving again. She was the one who was going to make sure this family stayed together. She took the envelope out of her bag and handed it to her mother.

"This should take care of you for at least six months."

It was the same envelope that Oliver and Kate had given her. Her mother looked inside. She had never seen that much money before.

"Do you have any money left for yourself?"

"Don't worry about me. But make me one promise; if any of the kids decide to continue with their education, please don't stop them. Do it for him. I don't know when I will be back again, but you can always count on me for financial support. I will send you enough money to raise the kids."

"I am so sorry to let you go. I am sorry to have given up on you, and I hope someday you can forgive me."

"We all have to live with our decisions. All I can tell you is that I am not any better than you. You did what you thought was right. I did my share of giving up also."

For the first time in her life, she felt close to her mother. They sat and talked for hours and days and got to know each other all over again. It was a time of peace and of letting go of their past. They forgave but not forget and took steps toward a better relationship.

Soraya spent her days watching her brothers and sisters play. It is so much easier to get over tragedies when you are just a child. She hoped they could live their lives not feeling the pain of losing their father the way she did. The pain was so deep, and there was no one to comfort her. No one understood how she felt, and she didn't bother telling them either.

Their last night together was so different from the last time she was there. This time she got to hold each and every one of them and say good-bye. One thing hadn't changed, she didn't know when she would see them again; but at least in her heart, she didn't feel that she had abandoned them. Everyone cried and knew that she was going to walk out of their lives once again. She left the next day, looking around at all the familiar grounds that she was leaving behind. With her father gone, for the first time, she didn't feel that she belonged to that place any longer.

She got off the bus and decided to walk for a few blocks. Suddenly a sign caught her eye. It was a small motel. She decided to get a room for the night, wanting to be all by herself. The room was small and simple and she put her small bag down and sat on the bed, feeling all alone. It was hard for her to say good-bye to her family, specially Zahra. She had an empty feeling. Somehow she felt lost, not knowing what she was doing in that motel room and not knowing what direction to go to next. She picked up the phone and dialed Oliver's number and waited, a few minutes later he answered the phone.

"Oliver Reed, may I help you?"

Holding the phone, she waited for a moment.

"Hi, Oliver."

"Well hello. I am so glad to hear your voice. Where are you?"

"In a motel room by the bus station."

"What are you doing there?"

"Just needed to have a day to myself to think."

"Would you like some company? Give me the name and the room number and I will be there shortly."

She put the phone down confused, wondering why she had called Oliver. And before she knew it, there was a knock on the door. She quickly opened it.

"Hi, beautiful."

"Hello, Oliver," she smiled.

"You look pale. Are you feeling okay?"

"I am just tired. That's all."

He held her in his arms tightly.

"Oh, I missed you so much."

It had been so long since he held her in his arms and smelled her hair.

"I love you."

He lifted her chin and looked into her eyes.

"Are you okay?"

"I have to be. What other choice do I have? My father is gone, and my family needs me. I have to be strong and face everything. At times I wish life could just stop until I am done mourning for my father, but that could be a lifetime. We only have one life to live and it goes on. Tomorrow, he will be just a memory to everyone; but to me his memory will never die."

"I know this doesn't sound right at this moment, but I promise you it will get easier. God gives and then takes away, but in the meantime gives patience and reasons to go on living. Maybe someday, all this will make more sense to you."

They talked for a long time, and Oliver was glad she finally opened up to him and let him help her in a small way.

"I need to sort things out in my mind. Tomorrow I will go back to the house.

For now, I think you should go back, too, and let me be by myself."

Oliver left with a heavy heart, knowing her love for her father was a lot stronger than he ever imagined.

Soraya opened the holy book of Quran and started reading it. She read the part about sins and read it over and over again. Then she knew what she had to do. Tragic events were going to keep happening to her unless she stopped her sins. Her relationship with Oliver was a sin against her religion, Kate, and all forms of life, and she had to stop it. She truly believed life would go on punishing her unless she stopped. She did not want anything to happen to another one of her loved ones.

"I can't control my feelings and my love for Oliver, but I have to end the affair once and for all."

It was like two deaths at once; her father's and the death of her relationship with Oliver. Her mind was made up. She was going to follow through with her plans, but the thought of it almost killed her.

She woke up early the next morning and left the motel room. She walked a few blocks and finally took the bus, going home to Kate, Oliver and her son Ali.

Kate was feeding the baby when she heard a key in the door. She turned around and to her surprise found Soraya standing there. The two women looked at each other and ran to each other's arms, crying. Soraya finally pulled away.

"Kate, I need you to forgive me for my behavior lately. And also for the way I left a week ago."

Kate didn't know what to say for a moment.

"You are forgiven for whatever you think you have done."

She felt Kate knew what she meant, but it was to remain unsaid.

"I am back, and I need this job more than ever, if you still need me."

"You are definitely needed, love. Welcome back."

It was a pleasant reunion and they both felt a sense of relief but they didn't know why.

"I need to take care of a couple of things this morning, and after that, I will be at your service."

"Take your time and let me know if I can be of any help to you," Kate said. "It would be nice to see all of us back to normal for a change. Too many tragedies have happened lately, and I am ready for it all to end."

Soraya changed her clothes and left the house. She stopped at a phone booth and called Oliver.

"I need to talk to you. Can you meet me somewhere?"

Oliver wondered what was going on and decided to meet her immediately to find out.

They sat across the table from each other at a small cafeteria. He almost didn't want to hear what she had to say.

"Oliver, I don't know where to begin. I know you are the only man that I will ever love this way. I am glad to know true love through you. You gave me something that I don't think most people experience in their whole lives. Our love is not wrong. It doesn't feel wrong, but it is unfair, and it can't continue. I want to be a part of your life forever, but that could only be through Ali. You and I can't exist anymore. It never was. I want you to be safe and loved, and Kate is the one who will give you that. I can't give you that safety. We will hurt ourselves and our loved ones if we continue. You and I are no more and will never be. Please understand me and don't hate me. Your love will never die in my heart. It will always be alive, but our actions have to stop for all of our sakes. I don't know what direction life will take us. Some day you will have to go back to your own country, but always remember you can find my love through Ali's eyes. Whenever you look at him, just remember how much I loved you. Ali is the sign of my love for you and Kate. My love for you will last a lifetime and so will Ali. I know you will never forget me, and I don't want you to, but give my son all the love that you have for me. With that, I can go on with my life, knowing he will be loved. That will be my happiness. I am going to leave this cafeteria in a few minutes, and I want the next time we meet to be like the old days, like good friends. You won't have a chance to say anything because I couldn't take it if you said anything sad to me. It would tear me apart and make this more difficult. I have said too many good-byes lately. This one is the hardest one. But remember, I am not going anywhere. I will be right beside you and your family as long as I can."

She squeezed his hand and stared into his eyes for a moment, then walked out.

Oliver sat there, stunned. In a way, he admired her for her strength, her honesty, and her love for him. But he wasn't ready for this yet. Would he ever be ready to leave her and say his final good-bye to her? He knew someday it would have had to come to this, but he could not bring himself to do that to her. He loved her too much to be the one to end it first. She had made it easier for him to bear. He loved her more now than ever; yet knew it was over and he would never be able to hold her in his arms and make love to her again.

He had listened to everything she had said and respected her wishes.

"I will love you until the day I die; and I will never forget you, my love. You have given me your son, and that will always be with me. I will see him grow up before my eyes and remember you. And I will know that somehow you know."

Soraya left the cafeteria feeling lighter than she had in a long time, feeling a sense of freedom that made her want to skip all the way home. She looked at the bright blue sky and smiled. She had freed Oliver to live his life without guilt toward her. She looked over her shoulder and felt a warm hand on her shoulder.

"I know you are here, Father. I know."

# CHAPTER SIX

Summer went by fast. Soraya had been accepted at the university and couldn't wait to start. She saved as much money as she could and helped her mother any chance she got. Kate had to go back for another check-up. This time Oliver decided to go with her, and Soraya was glad about his decision. They just couldn't risk being together alone. It was too early yet, and they both knew that. She was about to start school when they left and was pleased to have the time to herself.

Kate and she had gotten close again. It was a good feeling all the way around. Oliver was glad to see Soraya so much at peace with herself. He still loved her as always, and at times would give anything to hold her close but had learned to put his feelings aside.

Soraya had learned to live with her tragic past, and yet be happy; and he was happy for her. She started school the week after they left and couldn't believe how different it was from anything she had experienced in the past. She liked everything about being a college student. She also found herself a couple of tutoring jobs for high school kids and made good money. For the first time, she realized that her days of being a servant were long gone. She could make more money in one week tutoring than what she made all month working as a servant. Plus, she enjoyed teaching so much. She took everything in and enjoyed the college life; it was so different. Everything for once was going her way, and that pleased her to no limit. Most guys at school would have given anything to get one glance from her, but she was deep in her books and work and never saw or heard anything else. Soon everyone found out she had the highest scores to enter university that year, and she began getting a lot of attention. Still she kept to herself most of the time. She got many offers to go to parties and gatherings, but she turned them all down. Her life consisted of working, going to school, tutoring and studying, and she wanted nothing more. Soraya Noor was a mystery to most of her college friends. They knew not to ask her anything personal and not to get too close to her. It didn't interest her to get involved with anyone there. She had only one mission, and that was her education. Her professors got to know her fast. She was the one with all the right questions and answers. She often sat next to a young man with very thick glasses. He was quiet and never paid any attention to anything else except his work. It was safe sitting next to him; he never showed any interest in her personally. They had talked a few times about different school projects, and that was as far as they went. He didn't notice her beauty or the mystery that everyone was trying to solve. Actually, he didn't notice anything unusual about her which made it safe for Soraya to choose the empty seat next to him in most of her classes. There was nothing attractive about him, so most young girls left him alone, which made it easy for Soraya to spot him. He didn't mind her next to him; but then, he could care less who sat by him. All he wanted was to be left alone, like Soraya. She respected him for that.

"Excuse me. Do you have an extra pen?" My pen just ran out of ink."

He searched in his bag and gave her a pen.

"Thank you."

He just nodded. The class was about to end. The professor gave them their assignment as they all made notes.

"See you all next week," he closed.

"Here is your pen."

"That's okay. You can keep it."

"By the way, my name is Soraya."

"Hi. My name is Nader. Are you from Tehran?"

"No," she said.

"Well, it's nice to meet you."

"Same here."

He walked away, and for the first time Soraya noticed his warm voice. She liked him mostly because unlike all the other guys, he didn't try to hit on her.

"I wonder if he has a past that he doesn't like to talk about." She found herself with the same curiosity as the other students.

"This is stupid. All along I've been wanting to meet someone who doesn't care about who I am, and now I am judging him without knowing anything about him." She gathered up her books, left the class, and slowly walked to the bus stop. She saw him standing in the line waiting for the bus.

"Hi, I have never seen you take the bus before."

"Oh hi. My car broke down and it's in the shop getting fixed."

"Do you live near by?"

"No, not really."

They talked for a few minutes about their classes and their professors, and soon the bus stopped. They both got in.

"What school did you graduate from?"

"I went to Nasari night school."

"What's your last name?"

"Noor."

"Oh, so you are the one to enter university with the highest scores this year."

She smiled, "That was just luck."

At this he laughed out loud. It was the first time she had seen him smile.

"You are a very modest young lady."

It was a pleasant conversation, and she enjoyed talking to him. He seemed so shy, but there was a lot of confidence in his tone. He talked firmly and sounded very intelligent, which impressed Soraya, who had not been exposed to many male figures in her life.

"So, what are you going to be when you grow up?"

"I don't know yet. I am still deciding, and yourself?"

"Maybe be a teacher someday. I think it's a good occupation and at the same time very rewarding," he said with a smile.

"You know, I have been thinking about that myself," Soraya replied.

"Well, what do you know? We have something in common."

They both laughed.

The bus stopped and they both got out at the same station.

"Is this your stop also"?

"Yes, it is," she answered.

"This is very coincidental. I live about three blocks east of here. We are almost neighbors."

They both got off the bus and started walking toward the same direction.

"You don't happen to have a very strict father or brother who's going to get upset because you are walking with a strange man, do you?"

She smiled, "Relax; you are safe. Actually, I am on my own."

"That's strange in our country; don't you agree?"

"Yes it is," and she decided to leave it at that. "Well, I am almost home."

He looked at her and stopped walking for a second.

"I can give you rides from time to time, if you like."

"Thank you. That is very nice of you, she said after a pause well I better go now."

"See you later."

He kept walking as she stood there looking at him for a short time. He never turned around to look, just kept on walking.

For the first time, she felt safe with a man other than her father or Oliver. She thought that this could be the beginning of her healing process with the opposite sex. There wasn't any attraction between them, so she didn't feel she had to have her guard up. At the same time, she knew if anyone from school ever saw her get in the car with him, it would start a rumor; and she didn't want that. Many of the students dated each other, but it was all done behind their parents back. After all, they lived in a country that didn't allow their daughters or sisters to date. Of course that didn't stop any of the young kids from sneaking around behind their families' backs, but it still was a rule. The upper class people were more open minded, but even they had to sneak around most of the time. Most men dated these girls, but in the end they would choose a virgin wife and not someone who they dated. They would choose someone who was untouched and unseen by any other male. And that's what it came down to; virginity was the most important thing a woman could give her man on the day they wed, no matter what part of the country they were from. Young girls had sexual relations with their boyfriends, but they would stop before it broke their virginity. That was the rule. It was your reputation, and without it you would have a bad name. Every man would want to have you, but not for a wife. That's what Soraya was missing and could never talk about. She had to keep it all to herself. It was to be a secret forever.

She walked in the quiet apartment and missed not having anyone there. She still thought about Oliver often and loved him for not judging her for who she was and what was done to her. She missed him with all her heart. She missed his touch and the gentle ways about him which she could never forget, no matter what the future brought. As far as she was concerned, she had enough love to last her a lifetime. Now he was just a fantasy to her, someone she could never have. She learned to live with that fact. It was almost a month since Oliver and Kate had left and she began getting lonely. They were like her family now. And as for Ali, there was no way of explaining how she felt about this child who she had no right to any longer.

The night they were due back, Soraya was so excited to see them. She couldn't wait and did all her work and sat on the couch waiting for them to come home. She missed Ali and also Kate, but most of all she missed Oliver. In her heart, nothing had changed. She still loved him just as much. Often wished she could tell him that. But for now, she was just satisfied to see him and at least know he was near, not thousands of miles away. She was deep in her thoughts when she heard the door open.

"Hello. Anybody home?"

"Oh my God, it's Oliver."

She ran to the door and found all three of them at the front door. There was laughter and hugs and kisses. Then she turned to Ali.

"Oh God, look at how much you've grown."

She took him in her arms. "I missed you so much." She held him close and then noticed Oliver, watching her holding her son in her arms.

"Hello, Oliver." She gave him a hug, and he held her tight for a short few seconds. She could tell he missed her just as much. It was a nice reunion for all of them, and she was glad to hear Kate's test results had come out well for the second time.

"So, how does it feel to be a college student?"

"It's wonderful. I couldn't be happier, especially now that you guys are back."

"Tell me, have you met any cute guys at school yet?" Kate asked with an inquisitive smile.

She smiled back, "And what if I have?"

"Oh, that sounds very interesting. It sounds like you have been very busy since we left."

Oliver looked at Soraya, not knowing how to react.

"I am just joking, there is no one."

And then she smiled.

"Well, there have been a few offers, but I am just going to wait for my prince."

"So, you had some offers?" Kate asked, hoping to find out more.

"I am not interested in any of them. Except, there is this one guy. He is not good looking, but very smart; and I like him because he is not interested in me or my life. As a matter of fact, he is not interested in anyone. It feels safe sitting next to him in class, even safer than sitting next to some of the girls. They are all nosy and want to know everything there is to know. He is not like the rest. That's why I like him, just as a friend, nothing more. So relax, he is not my type. I don't even know who is my type.

Kate began to laugh, listening to her go on and on. It was nice to see her act her own age for a change. It was so unusual for her to act that way, and maybe this was the new Soraya who began to open doors and let others in.

Oliver, however, felt intimidated by this new friend of Soraya's. He didn't want anyone hurting her. He decided to use the opportunity when Kate took Ali to bed to question her.

"Do you want to tell me more about your new friend?"

"There is nothing to tell. He doesn't even talk to me that much. All I know is that his name is Nader and he lives a few blocks away from us. We are not interested in each other the way you think. He didn't ask me a thousand questions like everyone else, and I liked that about him. I felt comfortable with him."

"Are you sure that is all there is?"

"Yes, I am sure. You don't need to be so defensive. I can take care of myself."

"I am sure you can, but I do things my way, Darling. When it comes to you, I won't take any chances. I hope you understand that."

She sensed a little jealousy in his tone and she didn't really mind that. She still loved him and wished she could tell him that there wouldn't be anyone else who could take his place in her heart.

He stepped closer to her and grabbed her arm. He pulled her close and kissed her passionately and then parted from her quickly before Kate's return.

She stood frozen. Her heart was pounding. "You shouldn't have done that."

He just smiled at her and whispered, "Sorry, love. That one was out of my control," and walked out of the kitchen. That small kiss brought all her emotions back to life again. "I should never talk about another man in front of him again." She did want him to know how she felt watching him and Kate together, though.

Oliver was all mixed up again. He had thought about her many times while he was away and wished he could get her out of his mind;

but she always managed to find her way back into his mind. Every time he looked at Ali, he saw her. Their similarities were absolutely incredible. He had so much on his mind lately. Kate had talked to him several times about moving back home, but he had brushed it off. He wouldn't allow her to continue with the thought. Knowing it would eventually be brought back up; but, for now, he had to make her understand that the timing wasn't right. The truth was he couldn't leave Soraya behind. He often wondered if he would ever get over her and go on with his life, but he never had an answer. For the time being, he couldn't risk the thought of not seeing her ever again. It was too soon for her to lose all of them. Not to mention, he couldn't leave her because he wanted to be near her so for now, this is where he was going to stay, no matter what Kate said. He was going to fight it until the last possible moment.

Kate pushed him every chance she had to move back to America.

"I want to raise Ali in my own country. Is that too much to ask? It is hard for me to fly back home every three months for different tests, Oliver. I don't want to be here for Christmas anymore. I want my son to know what it is like to have Christmas in his own home, where he belongs."

"Kate, I have committed to this position for at least two more years and can't just pack up and leave. What about Soraya, anyway?"

"She can come visit us every year; we will send her a ticket. And when she is done with school, we can bring her to the U.S. if she would like. Oliver, I don't want to be unfair to Soraya, but I need to think of us first."

"I can't stop you from leaving, but you can't push me into making a decision that I am not ready to make yet. I need to be here two more years. You can move back if you like and find a house and decorate it the way you like. You could get settled until I am done with my obligations here. We could take turns visiting each other any chance we get, but that is all I can promise for now. The last thing I want to do is to let you and Ali leave without me and then not be there to witness his first step and all those other special moments. Kate, that is not what I want, but I will leave the decision up to you. My mind is made up, and you have to do the same thing."

Oliver knew in his heart that Soraya was the reason he couldn't leave; but he justified it by telling himself that he had to see her more situated before he decided to leave. He could never abandon her. There was too much love in his heart to just leave. He had to be there for her, even if that meant watching Kate and Ali leave without him. Oliver knew that Kate was influenced by her mother to move back home. He didn't blame either one of them, but he couldn't ignore his own feelings for Soraya either. Soraya knew Kate and Oliver were having problems, but she wasn't sure why. They hardly spoke to each other and neither one had confided in her. She had never seen the atmosphere so chilled between them and it worried her, not knowing what was happening in their life?

One night she came home after a tutoring lesson and found them shouting at each other. They both stopped when they saw her come in. Oliver picked up his keys and left the house, and Kate sat at the kitchen table holding her head.

"Kate, are you okay?"

She looked up and Soraya saw that she was crying.

"I don't know. We have never fought like this before. It's been impossible to communicate lately. All we do is scream at each other and walk out."

"What are you fighting about?"

"I know I am pressuring him, but it seems like he is obsessed with this place, this country."

"Are you thinking of moving back home soon?"

Kate felt guilty keeping it from Soraya, and whispered, "Yes I am. But he doesn't want to. That's why we have been fighting lately. I don't understand why he doesn't even try to get out of his commitment here. Soraya, I am so sorry. You must think I am very selfish, not even discussing it with you up until now; but be sure, I won't leave unless I know that you are taken care of. It is just that so much has happened lately. My parents are getting older, only God knows how long they will be around. My illness has made me think about some of those things and it makes me want to go home and be near the people I love. With my condition it is hard to travel every three months with a baby. All of these factors tie into why I think it is time for us to go home. I hope you understand and don't hate me."

"Kate, I do understand. I don't want you making any decisions based on me, either. I am fine and can handle my own life from here on. I can teach more nights and rent a small room somewhere. It was something that I was considering anyway. You two have enough to worry about; and I don't want you to think about me, not even for a minute."

"Well, at this point, I don't think Oliver is going to change his mind. So, I have to decide what to do? Stay here with Oliver or leave without him for two years."

"What would you do, Soraya?"

"I can't answer you that, Kate. You have to decide what's best for you and your family and do just that."

"I know it would drive me crazy leaving without Oliver, but I need to go on with my life. Most of all, I need to be home."

Their conversation lasted for a couple of hours, and Soraya finally decided to go to her room to give Kate some privacy to think about everything. She knew why Oliver wouldn't leave with Kate, and she felt responsible. It was going to happen someday anyway, why not now?

"I have to do this for Ali and convince him to leave with Kate. Life will never be the same for me if they leave, but I know only too well that the day will come sooner or later. I have to talk to Oliver and tell him it's okay for him to let go, that I want him to go on with his life. I need to let him know that he is free to go and shouldn't let me be a factor in his decision making. He needs to hear it from me, and he must know that his happiness is all I ever wanted."

She woke up early the next morning and got breakfast ready. Oliver came out, but she could tell he was in a very sour mood.

"Coffee?"

"Please." He sat at the kitchen table reading the paper.

"Oliver, we need to talk. Can you come by my school at lunch time?"

He put the newspaper down and looked up.

"What about?"

"I can't talk to you now."

"Did Kate say anything to you?"

"She didn't have to. I heard it myself, and we need to talk."

"Listen Soraya, no one can make this decision for me, not Kate and not you. I have to decide what to do, and she has to do the same."

He got up, threw the paper on the table, and walked out slamming the door behind him. She had never seen him like that before. She could tell that he was under a lot of stress, and she felt for him.

"Is he gone?" Kate asked.

"Yes, he is. He didn't even drink his coffee."

"I don't know what to do or say anymore. Somehow he is slipping through my fingers and I can't save him."

"This must be very hard for you, Kate. Just give him some time. He will eventually come around."

"I don't think so. Not this time. He seems so angry with me, and I don't know what to do. It was getting late and Soraya had to leave. She told Kate they would talk some more later. It was a very solemn day for her and she couldn't get anything done. Her mind was filled with thoughts of Oliver and couldn't wait to get out of there and call Oliver to see if she could talk him into seeing her that day.

As she walked out of the building, she saw his car waiting for her, and she ran toward it.

"Hi dear."

He looked at her. "Well get in."

She got in the car and he started driving.

"Where do you want to go?"

"Someplace where we can talk."

He began driving toward the park area.

"Are you mad at me, Oliver?"

"No, I am not," he said curtly, not wanting to talk until they got to the park.

They found a quiet corner and he parked the car. He turned toward her and said

"I am all yours."

"I don't know what to say now that I have you here." He smiled. "That's a first."

"Are you being sarcastic with me?"

"No, I am not. Sorry."

"I know you are going through a very rough time right now. I just want to help you like you helped me so many times when I was in need of a friend. I know you are having a hard time making a decision, but please don't let me be the reason why you are not leaving with Kate. Do it for yourself, for Kate, and for Ali. You belong to each other, and I feel responsible for your problems right now.

"I think I am partly the reason why you don't want to leave with your wife. But Oliver, you have given me so much. Now it is time for you to forget about me and get on with your life. Believe me, I will be okay. I didn't come this far to let anything come in the way of my getting where I am going. I will be fine and I want you to know that. Let go, even though it is hard. You have to free yourself and to not allow me to come in the way of your happiness with Kate."

Oliver listened to what she said and asked, "Are you done?"

She nodded.

"The last time you talked to me, you never gave me a chance to respond. You just got up and left, and I had to deal with everything you left behind. You made a decision for both of us, and I just had to accept it. I was not allowed to tell you how I felt, but still gave it a chance as you wished. Well, it didn't work. I can't let you or Kate decide for me anymore. It has to be me, because it is my life, and I am going to do it my way this time. She can leave if that's what she decides to do. And if you want to move out after she leaves, that's okay too. That's both of your own decisions. I can't, and won't, try to change your mind or hers but I have to find out what I need to do. Soraya, I don't know what goes on in your head. I do know what goes on in mine. Nothing has changed for me; I love you, and I want to be with you more than ever. I am even ready to tell Kate about us. I can't stop thinking of you all day and every day. When I lay next to Kate, I wish I was next to you. When I make love to her, it bothers me, knowing you are in the room next to me. My love for Kate has not ended, but it is not the same anymore, not since you have come into my life. Is it fair for me to leave with her when I have all these uncertain feelings? I don't know. Maybe time will decide. Maybe it's not a bad idea for her to leave for a while. Maybe we need time apart to work things out for better or worse, whatever that is. Soraya, I love you more than anything in this world. I want to be here for you, to protect you and to love you. You see, I can't leave like this. My body will be gone, but my heart will be left in this country, and it will tear me up. What we had wasn't just sex to me; otherwise, it would be over by now. For me, it was magical. It was beautiful, and it is worth risking everything I have to find out where it takes us. I want to share my life with you, to love you and protect you and be with you. That's why I can't leave, not until I know it is the right time for me and for you. I love Ali. He is my son; but I love Ali's mother even more. I hope you understand and maybe realize where I am coming from."

Soraya didn't know what to say after hearing Oliver out. This was the first time she listened to how he felt about her.

"Oliver, I love you more than anything in this world. Everything I've done was to protect you, and make things easier. I never thought you needed to worry about me. My life will never be dark and cold, not after what you have given me. Whatever you decide, I will be there for you and with you. To me, no other man exists in this world, but you. No one will ever take your place in my heart. Don't be angry with me for wanting the best for you."

She then took his hand in hers and kissed it with such an affection.

"I grew up in a village and until the day I die, the true value of life that was taught to me will not change. That's the way I was raised. You were the first man I chose to give myself to, and I am committed to your love for eternity. You are the one whether I am with you or not. That will never change in my heart. But, don't blame me for wanting happiness for you, something I never thought I could give you."

Oliver listened to this grown child, who was more honest than anyone he had ever known, and knew right then that he couldn't let her go, not then and maybe never. He felt her long hair through his fingers and lifted her chin.

"Are you willing to stand by me if I decide to tell Kate the truth?"

Tears filled her eyes.

"Oliver, I couldn't live with myself revealing our relationship to Kate. Please don't do that, not yet. I would rather die than face her. I truly don't think I am strong enough to do that. Oh dear God, what have I done?"

She stopped and buried her face in her hands.

"Listen to me, we didn't plan this. It just happened. Please don't cry."

He held her in his arms, comforting her and, for the first time in months, felt at ease. At least he now knew which direction he was going, whether it was right or wrong. Kate and Oliver sat across the table from each other at a restaurant.

"Kate, I've been trying to come up with a solution to our problem, and I know what you want to hear. Unfortunately, it is not going to happen, not yet. I need to finish what I am committed to do here. You surprised me with your sudden decision of wanting to leave and I understand your position, but two more years will not change anything. I don't want you to leave. I don't want to miss watching my son grow up by my side; but if that's what you want, I can't stop you. At the same time, I need you to respect my wishes and understand that I am not ready to leave yet. Kate, I love you and I always will. I just want you to know my love for you will never die, but might take a different direction, and that's something I can't help."

"It sounds like you are saying good-bye to me forever. Are you telling me everything I need to know?"

"There is nothing left for me to tell you. I just want you to know where I stand; that's all. You and I have never been separated for more than a few weeks, and this time it will be much longer. I don't know how to react to it all."

Kate looked away. "I don't either." And then she turned to Oliver and asked,

"How do you think Soraya will respond to me taking Ali?"

"I am sure it will be hard on her, but she has made it through tougher times. She realizes that someday it would come to this, and she would have to part with him possibly forever. The only problem is her staying in the apartment while you are gone. You know how people will think in this country with her and me in that place. So I thought maybe I could rent the room by the parking for her. That way she is still close for me to keep an eye on her, and also for her to still do the housework. What do you think?"

"I guess that will be fine as long as it is okay with her."

They talked about their marriage and relationship. This all seemed so final for them. Kate had felt Oliver had changed for months now, and she didn't know why. For the first time in her life there was another person whom she loved and adored and so was willing to take a chance with Oliver. Just as long as no one was going to take Ali away from her, she would be fine. He meant everything to her. He was going to be a reminder to her of a young woman who she adored and respected to no limit. Her love and respect for Soraya was the reason Oliver decided not to tell Kate anything at the time and also didn't want them all to part with bad feelings. Oliver never thought this would happen to them, for Kate leaving without him. Soraya had changed everything for him. He couldn't just leave her behind and get on with his life.

Soraya was watching Ali that night, knowing Kate and Oliver were out talking about their future. Ali would be leaving with Kate if that's what she decided to do. He was almost a year old now, and she knew these might be her last days with him. The thought of it depressed her and made her heart ache. She sat back and watched him play.

"I have made some selfish decisions in my life, but giving you up was the worst one yet. Maybe if I wasn't this close to you, it would be easier. Losing you is worse than death, even though I know you are loved. So what's the matter with me? Why can't I let you go and have a wonderful life? I just want you to know the truth someday, that I did love you, but my hands were tied. Someday Oliver will be with you, and I hope maybe when you grow up to be a young man, he will tell you about me. We will be far away from each other, my sweet love, but my heart will go with you wherever you are. My thoughts will always search for you. I know you will have a better life than your mommy. Who knows, maybe someday I can come and see you. I don't ever want you to know how you were conceived; but you know what, my darling? You are the symbol of my innocence. I sacrificed my whole life to give you life, and that is the sign of my love for you. You remember that your mommy loves you more than anything and that my prayers will always be with you, wherever you are."

Kate was to leave in a couple of days. Everything happened so fast. She had been in a strange mood for days now. She was busy mailing and packing so many things. This time she wouldn't be back. As for Soraya, she walked around in a daze. All she thought about was Ali. Her baby was leaving and she couldn't stop him. She had to let him go permanently. Everyone understood the other person's position, but they all were distant from each other, blaming themselves for what was happening.

Soraya had already moved downstairs and liked her room. It was nice and cozy, and she thought it was a good idea for her to make that move. They didn't need any gossip, even though not too many people knew them. Oliver had hardly spoken to her in days. He was busy getting everything ready for Kate; so Soraya decided to stay away as much as she could, getting herself used to the idea of not seeing Ali. She was deep in though when she heard a knock on the door.

"Who is it?"

"It's me, Kate."

Soraya opened the door and let her in.

"Can we talk?" Kate asked.

"Sure, sit down."

"Soraya, I haven't had a chance to talk to you much these days. Everything happened so fast. I don't know if I am doing the right thing by leaving. And I know this is just as hard on you as it is for Oliver and me. Don't think for a minute that I am unaware of your feelings for Ali. I know how much you love him, and I know this is in a way not fair to you. I know all this, but at the same time, I need to do what I think is best for myself and Ali.

"When I look at him and care for him, I don't think for a minute that he wasn't born to me. He couldn't be loved any more than if he were my own flesh and blood. I just hope that Oliver changes his mind and comes back to us sooner. I want you to know, we are never going to lose touch with you. My purpose is not to cut you off from Ali. That has never been my intention, and I hope you believe me. You are his biological mother, and I will never forget that. Someday I will tell him about you and show him pictures of you. He will know what a courageous mother he has and will be so proud of you, just as we are. My last wish is for you to take care of Oliver for me. Help him get through these rough times. I know you will, but I just had to ask you. I hope you don't mind."

Soraya was looking down as not to betray what she was thinking to Kate. She finally looked up.

"I know Ali will be loved to no end, and I am not worried. He is in good hands. I couldn't have made a better choice, even if I tried and searched my whole life. I want to thank you for loving him the way you do. As for me, I will be fine. Time is the healer of all wounds. Just send me a note in the mail every now and then and also some pictures of all of you. That is all I need and nothing more."

She took off the necklace that her mother gave her the day she left the village.

"I want you to have this. It's been in my mother's family for many years."

She then reached over and picked up a small box and opened it.

"This is for Ali. It belonged to my father, and I want Ali to have it someday. It's not a valuable ring, but it has come from a man who had more love in his heart than anyone I know. So maybe, in a way, I can pass that love on to Ali through this ring."

"Don't you want to keep these for yourself?"

"I would like you and Ali to have it. Kate you are a wonderful, kind, and caring woman, who has shown me more love than my own mother. I will never forget that.

I will miss you more than you know. I hope someday our paths cross again and that would be the happiest day of my life. But if it doesn't happen, remember me and tell Ali about me. But please don't ever tell him how he was conceived.

Promise me that. You and Oliver are the only ones who know what really happened after the rape, and I want it to be put aside and forgotten."

The two women embraced with tears, the future so unknown to them.

They all spent the last day together. Kate and Ali would be leaving the next morning. Oliver was distant. He never talked to or looked at Soraya all day. He just sat on the floor and played with Ali most of the day. It was obvious that he was going to miss him so much. He was bitter at Kate for taking him away and annoyed at Soraya also, but didn't know what it was that she had done. Everyone kept busy that night, and sad for what was about to happen.

Soraya decided to put Ali to bed that night after dinner. She took him to his room and closed the door. There she sat holding him on the floor and sobbing.

"Oh my God, give me strength to get through this. I am losing my baby, and I know that I will never see him again."

She just held him for a long time and inhaled his scent burying her face in his tiny face.

"I love you more than anything. I wish you could understand and remember that many years from today. Remember what I told."

She stood there crying like she had never cried before. Kate saw her and took her in her arms, and they both cried for a long time.

"I am sorry. I hope you can forgive me."

"Don't be sorry; I love you, Kate. Take care of yourself and please write me."

She held her tight for a few seconds more and ran out the door. She threw herself on her bed and cried herself to sleep. Kate sat in the car the next morning and looked around. This would be the last time she would see these streets and alleys. She knew she would never forget about this place. The magic would go with her wherever she lived. In a way, she would always have a special love for this place. She hoped to tell him of his birth place someday, this place that was still a mystery to her with its mysterious people and customs. She would never hear the morning prayer again. Even though she didn't understand the words, it still gave her a chill to that day. It was impresive and mystical, just like the rest of the Middle East, a special place with a special kind of people like Soraya. Oliver stopped the car.

"Tomorrow this time you will be home, and I hope you will be happy once again.

Call me when you get there. Take care of yourself and my little boy. Kate, I love you, and I always will."

She didn't like the way everything had turned out. Leaving Oliver behind was something she was not going to get used to any time soon.

"I love you too, Oli. You are the best thing that ever happened to me, and I will get you back sooner or later."

He smiled and took her in his arms and held her for a long time.

"I am sorry, sweetheart. This is not an easy day for me. This place won't be the same without you." Kate began to cry once again, and he was chocked up, too.

"My life won't be the same without you, either. No matter where I live."

He held Ali in his arms, having a hard time parting with him.

"You be a good boy for mommy, you hear? And don't forget about your daddy either." and he whispered in his ears, "I love you, Ali Reed. Don't forget that."

He stood there and watched the plane disappear in the sky. They were gone and he felt an enormous emptiness, feeling lonely. For the first time, he didn't feel like he belonged there anymore.

"I should have been in that plane with them. What am I doing to my family?"

Guilt and doubt took the better part of him as he left the airport. He drove around for a long time and finally went back to work and buried himself in his job so he wouldn't feel the emptiness as much.

Soraya woke up the next morning and realized right away that Kate and Ali were gone. She couldn't just walk upstairs and see them anymore. Her son was gone, and she thought this was an everlasting separation.

"Dear God, watch over him, wherever he is."

There were no more tears left. Her body ached and her eyes were swollen shut. Soraya also sensed the emptiness that Oliver felt earlier that morning and in a way believed she had lost Oliver, too. She knew this was hard on him, but thought it best to let him be for a while. It was painful for her to clean the apartment that day. Everything was a reminder of Ali and Kate. Suddenly she didn't feel like she belonged there anymore. It was a strange feeling and she couldn't describe it even to herself. She left for school shortly after and never heard from Oliver that night or the next six or seven nights. The longer it took, the harder it got for her to just stop by to say hello. She thought he would come and see her when he was ready. Was he ever going to be ready? She didn't know the answer to that; so one day she picked up the phone and called him at work.

"This is Oliver Reed."

"Hi, Oliver. It's me."

"Hello, stranger. How are you?"

"I am okay. How about yourself?"

"Okay, I guess. I just called to say hello and see if you need anything."

"Thank you. I know you have been cleaning the apartment every day, but I never get to see you."

"What have you been doing?"

"Just working a lot of hours and keeping busy. I talked to Kate and she said to say hello. She is going to write you soon. Ali is doing fine, I guess. She said he loves being there and getting all the attention from the family."

"It's been hard. I miss him so much."

"I know you do."

She waited for a second on the phone, but he didn't offer any more conversation.

"Well, I won't keep you. I just wanted to check in with you."

"Thank you. I will stop by soon. Your light is out most every night when I get home. That's why I haven't stopped."

"Well, take care of yourself," Soraya said sadly.

"You too."

She put the phone down and wondered what all this meant, his coldness and distance from her.

She didn't hear from him for another week, and she had decided not to call him until she heard from him. It was a busy morning for her and she went to the apartment to do the daily cleaning and saw his brief case on the table. For an instant she thought he was home, but then she realized his car was gone. She decided to leave and clean later, just in case he came back to get his case. She quickly opened the door to run downstairs and crashed into him.

"Hi, slow down. Where are you rushing to?"

"I was running late this morning and decided to clean later. I hope you don't mind."

"No, it's okay. I forgot my brief case and had to come back for it. I can give you a ride to school."

"You don't have to do that."

"I don't mind. I'll be down in a few minutes."

"Okay."

She ran down and went straight to her room and closed the door. She stood behind the door, her heart pounding, as she tried to catch her breath. How could he do this to her simply by his presence. Finally, she grabbed her books an out to wait for him by the car. He came down a few minutes later.

"Aren't you early for school?"

"I have to go to the library before my class. I need to do some research on a paper I am doing."

"How have you been?"

"I've been okay. How about yourself?"

"Okay. Sorry I haven't been around much lately. It's hard for me to be at the apartment. It's too quiet sometimes."

"I feel the same when I am up there cleaning. There are too many memories of Kate and Ali. It's not the same without them."

He just nodded. "How is school?"

"Thank God for school. Sometimes I think; what would I do if I didn't have school to go to everyday? Have you talked to Kate since the last time we spoke?"

"I talked to her a couple of nights ago. She is still trying to convince me to move back."

"And?"

"I am not ready to go yet. Nothing has changed for me, but that doesn't mean that I don't miss them."

"This must be hard on you, Oliver."

"And you. What about you?"

"It is different for me. She is your wife."

"Yes, but what about Ali. He is your son."

"No, he is yours and Kate's son, and I wish you would be there with him. I don't need a baby-sitter here, but Ali needs you."

Her words made Oliver tense again. He couldn't handle any more pressure.

"What about us, Soraya?"

"What about us? We both have so much guilt that we don't even talk to each other anymore. We run away and close our doors and pretend everything is ok. Is this how how you want everything to end Oliver? You living with the guilt of letting your family slip through your fingers? And me, feeling responsible for your being here? In the meantime, we don't even talk to each other. Who are you protecting here, yourself or me?"

"Maybe myself. I don't know the answer to that. And that's why I can't leave yet. I need to get my head straight, sort out my feelings and be able to leave you, or just the opposite."

"And are you doing that?"

"I don't know." He stopped the car as he said that.

"Oliver, I want you to do the right thing. I am not good for you. You have a different life waiting for you, and I don't want you to waste your time here on me. I want you to be happy, and right now you are miserable."

"You are not a waste of time, Soraya. Sometimes I wish you were, but you are not. You are special, and I just can't let go yet. I can live with the fact that I don't see you much, but at the same time, I know I can reach out and feel you. That keeps me going. Like I told you before, our relationship is not just a sexual attraction. God knows if that's what it was, I wouldn't feel this way. I haven't touched you in months. It's not sex that I want from you. Knowing you are close is what I need. That's all. Don't make me explain my feelings anymore. I don't even know what they are, but you will be the first one to know when I figure it out."

She looked away for a moment.

"So why are we doing this to ourselves?"

She wanted nothing more than to wrap her arms around him and tell him how much she loved him and make everything easier for him. But she decided to go easy and take one step at a time instead.

"Can I make dinner for you one of these nights?"

"That would be nice."

"Is Thursday night okay for you?"

He just nodded, "See you Thursday night."

She got out of the car and walked away. As he sat there watching her, he noticed how everyone looked at her in admiration, he knew he just couldn't let her go. No one knew anything about her except for him. That's why he was so protective of her, knowing what she'd been through and what she had accomplished. He respected her and loved her more than life itself. He simply didn't know what to do with all his mixed feelings. He was angry with Kate for leaving and taking the baby away from him and Soraya, yet he knew that he'd been unfair to her, too. Soraya, as young as she was, had resisted her feelings and emotions and was willing to let him go and never see him again, if that's what he chose to do. He began driving away more confused than ever.

Soraya was early to school and didn't need to go to the library. She had just told Oliver in order to avoid him. She sat on the steps holding her books and thinking about him. It broke her heart to see him so hurt and uncertain and angry, but there was nothing she could do for him. He had to decide what he wanted to do and made that clear.

"Hello, Soraya."

She looked up startled and saw Nader.

"Oh hi. How are you?"

"I am fine. How are you? I hope I am not disturbing you?"

"No, you are not."

"Are you okay?"

"Yes. Why do you ask that?"

"You've been so distant and preoccupied these days, like you have a lot on your mind."

"Thanks for asking, but I am fine."

They talked briefly about school.

"I drive by your place every day. Let me know if you ever need a ride."

"That's very kind, I like that."

"Well, see you later."

He walked away leaving Soraya wondering. She liked him. There was something about him that she couldn't figure out. Of course, there was so much in her own life to figure out that it seemed funny to her trying to figure out his life. That didn't stop her curiosity about him though. Later that day she stood at the bus stop waiting for the bus and saw him drive by and honk the horn. She paused for a second before running toward his car

"Need a ride home?"

"Sure." She got in and sat next to him in the front seat.

"I hope you didn't go out of your way just to pick me up."

"No. I didn't. This is the way I go home every day. I told you before, I can give you a ride anytime you want.

They spend a few minutes talking about the usual stuff before he found the courage to ask her a personal question.

"Are you seeing someone? And if the answer is no, I like to know why?"

"I could ask the same thing of you."

"Yes, but there is a big different between you and me; half the school is after you."

"I guess I haven't noticed that."

"You are a very smart girl, and somehow I find it hard to believe you haven't noticed all the attention."

"Listen, Nader. I am not in school to socialize and make friends. I am not interested in anyone's life, their past or future.

"So, you don't like talking about your past?"

"That's not what I said."

"It's okay. I have my own little secrets that I don't like to talk about, but it's still okay to have friends and to trust some people in life. I know you trust me a little, and that's why you are in my car and not in their fancy B.M.W.'s"

"And you. Why are you so withdrawn?"

"Oh, so you do notice the world around you. That's good. I am glad you do have a sense of curiosity. That's healthy"

"You make it sound like I am some kind of freak."

"Well, you and I have been called that before."

She looked at him in shock, "We have?"

"You don't seem like the typical young Persian girls."

"I didn't know that. Is there something wrong with going to school and wanting to be left alone?"

"But they want to know the reason, Soraya. Why is it that a nice attractive girl like you doesn't want any attention? It's not normal."

"What are you, some kind of a shrink?"

"No, I just like to analyze everything."

"Well, I don't like to be analyzed. I think if you like to do that you should start with yourself."

"Very defensive. That's a sign of a big dark secret."

She was starting to get a little annoyed with his attitude.

"Listen, Nader. Maybe I should get off here and take the bus. I don't need to tell you my whole life story because you are giving me a ride."

"The ride has nothing to do with it. Okay, enough questions. I won't ask anything unless you decide to open up to me."

"There is nothing to tell."

He smiled.

"What's so funny?"

"You are."

"I have never been told that I am funny."

"That's because you don't let anyone inside your four little walls that you have built around yourself, to know that."

"I can say the same about you, too."

"Oh, but I have already told you that I have some secrets I don't want anyone to know."

"That's your business."

"Yes it is," as he smiled and asked, "Would you like to get together and study sometimes?"

She looked at him in disbelief, "You don't beat around the bush do you?"

"Why should I? I am not interested in you in any way. It's all very innocent and friendly. I didn't ask you on a date, and I am not going to either. What I asked you is exactly what I meant and nothing more."

She thought for a moment.

"I do better on my own."

"That's a fair answer, and I respect that."

"You are not going to try a different way to get me to study with you?"

"Why should I? You do better on your own, and that is what you should do then. Soraya, I am not interested in anything more than an occasional chat. And if you need a ride every now and then, we could talk like we are right now. Nothing more and nothing less. I think we both know where we stand and hopefully can respect each other's privacy, so there should never be any questions."

Soraya looked straight at the road, not knowing what to make of this whole conversation, even though she had always thought he was a little weird. But she now was sure that's how she came across to others also; and if that was going to keep everyone away, it was okay with her.

"Well, here we are."

"Thanks for the ride."

"No problem."

She got out of the car and looked through the window at him.

"I think you are okay."

"Same here. See you later."

She walked toward the apartment smiling. That sure was an interesting ride. She kept smiling without knowing why. In a way, he was funny, with a strange sense of humor; yet, he appeared very smart. He definitely got her attention, if that's what he was after. She somehow wanted to get to know him better, but she didn't want to give him the wrong idea, even though he had assured her that he wasn't interested in her.

The next time she saw him in class he acted like a total stranger, like he didn't even know her. He was deep in his work and books. She wondered if he was playing a game with her, but that seemed too odd.

That night, Soraya rushed home and took the groceries upstairs. Oliver wasn't home yet and she got busy making dinner. It had been a long time since she had made a meal in that kitchen and was a little nervous. This was the first time they were going to be alone in this house since Kate had left. She finished with her cooking and rushed downstairs to get ready. She put on a simple dress and combed her hair. She put on the lipstick that Kate had given her and liked what she saw in the mirror.

"He will know it's because of him, and I don't need to lead him on."

She wiped the lipstick 0ff and walked out of her room. Oliver walked in and smelled the food immediately. He felt so at home once again. He hadn't felt that way since they all moved out.

He called out her name "Soraya?"

There was no answer and he went to his room to change his clothes.

Soraya opened the door and knew he was home. Her heart was beating fast, and she was mad at herself for feeling this way.

"He is going to look at me and read right through me." She took a deep breath and casually called his name.

"Oliver, are you home?"

"Yes, I'll be right out."

She went in the kitchen and began setting the table.

"It smells great. What are you cooking?"

"Chicken. I hope you are hungry."

"I am starved. It's been a long time since I've had a home cooked meal."

"Good. We can eat in half hour."

"How was school?"

"Just fine,"

"You look very nice."

"Thank you."

"Are you nervous?"

She turned around so her back was towards him, keeping busy with the food.

"Oh my God, he can tell," she thought. "I wouldn't call it nervous, just a little uneasy in this place."

"That's how I feel every time I walk in this place."

"I am sorry, Oliver. I know it's hard for you."

"It's getting better." He wanted to change the mood and walked over to the stereo and put on a some music on. He was tired of talking about how they both feel in the home they once shared with Kate.

"Why don't we sit in the living room until food gets ready?"

She followed him to the other room and picked the farthest chair from him to sit.

"Why don't you relax a bit?"

"I am relaxed."

"You could have fooled me. Why don't you sit by me on the couch, so I don't have to shout when I talk to you?"

She moved and sat on the couch next to him.

"That's better."

She couldn't look at him when he talked to her.

"Hey, young lady, you can look at me when I talk to you. I promise not to bite you or attack you, not unless you ask me to."

She looked up and smiled.

"That's much better. I was beginning to think you forgot how to smile."

Her expression suddenly grew serious.

"Why is everyone trying to analyze everything I do?"

"What do you mean by 'everyone? I am the only one here. Is there anyone else who tried to analyze you?"

She felt stupid for saying that.

"No, just that everyone at school questions what I do or say."

"Are they quizzing you?"

"Just a lot of curiosity, that's all."

She tried to steer him away from the topic.

"I don't blame them for wanting to know what goes on in that pretty little head of yours.

I wonder myself most of the time."

"You know everything there is to know."

"Oh, I am still trying to get to know you."

"There is nothing to know. I am not all that complicated."

"But I think you are, Soraya. I would like to talk to you tonight, but it could wait until after dinner."

"It seems like you have made some decisions since the last time we talked."

"Yes and no. It depends on how you feel about what I have to say."

"Sounds serious."

"No, not really. We just need to make some changes, but I don't want to get into it until I eat first."

"Speaking of eating, I think the food is ready."

She jumped to her feet almost afraid of what she might hear. They didn't talk about anything too significant during dinner, mostly small talk.

"Dinner was fantastic, thank you."

She got up and began clearing the dishes. He reached over and gently took her arm.

"Don't, we can do that later. Please sit down."

She sat there, but couldn't look at him. He was still holding her hand.

"Look at me." He wanted her attention without hinder.

"I have thought about us a lot. I've been trying to find a way to do what is right even though I don't know what the right thing is anymore. What I want is for you and I to get to know each other better. I would like us to put the past behind us and start all over again. I want to take you out once in a while and for you to come up here and have dinner with me more often. I would like to talk to you and get to know you. We don't have to sneak around anymore; Kate is not here any longer. She chose to leave, and I stayed behind mostly because of you and my feelings for you. I can't ignore these feelings any longer. I want to let them take me to wherever. It's not fair to you and me to let our love die without giving it a chance to grow. Kate is very happy with her choices and I want to feel the same. If our love grows, that's great; but if it doesn't, at least we can each go our own way knowing there was nothing there. Soraya, I know I love you, whoever you are. That is just the problem: I am in love with someone I don't even know and don't even know if I am allowed to love or not. What I am asking you is to give us both a chance and wait and see what happens. We are not going to plan our whole future, but just take it one step at a time, nice and easy."

He reached over and held her hand gazing into her eyes. She didn't know what to say.

"I always have this guilt."

"There is nothing to be guilty about," Oliver assured her, "you have given me and Kate every chance to get our lives back together. She chose to leave, and I chose to stay.

She took Ali and left what we had behind, and I decided to stay. What if I met someone else? What if she meets someone she likes? Soraya, we found ourselves in a situation that was very emotional and hard to resist. That's why I want it to be different now. There is no more

156

pressure or guilt. I am very comfortable with my choices. I just want to give it a fair chance.

Soraya listened to him and smiled. "And how are you going to get to know me better?"

"By shutting up and letting you talk for a change. By looking at you and listening to you and hearing everything you say, getting to know your likes and dislikes and all your desires, to find out what kind of music you like, what you like to eat and what your favorite color is. There is so much I need to know about you. I need to know the person that I am in love with. Is that a crime?"

"No, it's not. I just wanted so much more for you." Oliver looked at her with agitation.

"And who is to say Kate is more and you are not? That's not my opinion. I don't want you to think of yourself as lesser to anyone, absolutely no one. You are the smartest, bravest, and the most unselfish person I have ever known."

"So you do know me pretty well, Mr. Reed, don't you?"

"Yes, but there is so much more to you than meets the eye. I want to know it all."

He gently kissed her hand, looked her in the eyes for a long time, not saying anything more. There was nothing to say. He hoped she could see how much he loved her through his eyes. She was elated, knowing she hadn't lost him. Yet, there was still a tremendous guilt that she couldn't run away from. She wanted to let her feelings carry her away. Tired of doing the right things all the time. If this was what her heart wanted, she was not going to fight it any longer. She looked up at him and said, "there is nothing I want more in this life than to be close to you and be a part of your life. I fought all my feelings for a long time, hoping you could come to a decision without any pressure from me. The selfish part of me always wanted to hear you tell me everything you just said, though. And then there is this other part of me who tried to walk away from you just to be fair. I have always wanted you and I want you even more now." The two of them just held one another. They had found each other for now, and that was all that mattered, nothing more. There was so much they both wanted to know about each other. They were two people who grew up so differently, yet now wanted the same thing. They didn't want to part and let go of the moment. They had captured it and were going to hang on to it as long as they could.

"I should go back to my room. It's getting light out."

"When am I going to see you again?"

"Any time you want. But if you are going to keep me up all night, it has to be a Thursday night; so I can sleep in the next day. She could see comfort in him that she hadn't seen for months. It made her feel at ease, too.

"It's a date. Every Thursday and a night cap every now and then, as long as I send you back to your room at a decent hour."

He then walked her to her room and came back in, feeling like a kid. He knew he had finally got through to her. It had taken a long time to get her to this point, and he couldn't have been happier. At least he had got his chance, even though he had no idea where it was going to take him. But that didn't matter. For the first night in a long time, he went to bed and slept like a baby.

Soraya sat on her bed, wanting him more than ever. She wanted to take it slowly this time. Her thoughts took her away, and she found herself talking to her father once again.

"I know you are looking down at me and not approving of our arrangements; but you have to know, I can't resist him anymore. My love for him is too great. I hope you understand and do not hate me. I hope God doesn't punish me. He should know better than anyone that I have paid for my share of sorrow. To me, Oliver is life and happiness; so I hope you can forgive me for my actions. This time it truly is beyond my control."

She laid down on her bed holding her pillow and closed her eyes, pretending to be near Oliver. She too slept more peacefully that night. She even slept the morning away. It was almost noon before she opened her eyes and looked at the small clock near her bed. It showed ten to twelve.

"I hope he is still sleeping, so I can go up and clean last night's dishes."

She hadn't forgotten her normal duties, even though things had changed and he didn't expect her to do anything but be there for him. The apartment was quiet as she slowly opened the door and walked in. She suddenly turned around and found herself in his arms.

"Hi. I was hoping you would still be in bed, so I could clean up the dishes."

"Too late, I beat you to it. They're all done, but I will share some of my coffee with you. First, however," he trailed off, taking her head in his hands and kissing her passionately for a long time. Finally he parted from her and continued, "now would you like some coffee?"

"I would love some."

They sat in the kitchen and talked some more, drinking coffee and enjoying each other's company.

She had to study for a test and decided to excuse herself to go back to her own room but she looked forward to the following Thursday when she could spend some more time with him. For once everything was so peaceful. She felt a sense of freedom knowing there was no one there to judge her or ask her for an explanation. Oliver belonged to her now, and no one could take that away from her. The thought warmed her heart. She had lost that warmth for a long time and had thought nothing could ever give her that again.

The next day she walked to the bus stop, still dreaming of her weekend with Oliver, when she heard her name. She turned and saw Nader. He brought a smile to her face. For some odd reason, she liked her new friend and was glad to see him.

"You need a ride to school? That's where I am going."

She smiled and jumped in.

"How are you this morning?"

"I am great," she said with a smile.

"Why are you in such a good mood? It's Saturday, remember, the first day of the week?"

She just smiled, "I know."

"You look like you are in love."

His statement caught her off guard. "Do you always say whatever comes to your mind or do you think about it first before you say it?"

"No, I just say it."

"You should be more careful. That might offend some people."

"I don't care what people think, as long as I am honest with them. So who is he, one of the rich boys at the university?"

"Of course not."

"Would you like to tell me?"

She didn't know the reason, but she had a need to talk to someone.

"I don't know, depends on how sealed your lips are."

"They are sealed. I promise."

"Well, the answer to your question is, yes, I am in love."

"How does your family feel about that?"

"You know perfectly well no Iranian family approves of their daughter seeing a man when they are not married, but I don't have to answer to anyone. My family is not here."

"Do you live alone?"

"In a way. I have my own place. I used to live with an American family, but the wife left; and I moved downstairs." "Is the husband still here?"

"Yes he is."

"He is the man you are in love with, isn't he?"

He didn't need to wait for the answer. The look on her face said it all.

"An American. Not bad Soraya. No wonder you don't even look at any of those boys at school; you have yourself an American man."

"Now you know; but you don't have to act so sarcastic. I don't know why I trusted you, but it is too late now."

"Hey, don't worry. I admire your honesty. I am glad you told me. Now we can be friends. I hope your friend won't mind."

"Why should he? Like you said, we are just friends.

She felt she had already said too much and wanted to change the subject.

"Tell me about you. If we are going to be friends, I need to know more about you."

"I live at home with my family. I am twenty-three years old. For some medical reasons I was held back a few years in school. Reading is my first love, and I have a very boring life. There is really not much to tell."

"What kind of books do you like to read?"

"I like history and politics, even though they are not available in this country."

"Why not?"

He looked at her in astonishment!

"Where have you been Soraya? Did you grow up in this country or not?"

"Yes, of course. I grew up in a village near the Damavand mountains."

"So, you are a nice little village girl. You have come a long way being from a village. I am shocked they didn't have you married with kids by now."

"They tried, but I had other plans in mind."

"Obviously. Anyway, you know how it is in our country, we are not even allowed to read what we want."

"Why not?"

"Because it's not being run the right way. We have a very rich country, yet half of our people live in poverty, like you, and I am sure your family. Our people are not being taken care of like they should. That's why they don't want you and me to know much and they stop us any way they can. They like to see half of this country, or even more, in the dark. Listen, whatever you hear from me has to stay between us. You can't talk to anyone about it. It's very dangerous. Savak is everywhere."

"What is Savak?"

"They are one of the biggest secret police in the world. They are his chains around our necks."

"Whose chains?"

"The Shah of course."

"But, I thought he is a nice man."

"That's what they want us to believe. Listen, I will talk to you more about this if you like, but you have to promise me that you won't trust anyone to talk about this, not even your American friend. Who does he work for?"

"An American company, but he spends a lot of time at the embassy."

"Oh shit. Listen to me, they are all connected. The Shah is their puppet, and believe it or not they have so much control over this country. You can't trust anyone, certainly not your American friend especially if he has connection to the American embassy.

He seemed nervous, as if he had spoken too soon and said too much.

"I promise," she said, "Don't worry. I would like to know more. Can we talk again soon?"

He rubbed his face, doubtful.

"We will, but there are certain things you should know first, before I can tell you anything else."

She was filled with questions, but just then they arrived at school.

"Do you need a ride home?"

"No, I tutor tonight after school."

"Okay, I will look for you at the bus stop tomorrow, but let's stay cool about everything we talked about."

She thanked him for the ride and got out of the car with a lot of unanswered questions. For some reason, she trusted and believed him and knew he trusted her, too. It all interested her so much. She also felt so naive.

The next twenty four hour she was busy but their conversation occupied her mind most of the time. She waited at the bus stop the next day like he asked her to, looking for him; but he never showed up, and she ended up taking the bus to school that day. For the first time, he didn't make it to school. She didn't see him for a couple of days. During the same time, she never heard from Oliver either.

"What's wrong with all of these men? They want your attention, and once you give it to them, they just disappear." She was deep in her own thoughts when she heard someone call out her name, and then she saw him. It took her a second to respond before she ran toward his car and got in.

"Where have you been?"

"I've been around."

"Not at school. Were you sick? I was worried about you."

He smiled, "We must be getting to be old friends if you are already worried about me."

"You know what I mean," she said.

"Yes I do. I decided to study at home and give you a couple of days to think about what we talked about."

"I haven't thought about anything else the last few days."

"Is that good or bad." Nader asked.

She smiled, "Its good, and I am fascinated."

"It is not a very good idea for you to rush into this. Take it slow and think about it before you make any abrupt decision."

"Why do I have to make any decisions?"

"There are people who learn a little and decide then they don't want to know more. It might get them in trouble; so they get out of it and let it be."

"I guess I have to do the same and decide on my own." "That's good, Soraya. Don't let anyone push you, not even me. Take your time and digest everything. Think about it and then go to the next step."

"Sounds fair," she said, "so where do we start?"

"Okay, we can start with you for example. It would be easy for you to understand and comprehend everything if you start with real people and real life. Most people who live in the cities know what's going on, but they choose to live their life and close their eyes to what's happening. That's okay; most of these people have no other choices," and suddenly he stopped talking and looked very distant. "Soraya, I am not sure why I involved you in my thoughts."

She looked puzzled.

"Well, I do, Nader. There is so much that I don't know about my own country and our government. I always thought of the royal family as these magical people who can do no wrong, but you see it differently, I want my eyes open to what's happening in our country."

"Soraya, you have to promise me not to trust anyone. What we discuss has to stay between us. I can't stress enough how dangerous it is for you to repeat anything that you hear from me. It could jeopardize both of our lives. Do not trust anyone."

"I have already told you that I won't tell a soul." He looked away and took a deep breath asked himself for the hundredth time why he involved her?

"I am involved in a group that hopes to overthrow the Shah and his family someday. We are against everything he does to our people. Savak, like I told you, is one of the most powerful secret police in the world. These people get trained out of the country, mostly in Israel and by the Israelis. Their mission is to stop people, like myself or my group. They are brutal, and that is what they get trained for, to lose all sight of humanity in order to protect their master. We live in a very rich country, yet most of our people live in poverty. They have it all, our country's fortune. This is not a crusade for me. I live in a nice house, and we live very comfortably. But there are so few of us out there who live like that. You know better than anyone how our people live in the villages: total poverty, no electricity or running water, hardly any education, or any kind of medical facility. The Shah's government has a hold on everything that belongs to them. They like to see very little education in these areas because they don't want them to be empowered to what they are doing. They are a bunch of bastards who control our lives and our minds with complete authority. They have a life of total comfort at the cost of our people's suffering. It's not right. We have oil; our people shouldn't live the way they do. They deserve more, much more."

Soraya cut him off, "What does Savak do to people after they capture them?"

"They interrogate them, torture, play sick mind games and ultimately death for many people. It goes on and on. They are all crimes against humanity. No mercy toward anyone who is against the regime. We live in a society in which people are not allowed to speak and say what's on their mind. Our media is controlled. Our lives are in the hands of these people. We have no right except to exist from day to day. Even animals have more rights in the western countries. We can't even compete with animals; think about that." He then paused to allow her digest everything.

"My uncle was arrested a few years ago by Savak, and we didn't see him again until his body was given to us six months later. He was tortured to death, and our family has been under close watch to this day. I have to do this for my uncle and for all the people who lost their lives."

She had tears in her eyes listening to him.

"I am sorry, Nader. I don't know what to say."

"It's okay. It happened many years ago, but the unfortunate fact is it's happening right now as we speak to someone else's brother or father and even sister. It has to stop. People fear for their lives, and that's why no one says anything. We lost a friend just a few months ago, and we were all nervous that he might talk; so we all went in hiding for a while. But once they figured he wouldn't talk, they killed him and turned over his body to his family. He was missing an eye and three fingers on his right hand. His body bruised badly. He had a very painful death, but he never talked. He knew they would kill him in the end anyway. He saved all of our lives with his silence."

"How do you know for sure that he didn't give any of your names?"

"I wouldn't be sitting next to you if he did. Once you get arrested, the key is to count yourself good as dead; so why even talk? Of course, the torture is what breaks down many of our people; and this one, he took it to the last breath and never said a word. In my eyes, he is a hero.

He will forever be my hero, and I will never forget him. We are in touch with his family from time-to-time. They are so angry and will never forgive the ones responsible for his crude death, and neither will I. We will fight to the last breath to get rid of them. Someday it will happen, I promise you that. I just hope to be around to see it."

"What can I do to help?" "We are always recruiting new members, but you have to learn more and then decide if you want to join the group. We need as many people and as much help as we can get. "Remember what I've said and don't trust anyone.

Your best friend could be a Savak member, and you would never know. They turn on you so fast that it is beyond belief. They would even participate in your interrogation and torture and finally death. You see, they are trained to shut off all their emotions, just like a light. From your best friend, they turn to be your number one enemy in less than one minute. Once they turn on you, they are not capable of any remorse or feelings. This could be your father, husband, lover, or a friend from some other country. They come in all shapes, sizes, and colors. You are to trust only the people we tell you, and no one else."

Soraya was taken aback with all this information and was speechless for a while.

"Why did you trust me and tell me everything?"

Nader felt uneasy answering her question, fearing he might lose her trust; yet he had no other choice, but to be honest with her.

"You passed the test."

"What test?"

"You have been under our watch for a while now. There is nothing we don't know about you, and that includes the child you gave up for adoption. The only thing we don't know is who fathered your child."

She looked at him in disbelief.

"Why didn't you tell me you have known about me all this time?"

"That was one way of testing your honesty. I am sorry. You have to understand that if we don't do our homework right, it is our lives that we are playing with. We need to recruit as many people as we can in order to keep the organization going."

"Has anyone ever turned your people in due to extreme treatment?"

"No, not to our knowledge. Sometimes Savak sits on some information for a while, in order to get more people; but usually they don't wait too long. They prefer to eliminate as many of us as possible."

"Are there other groups beside your organization?"

He smiled, "oh, yes. There are communist groups and some religious groups and freedom fighters and some others. None of these groups agree on anything except to see the present government overthrown, and that is our mission also."

"What happens then?"

"I guess we will have some kind of revolution for power and hope the best man wins. But all that involves a lot more, and we are not even close to that point yet."

"How soon can I meet the group?"

"Not yet. I will let you know when you are ready."

"And when would that be?"

"Like I said, I will let you know. For now, I will give you some reading materials to open your eyes. Keep them in a safe place. Don't ever bring them to school, and never let them be visible in your house for anyone to see. They should be kept in a safe place."

"I have to tell you something else. It's about your friend. You have to realize how the American government feels about the Shah. He is under their control, like a robot. He does as he is told by the Americans. They want him in power right now, and they don't get involved in what he does to keep his power. As long as they can control the gulf through him, that is all they need. They are not interested in knowing what he does to his own people. As a matter of fact, the more people that stay in the dark, the better it is for them. Right now he keeps them happy and our countries are best pals. But the Shah is getting to be too powerful in the Middle East for his own good. They could turn on him, and they will. That would be the end of him."

"I can't believe what I am hearing. To me Americans are the nicest people, and America is this wonderful free country, and they are everyone's friend."

"Soraya, people are people, but you have to realize that people who run these countries are not who you think. The United States is this nice country that you think, and there are many nice people who live there, but those nice people don't actually run their country. Most American don't know what their country is involve in particularly in the middle east, and don't forget about Israel."

"Where do they fit into the picture?"

"The United States is the biggest supporter of Israel. They pay one fifth of their total national income. Of course, the Shah is in bed with both of them. Of course most middle eastern countries are not happy with the treatment of Palestinians by Israel.

The Jews don't like to see anyone with too much power in the Middle East; that's a threat to them."

Soraya, there is so much more for you to comprehend that I can't possibly fill you in all in one day. Like I said, I have some reading materials for you. Are you going straight home?"

She nodded.

"Good. Then I will give you a ride home and give you the stuff at that time."

They said good-bye to each other and each went their own way once they got to school. Their conversation left Soraya with so many thoughts, things that never before entered her mind. For the first time she felt stupid to think she had a hard life, knowing there were people out there who died for what they believed in everyday, according to Nader. It all seemed so unbelievable and cruel.

She waited for him at the bus stop and saw his car a few minutes later. She ran toward the car. They talked all the way home. He stopped the car at a quiet corner, about a block away from her house. He then got in the back seat, and it seemed as though he tore open the back side of the passenger seat, but it was only the seam; and he took out some papers. He hid them between a newspaper and handed it all to her.

"Don't forget what I told you. If anyone finds these in your possession, and you are dead."

She looked at him nervously, reached over with shaky hands and took the papers from him like she was holding a bomb.

"Go straight home and I will see you later."

And that's exactly what she did. She started reading the materials as soon as she got in her room. There were at least twenty pages of documents, with many different names and addresses. At first she thought they were the names of people who belonged to the group, but soon she realized who they really were. They were the people who had been killed in the last two or three years by the government. There were at least two thousand names there. Attached to the list of names was a small memo which explained:

"These are the names of people who have been slaughtered by our vicious government. Some of these people were caught for just reading some materials without ever belonging to any groups or organizations. Some were killed just for saying a few frustrated words to someone; but they said it to the wrong people, and for that, they died.

The first thing Nader wanted her to know was the danger and the risk of her involvement in the group. He wanted her to know what she was getting herself into. And that was only fair. As a matter of fact, Soraya could have easily been killed for her curiosity at this point. People had died for a lot less. She was learning that she was playing with fire and was already afraid for her and Nader's lives. She couldn't believe her eyes and wondered if it was all facts or if some of the stories were made up. But how could the names and dates be wrong? Anyone could check the names and find out the truth.

"Don't they have any fear? My God, our government is having a war with its own people, and the sad part is that only one side was paying the price with their blood. The other side keeps getting more powerful. They don't have to justify their brutal murders and actions to anyone. They give the bodies to the families, if they are lucky, and that is the end of it for them. We are living under strict dictatorship, and people's lives are being destroyed everyday yet the world is sitting back and watching it. Why is it that no one tries to stop him? The United States was the hero in

World War Two, but they are his allies. Are the oil and gulf that important to them that they simply turn their backs to these mass killings of innocent people?"

She continued to read and realized that just for reading the pages in front of her, she too was considered a traitor. And her penalty was death. She kept on reading through her tears, wondering what could be done to stop them once and for all. She read them over and over again. Her people were robbed of their freedom and the country's oil fortune. She was still reading when she heard a knock on the door. It startled her for an instant and she jumped to her feet, not knowing what to do. Her mind was blank. Then she hid the papers under her mattress, even though she knew if it were the authorities that would be the first place they would look.

She was paranoid, and as she took a deep breath, she asked

"Who is it?"

"It's me, Oliver."

"Just a minute." Her heart was pounding as she walked toward the door and opened it.

"Hi, Oliver. How are you doing?"

"I am doing fine. How about yourself?"

"Okay. What are you doing here?"

"I thought maybe you like to come up for a while."

She looked nervous and it was obvious by her expression.

"What's the matter? Are you okay?"

"Just fine. Give me a few minutes to finish here, and I'll be up shortly."

He looked at her suspiciously and took a step back.

"Okay. See you upstairs."

And he walked away.

She closed the door and leaned against it for a second, knowing Oliver was probably wondering what was going on with her. She tried to get her composure back and made sure the papers were all hidden and walked out of her room. It was the first night she hadn't thought about Oliver once. She walked into the apartment and was greeted by him at the door.

He wrapped his arms around her waist and pulled her close to him.

"How is my Persian princess?"

This struck her attention negatively, "Don't call me that."

It caught him off guard. "What's the matter with you tonight?"

She instantly knew it was the wrong thing to say and looked at him apologetically.

"I am sorry Oliver. It's been a long day. I didn't mean to take it out on you."

"That's okay."

He looked at her with worry and asked, "Do you want to talk about it?"

"No. I would rather forget about today and not talk about it, if you don't mind."

"Okay, why don't we start over again?"

She walked in the living room as Oliver went back in the kitchen and brought them each a cup of coffee. It was a stressful evening for her and she tried to try lean back and relax more. He sat across from her and wondered what was going through her head.

"Have you heard from Kate lately?"

"I talked to her yesterday. As usual, she is not giving up on the idea of me moving back yet."

"How is Ali?"

"He is doing fine. She just put some pictures of him in the mail for us."

Soraya suddenly sat up and asked, "Oliver, what do you know about the Shah?"

It was the last thing he had in mind and was lost for words.

"What about him?"

"Just wondering what you think of him?"

"Well, I think he is the best thing that ever happened to this country. Without him, Iran would be like all the Arab countries, hundreds of years behind time. He is too strict, in my opinion; but then again, you almost have to be in a country like this."

"Why is that?"

"I don't know. I guess because it's the way it is in the Middle East."

"Do you think Iranians couldn't handle freedom like you Americans?"

"Probably not. We were born that way. You, on the other hand, have gone through two thousand years of history and oppression; you people are too committed to your culture, and freedom was not always a part of your history."

She was a little troubled, listening to him, but thought it was best to hide her feelings.

"I would much rather talk about you than the Shah; can we change the subject?"

Soraya just smiled.

"How was your day?"

"Very busy, but in the back of my mind, I knew I was going to see you tonight; and that made all the difference."

And with that he went and sat next to her on the couch.

"Why do you look more beautiful to me every time I see you?"

She laughed, "You are a silly man, Mr Reed."

He began touching her hair, he was so close that she could hear him breathe. Slowly he got even closer and their lips met. He kissed her gently and she closed her eyes.

"I love you."

"I love you, too," she said.

"Do you want to wait?" Oliver asked.

She gazed into his eyes. As much as she wanted nothing more than him making love to her, she decided to resist and nodded. Her lips broke into a smile.

He slowly pulled away with a half a smile on his face.

"I admire your determination to stick to our rule. So in that case our date is on Thursday but there is something I want you to do."

"What's that?"

"It's going to be our first date, so I want you to go pick out a new dress on your own, and I would like to buy it for you."

"Oliver, you don't have to do that. I have some money saved up."

# CHAPTER SEVEN

It was a new beginning in Soraya's life. She felt like a new person. What she had learned through Nader had changed her, but knew better to make those changes obvious. A new chapter in her life was beginning to take root, but the branches were not to blossom until later.

She was excited to buy a new dress that day after school. She saw Nader waiting for her before she even got to the bus stop.

"Well, did you have a chance to read the memos that I gave you?"

"Yes, I read all of them."

"What do you think?"

"If everything I read is true, it means we have a nasty and heartless government. What surprises me is that there are not more people speaking out."

"Because they fear for their lives. You could have a nice life in this country if you are middle or upper class as long as you keep your mouth shut. The Shah doesn't give us any right to question him or his government because he is fearful of a revolution. Knowing how fast it can get out of control, that's why he has such strict rules and laws; and, that's the reason he created Savak. They are there to protect his kingdom, and they are the most important organization to him. He pays these people well, and they live like royalty. As Iranians, we should have the right to know what happens to our country's fortune. Where does the money go, and why is it that there are so many poor people in this country? He should have a salary like the Queen of England and not an open hand to everything. He should have to answer to people what he does with our money. Soraya, we should have more freedom than we do, and this is a fight for our people's freedom. It opens your eyes. It gives you more of an opportunity to move ahead. Look at the western world;

they are so much further ahead of us; yet we are the ones with two thousand years of history. Our government has its weight on us, and we can only grow so much before they will stop us. We have oil and should have the opportunity to grow a lot faster than we have in the past. Most of the western countries are not nearly as rich as we, yet their people live better than we do. That's what freedom does for you. It gives you the opportunity to grow. Our government is paranoid because they know that what they are doing is wrong. They are guilty, and that's why they have to go to extremes to protect themselves. We have no freedom of speech. We can't read what we want, and we are kept in the dark. I am telling you, someday it will backfire, and the Shah will be one sorry king for treating his people like he has. By then it will be too late for him. Facts are, you, as a straight A student who has done nothing wrong, could be put in prison and tortured to your death for just reading the materials I gave you. You can be killed for the conversation we are having right now, and that's why most people prefer the life of darkness and they don't risk their lives. They have their families to think about. So they go on with their lives and keep silent. I am not one of those people. I would rather die someday fighting for what I believe in, so the next generation can live in a safe and free country.

Death doesn't frighten me, and I will fight until the day I die. That is my mission in life. If I can open one person's eyes during my whole life to what's happening, it is worth dying for."

Soraya was captivated by what she heard, and it took her a while to get her composure back.

"Has your group, or others out there who are fighting the system, accomplished any victories so far?"

"They know we are out there and that keeps them on their toes. They know we won't give up. Believe me, life could be much tougher if it wasn't for people like us. We are making a difference, even though it is not visible to common people and though they try to cover it as much as they can. So, to answer your question, yes, we are making a difference and accomplishing a lot. And we are proud of it. Our mission is not revealed to people because we have no way of doing that. But we know where we stand, and they know where we stand. We keep our guard up and hope that someday we can change things so Iran can become what it should be, once and for all.

"Let me give a you a little history. Many years ago, the Shah's father, Reza Shah, ordered no freedom of dress code; so all these religious women, who wanted to cover up, were stripped of their Chadors and vails in the streets throughout the country. Don't forget, we live in a Muslim country. Our people should have had the choice to cover up if they chose to. Many people got killed during that time to fight the ruling. Even people who didn't cover up were angry. What if something like this were done to them? They eventually won some years later, but at the cost of many innocent lives, of people who believed in the freedom of choice.

"It's almost like it ran in the family, his father was as much a dictator as he. Like father like son. He is very smart and does do things differently, but still, it is no different if you look at it from the inside. He is doing the same crap as all the other dictators did throughout the history of the world. As always, history is repeating itself, and none of those dictators lasted and neither will he."

Soraya was listening to everything Nader had to say with great intensity. She had lost all her excitement, and it made her feel stupid to be happy about buying a new dress and having a date with Oliver. Nader could see it in her eyes.

"I am sorry. I didn't mean to get you down. We are a very happy group. We enjoy our lives to the fullest because we know it might be our last one. We enjoy every day and do what all the other people do; yet we have a mission to accomplish, that's all. I don't want you to feel down or depressed. You won't be good to anyone, not yourself or us. You should be proud to have come this far. Now you know what goes on out there and that is an accomplishment."

"Is the list of names you gave me for real? Have all those people been killed by the government?"

"We don't just make up names to get people's sympathy. You can choose a few names randomly and call to find out for yourself."

"Did you know any of those people?" Soraya asked sadly.

"I knew some of them. Some belonged to our group. Don't forget, these are the people we know have been killed by the government for sure; there are so many that we don't know about. Unfortunately, the list is not complete, and it won't be until this war is over."

It was time for them to part and go to school, and there was so much more that Soraya wanted to know; but for now, they had run out of time. She left the car bitter and disappointed, knowing she couldn't make an overnight decision. She had to think about it and study it more. So far, she didn't like what she heard. And she knew one thing already, there was a feeling of hostility deep down in her heart for the Shah that she couldn't explain.

She sat in the class, numb from the whole event that took place in Nader's car. She turned and saw him busy at work. Just like he said, they all had their own lives and did the best they could to enjoy each day. How could he act like a normal student? Soraya wondered if he had talked to any other students beside her.

The long day finally ended and, as usual, she walked over to the bus stop. This time she wasn't going home, she was to buy a dress and had no idea where to go. She had never bought anything on her own before. It had all been given to her or bought for her by Kate.

"You need a ride home?"

"I am going shopping, but I don't know where to go."

"What are you buying?"

"A dress."

"Well, well. Maybe I can help you. I have a couple of sisters and have a good idea where they go shopping most of the time. Would you like that?"

"Are you sure it is not too much trouble?"

He smiled. "No, it's not. Get in but don't ask me to give you my opinion. I am not very good at that sort of things."

She let out a short laugh and got in the car with him, somehow pleased to have him as a friend.

"Do you want to go and have lunch somewhere, my treat?"

177

"Why are you so nice to me?" She asked him.

He grew kind of serious.

"Because I think you are a very special person, and I like to think of you as my friend."

"I am your friend, you silly man. Actually, you are the only friend I have."

"What about your American friend?"

"I trust him with all my heart, and I love him very much, but there are mixed emotions there. I can count on him for everything, but at the same time, I couldn't tell him what goes on in my head. Do you know what I mean?"

Nader nodded.

"It is different with you. I couldn't have this kind of conversation with him."

"So, what do you say? Are you hungry for lunch?"

"Hungry is not the word; I am starving."

He drove to a nice little restaurant and she placed herself across the table from him. Looking back at her life, never did she imagine it would take such a turn that she would be sitting across from this man she called her friends. Enjoying a meal and laughing. They had established a bond and their friendship grew stronger. He was very intelligent and his sincerity and frankness made is easy to trust him.

She truly cherished that. After lunch, their mission to find her a new dress began. It was mid-afternoon when she came out of the dressing room of a small boutique, wearing a navy dress, and Nader was speechless. She looked exquisite in the dress and it fit her perfectly. He told her so.

"Well, I think the American might have a hard time keeping you all to himself. With that dress, he will have lots of competitions."

Soraya was pleased with her purchase and she was happy to have spent the afternoon with her friend.

She came home later and couldn't be happier to have Oliver to love and Nader as a friend. He was someone she could trust besides Oliver. Considering herself very lucky.

It was hard not to think about everything that they had talked about, and she had convinced herself to join and help any way she could. But she decided to keep it to herself for now. She didn't want him to think she had made a hasty decision.

That night she stayed in her room and decided, for once, not to even open her books. She shook herself as though to rouse her mind from a trance. Her eyes got heavy soon, and she fell sleep without even trying. She once again dreamed of her father.

He was walking through a corn field, and she was trying to catch up with him but couldn't. He turned around and looked at her every now and then, and all she could see in his face was sadness. She kept on running after him as fast as she could, but it was impossible to catch up with him. He was disappearing, and at the last moment, he turned and pointed his finger at her and yelled.

"You are playing with fire!" And with that he vanished in the corn field. She opened her eyes with a gasp, and sat up, trembling.

"Is he aware of what I do? Oh dear God, he doesn't approve. Am I doing the right thing? Is he trying to tell me something?"

She was so confused. The thought of him being mad at her broke her heart. The last thing she wanted to do was to disappoint him.

"But this is real life, Father, and I have to do what I think is right. That's what you taught me. It was a strange dream, and she finally convinced herself that it was just that. She decided to read to get her mind off of the dream. The memos that Nader had given her were still hidden under her mattress. She pulled them out and read them again, and that made her more determined to join the group than ever.

The following day, she never had a chance to talk to Nader and took the bus home. It was a beautiful afternoon and the sun was as bright as could be, beating through the window of the bus she rode. All she could think about was her first date with Oliver, knowing it was a true beginning for them. Holding her books in her arms and pressing them against her chest, she whispered "Life is good. Life is good."

That night, she did nothing but pamper herself before Oliver picked her up. It was something she had never done before in her life. It felt so good, and once she was done with her hair and makeup, she put on the silk dress. The feel of silk against her skin made her feel different, like she was not the same person anymore. She was in a dream world and her prince was to come and lift her off her feet. It was okay to dream, but for the first time, she didn't feel this was a dream. Some of her fantasies were becoming a reality for her. She looked at herself in the mirror and was pleased with the result of her efforts. There was a knock on the door and she opened it, knowing it was Oliver. he stepped in, but couldn't believe his eyes.

"You look absolutely stunning."

He couldn't keep his eyes off of her.

"Thank you. You look very nice, too."

He couldn't hear a word she said. All he could do was to look at this magnificent woman who belonged to him. He remembered the first time he had seen her. She was like a frightened child in old clothes that belonged to Kate. She had come a long way, and he was so proud of her. The night belonged to them, and he planned to make it as memorable as possible for her.

"I am going to have a hard time keeping you all to myself tonight."

She laughed at what he said, remembering Nader's words which were so similar.

When they walked out, Oliver opened the car door for her. She climbed in and felt like a princess. And he couldn't help but keep staring at her while he was driving.

"Where are we going?"

"We are going to have dinner at an Italian restaurant that recently opened up. It's very cozy and dark. I don't want to show you off too much tonight. I would rather have you all to myself."

"I have never had Italian food before. What is it like?"

"Well, it's pasta and pizza and good homemade sauces. I hear it's pretty good."

He had called and made a reservation. It was a busy night for restaurants, and he wanted to make sure they had a nice table.

They entered the restaurant and noticed a lot of people waiting to get in. And as Oliver predicted in his own mind, she turned everyone's head as they followed the host to their table. Oliver could see the excitement in her eyes. She was so easy to please when it came to material things in life. She was so content with just simple things.

"What are you thinking about?" he asked her.

She looked up and smiled.

"How happy and lucky I am to have you in my life right now."

"That goes both ways, sweetheart. You make me just as happy."

The waiter stopped at their table and Oliver ordered some wine for both of them.

"I have never drank wine before," she told him.

The waiter showed up with a bottle of wine and filled their glasses. Oliver picked up his glass, she copied him as if she had done the same before.

"This is to you, my love, for all you have done and for being such an important part of my life."

She smiled, and took a sip, and immediately made a funny face.

"This is so bitter and dry. How can people drink this stuff?"

He laughed.

"Just take small sips and keep it in your mouth for a few seconds, to taste all the wonderful stuff that goes into making it. After a few sips it tastes much better, I promise you that."

She did as she was told, and to her surprise, it started to taste much better. Her mind drifted off to her family. If they could only see her now, in an Italian restaurant, which they would have no way of comprehending, and drinking expensive wine, all dressed in silk. They wouldn't believe their eyes. For that matter, she couldn't believe it herself.

"What are you thinking about?"

"My family."

"What about them?"

"I was thinking, if they could see me now, being in this place with you, dressed in a silk outfit. Oliver, they wouldn't have a clue and probably never will. It sure is a different life. And you never think life exists in other places when you live in a village like where I grew up. They all stop growing after a certain age and become these robots that are programmed to do certain things and only say what they are told to say. Life is dead there. It doesn't grow and it doesn't go anywhere. It just stops. I always dreamed of a different life. Dreaming is okay, the real challenge is to make dreams come true, and I owe all my success to you."

"You don't owe me anything. Giving Ali to Kate and me was more then we could have ever imagined. He is a gift of love and how could we ever begin to pay you back, I don't know.

You have given me more love, and that alone is all I need."

It made her sad thinking about Ali and how quickly she lost him to Kate. Oliver noticed the sadness in her face.

"I miss him too, darling. It pains me to know that he is growing up and I am not there to share his life with him. But I know he is in good hands, and that's the only thing that makes me feel good. Soraya, I made my own choices, and to me, they were the right ones. So I go on with my life, hoping someday it can be a life filled with his love and also yours."

"I am very thankful to Kate. There is not a day that I don't pray for them. She is always on top of my list. She is raising and loving my son, and I hope and pray that she lives a long life and enjoys watching him grow up. That is my only salvation."

Oliver ordered dinner for both of them as Soraya took more sips from her wine glass and began enjoying it more. Once her first glass was empty, she felt pretty good. She felt tingly and had never experienced anything like that before.

"Would you like another glass of wine?"

He could see the answer in her face as she smiled and nodded. Her glass was filled. She looked at the deep red color of her wine, having a hard time taking her eyes away from it. Their dinner arrived soon and they both enjoyed it. She decided that she liked Italian food. They talked about many different subjects and, as she finished her third glass of wine, Oliver could see the effect of wine on her. She was feeling no pain. He enjoyed watching her giggle and have a good time. He had never seen her like that before, relaxed with not a care in the world. He thought that was good for her, to let go and feel so free. They went for a nice long drive after dinner and she kept on asking him for another glass of wine.

"No, I think you have had enough for your first night."

He parked the car as Soraya wrapped her arms around his neck.

"I don't want to go home yet."

"Okay, then come upstairs with me and we can have a cup of coffee together."

She let out a laugh.

"You can have coffee and I will have some more wine."

"That's a deal."

He realized she was a little drunk and almost had to pull her out of the car and carry her half-way back to his place. They stumbled in and she kicked off her shoes and threw her purse on the chair.

"Okay, I am ready for some more wine."

Oliver went in the kitchen and told her to sit and relax until he got back. She went to the bathroom and stood in front of the mirror, looking at herself. Her cheeks were red and she had a hard time focusing her eyes. It didn't take her long before she decided to go back to the room and check on Oliver.

"This is mine, and this cup of coffee is for you, my love."

"It doesn't look like wine to me."

"I know that, but I want you to drink this first."

"What for?"

"It's good for you and is what you need right now. Come here and sit by me."

She threw herself on the couch next to him.

"Oliver?"

"Yes, my love."

"Do you love me?"

He just smiled. This was so unlike her.

"More than you know."

"Why haven't you told me that lately?"

"I am telling you now."

And she smiled.

"Do you mind if I get comfortable?"

He thought she was going to lie down, but instead she turned around and sat straight up with her back toward him.

"Will you open my zipper, please?"

"Listen, sweetheart. You don't want to get too comfortable."

"Yes I do. Please help me."

Oliver grabbed her hand.

"No, I said. Now drink your coffee."

"Okay then, I'll do it myself."

"Don't do that. You've had a couple of drinks tonight and I don't want you doing anything that you will regret later."

She gave up on the idea and a moment later collapsed on the couch.

"Oh Oliver, you wore me out. I am so tired."

He sat there, holding her for a while, looking at her beautiful face and laughing at times at how silly she acted. And finally he decided to take her to his bed and he covered her with a blanket, kissing her on the forehead. He loved her so much. He had almost given in to her when she insisted on getting undressed, but he was glad that didn't happen. He only wanted to make love to her when she was ready and willing. And, at the time, she was too drunk to make those kind of decisions. He was not going to take advantage of her.

Soraya woke up the next morning and found herself in Oliver's bed. She still had her silk dress on and couldn't quite remember everything that happened the night before right away. She remembered Oliver holding her on the couch.

"I must have fallen sleep in his arms," she thought aloud, hoping she hadn't made a fool of herself.

The house was quiet as she peeked her head out of the room and found Oliver sleeping on the couch. She realized for the first time that nothing happened the night before.

Not wanting to wake him up, she decided to take a shower. She stood under the hot water and thought about how much fun they had that night and wished it could have lasted forever. Oliver truly loved her. He could have easily taken advantage of her if he wanted to, but didn't. For that, she respected him even more. She wouldn't have been mad at him or loved him any less, even if he did make love to her and gave in to her demands while she was drunk. It was so easy for her to think of a future with him after the night they spent together.

Like any young woman she wished the man of her dreams would someday take her away and start a new life with her. She turned the water off and got out of the shower. She wrapped herself in a towel and found Oliver in the bedroom reaching for his robe.

"You are not looking for my robe are you?" he asked her, smiling.

"As a matter of fact, I was."

He held it up for her.

"Climb in."

"Turn your head and I will. No looking either."

She dropped her towel and stood before him totally naked.

He turned his head facing her.

"Do you really want me to turn my face?"

She looked up at him and replied, "Not if you don't want to."

And he dropped the robe on the floor and pulled her naked body close to him.

"My God, you are beautiful."

He was filled with desire as he spoke. He covered her lips with his and then lifted her up and carried her to his bed. He laid her on the bed while still kissing her. She hung on to him and didn't want him to stop loving her. He kissed her until she was breathless, and then he slowly pulled away from her.

"Please don't stop. I want you with all my heart."

"Listen to me, angel. There is nothing I want more than to make love to you right now, but I don't want you to regret it later. Remember, we decided to go nice and easy."

She was still holding on to him.

"I have never regretted making love to you, ever. Those were the most beautiful moments of my life, and I love you now more than ever."

There was a more aggressive way about her, and it made Oliver give in to her desires. He laid her back down and their lips met once again. He studied every inch of her body and felt her soft skin, holding her soft breast in his hand until he couldn't take it any longer, and he made love to her more passionately than ever. They had an uncontrollable desire for each other and they were both left without a breath.

Soraya didn't feel any guilt or sorrow for Kate this time. She just felt so loved and was glad with all her heart that he had stayed behind. He loved her so tenderly and passionately that she couldn't believe it was possible. They both lay back, catching their breath, each in their own thoughts. Oliver knew he could never let her go, no matter what the cost was. He couldn't imagine life without her. He was almost twenty years older than her; but to him, this match couldn't be more perfect. No one had ever made him feel the way she did. It was more magical than anything he had seen in the movies or read in books. He turned over, pulling her close to him.

"Why is it that I can't get enough of you?"

They wrapped their arms around each other once again and lost themselves in their love making, closing the world around them.

Peacefully they fell asleep in each other's arms, feeling safe and loved and more than ever satisfied.

He opened his eyes some hours later and looked at her sleeping peacefully next to him. So much had happened and his feelings for her were so strong that he didn't want to see her live in that small room by the parking area. He wanted to take care of her forever and didn't want her to clean his house any longer. What he wanted for her was to go to school and spend all her free time with him, making life as easy as possible for her and treating her like his lady. That's what he decided to tell her once she woke up.

He made them breakfast and decided to wake her up, anxious to talk to her and tell her what he really felt.

"Wake up sleeping beauty. Let's not spend the whole day sleeping. I made breakfast for us."

He began stroking her long black hair. She opened her eyes and smiled, seeing him next to her, knowing what happened between them earlier wasn't just a dream.

"Good morning. Smells good. What is it?"

"First of all my love, it is not morning anymore. It's afternoon, and I made us some omelets. I hope you are hungry."

She got up and wrapped his robe around her.

"I could live like this for the rest of my life."

And she smiled as she took a bite of her omelet, enjoying their time together and wishing it would never end. Oliver thought it was a very good opportunity for him to bring up what was on his mind, as long as she had mentioned the same idea.

"Now that you mentioned that, it brings up something that I've been wanting to talk to you about."

She looked at him with concern in her eyes, not wanting anything to spoil their time together.

"What is it, Oliver?"

"Well, I guess the best way is to just tell you and see how you feel about it."

He took her hand in his and continued, "Darling, there are so many things I'd like to do for you that I don't know where to begin. The first thing is, I don't want you living down in that room any longer. It is not where you should be living, not when I have all this room up here. It bothers me to know you live down there. I want to have you near me and come home from work to see you up here with me, where you belong. I don't want you to feel obligated to clean my house anymore. Do it because this is where you live, but not because it's your job. With my income, I can easily support you, and that's what I'd like to do, to take care of you, like you are mine to take care of. I hope I don't sound too chauvinistic; but when it comes to you, in a way, I am kind of old fashioned. I am not ashamed of that either. It has to do with me loving you and wanting more for you and being able to spend more time with you. So, what do you say? Will you at least think about it and try and see it my way?"

She was very touched by what he said, but she still liked her independence and didn't know what to tell him.

"Oliver, this is very generous of you, but I don't feel right taking money from you and allowing you to support me, plus I have been sending money to my family from tutoring and have thus been supporting them."

Oliver looked at her confused.

"You mean you have been sending them money from your tutoring jobs?"

"Yes, I have."

"Oh, my dear love, the more I get to know you, the more I fall in love with you. Why haven't you told me that before? I could have helped you. You must have been living on absolutely nothing at all. Listen to me, nothing has changed. We will help your family just as you have been in the past, and I don't want you to worry about that."

He pulled her close to him, feeling so fortunate to have her in his life. She had done so many unselfish acts in her young life that it melted his heart. He wanted to do more for her, especially since he found out that she had been sending practically every dime she had to help her family.

Soraya looked at him in appreciation.

"What would I do without you, Mr. Reed?"

"You would do just fine, but I just want things to be a little easier for you, that's all."

He decided to drop the whole thing before she change her mind.

"So what would you like to do today?" he asked her.

"I just want to be near you."

"That sounds like a good idea. We will just hang out and do absolutely nothing. Well, maybe some things, but nothing that will take a lot of effort."

With that he kissed her, letting her know what he meant.

"There is going to be a big party at the embassy in a couple weeks, and I would like you to go with me."

"Oliver, I can't do that."

"Why not?"

"Because, there are going to be a lot of people there who know you and Kate, and that would be very embarrassing for me. I don't think I am ready for that."

"Listen, love. You better get used to the idea of being with me. Kate isn't here and chose not to be here. She made that choice, and as far as they are concerned, we are separated at this time."

"Is that what you have told them?"

"In a way, yes, I have."

She was a little annoyed.

"What do you mean; in a way?"

"They know she didn't leave on good terms and that we had some problems."

"Oliver, I can't expose myself to gossip, and that's what it would be like."

"At some point you have to come out of this apartment with me and face other people. You have to be comfortable with your choices and not let people intimidate you. Soraya, I don't care what people have to say, I only care about us."

"If you care about us, you wouldn't ask me to do this."

Oliver began raising his voice and didn't like where the conversation was headed, "What do I have to do in order to be with you whenever I want, in public or in private? Marry you? Is that what it is?"

Soraya looked at him with wide eyes.

"Oliver, you are married to Kate. How can you talk like that or suggest that's what I want you to do?"

"Well, if that's what it takes, I am willing to marry you."

"Oh my God, now you are talking about marriage. Oliver, listen to me. I want us to get married someday, there is nothing in this world that I would rather do than to marry you, but I want us to get married for all the right reasons, not because we were pressured by other people."

"I know that, but you have to understand; there is nothing I want more than us being together. I want to be able to take you out and show you off as mine, my lady. Do you understand that?"

Soraya couldn't believe what he was saying.

"You are going a little too fast for me. There are a lot of things we have to work out before having this conversation."

"Like what?"

"Your marriage to Kate for one thing. Ali, remember him? How do you think he will react when he grows up and tries to understand this situation. Plus, you and I are from two different countries, cultures, and religions."

"Love doesn't understand any of these things you are telling me. If we love each other, we will work them out one by one. My first step is to tell Kate about us, and then we go on to the next step."

Soraya always felt anxious when it came down to having to tell Kate about their relationship. She wasn't ready to discuss that yet.

"Let's not talk about all this right now. It's too complicated, and I don't want to spoil our day. Please let's stop."

"Okay, but we have a party to go to. Don't forget."

The next day, they both got ready for work and school and Oliver reminded her of their arrangement.

"I want you here when I get home from work, not downstairs."

She laughed sarcastically, "Okay, Master. Anything you say."

And they both went their own ways for the day. She got ready as fast as she could after Oliver left, hoping to catch Nader at the bus stop. She found him waiting for her.

"Good morning."

"Hi, Soraya. How was your weekend?"

She smiled and replied, "It couldn't have been better."

"I wouldn't have guessed. You have it written all over your face."

"Is it that obvious?"

"Yes, but don't worry. No one else will know."

"Thank God for that. How was your weekend?"

"It was the same as always, meetings, gatherings, and a lot of discussions; nothing unusual."

"Nader, when can I go to one of these meetings with you?"

"I told you; I will let you know when I think you are ready."

"Come on, I am ready. I want to be more involved."

"And you will be when the time is right."

Soraya didn't like the explanation he was giving her.

"Who will decide?"

"I do. End of discussion."

"Okay, at least tell me what you talked about this weekend."

"Only after you tell me exactly what you did this weekend."

She blushed.

"That is none of your business."

"And I could tell you the same thing. Anyway, I have more stuff for you to read."

Soraya looked a little annoyed.

"Listen Nader. Oliver will be around a lot more and I can't take everything home with me."

"Well, that's why I don't want you to get involved yet. Once you are in, it will take a lot of your time, and he may be suspicious. Being involved doesn't mean you just show up at the meetings whenever you want and then leave. It means you will work for the group and put in time.

"I can handle that."

"You can't even handle taking home some reading materials because you live with a Yankee."

"Who told you that I live with him?"

"You did, just a few minutes ago. Remember? You said you can't take things home because he is going to be around more. I am not as stupid as you think."

"I know that, Nader. I didn't mean to insult your intelligence. I need to ask you something. Oliver asked me to go to an embassy party with him. There will be a lot of the royal families there. Do you think I should go with him?"

She totally caught him off guard.

"Is the Shah going to be there too?"

"I don't know that for sure, but I know he has gone to gatherings with him there in the past."

Nader was all business now.

"Yes, you have to go. It would be to our benefit if we had someone like you there. Find out who is going to be there; get me some names."

Soraya got a little suspicious, noticing his interest in the whole matter.

"I can't do that to Oliver."

"I know that, but this has nothing to do with him. This is our war, not his."

"But you want me to use him in order to get information."

"Well, we are just turning the tables around for once. They have been using us for many years. But personally, you are not doing anything to him."

Soraya knew she was stepping into muddy waters and there would be no going back anymore.

"Okay I will, but on one condition. I need to meet the rest. I want to know who I am dealing with."

Nader noticed how she manipulated the situation using the information she had. Her clever style made him feel even better about recruiting her.

"I will work on that."

He knew this was going a lot faster than he anticipated.

She was filled with mixed feelings after she parted with Nader. She felt like a spy, not knowing what Nader and his group were intending to do with the information she was about to give them. What made her feel uneasy was that the information would come from Oliver, and she didn't particularly like that. She didn't like using him like that and decided not to say anything to Nader unless they gave her all the answers she needed.

"This game goes both ways. I am not going to jeopardize Oliver in any way."

She was going to tell them once she got to meet them.

"I don't care how much they hate the American government; Oliver is not going to be used and stepped on, and I will see to that."

She was trying to convince herself of her choices and decisions, not knowing if she was doing the right thing or not.

That night she decided to find out more from Oliver after she got home.

"Hi, sweetheart. You look tired."

"It was a long day. Plus, you didn't let me get much rest this weekend."

She smiled.

"Well, I will make it up to you now. Are you hungry?"

"Yes, I am."

"That's good. Let's eat dinner."

"You made dinner?" she asked, surprised.

"Of course, my love. You just sit right here, and I will do the rest."

He put a plate of food in front of her and said, "Wallah."

"This looks wonderful."

"Thank you, madam. Compliments of Sir Oliver to my lady."

This made Soraya laugh. And he sat next to her and they began to eat.

"I thought about the party, and I decided to go with you."

"What changed your mind?"

"Oh, I don't know. I guess I feel the same as you do." She hated keeping the truth from him.

"Good, I am glad. You won't be sorry. And it's good for you to wine and dine with the royalty."

"Who will be there?"

"The Iranian Ambassador from Washington is in town, and a few others. They don't give us all the names, for security reasons."

"Do you think the Shah will be there too?"

"He might. We never know until the last minute. I am the last person to know that information because even though I do some work for the embassy, I am not actually employed by them."

"What about the Prime Minister?"

"Same with him. Are you getting more interested in politics lately?"

"No, not really."

"That's good; because in this country, the less you know, the better off you are."

"So, you expect us to act like a bunch of idiots and just do as the government wants us to, no questions asked? Could you live that way?"

"No, I couldn't; but like I told you before I was born in a free society, that's the way it has always been for us."

"Well, maybe we need to change some things in this country too."

"Yes, but it may cost you your life. Is that what you want? Soraya, I don't know how much you know about your government, but I guarantee you they have no mercy toward anyone who wants to know more or wants to change things. I know that for a fact."

He was clearly upset and Soraya could tell. She decided not to continue the conversation, in case he got suspicious of why she was asking him all those questions.

She met Nader a couple of days later at a cafeteria and was anxious to talk to him.

"Did you find out anything?" Nader asked her casually, like it wasn't all that important to him.

"Just that the Ambassador from Washington will be there. At this point, I am not sure about the Shah or Prime Minister Hovaida. He said they usually don't know until the last minute, for security reasons."

"You think he was telling you the truth?"

"I am not sure."

"Did you tell him that you are going to the party with him?"

"Yes, I did. He was kind of curious why. He questioned my sudden interest in politics."

"You have to be more careful and not cause any suspicion."

"He won't do anything to hurt me."

"Let me tell you something, Soraya. When it comes to the U.S. and its interests, they'd sell their own mother in order to protect their country. Don't let him fool you for one moment."

"There is nothing wrong with loving your country, is there?"

"No, there's not, and that's what I am trying to tell you; I will risk my life and my whole family in order to save my country, and so will Oliver. To them, we are nothing but a bunch of barbarian camel kissers. They need our oil and our geographic position. It is very important to them. We are being used for the moment, and when the time comes that we are not of use to them, they will drop us like a hot potato. That's the way it is."

"You think the time is coming?"

"I think we are getting close. There is a revolutionary who is trying to overthrow the Shah, which seems impossible at the moment, but he is making a lot of headlines in Europe."

"Who is he?"

"I can't tell you his name yet. I am sorry."

"How do you know about him?"

"We have our sources."

"Is he a good choice?"

"It doesn't matter at this point. We can only do one thing at a time. Right now, our goal is to get rid of the Pahlavi regime. We'll deal with the rest later."

"So you are working with other groups who are not necessarily in agreement with you for a common goal? What will happen later, if you get rid of the Shah? Will you fight over power then?"

"Like I said, we will work out the details later. Right now, we are shooting at the same target."

"But eventually you will be shooting at each other."

"If that day comes, there will be a revolution, a civil war. But in the end, it's worth it. We know it couldn't be worse than it is right now."

"How do you know that for sure?"

"I don't really, but it is a risk that we are willing to take."

"What about the U.S.? Aren't they going to step in and help the Shah and his regime?"

"They probably will. That will be one bloody day in our history."

He was very distant as he spoke.

"Nader, do you think in the end, it's all worth it?"

"We don't know for sure. But maybe someday we will have a free country, and that to me is worth risking everything."

"I hope you are right."

He smiled, "me too. We better leave, it's getting late."

She looked at him, almost frightened of the unknown future.

"Be careful. This makes me very nervous."

"Don't do that. We are going to need your help, and I have a feeling you are going to be a valuable asset to our group."

"And when will that be?"

"Sooner than you think."

He walked her out, and they each went their own way.

Soraya didn't know exactly how she could help. For now, more than anything, she was curious and wanted to know more about the group and their activities. It was all kind of exciting to her, and all she knew was that she didn't want to get Oliver in any kind of danger. At the same time, joining the group would give her a thrill. She liked the thought of belonging to a group. She walked in the apartment and sat on the couch, still holding her books in her arm, deep in thought.

"He is either going to get me in at least once or I will tell him that I am not interested in being a part of the group. And I won't give any information unless it is known to me who I am dealing with. And what if they are using me?"

She changed her mind on that quickly.

"No, they wouldn't do that. All I have to do is open my mouth and Nader would be history. They are probably just being cautious."

And she didn't blame them for that. But she was going to stick to her guns and let Nader know that she wouldn't take another step unless she met the group members.

Oliver walked in and he wondered what was going on in her head.

"Hello, beautiful, what are you thinking so hard about?"

He startled her, and that made her kind of nervous.

"Oh hi. I am sorry, I didn't even hear you come in."

"I guess not. Are you ok?

"Just fine. I am fine."

She wasn't thinking straight for a minute and nothing was coming out right. Oliver of course noticed.

"What did you do today?"

"Just the same old stuff."

He had a suspicious look on his face, and for the first time she noticed it.

"I stopped by your school today to pick you up."

"What time?"

"Oh, about four. And I saw you walk into a cafeteria with a young man."

She felt like a small child being caught with her hand in the cookiejar her heart pounding, but got a hold of herself quickly.

"Why didn't you stop in?"

"I don't know, maybe because I didn't want to intrude on your privacy. Do you go there often?"

"No, not really. Oliver, we are just friends. We talk about school and other things, like all friends do. I like to listen to him. He is a very intelligent individual."

"Is he the one who got you interested in politics?"

"Why do you say that?"

"Just because of your recent interest in the subject. Am I wrong?"

She avoided answering him.

"We talk about school and the work that we are assigned to do together, and basically small talk."

She hated keeping the truth from him, and she knew that she wasn't very convincing.

"I just want you to be careful. The University of Tehran is where every political problem starts. I just want you to stay away from it all. Don't get involved in anything that you may resent later. And don't allow anyone to get you mixed up in even a simple conversation. You are too trusting sometimes, and that makes me very nervous."

"No one is trying to do anything to me or get me mixed up. You are making a big deal out of this whole thing. Believe me, there is nothing to worry about. He is just a nice guy, that's all."

"I don't want you to think for a moment that I am being jealous. I trust you and believe in you. All I am doing is making sure you are protected and not used by anyone."

They went on discussing the matter a little further and finally decided to drop it as long as they both understood where they stood. But Oliver still had a funny feeling about the whole thing and wasn't sure where the feeling came from.

# CHAPTER EIGHT

Soraya met Nader at the bus stop as usual.

"Oliver saw you and me the other day, going to the cafeteria. I had a hard time deciding what to make of the conversation we had."

"That shouldn't bother him. After all, he is the one who claims to be from an open-minded society; so these kind of things shouldn't bother him at all."

"Don't be sarcastic, Nader. He wasn't jealous. He was wondering why I haven't told him about you, and also if you are the reason for my sudden interest in politics."

"What did you tell him?"

"Just that we are friends, and there was nothing more to it."

"Did he ask you for my name?"

"No, he didn't. Why?"

"If he does, give him a different name. Don't give him my real name," he said very seriously. "Tell me exactly what He asked you."

She went through the whole conversation they had the night before.

"Is this guy for real, Soraya? Does he really care about you like he says he does?"

Soraya didn't like talking to Nader too much about her personal life, but she said, "yes, he does. He practically left his wife and son for me."

"You mean, your son?"

"He belongs to her now."

"Is he the biological father of your child?"

"No, he isn't. I wish he were."

"Who is the father then? I don't know of any Iranian man who would let his child be raised by another man, especially an American."

She didn't know how to answer him. There was so much that he knew about her life already; what was the use of keeping the rest from him? So she decided to tell him the truth once and for all. Then she could be done with it and go on living her life without the fear of the group ever finding out from a different source. She bit her lip and looked down for a moment.

"I was raped."

"You what?"

He looked shocked and couldn't believe his ears.

"Where, by who?"

"I don't know. It happened by a little pond I used to go to near my village," she looked so distant as she went on, "my little hiding place, where I used to get away from everyone. I don't know who they were. I had never seen them before."

"What do you mean, `them'?"

"There were two of them. All I know is that they weren't village people. They were city men. I could tell from the way they were dressed."

She was pained by the memories, and he could clearly see it in her face.

He took a deep breath and said, "I am sorry. I had no idea and would never try to push you into telling me if I had." She continued telling him the story of her youth, and he had to pull over to the side of the road half-way through her story, unable to drive. He just sat frozen, listening to her. For the first time, he realized how far she had come with so many odds against her. Now he understood why she was so protective of Oliver and the reason behind all her secrets. Without Oliver, who knows what would happen to her. Nader had completely turned around emotionally; an hour earlier he was willing to use Oliver anyway he could; but now, he felt differently and didn't want to do anything to jeopardize his position. Not after what he just heard could he do such a thing to Soraya. He knew he had a lot of thinking and talking to do, as the group was ready to meet with her soon, and they needed to know everything about her.

To invade her privacy would be cruel. He had to think of a different way to protect her from wondering eyes and minds.

"I could kill those bastards with my bare hands. I am sorry for pushing you to cut ties with Oliver in any way."

She looked up, surprised, and asked, "Is that what you were trying to do?"

He nodded.

"Eventually yes, I was. To me, he was an outsider and didn't belong to this war."

"I know how you feel, Nader, but you have to understand where I am coming from. My feelings have not changed. I still want to get involved and be a part of this so- called revolution. This is my choice. I am the only one who will make that decision, but I still don't want to use Oliver in any way. It's just not fair. You, or any members of the group, don't use your families to accomplish your goals, and my loved ones should be left alone too."

He nodded in agreement.

"I understand and promise you that I will think about it and give you an answer very soon. There was so much that I didn't realize, but now everything makes sense."

Taking her hand in his, he continued, "I want you to know that I am your friend and want to be a part of your life. You are a very special woman, and Oliver is very lucky to have you."

Nader was filled with emotions when he left Soraya. He had to find a way, and explain everything to the group, without invading her privacy. The group was to meet that evening. He drove to the location to meet with them, and found everyone there waiting for him to start the meeting.

They all sat around staring at Nader. He had to play this right; so he decided to be honest with them.

"I want you all to listen to me very carefully. Soraya has been through a lot more than you can imagine. I don't feel right going through all the painful details of her life to tell you about her. All I am asking is that you respect her privacy. We all have our secrets, and we are all entitled to them, as long as they are not a threat to our group in any way. I want you to know that I trust Soraya fully. And I promise you that her intelligence and honesty will be a benefit to our cause. She will never jeopardize our life or mission in any way. I need you to trust my judgment and not put her through any more pain by questioning her about her past. There is nothing that I don't know about her, and I promise you, she is to be trusted. She would like to help as long as no one she cares for gets hurt or used by us on purpose. She knows the risks otherwise."

He stopped talking for a moment, and then said, "I am ready to answer any questions you might have."

There was a silence. And then Mohammed, the group leader began to talk.

"You understand that we are putting our lives in her hands and are trusting her unconditionally?"

"Yes sir, I do. As long as you trust me, you can trust Soraya also. I don't know how else to put it."

"Is she ready to meet the group?"

"She's been ready for a long time."

"Why don't you arrange it? Tell her of the procedures and we will meet again soon."

Nader was relieved that he could present his side the honest way, without hurting either party. He thanked the group for their trust and understanding, excited to share his news with Soraya.

The two of them met at the cafeteria again, and she was anxious to find out about the meeting. Nader was calm, which made Soraya even more anxious.

"So tell me, did you have a chance to talk to them?"

He casually nodded, replying, "And they would like to meet you as soon as possible. There won't be any questions. All you have to do is to listen to them and swear on the holy book that you will be faithful to the group, no matter what. This will be your marriage vows to the group, and then you will become ours. Are you ready for all this?"

She looked at him with uncertainty.

"Up until now I wasn't so sure that they would accept me. Now I feel strange."

There was so much more she wanted to know, yet it was impossible for her to find out unless she joined. The moment had come, and she felt so unprepared for it. She did not want to act stupid, yet there was so much she needed to discover.

"I don't know if I am ready for all of this; or even if I will be any help when I feel so uncertain. There are so many unanswered questions flying around in my head. A part of me is pulling me away from it. I am so scared; but, at the same time, there is a thrill within my body which makes me want to close my heart to all the other emotions and give it a try."

Nader looked at her for a moment.

"Soraya, this is not a game. You can't just give it a try. It's very important for you to understand that once you are in, it means you are in it forever. You will be devoted to the group and their needs. We don't have many female members, and you will not be expected to do as much as other members, either. We understand your position and will not risk it. We are aware of your relationship with Oliver and respect your privacy. But you have to know where we are coming from also. This is a very dangerous mission. You may not live to see your twenty-first birthday. We don't like to think of it that way, but it is a risk that we are willing to take; and it will also be expected of you. So you can't just give it a try. You will give it your all, your best. And remember, the cause is so rewarding; it is for our land and our people. It is so our children can live free at last."

"When is the next meeting?"

"In a couple of days. Remember, they won't ask you anything personal. You just have to be there and listen for the first couple of weeks. The more you get involved, the more you will feel at ease. There won't be any pressure, and you make your own decisions."

Soraya tried not to show Nader her true feelings. She felt trapped in the situation and didn't know if she wanted in or out.

That day, Oliver came home hoping Soraya wouldn't be there until he was ready for her.

"Hello! Anyone home?" Oliver didn't hear anything and quickly put the flowers he'd bought in a vase and got out the bottle of wine from the fridge. He had ordered food to be delivered to the house and couldn't wait for Soraya to get home to share his exciting news with her. He put on some soft music and sat on the couch waiting for her, reading the paper and wondering what was keeping her.

Soraya got out of the bus a stop early and decided to walk home and think. There were so many things she needed to sort out. Plus, Oliver could never find out; it would destroy their relationship. Her heart pounded at the thought of him ever finding out. In a way, she didn't understand why he would be so against it when he came from a country that was based on freedom. Why could he not understand that she wanted the same things for her country also. Was it because he had been brainwashed into thinking Iranians deserve no more than what they already had? There were so many questions in her head that were starting to upset her and even make her mad at Oliver without him even being there.

"Why should I be afraid of telling him my feelings? I haven't made any commitment to him when it comes to anything other than my heart. Would he turn me in?" But she truly didn't believe that.

"God, help me make the right decision." She walked into the house with a very heavy heart and surprised to find him sitting on the couch

"Hi, Oliver. You are home early."

"I know that, but you are not."

She looked at him, feeling annoyed that he was timing her.

"I felt like walking home. Is everything okay?" She wondered if he had seen her with Nader again at the cafeteria.

"It sure is. I have a surprise for you. Come here and sit by me. I have been working on this for a while and didn't want to tell you in case things didn't work out. But I got everything done and put the finishing touches on it today."

He handed her a white envelope. Soraya looked at it, wondering what it was and hesitant to open it.

"Go ahead and open it."

She looked at it again and slowly began to open the envelope. Inside she found two long thin booklets.

"What are these?"

He figured she had never seen such booklets before, so decided to help her with what they were.

"They are plane tickets."

"For who?"

"For us, darling. You and I are going to Paris for ten days."

She looked at him in a state of shock. She couldn't believe him.

"I don't have a passport."

"Well, that's what I have been working on, and that's why I didn't want to say anything to you until everything was worked out."

"Oh, my God, Paris? To me, Paris is just a name, a place forever out of my reach. I know there are a lot of wealthy families who go there, but me?"

"Yes, darling. You are going to Paris, and you won't believe your eyes. To me, it's the most beautiful and romantic city on the face of this earth."

Soraya was still in shock. Her life had changed so much, from a village in the mountains, to Paris, the most famous city on earth. She suddenly knew her life's destination was going to take her places she had never expected.

"Well, what do you think?"

"I don't know. I can't believe you did all this without me even knowing about it."

"There are so many things I want to do for you, so many places I want to take you. And my love, this is just the beginning for us."

He was filled with excitement and Soraya could see it in his face.

"Do you think it's right for me to just pack and leave the country with you?"

"Why not? Who has to know about it? Just tell everyone you know that you are going to see your family. This is all legal, and you are not breaking any laws. Trust me, everything is taken care of."

She threw her arms around him.

"Why are you so good to me?"

His love for her was so fierce, he would do anything to show her his true emotions.

"I don't know. Maybe because I am just in love with you. Is that a good enough reason?"

"Good enough for me."

They celebrated their night together and lost themselves in each other's arms and made the night theirs once again.

She struggled with the idea of telling Nader about her trip or to keep it to herself for now.

She finally decided to be honest and tell him the truth. She could never get in trouble for telling the truth, so that's what she decided to do.

He caught up with her in the school hallway, saying, "slow down a bit, lady. What's the rush?"

She smiled and turned around.

"What's up?"

"We are meeting today after school. They want you there too, can you make it?"

She looked calm.

"Yes I can."

"Wait for me outside by the bus stop, and I will pick you up."

He walked away as he finished his last word.

Soraya stood by the bus stop waiting for him. As soon as she saw his car, she jumped in, not knowing what this first meeting was going to be about. She decided to wait until later to tell Nader anything about her trip.

"Are you nervous?"

"No, I am not. Don't ask me why. Even though I have always had a hard time being around strangers, I feel like I belong with these people for some odd reason. I hope they are all as good as you."

Suddenly tears filled her eyes and she didn't know why.

"You have been a good friend to me, and I truly appreciate you."

He smiled. "Now don't get sentimental on me."

And she broke out in a laugh.

"I am not, you fool."

"Okay, here we are. Let's go for a little walk."

She didn't ask any questions, just followed him. They walked for a couple of blocks, and then he entered a small drug store. There were some people in the store, and Nader wandered around looking at things. Then he quickly grabbed her arm and pulled her through a small door toward the back of the store. It took her by surprise, but she said nothing. They walked through a narrow hallway and then went through another door, entering a bigger room. There were about twenty men sitting on a big Persian rug on the floor. Nader took his place close to the door and told her to do the same. No one looked at her and she appreciated that. Moments later, a few more men joined them, and then someone got up and closed the door.

Soraya heard her name being called from across the room.

"Yes?"

"I want to thank you for being here today. It takes a lot of courage and understanding to make this first step. We are all like a family here. After today, you can count on any of us as a member of your family. You can trust us and put your mind to rest that you will never find better friends than these people who are sitting next to you. We respect your privacy, but we also know enough about you to trust you as one of us. We will support you in any way we can financially, emotionally, and so on. But the group only asks you one thing, to be as honest as you can with us. We don't like any surprises. Just tell us what we can expect of you and what we can't, so we know at what level we can count on you. What you are doing is a big commitment here, so be honest with yourself first, and then with us. I will protect you until the day I die. That day could be tomorrow or many years from now, but until our mission is completed, you can count on me like you have known me all your life, just as you can every member of this group. You will become closer to these individuals than anyone you have ever known. You go on missions with them; you will risk your life with these people; and they become a part of you, and you of them. We don't have a name for our group, nor do we believe we need one. We know who we are and know exactly what we want. Our mission is to eventually have a free Iran, freedom of choice, religion; and most of all we want a new government who will stop the killings and torturing of our people for reading a book or saying the wrong things. We want, above all, freedom for our people. Our mission is not hurting the people to accomplish our goals, but we do know there will be sacrifices. You can't look back. You can only look forward and learn from your past. Don't stop. Keep on going, and always keep your chin up high. Be proud of your mission and what you stand for. Remember how far you have come and that this is just the beginning for you. Learn facts that will make you, not break you. We are confident in our choices in you, and we know you are tough enough to hear them and not let them stop you from making the right decisions. Your friend Nader has been on more missions than any soldier on a battle field. Yet you, as his good friend, would never know. He keeps up with his private life, school, and whatever else he needs to do. You are not expected to change your lifestyle or put anyone else you care about in any danger. Remember, we are not after fame or wealth or excitement, our mission is far from that. Once we have reached our destination, we will all go our own ways. In our hearts, however, we will always be a family. Take a look around and remember everyone's face. This is your new family, people you can trust and be trusted by." What you have heard just now are our vows to you, brother and sisterhood, love, trust, and most of all, honesty. You will, under no circumstances, risk our lives even if it costs you yours. You don't know us outside of this group, unless you are on a mission. You will forever forget our identity and remember there is nothing higher than death. If you ever get caught, death is above all. You will take it with dignity and pride so that our mission continues. They will torture you to the point that death will become a sweet sound to you. Remember again, death is above all, and you will give your life before you will risk others. That is something we have all had to promise before we could join in. Do you have anything you need to tell us at this point? You can share anything and it will not change our opinion of you."

She looked around for a moment.

"Yes, I do. I am sure none of you is interested in where I came from, but you might like to know where I need to go or where I stand? I am very much involved with an American man who has saved my life and taken me where I am today. Without his help and support, I would be a maid at one of your homes, with no education and of no help to you today. There is something else you should know; I will be going out of the country with him for a short trip and I don't yet know the timing, but will inform you of it as soon as possible."

Nader got up, brought the holy book to her, and held it out.

"In your own words, give us what we need to hear."

She looked up at him with tears in her eyes. She had always had a special place in her heart for her faith.

"My holy book, I am not good enough or decent enough to put my hands on you, and I wish I could forever be lost within your holy pages, but I am not cleansed enough to even touch you. I ask your forgiveness for all my sins and also ask you to be my witness in the presence of all these people. I swear that I will be honest and faithful to this group and their mission. I promise I will not go back on my word. I will protect them and their identity, even if that costs me my life."

Tears continued to wash down her face. There was a feeling of security and protection that came upon her which she couldn't explain. She kneeled down and kissed the holy book and rested her forehead on it and whispered a prayer.

The whole room was silent. Everyone was bowing their heads, and they knew a great journey had just begun for her: the journey of unknown danger and total commitment.

"Nader will inform you of your first mission. There might be late-night missions or meetings. Remember, if it causes any inconvenience, you let us know. We don't need anyone being suspicious; you have to be the judge of that and only commit to missions that you know will not risk anything. Do you understand everything you have been told?"

She nodded.

"Okay, the meeting will begin. We have just received information that Reza has not spoken a word, and also, he is in a very bad shape. He doesn't have much time left; so it looks like we have lost another member forever. At this stage, he is not coming back to us. We will be helping his family financially, but they are not to know where the money comes from." Then, looking at Soraya, Mohammed said, "you can start your first mission tonight if you are ready. It is not a dangerous mission and Nader will assist you and fill you in on what you need to know."

Soraya looked surprised at how fast they got her started in the mission.

"What time?"

"Right after dark."

She let out a little sigh of relief knowing Oliver was working late that night.

"Is there a problem?"

"No, I can do it."

Without hesitation Nader got up and told her to follow him. They took the same route back to his car, and she felt numb as she sat next to him. He drove her home giving her the necessary information.

"I will pick you up at seven."

She didn't have a clear idea of what they were going to do and never asked, thinking the less she knew the less nervous she would be. He dropped her two blocks before they reached her house, and she walked home the rest of the way. Her head was filled with emotion and questions, remembering Mohammed's words about a man's name, Reza. The thought of someone being tortured to death made her cringe. How could they be so heartless? She walked into her house still thinking of a man she didn't know, her eyes filled with tears. She somehow felt a bond with this man, feeling his pain and thinking about if it had been Nader. Mohammed said he had been on more missions than any soldier on a battlefield. What if he got caught one of these days? Her tears turned to a quiet sob. Once again she remembered his words.

"There will be sacrifices, you can't look back. You don't stop, you keep going and always keep your chin up high. The truth will make you, but not break you."

She felt broken already, and told herself to stop.

"I can't do this. What if Oliver walks in and sees me like this. What would I say to him?"

The whole meeting had affected her more than she had thought. She felt drained and exhausted and decided to wash her face and lay down for a nap to take her mind off of the subject. She felt relaxed lying down. She read a book until her eyes got heavy and she couldn't keep them open any longer.

In her sleep, she once again found herself back at the village, walking in a corn field. She saw her father sitting down, playing with Ali.

"What is he doing with my father?"

She ran toward him, but her father picked up the child and began to walk.

"Wait a minute, Father. Where are you going?"

He looked back and held the baby even tighter, and then he started to run. She could see anger in his face.

"Please wait. Let me hold him. I miss you both so much. Please wait."

But he only went faster, and soon he was only a small vision in the cornfield. She gave up following him and sat down, sobbing.

"What have I done? Why is he treating me like this?"

She slowly opened her eyes and realized it was only a dream; another dream that left her questioning its meaning. It was close to seven when she awoke. She got ready and ran out to meet Nader in time to find him waiting for her.

He looked at her with a smile.

"You look like you just woke up."

"I did. And it's not funny." Wondering how he could keep it togethere?

"Who said anything was funny?" He looked at her more carefully.

"Have you been crying?"

"No, I haven't."

Nader didn't believe her.

"What's wrong? Are you having second thoughts about the group?"

She just shook her head and looked out the window.

"I don't know if it is going to be as easy for me as it is for all of you, to deal with everything and go on missions and pretend nothing is wrong. I don't even know this man who is dying, but it bothers me so much. Why do I feel this way?"

He suddenly looked serious and turned to her.

"Because, in a way, you bonded with him today. You joined in with what he believes in, something that he will probably die for. You have taken his place, and for the first time you are sympathizing with what he is going through and you realize that it could happen to you."

"What about his family? They must be beside themselves."

A faded smile crossed his face and she knew it pained him to talk about Reza.

"They are devastated, and you are going to help them tonight. It might make you feel better knowing that we don't forget our people."

She looked surprised.

"How can I help them?"

"By making sure they get this small bundle. We have got together some money for them, so they don't have to worry about finances. They should spend their time mourning his loss; they deserve at least that. This is the least we can do for them. His wife knew of his involvement with the group, but she doesn't know any of us personally. What you have to do is to wear this Chador and cover yourself. You knock on the door, and if a child answers the door, ask him if you could talk to his mother. When he leaves, you leave the money and walk away as fast as you can."

"What if the mother answers the door?"

"You just tell her you found the package by their door and give it to her and leave. We have a letter in there that explains everything to her. I will pick you up one block closer than where I will drop you off, and that will be the end of it. Any questions?"

She shook her head and reached in the back seat and grabbed the Chador as he kept on driving. He showed her the place he would pick her up.

Soraya got out of the car and began her walk. Her heart was pounding and her hands shook under the Chador holding the money. She was glad to have the Chador, so no one could see how nervous she was. Looking around she felt a sadness in the neighborhood as if they knew his presence was never to be around. Soon she reached the family's front door. There was no time to waste, so she did exactly as she was told. A few seconds past and then she heard footsteps and the door opened. A small girl appeared on the other side.

Soraya felt speechless for a moment, but soon got ahold of herself.

"Hello, can I talk to your mother, please?"

"Would you like to come in?"

"No, I will wait here."

"The little girl turned around and started walking away from her, but then stopped.

"Who should I say is waiting?"

"Just a friend."

The little girl ran inside and Soraya quickly put the bundle of money down and closed the door. She began walking toward the car as fast as she could turning around to see if she was being followed, but didn't see anyone.

Holding on to her Chador as tight as she could, she hurried to the car waiting for her. She quickly got in, and he took off immediately.

"How did it go?"

"Fine," and took a deep breath, "I did exactly as you told me. I don't think anyone noticed me."

Nader smiled.

"Good job. Congratulations; you just finished your first mission. It wasn't all that hard was it?"

Soraya smiled. She felt a thrill and a high that she couldn't explain. It felt good, and it was almost impossible for her to stop smiling. For the first time, she felt like part of the group, like she belonged to them now. This made her feel satisfied. It was just the perfect mission for her first time, and that's what they were hoping for. She hugged Nader and gave him a kiss on the cheek.

He laughed out loud. "We should give you more things to do from now on. It gets you out of your sour mood."

Nader finally stopped the car.

"Good job, Soraya. I thank you, and so does Reza's family."

She nodded and rested her hand on his.

"Thanks for being my friend; it means a lot to me."

Getting out of the car she stood on the side of the road and watched him drive away, feeling so close to him and knowing he felt the same. So much had changed, and she knew there was going to be a lot more changes in the future. The idea concerned her about Oliver. Living with him was going to tie her hands when it came to helping the group. Somehow she had to convince him to let her move back to her room, without raising his suspicions. She decided to talk to him once she got home.

Oliver was sitting in the living room reading the paper when Soraya walked in.

"Hi, sweetheart."

"Hello," she said as she walked over to him and kissed him. Feels good to be home. It's been a long day."

"Did you work tonight?"

"No, I was bored so I decided to get out of the house for a while and go for a walk."

"Is everything alright?"

She paused, smiled and said, "Everything is fine, but I would like to talk to you."

"Sure, what's on your mind?"

"I want you to listen to me first and let me finish. Oliver, I know you want me here with you all the time, but the neighbors are starting to look at me in a strange way. It's getting harder and harder on me living here and looking anyone in the eye. You know how it is here. No matter how much we try to ignore their judgmental stares, it still bothers me. I think it is best if I move back to my room. Nothing is going to change between us, and I will still be here with you every weekend. But during the week, we should stay in our own places."

She got closer to him and took his hand in hers.

"This doesn't mean we can't sneak around once in a while during the week. I hope you understand, sweetheart, and don't question my love for you. That has not changed. We just need to be a little more careful, that's all."

He understood, but didn't like it.

"If that's what makes you feel more at ease, I am willing to give it a try."

"It's not what I want, but I think it is the right thing to do."

She hugged him and added, "Besides, it will be more exciting for us, and you won't get tired of me."

"I will never get tired of you. I love you more than anything in this world. But we can start this new arrangement as of tomorrow. Tonight, I want to make love to you all night and forget about our nosy neighbors."

With that said, he began taking her clothes off and soon they were in each others arms making love. They loved tenderly and passionately and ignored the world around them, the world that banned them from being together. Nothing else mattered anymore. They enjoyed the moment and let their love take them away to unknown places. Their love was stronger than anything else around them, and this, they both knew. They closed their eyes to the world and only opened them when they could see each other and nothing more. As they saw it, what they felt for each other was stronger than anything one reads in a book or sees in the movies. There was no greater love than theirs.

Soraya left early the next morning, and Oliver was already gone for an early meeting. So many things had to change from that point on. She had already started those changes with Oliver. She hated to lie to him, but there was no other way she could do that without making him get suspicious. And now she had to make some changes with Nader. She was told that once she joined the group, they couldn't be seen together anymore. They had to make it so no one would know they had any relationship outside of school. That was the only way they would both be protected.

She was surprise to find him waiting for her near the bus stop.

"what are you doing here?"

"I had to talk to you before school. There will be a meeting this afternoon and we need to have you there; but I won't be able to take you there. It's too dangerous. We shouldn't be seen together after school at all, not if we can help it. So what do you think? Can you make it?"

"Yes, I'll be there."

Nader dropped her off a few blocks away from school and she got out of the car wondering what this sudden meeting was about. She had a hard time concentrating on anything that day. Her mind kept drifting off to the meeting they were to have that afternoon. She couldn't wait to get out of there and find out what it was all about.

The taxi dropped her off near the same drug store she had gone to with Nader. She walked in and looked around, just as they did before and then slipped through the door without anyone seeing her. She never noticed Mohammed standing in the corner, watching her enter the room.

"You are a fast learner, lady."

She turned around and saw him.

"Hello, Mohammed."

"How are you?"

"I'm fine, thank you."

"I hear you did wonderfully on your first mission."

"Thank you. And I am ready for more."

"Just remember what I told you, rushing into things is always dangerous. You go slowly and carefully. Well, let's go and join the rest. The meeting is about to start."

She took her place on the floor, curious to find out what went on in those meetings. Her first time around was all based on her getting started. This would be the first time for her to sit in and listen to what really went on.

Mohammed cleared his throat and began, "Our next focus is on Taimoor. In case you don't know who he is, let us fill you in, Soraya. He is the man who is in charge of all executions and tortures within the Savak system. Everything runs through him, and what Reza is going through today is due to his orders. So, it is time that he pays for his crimes. We have the bomb in our possession and our next step is to plant it in his home."

Soraya was shocked. She couldn't believe what she was hearing. She stopped him immediately.

"Does he have any family?"

"Yes, he does and this will put all of their lives in danger." He could see the horror on her face.

"Remember, Soraya, there will be sacrifices, but it's the only way to stop these men. They are heartless. If you have no heart, then you should not live. And that's our belief. People with no heart will cause pain and suffering for others. Our mission is to stop and eliminate them. We can't make a mistake; this bomb is very costly."

Soraya cut him off again, "How can you not care about the innocent little children? They haven't done anything wrong."

"We know that. But think about it for a moment. Do you think Taimoor cares about what happens to Reza's family? Once they are done with him, his family will be lucky to get his body for a proper burial. The

Savak doesn't care what happens to people like us. They would like to see us all dead. We are the reason why Savak exists. Soraya, you haven't been around long enough to witness what we have. For now, I want you to sit in the meeting and control your feelings. Don't forget the face of the child who opened the door for you on your first mission. She will grow up not knowing her father. She will never know what a kind, giving, and intelligent person he was. They took him from her. She is fatherless for life."

Soraya argued back, "But at least she lives and will hear about her father. Taimoor's kids will never have a chance to decide for themselves what an evil man they had for a father."

Mohammed was patient with her and liked her courage.

"We hope they do; but if we think about what happens to every little child who belongs to a bastard, we could never accomplish anything. I understand your concern and pain; but remember, in every mission or war or revolution, there are always innocent lives that get destroyed. We don't like that either, but what other choice do we have? We have to continue with our mission even though there will be sacrifices. These are facts of life; and we have to go on hoping that the person who takes his place, at least out of fear, will think twice when he orders those inhuman acts. Because in the end, he will die too. Sooner or later we will get to him somehow."

Soraya looked away with tears in her eyes; she was thinking about her own child and how innocent he was even though he was conceived through a brutal rape and his father wasn't any better than these men. Did Ali deserve to die because of that? She knew the answer to that; no matter what reasoning they gave her, she believed those children should not be put in any danger. They didn't deserve to die because of their father. She kept quiet and listened to the rest of the conversation, but it left her uncertain and in pain.

Nader approached her after the meeting.

"You ok?"

"I don't know, Nader. If we act like them, then there is not a difference between us. There will be no peace, ever, if we just go around hurting each other."

"Listen to me, Soraya. We didn't start this war, and we don't go after anyone unless we know that they are guilty of crimes against humanity. It doesn't matter how many innocent people they kill, one or a thousand, it shouldn't be. You and I shouldn't die because we'd like to see our people live better or have more freedom or demand to know what happens to all of our wealth. Our government has such a lavish lifestyle that it doesn't leave much for others. You and I should not die for these beliefs. When they execute people like us, they should pay the consequences. It is an eye for an eye, and they started this war not us. We are just fighting to protect our rights as individuals. Ask your friend about freedom and rights and see how far he would go to protect that right. See if he thinks it's worth fighting for. We just want the same thing, that's all. We are tired of being called ignorant because our government doesn't give us any breathing room, let alone freedom."

She understood his views, but children had a special place in her heart.

She wanted them to be protected no matter what the cost was, and she wasn't going to change her mind on that. No one should pay for someone else's crimes, especially when it came to the innocent and vulnerable.

"Please, Nader. Do your best to protect those children. I just don't feel right about this mission. If we don't do the right thing, we will pay a higher price in the end. We should have the fear of God in us; and do the right thing, if it is possible at all; at least try."

"The security is way too tight at Savak. As far as planting the bomb in his car, that's out of the question, too. Because of security reasons, he changes cars all the time. His home is the only place we can possibly destroy. But we have always done this sort of thing in a way that there would be as few casualties as possible. Now just take it easy and don't be too emotional. We will do our best."

"Do you know who is involved in this mission?"

He nodded.

"You and I are part of this mission."

"Why me?"

"Because you have to get over these feelings and this is the only way."

She began walking away from him, and he could tell that she was angry about their decision; but he decided to let her leave and think about it first. He stood there, watching her disappear in the crowd and knew her pain only too well. It hurt him, too; he was just used to it now. So many of his friends and family members had been so brutally murdered that it didn't leave him much room to feel anything toward these people or their families. He knew she would come to the same conclusion someday. It would take time, but she would be there sooner or later.

It was about one in the morning. Soraya stayed in her room, was dressed and ready to go. She took a look around, knowing the next time she would see this room things would be different for her. She would be a changed person. This was a mission that meant bloodshed and death. The group had trained her for weeks. Now she was going to put it into action. There was no fooling herself, it frightened her to death. Her job was basically to run a C.B. and keep an eye on the guards. She was to report to the group if anyone unexpected came or anything unusual happened. They would do the rest. They had dug a tunnel through the underground pipes which ended right in the back yard. Once they were inside of the mansion gates, they could get to where the bomb was to be planted. One of the guards was a group member, but he was not going to be there at the time the bomb would explode.

She got out of the car with the others and placed herself so she had a good view of the guards in front of the house. The mansion was under watch from every angle by someone like her. They had figured it would take about an hour to have the whole thing set up. At times, she thought the C.B. was going to break into pieces because she was holding it so tightly. Soraya and the others with a C.B. reported everything they did to the rest of the group so they had a good idea of their whereabouts. They all had a small map of the tunnel, and everything was going smoothly.

This place was so close to her house that, from there, she would hear the explosion when it happened. It was going to be a massive bomb. She looked at the guards that would not see the sun come up the next day, or at best would be seriously wounded. To her relief, the kids were not in the mansion. The group had waited and planned the mission for a day that the kids had gone on a trip with their mother to the northern part of Iran, by the Caspian sea. Mohammed had eventually given in and promised Soraya that they would do their best to avoid the kids from being hurt. He kept his promise, even though it postponed their plans for a few days; and she was thankful for that. She was filled with anxiety as she sat there praying that everything would go smoothly, and that no one would get hurt but Taimoor. She honestly didn't care what happened to him. She wanted him to feel the same kind of pain that he had caused others. Time was passing by, but not fast enough. For the first time, she noticed the guards were being distracted by something. There was some movement, but she didn't know exactly what it was. She reported it immediately. Minutes later, everything was calm except her heart. It was pounding so hard she could hear it. She thought about Oliver and how she had to lie to him about being tired and having a lot of homework so he would leave her alone that night. Her emotions were on a roller coaster ride lately. She had learned much more about the government that disturbed her. That was what the group was hoping for. They knew in time she would come around. There was a signal which meant the planting of the bomb was all over with, and it was time to leave. She moved away from her spot slowly and quietly. It was hard to believe that it was over and once she left, the turn of events would be beyond her control. She felt a chill as she jumped in the car, and it pulled away immediately. Everyone in the car was pleased with the mission so far and they congratulated each other. Mohammed looked at Soraya, uncertain of her feelings about the mission. Yet, he did understand her mixed emotions. They dropped her off without exchanging many words with her.

Once in her room, she closed the door behind her and went straight to the bathroom. After emptying out her stomach in the toilet, she opened her medicine cabinet and drank down some sleeping pills with a glass of water. It was a difficult mission for her, and she didn't want to hear anything. She covered her face with a pillow, shut her eyes, and cried herself to sleep.

Oliver knocked on her door, but there was no answer. The explosion had woken him up, and for a moment, he wondered if it was an earthquake. He heard the sirens a few minutes later and turned on the radio, but there was no news of anything. He wondered if it had been a bomb. He called the embassy to find out, but they didn't have any information on it yet. So he left for work earlier than normal in case of anything unusual that might concern the embassy. Although he didn't work directly for the embassy, he did a lot of work for them. They were all his friends, and he could always count on them.

Soraya rolled over and opened her eyes. She was still tired, and wondered if the bomb had exploded. She turned on her radio and left it on to find out if they would report it.

She was busy brushing her teeth when the news came on later. They called it an act of terrorism that was under investigation. No one within the mansion had survived the explosion. The government has indicated that they had leads on who was responsible and threatened to punish them severely. Taimoor was dead, and a few minutes later they reported his death. She wondered if they really had any leads, or if they were just saying that.

She got dressed and left her room for the meeting they were holding that afternoon. She had missed a whole day of school and wasn't too thrilled about that. When she walked into the meeting, she found everyone joyful. They were hugging each other and congratulating one another on the successful mission.

It was one of their biggest accomplishments yet, and they were all thrilled. The next mission was to distribute as many fliers as they could explaining to the people about the explosion and to let them know of all Taimoor's crimes. Even though everyone knew him only too well, his name brought a chill to people. They were glad to hear of his death, but no one could show any negative emotions toward his death.

The next few days, the government showed all the good things he'd done in his life and that he served his country until the day he died. They gave his family a medal of honor for all of his achievements. They simply left out some minor details, such as all his crimes against Iranians.

Reza didn't live long after that. The news of his death came only a week later and saddened everyone in the group, including Soraya. His family never received his body and they were not even allowed to have a memorial service for him. It was like he never existed. The family was told that he was a shame and embarrassment to his nation and didn't deserve to have anything. They had probably burned his body and thrown the ashes in the sewer. Soraya was beginning to understand the group's view more and more. She no longer let her feelings get in the way of doing what the group asked her to do. She understood her position and knew that there were good reasons why they handled things the way they did.

She came to understand and admire the group and their dangerous mission. Keeping as many people in the dark was to the government's benefit. Most of these people, especially the villagers, had accepted living like a bunch of cattle and they didn't expect anymore. Actually, they didn't know any better. Life outside of the village for them was a threat and even sacrilegious. They were kept in the dark without them even knowing it. They thanked God for the dry piece of bread they ate every day. These were good honest people that had been forgotten. They were truly the forgotten people. This is where it hit home for Soraya more than anyone else. After all, she knew only too well how these villagers lived. She wanted more for her people: more education, more food, more medical facilities, and most of all, more life. Deep inside, these people were all dead, and life barely existed for them.

Soraya's spirit was getting a lot harder and colder. Tears didn't roll down her face as easily as they used to. For the first time, she wanted revenge for Reza, someone she had never met. Listening to his tape giving speeches and lectures many times helped her get to know him. She became less tolerant of stupid people who had no goals in life other than to get more material things and live a better life, never fighting for what's right or wrong. Eventually, she even got negative feelings toward the western world who supported the Shah who destroyed anyone or anything in his country that questioned him or his lifestyle. She became aware that her country was being used for their oil resources and their geographic position in the Persian Gulf. Nothing mattered to them. Holocaust was alive and well and was being fully supported by the westerners, who never even questioned him or his regime. As long as they were on his side and he was on theirs, it didn't matter how many people were wasted for their beliefs. In time, she had changed. Her thoughts began to turn and show a different color.

"They can call me a terrorist or whatever the hell they want. I am proud of who I am and what I do. I will put my whole life on the line to protect the innocent and destroy the evil. And yes, there will be the ones who die, who have done no wrong, who don't deserve to die, but aren't those the bitter facts of life? War will never end in this world, not in our time or our children's time or their children's. It goes on forever and innocent people die in the name of God, land, freedom, and so on. This is my war against the evil, against crimes, and most of all for freedom. I will fight and use the last drop of blood in my body if I can make a difference. I will give it my best shot, and if that shot hits an innocent bystander, then I will live with that fact. Freedom has a sweet sound to it. How many lives does it take to have a whole nation free? I guess that would be a good question for the westerners to answer. Not for me, I have never had it and my fight for freedom is called an act of terrorism. So be it."

With all her callousness toward life lately, she still had a very soft spot tucked in her heart and that was her love for Oliver. That was something she had no desire to change. Sometimes she felt it was the only sign of humanity left in her, but she knew that her hardness was just her outer look, not her inner soul. At times she would lose herself in his protective arms. That was something she needed more than ever.

It was getting closer to the time when she was to leave with Oliver, and she was looking forward to having some time away from everything. She was curious to find out how people lived in other countries and how the western world enjoyed their lives as free nations. She had no idea what it would be like. She was aware of other countries in which women had absolutely no rights, like in Saudi Arabia. They had to cover from head to toe and weren't even allowed to drive a car. They were treated like a bunch of little kids that weren't allowed to grow up except enough to have children and care for their families, just like the villagers. Iranians never like to be called Arabs; they didn't want to be associated with them. They shared the same religion, and that was basically it.

She had done a lot of growing up in such a short time. In fact, she often wondered if she'd been brainwashed or if this was the real Soraya who suddenly came to life. For now, she was going to keep up with everything and find out as much as she could.

Soraya heard of some uprising in Paris. She heard about some religious groups and that their leader had been in exile for many years and was starting to cause little waves here and there. She wasn't sure if her country needed a religious leader, but at this point anybody was better than the Shah. This became a topic of much discussion, and her group had been in touch with Paris. For now, they all held hands and decided to deal with the rest later. After all, it couldn't get worse; it could only get better. It was beyond their belief that anyone could commit as many crimes against humanity as the Shah and his regime. Things would only get better if he left, and that's what they kept telling themselves.

Oliver talked about nothing but their trip. They were going to stay in Paris for ten days; and he was going to meet with some members of his company there, discussing some future plans. The group wanted Soraya to somehow meet with the religious group in Paris, and she just hoped it could be done. She would have to do it when Oliver went to his meeting because that would be the only time she could get away from him.

Given all the necessary information by the group, all she had to do was dial the number she'd been given, and they would take care of the rest to set up a meeting immediately.

Nader was at her side every step of the way, guiding her and teaching her how to deal with these people so she wouldn't feel intimidated by them. She was to be their messenger and they had great confidence in her, but at the same time, they were aware of her sour moods and didn't want her to lose control. It was important for them to have everything worked out the right way. They knew this group had a lot of money behind them, and that was one thing Soraya and her group were lacking, the financial backing.

Nader and Mohammed discussed with her everything that they thought she should know, the rest was up to her. They both felt she was a good choice for the job, as she would not let the other group run the show. On her own, she did as much research as she could and was ready.

It would be a challenge for her, but it certainly wasn't her first challenge in life. This one, however, was for real and all her college education and studying could not compare with what she was to face soon.

The night before her departure Nader hugged her and wished her luck and told her to be herself, no one else but herself.

"And that, my dear, is the key to all your success in life so far."

She thought about his words as she packed her bags that night, and they brought a smile to her face. She truly cherished her friendship with him.

The following day, Oliver was out getting last minute things before their departure the next day. He knew how nervous she was getting on that plane. He planned to get her some pills to make her more relaxed; he didn't want to waste a minute of their time worrying about anything.

He had talked to Kate a few days before and told her he was going on a business trip, but never told her that Soraya was going with him. They both decided to wait until they were back from their trip before telling Kate about their relationship.

Oliver walked in that evening to find Soraya nervous and stressed out. She got sick to her stomach every time she thought about flying. She would rather die on a mission than die in a plane crash; there was no doubt in her mind about that.

Oliver decided not to wait until the next day to give her the pills.

"Listen, sweetheart, I got something that will make you feel a little more relaxed."

He gave her the pills and a glass of water.

"This is not going to put me to sleep, is it? I've got so much to do yet."

"It won't put you to sleep if you don't want to sleep; it will just help you relax."

He decided to get out of her way to give her some time to calm down. It was going to be her first time on a plane and he knew it could be a frightening experience. She kept busy the next hour and was almost done with everything when Oliver walked out of the kitchen with a small tray of sandwiches for them. He found her in a much better mood.

"Let's take a break and have something to eat.

They sat next to each other on the couch. In a way, they had already started their vacation. They were not going to see or talk to anyone, just finish packing and leave the next morning.

It was so strange for her to remember the last time she had to pack. Everything she owned was put into a small sack, and she could easily carry it under her arms. It seemed like nothing compared to what she had to pack now. Even the simple things in her life had changed. She could see that more clearly every day.

It was getting late and Oliver took their suitcases to the car that night. It was something that they both wanted to do at night so it wouldn't raise any questions by the neighbors the next day. They looked at each other with tired eyes and all they could say was good-night before going to sleep.

# CHAPTER NINE

Oliver showed her how to fasten her seat belt, and she just sat there holding on to the arm chair. The plane slowly began to move, and Soraya felt like her soul was flying right out of her body.

Oliver had given her another pill just moments earlier, and she was hoping to close her eyes and just fall sleep. She didn't like flying already and the plane hadn't even left the ground. Oliver held her hand and said, "I love you."

"I love you, too, but right now I could kill you for talking me into this."

She looked around and couldn't believe she was there. The plane started going faster on the runway; and she rested her head back and shut her eyes, holding on to Oliver's hand. They were flying first class, but Soraya didn't know the difference. At that moment, she could have cared less what part of the plane she was in. The plane took off and she prayed that it would get them there without any problem.

Oliver just sat back and watched her. He couldn't believe how beautiful she was. She didn't even move and he was glad that she had fallen sleep. The longer she slept, he thought, the better she would feel. When they brought their food, Oliver told the flight attendant not to wake her up.

"Could you save her tray for later?'

"Sure, no problem," the flight attendant replied.

Soraya turned her head and opened her eyes. She had slept for hours and saw Oliver next to her reading a book. It was hard to tell how long she had slept for. She looked out the window and saw the beautiful puffy clouds underneath the plane.

"So this is what you look like close up."

She smiled, still not believing she was in a plane way above the clouds in the sky.

"Well hello, sleepy head."

She turned around and looked, with loving eyes at the man who had made it all possible for her.

"I feel like I've been sleeping for hours."

"You have, my love. You've been sleeping for almost three hours."

"Oh my God, what did you give me?"

Oliver smiled. "You've been so tired lately, so you just crashed. That's all."

She had been doing a lot lately, much more than Oliver knew, between getting ready for her trip and school and most of all, the group was taking every free minute she had. It left her exhausted.

"Are you hungry?"

"I am starved."

Oliver pushed the button for the flight attendant and she came back a few minutes later with a tray of food for her. It was all so amazing to her, to have this beautiful blue eye, blond haired woman wait on her and bring her food. She wasn't used to such service. She looked around the plane and saw a lot of Iranian people on board.

"So, this is how the rich lives," she told herself, practically inhaling her food.

"You weren't hungry, were you?" Oliver asked her.

"Tell me what's it like in Paris."

Oliver took a deep breath, "It's old and beautiful. It's romantic, with some of the best restaurants and shops in the world. Beautiful countryside. You just have to wait and see it for yourself, darling. You can't even imagine, and I know you will love it. I promise you that."

It was still hard for her to believe that she was on her way to Paris with Oliver at her side. She finished her food and decided to use the bathroom.

"Oh my God, I look terrible," she gasped as she looked at herself in the mirror.

She quickly brushed her hair and decided to put on some make-up. She felt out of place at times. There were so many people with beautiful clothes on that plane. Oliver wouldn't let her buy any clothes before they left, but told her to wait until they got to Paris. He planned on buying her all new clothes and didn't want her to waste her money on anything before they left. She looked at herself in the mirror and was much more pleased.

"You look beautitful," he said.

"At times I don't feel like I belong here."

"Sure you do. You are my Persian princess."

"I don't like to be labeled as a princess. I am far from that."

"That's just a compliment, my love. Plus, why wouldn't you want to be called that?"

"Because it doesn't impress me. To me being identified as a princess for example has a different meaning than most people think. In my world it means being clueless of other people's suffering and hardship."

"How is it that you are so informed about all that?"

"I grew up in a very harsh environment. I am sure it's hard for you to believe that I went to bed hungry more times than I can remember."

"Sweetheart, listen to me. I have sensed some very negative reactions from you the last couple of times we have talked about your country, and I don't like it. You can't talk like this to anyone. It is very dangerous. People have disappeared for less reasons than that, and you can't trust anyone. Do you realize what can happen to you if the wrong person hears you talk this way?"

"I realize much more than you think and I don't like it one bit. I don't have to pretend with you. Things shouldn't be this way in my country. You just said it yourself; people have disappeared for absolutely no reason at all."

"You can't change centuries of abuse and dictatorship. You will only jeopardize your life and also our future together. You can't risk that. Plus, you don't have to put up with it but a couple of more years. I am going to get you out of here."

"What if I choose not to leave my country?"

"Then you have to learn to keep your mouth shut, like everyone else."

"That's your opinion."

"Soraya, you alone can't change anything. It takes a lot more than you think. It takes a revolution, and that will never happen. The Shah is too powerful and he has powerful countries behind him. We are one of his biggest allies, and will never let him down."

"So what you are saying is the U.S., with all its so-called human rights activists and all its searches for war criminals from World War Two, knows what the Shah is capable of doing to his own people, and lets it go on? And to top it all off, they stand behind him? I don't know, Oliver. Would you live in a country that supported someone who would destroy your people for something as simple as freedom of speech?"

Oliver was starting to get a little irritated.

"If it meant my safety and the safety of the ones I love, yes I would. Soraya, your country has a history of a dictatorship for centuries. If it's not him, it's going to be someone else just like him, or maybe even worse. We didn't choose him to be the king. He was already there. All we did was support him and become friends, economically and otherwise, with someone your own people chose. His father was a king before him. It goes back for centuries of kingdom in Iran. You have never had a free election in this country. It's not our fault, and we can't control who runs your country."

She was angry listening to him.

"Oliver, maybe it is time that we have a free election and choose who runs our country. I think the western world has a bigger role than you and I think. Just because you work closely with the embassy, do you think you know all the political maneuvers that they make? I think they have a lot more control than you know. All I know is that the western world supports someone who has committed a lot of terrible crimes against the Iranian nation."

"And how do you know that for sure?"

She bit her lips for a second and responded, "I just do."

"Soraya, are you involved in anything you are not telling me?"

"Like what?"

"I don't know. But I want you to tell me if you are."

It was time for her to end the conversation before it got any worse.

She looked out the window knowing she has gone further than she should have.

"we should just drop it."

"You haven't answered me. Are you involved with any political groups?"

"Of course not, but that doesn't mean I don't have a view that is different from yours."

Oliver looked at her, unconvinced by her answer. "I'd like to know where you are getting your information. Who is telling you all this?"

"Don't try to intimidate me, Oliver. I am not a child. I read; I go to the library, and I can decide for myself what is wrong and what's not."

"There is not a book available in this country that would give you this kind of information. You and I both know that,"

He was upset and was beginning to get a strange feeling that She was involved in something that she couldn't tell him. She noticed the look on his face and decided to drop everything and find a way out of this whole conversation.

"Oliver We are going on a dream vacation and I would rather just enjoy the time we have together and not discuss anything that would make us argue like this." Her efforts didn't work and she could tell by the way he was still looking at her.

"Just to put your mind at ease. I had a conversation with some kids at school. But don't worry, I never said anything. All I did was to listen and make up my own mind without getting involved."

He prayed she was telling him the truth.

"I just want the best for you and getting involved even in a small conversation is not safe. Please promise me next time you'll just walk away from the whole thing."

She tilted her head. "I promise. Don't worry, you silly man."

With that, she kissed him on the cheek.

Oliver stopped, but for some reason he didn't believe her. How much could she be involved? And who was she involved with? His imagination took the best of him. The bomb the other morning, would she be mixed up in anything like that? He got mad at himself for even thinking she was capable of being part of a terrorist act like that. No, she wouldn't. At the same time, he wasn't sure what all this nonsense was about? "What are you thinking so hard about?" she asked, knowing the answer to her own question. She had gone too far this time, and it wasn't a very smart move on her part.

"We are about to land, please hold my hand. I think I am going to get sick."

"Just put your head back and close your eyes and relax. We will be there in no time. And remember, if we crash, we will both die together."

"That's a comforting thought, Oliver. I guess I never thought about it that way. It makes me feel much better," she said with a sarcastic look.

It brought a smile to his face. He loved her so much, this mysterious young woman, so different from anyone he had ever known before. He held her hand and just stared at her sitting there with her eyes closed. A few minutes later the plane landed.

"We are on the ground. You can open your eyes."

The plane came to a complete stop.

"I can't believe we are here already, in a different country."

They got out of the plane and walked toward the line for a passport check. She hung on to Oliver's arm like a child who was out of her familiar territory. Soon they got done with the customs. She was all eyes, looking at all the people while Oliver got a taxi to take them to their hotel. She couldn't believe they were in Paris, so far away from home, where no one knew them or judged them for who they were. A couple got her attention. They had their arms wrapped around each other, kissing one another. One would never see that in public back home. Holding hands was the extent of what you would see in her country. Oliver pulled her in the taxi and broke her train of thought.

"Well, my darling, here we are, in Paris, my favorite city in the whole world."

"It looks so different."

"You haven't seen anything yet."

The taxi took off and she was amazed. There were so many people with blue eyes and light colored hair. She was the one who looked different from anyone else here. It was so clean and beautiful, she didn't know which direction to look at. Then the taxi pulled in front of a beautiful hotel and stopped. They both got out and a man in a uniform ran toward them and helped them with their suitcases. Oliver walked over to the reception area and checked in and they gave him a key. She followed him all around and they got out of the elevator on the eleventh floor. He opened the door with the key that they had given him and told her to wait. He put everything down on the floor by the front door. He picked her up in his arms and walked in the room.

She giggled, "What are you doing?"

"We are going to do this right," he replied and kissed her passionately.

The bell man brought their suitcases in and Soraya blushed seeing him in the room while Oliver was kissing her.

"Oliver, put me down. It's not right."

He put her down and tipped the man and closed the door.

"You are in Paris, the city of love and romance. Anything goes here, and it's okay to kiss in public in the presence of other people. There's nothing wrong with that."

"I know that, but I just feel so uncomfortable having some strange man watch us kiss."

"You shouldn't. It's okay to love and show it here.

"Well, I thought for our first night maybe we would just order room service and have a glass of wine and stay in. Tomorrow we will start exploring this town. What do you think?"

"It sounds good, for some reason I feel safer here."

"Honey, you will always be safe with me, no matter where we are, and don't forget that."

Soraya looked around the room and noticed at an oversized bathtub.

"What on earth is this?"

He laughed out loud.

"This is called a Jacuzzi hot tub."

It overlooked the beautiful city of Paris. Everything was so foreign to her, and she didn't like the feeling of being so lost with all the new surroundings. She decided to unpack and take her mind off other things that made her feel so uneasy. Oliver got on the phone and ordered their food. She didn't understand a word he said, she just figured that's what he was doing. She disappeared into the bathroom once she finished unpacking, to freshen up and change her clothes. She heard some soft music. It was a French song and sounded so relaxing. Soraya walked out of the bathroom and he handed her a glass of wine.

"Here is to us, my love. To our first vacation together, and may we have many more to come."

She gently touched his glass with hers. They sat on the couch looking out on the city lights. It was a magnificent sight. She was much more relaxed and began to unwind.

"This is just too nice. I still can't believe that I am here in Paris so far away from everything. I could stay here for the rest of my life and not one person would notice that I am gone." She looked at Oliver.

"Do you realize that no one waits for me to go back home? No one would ever know if I just vanished from the face of the earth? It is a lonely feeling."

Oliver knew that she was right and that she was a lonely child.

"My darling, you are probably loved more than all of those people and their families combined. You have my love and it is greater than anything you can ever imagine. So just remember, it's not the quantity, but the quality. And you should know, if you were to vanish, I would bring the heaven and earth together to find you and wouldn't rest until you were safe and protected in my arms."

She looked at him with loving eyes.

"You are just too good to me and I don't know what I would ever do without your love."

"I may be good to you, my love, but you are good for me. You have shown me a kind of love that I never thought existed. You are everything a man could dream of. I am not just a young man in love. I've been married for many years. I understand what it is to be in love, but at the same time, the love you have shown me is something that I don't think more than a handful of people ever experience in their life. It is so complete that I pinch myself at times to make sure that it's not a dream, and if it is, I don't ever want it to end. I could spend the rest of my life in a dream with you and never wake up."

She was touched with what Oliver told her. She loved him so, but when she thought about her life with Oliver, it made her feel that it was just there for the moment and someday it would be taken away from her, just like everyone else that she loved so much and in the end lost. So she cherished the moment and hoped it would last forever. God had given her the power to love but not the power to keep the ones she loved so desperately, and the thought of ever losing Oliver was more than she could bear.

"I feel so blessed being loved by you, Oliver, and I am thankful that I have given you the kind of love that you just described to me. I hope we can make it last forever. I just can't help thinking that someday you will need to leave and go to your own land and I wouldn't have enough courage to leave with you. For some reason, I think the day will come, and it won't be our choice. Do you know what I am trying to say?"

This brought tears to his eyes, but he didn't want her to see them; he looked down for a moment.

"Our love for each other is so strong that I think in the end it will pull through anything. You have to think positively and have faith in our love. In the end we will both see sunshine, everlasting sunshine; and that is my promise to you, my love."

They could sit there forever and look out the window and let the whole world go by them and they would never feel anything but their love for one another.

There was a knock on the door and it startled both of them. Oliver jumped to his feet.

"It must be the room service with our dinner."

He opened the door and let the man in. It was all so new to her, food being served in her room and a change of sheets and towels every day. She couldn't believe it was happening to her, yet she took it all in without acting like someone from a twilight zone. Oliver knew that she had never been exposed to anything like this before and was amazed at how well she absorbed everything and acted as though she were accustomed to it all her life. Some people could be born with no money, yet have a class that no money could ever buy; and to him, Soraya was one of them. He noticed how everyone looked at her everywhere they went, but to Oliver it was not all because of her beauty. It was the way she handled herself. She had an air about her that made others think of her as someone with a special background.

"Smells wonderful. What is it?"

"It's fish, and I hope you like it."

He took the top covers off. She looked closer.

"It looks delicious, so fancy you almost don't want to touch it."

He smiled.

"It looks good enough to eat, darling, and that is exactly what we are going to do."

He invited her to sit at the small table by the window and pulled the chair out for her. She sat down and Oliver sat across the table from her. He knew she would find it difficult to use all the right silverware, so he casually talked to her as he picked up his fork and knife and she followed. She was glad to have this little practice in a safe place with Oliver and not in a fancy restaurant surrounded with strangers. It was a wonderful meal, and they both enjoyed every bite and carried on with their conversation.

He put on some more soft music after dinner.

"Come here, let me teach you how to dance."

She slipped into his arms and let him gently move her around. She was so relaxed that he could practically lift her off the floor.

"Are you sure you haven't done this before?"

It made her laugh.

"Oh, maybe a few times."

He held her close. "My little angel, you are so pure and I feel so lucky to be the one to show you things that you have never been exposed to before."

They just danced in each other's arms until the music stopped.

"What would you like to do now?" he asked her.

"Whatever your heart desires."

"In that case, why don't we try this bath tub and see if it works?"

"I thought you'd never ask."

She slipped into the bathroom and took off all her clothes and returned with nothing on.

He helped her in, but couldn't take his eyes off of her magnificent body. Gently rubbing her shoulders with the soft oil, he gave her a massage that left her breathless. He kissed every part of her body, and slowly entered her, and they made love under the stars. For the first time they didn't care if the whole world witnessed their love making. It was a celebration of their love and it lasted way into the night. Nothing mattered to them. It was so passionate that they could not stop. He touched her soft skin and kissed her again and again. He understood her body and all her desires. It was an unforgettable night for them and he finally picked her up and gently laid her down on the bed. Looking down at her filled him with more desires. What she did to him was something that he had no control over and he knew this woman belonged to him forever, no matter what the cost was. She slowly drifted off to sleep and he just lay next to her watching her sleep so peacefully. He fought sleep, not wanting the night to end.

The next day he opened his eyes thankful that the previous night wasn't just a dream.

Soon his lips met hers and she slowly moved and opened her eyes. His heart was filled with so much love for her. He wanted to lose himself in the heat of her arms and make love to her ever so passionately and before she was fully awake he was making love to her.

"Well, my love, what do you think? Should we leave this bed before we get started again, or do you want to spend the rest of the day naked in my arms?"

"I think we better get up and get dressed. I'd like to see this city you've been telling me so much about."

They both showered, got dressed and left their room.

"Where are we going?" she asked with curiosity.

"To have breakfast and then whatever we like."

They got in a taxi and a few minutes later got dropped off at a busy part of town. Holding each other's hands, they walked around and watched the crowded streets. Soraya looked like a little kid in a candy shop. Everything was so new and exciting to her. They finally came across a small cafe with the wonderful aroma of coffee. It was an automatic move on both of their parts, wanting to go in and have some coffee. They picked a small table near the window. Oliver ordered breakfast, and Soraya understood for the first time why he loved Paris so much. Even eating breakfast in a small cafe was somehow romantic.

They walked around for a while after leaving the cafe and suddenly came across a beauty shop, the kind you see in the movies, with high tech fashions and makeovers.

"I have a good idea," Oliver said with a grin.

"What's on your mind?"

"Just follow me."

And he almost pulled her in. He talked to the receptionist for a while and Soraya wondered what he was saying as they both kept looking at her. It was obvious to her they were talking about her, but had no clue what they could be discussing.

"Oliver, what are we doing here?"

"Trust me, love, you will love it. They are going to give you a makeover and do a little pampering. You deserve it."

She didn't mind getting a haircut by a professional. It was something she had never done before.

"Just tell them not to cut my hair too much, and also not too much makeup."

"Just relax, darling. She will take care of you and I will pick you up in a couple of hours."

She pulled her arms and told her in English to follow her as she waved goodbye to Oliver and left the room with the lady. She handed her a robe and told her to change into it. For the next three hours she got a complete makeover. It started with a mud mask and went to a body massage, a skin cleanse, manicure, and a haircut. It was relaxing, enjoyable and she trusted the girl to do the right thing. The lady didn't have to do much of a makeover, noticing how beautiful she was. Her skin just glowed.

"You look beautiful and he will be very happy," the girl told Soraya in broken English.

She smiled and looked at herself in the mirror and was pleased with the result. It was such a classy haircut and it made her look sophisticated, yet in a way kind of sexy. The woman also showed her all the makeup she used on her and the right way of using it.

Oliver walked in and was amazed at his changed beauty. She looked like a model right out of a Vogue Magazine.

"You look gorgeous."

The beautician turned to him and said, "You better be careful with her; French men love beautiful women."

Oliver couldn't get over how beautiful she looked. He had a hard time not staring at her. He paid the bill and gave the girl a generous tip. He was truly pleased with the results.

"What do you think? Do you like it?" he asked her.

She smiled. For the first time in her life she felt beautiful. It was something that she never gave a lot of time and attention to, and it had never been a priority in her life to make sure she looked good at all times.

They continued with their walk. He was planning on buying her some new clothes and thought it was a good opportunity to do exactly that knowing she was a little more motivated than usual about her appearance. A small boutique caught their eyes and they walked in. Everything was displayed so beautifully, and she had a hard time deciding which to choose. She finally decided on a couple of outfits and tried them on and he thought they looked great on her. He wanted her to buy enough clothes so she didn't need to wear any of Kate's old clothes any longer. For the first time, she didn't fight him on buying things. She decided to let him spoil her and get whatever she wanted. Their shopping spree lasted all day. Their arms were so full, they could hardly carry any more packages. She bought everything from clothes to shoes, perfume and makeup; and in the end, felt a little guilty.

"Oliver we have to stop. I have no place to wear all of these clothes to."

She finally convinced him to stop and go back to the hotel. She was so happy. No one had ever done anything like that for her before, and she wasn't used to spending so lavishly without worrying about where the money was coming from. They sat next to each other in the taxi, and as she looked him in the eye, with so much sentiment. "how am I ever going to repay you for everything that you do for me?"

He squeezed her hand, "all I want from you is your love and that's how you can repay me, my love, just your love."

He saw the look in her face when he said those words, knowing she was hiding something from him. He knew it wasn't another man, but he still believed somehow she was involved in something he didn't know about. The look on her face said it all. He knew her well enough to know.

It hurt her terribly to hide from him what was happening in her life, but she could never tell him; it could jeopardize his safety and their future together. In a way, she thought it was for his own protection, but he would never understand.

"I will always be as honest as I can with you. And as far as loving you, I don't believe I am capable of loving anyone any more than I love you. You are all I have, and I am committed to your love for the rest of my life, I hope you know that."

That alone told him there was more to it than what she was willing to admit. As far as her love for him, he never doubted for a moment that she loved him with all her heart. It was obvious to him that she was truthful when it came to that.

They rested at the hotel for a while before getting ready to go out for dinner that night. He had reservations for them at one of the finest restaurants. He was determined to make this trip as memorable as possible for both of them. She didn't know which outfit to wear. It had never been a problem for her in the past considering she didn't have many choices.

"What should I wear?" She asked.

"Surprise me, darling."

"Is it a fancy place?"

"It is, but you can wear anything you want. The way you look today, I'd like to take you out there wearing nothing at all, but I don't think I can stand having every man in the restaurant staring at you."

She laughed, and picked out a short black dress that fit her perfectly. She finished doing her hair and makeup and walked back in the room.

Oliver turned around and was stunned at what he saw.

"Well, well, maybe I'll just order another room service instead."

"No you don't, not after all the work I went through getting ready. This is a lot of work, looking good."

"You look absolutely beautiful," he said proudly.

"Thank you. You don't look too bad yourself," she said with a smile.

They left the hotel room and walked down to the lobby. It didn't take long before everyone in the lobby turned and looked at her. It made her feel a little uneasy.

"Haven't they seen a foreigner before?"

"Not one as pretty as you, my love."

"It makes me feel very uncomfortable to be stared at like this."

Oliver laughed out loud. "Why is that? Anyone else would be thrilled to get all this attentions, and you get uncomfortable."

"I don't think it is polite to stare at other people," she said with a frustrated tone.

"Come on, silly girl, just get used to it and don't let it bother you."

They got to the restaurant and the host showed them to their table.

"This is a beautiful place," she said quietly, noticing the white table cloth and fresh flowers throughout the restaurant and the crystal candle holders on each table.

It was so romantic. Soraya couldn't help herself and leaned over and kissed Oliver.

"What did I do to deserve that?"

"For being so good to me. I will never forget these days; they will forever be cherished in my heart, and it is all because of you."

Oliver ordered a bottle of wine; the waiter poured them each a glass; and they toasted to each other. Everything was perfect: the atmosphere, the food, and the wine. It was a brilliant night. They danced to the soft music and enjoyed the moment to the fullest. Soraya kept up with Oliver drinking the wine and soon felt the effects of alcohol. She looked up with a silly grin on her face.

"What are you smiling about?" he asked.

"Oh, I was just thinking about some of the kids at school. If they could only see me now."

"Is there anyone in particular you are talking about?"

She looked away and smiled again. "Yes, there is."

"And who is that?" he asked, knowing this was his chance to find out some things. He noticed a warm look in her face, like she was thinking of someone wh o was dear to her.

"His name is Nader. He is a good guy and the only friend I have."

244

"Why haven't you introduced me to him?"

"Oh, just because."

"Because why?"

"He wouldn't like that. He is very different."

"In what way is he different?"

"I don't know. He is just someone you don't meet more than once in your life, maybe never."

"What do you two talk about?"

She looked up almost like waking up from a dream and realized she was talking about Nader to Oliver. Somehow it didn't bother her. It was easy to talk to him about anything when they were so far away.

Oliver decided to continue questioning as long as she was willing to talk to him, and felt guilty, knowing the alcohol had something to do with it.

"Is he the one who's been talking to you about the Shah?"

Soraya ignored his question but not on purpose.

"I like him because he has never tried to ask me out or use our friendship. He has never even gone as far as giving me a simple compliment. He is just not into all that."

"Is he handsome?"

She laughed out loud.

"You are jealous, Oliver. I can tell!" She laughed again.

"Depends on what is attractive to you, he is very smart and knowledgeable. He knows about everything. I can talk to him about anything and he would have the right information. Do you know what I mean?"

"Does he know much about politics?"

"I am sure he does, but he doesn't ever talk about it."

Oliver looked at her, not believing her for a minute, but decided to give her the benefit of the doubt.

"He is a smart man, and you should learn from him."

"I do, and he taught me everything I know."

He could tell she was going back and forth on her words and was contradicting what she had said earlier.

"Like what?"

She looked him in the eyes, but had a hard time focusing.

"Shame on you, Oliver Reed. You sound like a spy," she said laughing out loud.

He laughed too, knowing she had not lost her sense of intelligence even though she was a little drunk. He was taking advantage of her but didn't know what he would do even if he found out things that would not be to his liking. All he wanted to do was to protect her. He didn't want anyone using her in any way. It was time to stop the conversation before she got too suspicious, and that's exactly what he did.

"Okay lady, are you ready to go back to the hotel with a spy?"

She smiled.

"Sure. Spies like you turn me on."

Soraya opened her eyes the next morning knowing it was early and decided to get up quietly without waking Oliver. She put on her robe and sat on the couch looking at the lights. The city was not awake yet, and she stared out at the stars that still shone through the early morning light.

"I wonder if my family is looking at the same stars as I am."

They were so far away from her. She wondered if her sister, Zahra, was as happy as she was. Soraya couldn't even imagine having her life and being happy, but they were so different and she didn't belong to that world any longer. In fact, she had no idea where she belonged anymore.

All she knew was that the day Oliver walked into her life, he changed everything toward a new direction, and Nader pulled her away into a different path. She didn't know where she was going or who had more control over her, Oliver or Nader. She knew there would be a time when she would need to make some choices. For now she lived two lives, but that wouldn't last forever. She was loving and warm and compassionate when she was with Oliver; whereas Nader brought out all of her frustration and the hard life she had as a child. In a way, she almost had two different personalities. She was the beauty and the beast, and they both appealed to her at different times in her life. Her mind drifted off to the night before, and she remembered her conversation with Oliver.

"I hope I didn't say too much." She knew Oliver was suspicious; yet he had to respect her privacy. The sun began to come up and she looked at the city and wondered to which part of town she would have to go to meet with these people. Oliver hadn't mentioned anything about when he was going to his meeting. Her mission had to be done when he left her alone to meet with his people. In a way, she felt like a spy with a mission. She sat there on the couch with her knees tucked under her arms thinking of everything she has to accomplish during the short time she would have with a new group.

Oliver opened his eyes and didn't see her in bed. He leaned up and saw her sitting on the couch looking out the window, deep in thoughts. He wondered what went through her mind. She always seemed so mysterious to him. There were times that she was so far away that he couldn't even try to catch up with her and enter her world of silence. He wondered if he would ever be allowed to get close enough to be a part of her world, but he didn't know the answer to that.

"I hope I didn't wake you up."

"No you didn't. What are you doing up so early?"

"Just woke up and couldn't go back to sleep; so I sat here and watched the sun come up. It was so beautiful and peaceful."

"Come back to bed with me."

She got up and crawled in bed with him and lay in his arms.

"What are we going to do today?" she asked.

Oliver rubbed his forehead.

"I am going to make a couple of calls and set up my meeting. I'd like to do it tomorrow. Would you like to come with me and hang around, till I am done?"

She thought for a moment.

"I would rather just stay here and maybe go for a walk. I hope you don't mind."

"No, if that's what you'd like to do. I will call them after breakfast."

They ate at a small restaurant near the hotel and decided to go for a short walk. Soraya wrapped her arm around his and they walked to the park right across from the hotel. Anyone who saw them walk by could tell they were a couple in love. They strolled through the park talking and laughing at times, and every now and then they stopped and kissed each other passionately. They were lost in a world of their own that was so special and forbidden for anyone to enter. It was their private world and they intended to keep it that way.

Oliver made his calls when they got back to the hotel and set up his appointment for nine in the morning the following day. Soraya had to do the same, but not until Oliver went to take a shower. She dialed the number, and as soon as she heard a voice on the other end, she introduced herself and asked for a man by the name of Davood. He got on the phone immediately.

"I can't talk very long, but I can meet you tomorrow morning around eight-thirty.

She gave him the name of the hotel where they were staying. He told her to look for a dark blue Benz. She quickly made a mental note and put the phone down.

Soraya took a deep breath and listened for the shower. Oliver was still in there, and she decided to forget about everything for the time and enjoy the day with him.

He rented a car with a driver and asked him to show them all the interesting sites. They visited a couple of museums and also the Eiffel Tower and ended the day walking around a beautiful lake, holding hands. The driver almost envied them. They were so much in love, and for all he knew, they were probably on their honeymoon. It was a day of love and romance, and they enjoyed it fully.

That night they stayed in the hotel and decided to repeat their first night. They fell in love all over again, and in the end lay peacefully in each other's arms and drifted off to sleep. The next day they both got up early. Oliver was to meet with his company over breakfast, and Soraya told him she was going to get something to eat at the hotel.

"Are you going to be okay while I am gone?"

"Of course I will be fine. Don't worry about me."

She waited for five minutes to make sure he was gone and then left the room and went down. It was the first time the hotel staff saw them apart. She decided to use the back door of the hotel and walk around the building to look for the car. It didn't take her long before she spotted the blue car and looked around to make sure no one from the hotel staff had seen her. She quickly ran toward the car and got in the back seat. There were two men in the car.

"Hello, I am Soraya."

The man in the back seat introduced himself as Davood.

"This is Hasan."

"How much time do you have?" he asked, intrigued by her beauty.

"Just a couple of hours."

He nodded.

"Would you like something to eat?"

"No, thank you."

Davood turned to Hasan.

"Why don't you go to the park on Second Avenue and park the car?"

They pulled away from the curb, and Soraya felt a little nervous being with two complete strangers in a strange country. She decided not to let them know how nervous she was, though. A few minutes later he stopped the car and parked.

"Would you like to go for a walk?"

She was glad to get out of the car and got out right after him.

"So tell me, what's happening in our country these days?"

"Same old stuff as you know. I am sure you heard about the bombing at Taimoor's mansion. They now know that they are not just dealing with a bunch of demonstrators. The plan was very sophisticated and costly, but it was successful. We have more plans, but need more funding."

He cut her off.

"What did you accomplish out of the bombing of Taimoor's house?"

She didn't appreciate being cut off like that, and her look told him not to do it again.

"Our first goal is to create a revolution, and at this point we don't want to plan any further."

"Does your group have a leader in mind?"

"Of course we have our preferences, but at this time our main goal is to have a government that allows us to have a free election. People should choose and no one else."

"You do realize that you have to have a leader who would take over the power, and then you can go on to your free election and so on?"

Soraya nodded and said, "Yes, we do."

"Are you willing to work with us for one common goal at this point, and that is to get rid of the Shah?"

She didn't like the terminology but knew it was how the game was played.

"We will go with you to that point, but that is as far as we can go. After that, it is up to the people. Dictatorship is out. We want to eventually have a free democracy."

Soraya didn't want to allow him to go on to his next question, so she asked, "so tell me, Davood, how many are there in your group?"

He smiled. "You know we have to trust each other if we are going to fight for the same cause?"

"I understand that, but trust should go both ways."

Davood grew serious.

"We have enough people in each city in Iran to start a revolution when the time comes, and we also have plenty of funds. What we are lacking are people who can plan a mission like the one you just did. That's why we would like to merge with your group. We will supply the funds and as many members as you need, and you have to do the rest within the country; but nothing gets done without our approval."

"Are you a religious group?" she asked.

"Yes, we are, and we have a powerful leader with many followers inside Iran and also outside. He has been an outcast for many years and he is ready to go back home."

"Is he willing to give up leadership after the revolution?"

"Of course he is. He is not after fame or anything else. He wants the same thing as you and I and has no desire to be another king. He is all for the people and their needs. Listen to me carefully, Soraya. The message I want you to pass on to your group is that they cannot do it alone. We all have to play as one. All of us will be in it together, to make history and have the biggest revolution in the history of our country. It is the only way. We have to trust each other and be a team if we are going to do this right. There is no other way. Remember, we are going to fight the whole army in every city. Our weapons are limited. Making a commotion within the country is the first step and that is how it should be done."

They went on discussing the matter further until it was time for her to get back before Oliver returned to the hotel. Davood gave her a phone number.

"This is how you need to get in touch with our people. And don't forget, we need honesty above all. You didn't come to us. Our sources told us about your group, and they are doing their best to find smaller groups, like yourself, who are fighting for the same cause."

She memorized the number and remembered one of the last things he told her: honesty was above all. In a way, it touched her because that's what her group was based on. It was a good meeting and she felt good about it. They obviously had the funds and the followers that her group lacked. Her group could get enough money to purchase what they needed and also enough members to fight back. In order for them to accomplish anything, they had to join forces.

They got back in the car and drove her back to the hotel. Davood looked at Soraya, still intrigued by her.

"Could you get away sometime and join me for dinner during your visit in Paris?"

She smiled.

"My visit is very short, but thank you for the offer. Maybe we can have dinner in our own country some day."

He smiled sadly.

"I'd like that. Good luck with your journey."

She got out of the car a block away and walked back to the hotel. She slowly opened the door to their hotel room and called out Oliver's name, but there was no answer. She was glad to be back before Oliver's return and sat on the couch taking a deep breath. It was over, and she had done her part. From there on, events were to take place beyond her control. She remembered Oliver's words.

"It will take a revolution to overthrow the Shah," and this was a revolution they were planning. It was exactly what they had in mind. She knew everything would happen a lot faster than anyone ever anticipated. What worried her most was Oliver's safety, knowing that both groups were anti-American. She had to find a way to protect him. At some point, she would have to tell him the truth; but that couldn't be until the very end when he could leave safely. She would eventually join him at a later time, but she needed to finish her mission all the way to the end. It was something she had to do for her people and her country. She needed to do that before leaving everything behind. She had no idea how it would all come about, but she knew when it came down to it, Oliver would be the one with whom she wanted to spend the rest of her life. Maybe someday she could be close to her son and even be a part of his life. That was a dream that she didn't think about very often. The future did not seem within her reach, but she didn't stop thinking and dreaming about it either. Oliver walked in a few minutes later.

"How did your meeting go?" she asked curiously.

"It went great. By the way, I came back earlier than I thought, but I couldn't find you anywhere."

"I just went for a walk. It is such a beautiful day that I lost track of time."

"I want you to go on another walk with me," he said with a strange look in his face, which made her wonder if he had seen her get out of the car.

She grabbed her purse and followed him out of the room. They walked to the small park across from the hotel again, and he picked the same bench as the other day and held her hand in his. He then reached in his pocket and took out a small box wrapped in beautiful paper with a big golden bow on top and handed it to her.

"Go ahead and open it."

She carefully opened the box and saw a simple gold ring inside of the box. She took the ring out and looked at it.

"Oliver, this is beautiful."

He went down to his knees, took her hand in his and said, "with this ring, I'll give you my love and heart forever. I promise to always be there for you and love you. This ring is the sign of my love for you; and with it, I will give you my heart and soul. I love you so much. Soraya slipped it on her finger as tears welled up in eyes. Lost for words, she was so touched knowing he never stopped doing nice things for her.

She couldn't talk anymore. Instead she just held on to him.

He lifted her chin. "I didn't mean to make you sad."

"You don't make me sad. These are happy tears. You are the only one in my life who knows how to get to the roots of my emotions. You touch me in ways that I can't explain. Your love has carried me through so many rough times that I don't know what I would ever do without you."

She looked at him with loving eyes.

"Oliver, would you marry me someday? Would you make this ring for real and forever?"

There was no hesitation in his voice "Of course I will, my love."

He smiled at her and held her close to him.

"Soraya, I am thinking of transferring from Iran, but at the same time I am not ready to go back home yet, not until I work things out with Kate. I have to take care of that situation first. You see, I brought you here to see if you like it. There is a very good chance that I could transfer here in the near future.

That doesn't mean the immediate future, but close enough. That should give me enough time to settle everything with Kate. Then we can move here together and get married right here in Paris."

Soraya didn't know what to say.

"Live here in Paris? What about my school?"

"You can finish school right here."

"But I don't speak French."

"I know that, but you can learn. You can take classes, just like how you learned English."

"How long are we talking about?"

"Maybe eighteen months. I don't exactly know, but around that."

"Eighteen months is too early."

"No it's not. It's long enough for us to plan everything. It will give us plenty of time."

Her main concern was her commitment to the group. What if it took longer for the revolution to take place? But for now, she couldn't argue with him and raise a red flag.

"Okay, I will leave with you, but on one condition."

"What's that?"

"I want you to marry me in Iran. I want to move here with you as your wife and not your mistress. And we have to get married by a Muslim minister. In order for you to do that, you have to become a Muslim."

He looked at her with a grin.

"You drive a hard bargain; but if it makes you happy, I am willing to do all that."

They had made some important decisions, and that left them much more at peace. At least they knew where they were headed and had made some plans for their future together. They spent the last few days of their vacation making as many memories as they could and talking about their future plans together. They would have their own kids someday and begin their life together with a fresh start in a new country. It was a trip they would never forget. Every corner of Paris was a reminder of a special moment for them. Oliver wished they never had to go back, not as long as he had her by his side. He wished they could start their life together right then, but knew he had to finish his obligation in Iran. He looked forward to nothing but his life with Soraya.

On their last day in Paris, they walked around the little pond in front of their hotel looking, one last time, at their special place, where they planned their future together. The next day they would leave this place, hoping to return someday and start their lives as husband and wife.

The plane took off and they both looked grim. Soraya had tears in her eyes. She was sorry it had all ended so fast and that soon they had to go back to reality. It was hard for her to hide their relationship from everyone around them again. She has gotten used to walking with him and kissing him wherever she wanted to. Now it all had to stop. Oliver knew it would go faster than they thought. He was going to call Kate and get the divorce procedures started right away. They hardly spoke about anything but Ali, and she had finally given up on the idea of him moving back home anytime soon. Kate sounded content and happy and that pleased Oliver. In a way, he would always love her, but not in a romantic way. What he missed the most was Ali, and he knew Kate would never hear of sending him back to Iran to see Oliver. He had thought about taking a trip back to U.S. for a couple of weeks. He knew it was time to let Soraya in on his decision, knowing she would understand and encourage him to go, especially when it came down to spending some time with Ali.

He held her hand and kissed it.

"I need to talk to you about my plans with Kate. I hope you don't mind, but the sooner we discuss the situation, the sooner I can get things started. I want to go back home for a couple of weeks."

"When?"

"In a couple of months. I don't want to tell her over the phone. I owe her at least that much. And I also need to see Ali. Soon he won't even remember me, and I can't take that chance."

"What will you tell Kate?"

"The truth. I need to tell her everything. She has to know. I realize this is hard on you; but the sooner I talk to Kate, the sooner we can start our plans together."

She looked down and played with the ring Oliver had given her just days earlier.

"I don't want you to worry about anything. It is over for Kate and me."

"Are you going to stay with her when you get there?"

"I have to. It is my home, and my child lives there."

"Are you going to sleep with her?"

He reached over and turned her face toward him. "Sweetheart, I will never sleep with anyone but you. Kate is my wife, but not for long. I couldn't make love to her even if I wanted to. You are the one I love now. I know this will be very hard for Kate, and it will also be hard on me. The last thing I want to do is to hurt her, but I can't go on any longer living a lie. She has to know, and I want to be the one to tell her."

"How do you think she will react?"

"She will hate me, but I understand her anger. I didn't keep my commitment to her; I am breaking my vows to her. She will be devastated and hurt; but then again, she may be ready to split. I don't know. All I know is that it is time to tell her the truth."

Soraya nodded.

"You have to do what you think is best. Still, my feelings have not changed. I still have this guilt, and I don't know if I'll ever get over it. She is the innocent victim in this situation. We have to do our best to make it easy for her. Even though that seems impossible at this point.

# CHAPTER TEN

They walked into the apartment and put their suitcases down. It was a long day, and they both were exhausted from the day's events.

Soraya didn't have anything planned the next day except to meet with the group; whereas Oliver had a full day's work. He had to catch up and the thought of it made him cringe. He knew his desk would be full of paperwork waiting for him to get done.

That night they lay in their bed and both thought about their trip. They had a hard time believing that they were back in their apartment. He kissed her and held her in his arms and wished they had more time together.

Oliver got up early the next morning and got ready for work. Soraya felt sad.

He kissed her good-bye and left for work. She immediately called Nader to find out the time of their meeting that day. It was nice to hear his voice again. She had missed him and was anxious to meet with him and Mohammed.

She got ready and left the house shortly after and met them both at their usual place. She walked in and saw them both waiting. Nader looked at her in surprise.

"What did you do to your hair? It looks great on you." She smiled as she looked at Mohammed from the corner of her eye. She was embarrassed to talk about her hair in front of him as she wasn't all that relaxed with him yet. Soraya noticed the way he was looking at her, too. He smiled in agreement with Nader but was eager to find out about her meeting in Paris.

"So, how did your meeting go?" Mohammed asked feeling uneasy.

"It went fine."

She went on explaining all they had discussed and also told them about Davood's invitation for dinner.

Mohammed was curious.

"And did you?"

"No, but I told him I will once they get back home."

She sensed a different feeling from Mohammed that she couldn't explain, like a jealousy, but wouldn't dare think twice about it.

"What do you think? Are they for real?"

She nodded.

"I truly think they are and also, we can get in touch with their people and find out more about their activities. I got the impression that there will be a revolution a lot sooner than we think."

Mohammed listened to her carefully.

"That's good. It means that they are further into the operation than we thought. Tell me what they want from us." "They want the same thing we do, maybe a few more missions like the one at Taimoor's house. They are willing to give us the funds we need. Money didn't seem like a problem to them." She had certainly told Mohammed everything he wanted to hear and even more. He was anxious to get in touch with them and get some first-hand information on his own. Their meeting lasted a couple of hours, and they all felt comfortable discussing further plans.

"Are you ready for some serious work?" he asked Soraya with a smile.

"I think so," she answered. "It's time."

"That's good, because we are going to need you."

They didn't waste any time; the following week, they accomplished several small missions. Things were moving fast, and people were beginning to talk. There were rumors everywhere. The University of Tehran was the center of attention. Most everything got started there and no one knew how it began. A few days after their meeting, they planted a bomb at the government center that exploded at four in the morning. Fliers were distributed immediately after, and they claimed victory for the bombing. For the first time they gave themselves a name: Freedom Fighters.

They urged people to speak out and help in any way they could. Soraya and Nader were personally involved in most missions. They were the center of all distribution at the university, but no one ever thought that it was them. They noticed how students were talking more freely and discussing the events that were taking place in the country for the first time. The guards were there with some Savak members, ripping all fliers off the walls and making threats to close the university if it didn't stop. They promised severe punishment for those responsible. Oliver was starting to get a little nervous. He knew that the embassy would be one of the first targets if things didn't settle down soon, and that concerned him.

The government had tightened security on all American owned companies and also at the embassy. Rumors were everywhere. People whispered, and it was obvious to many people that something was about to happen, but most people had no idea what that would be.

There were twice as many guards and security personnel in the streets and also at the university, which worried Oliver. He wouldn't have minded if Soraya quit school for the time being and sat at home where she was protected; however, he knew only too well that she wouldn't hear of it.

Soraya noticed Nader was not being himself lately. His excitement was gone, and she didn't know what was happening with him. She finally decided to get him alone somewhere and find out.

"What's going on with you lately? You are so distant."

He looked at her reassuringly.

"Nothing. I am fine."

She knew him better than that so pressed on and said, "Nader, I thought we were better friends than that. Please let me in on what's bothering you."

He looked away not wanting to give away all his emotions.

"I may be wrong, but I think someone saw me the other morning putting fliers up on the wall. I just have the feeling that I am being watched by someone. Maybe it is paranoia, but it is a scary feeling."

Soraya was horrified at what she heard.

"Oh my God, you have to go into hiding. Have you told Mohammed?"

"Yes, I talked to him; but you see, I am not sure if all these feelings are for real. If I do go into hiding, it will give them their answer, and I know they will go after my family to find me. At this point, I can't risk that. I don't know, Soraya. It would be a shame for me to get busted this close to our goal and not see the day."

It broke her heart listening to him.

"There has got to be a way to protect you without them getting suspicious."

"Soraya, every student here is under watch right now. They would know if someone just disappeared. They would want to know why. I wish they would close the school so I could go into hiding. I don't want to worry you too much. It could be my own illusion and nothing more; but you wanted to know, and I had to tell you. It's going to be hard for me to show up at the meetings from here on out. Mohammed wants me to stay away for a while and see what happens. It is too big of a risk for the rest of the group; and we can't take that chance, not when we are so close. You can't be seen with me anymore either. It is too dangerous. They can put two and two together, so just be careful and try not to talk to me too much at the university."

Soraya left him that day with a heavy heart. She didn't know what to do. She talked to Mohammed and he told her not to worry too much. It was just a cautionary step that they were taking.

She worked without Nader for the next couple of weeks and missed him every moment, but nothing had happened. Every day that went by that Nader was free was a good sign. She had taken over all his assignments and was beginning to be known to everyone as one of the most important members of the group.

Soraya showed no fear when she was doing a mission. It was almost like she closed the world around her and only concentrated on her mission. Mohammed was proud of her and cared for her more than he wanted to admit. She was at his side every step of the way, and they both made sure Nader was informed about everything they did. Her life was much too busy, and Oliver wondered why she was so tired all the time.

At the time, he was too busy himself with everything happening at the embassy and also at his company to get too upset. They had to consider closing the company if things got worse. That was something they never thought they would have to face.

The timing couldn't have been worse for Oliver. He was planning on going back to the U.S. to finish all his business with Kate, but was afraid to leave, thinking he might never be able to get back. The thought of leaving Soraya behind and not being able to be with her if something happened was more than he could bear, but it was something he had to take care of soon. The longer he put it off, the harder it was going to be.

On the other hand, Soraya didn't mind seeing Oliver leave then. It was the only way she could protect him from what was happening. At times, she hoped they would stop him from coming back. It was a thought that she hated herself for, but she knew how stubborn he was. If things got worse, he would never leave the country without her. She was nowhere near ready to leave her country and knew that as long as she chose to stay behind, Oliver would too.

Nader went to school every day and things seemed to settle down a bit. He was beginning to feel more confident and was getting anxious to get back to the group. Mohammed felt the same way and they discussed the timing for his return. The danger had passed, so they all agreed it was a good move on their part to be cautious and that now there was nothing more to worry about.

Of all people, Soraya was the most excited about his return. She couldn't wait to have her friend back at her side on missions. The following week Nader began his work, but they still took all the necessary steps to make sure nothing jeopardized the group and their safety. Soraya felt like a little kid having Nader at her side on their first mission after his return. He could clearly see in her face that he had a friend for life, and nothing was going to break what they had. It was a special bond that even they had a hard time describing. Mohammed was glad they had each other, seeing as they were both a little different and didn't make friends as easily as the rest of the group. They were good for each other, and did their best work together. They had a partnership, and everyone in the group knew they were inseparable. Nader had a new energy now that he was back, almost like he was charged up. He had some new good ideas that the group put into action, and they got great results. This was a new beginning for them, and they were all motivated by events that took place every day. Things were moving according to the plan. The government had a hard time keeping up with everything that was happening at the time. They began showing stress, which was to the group's benefit. The group used it to their advantage, making life very difficult for them. For the first time in decades, people felt a little sense of freedom, knowing the government couldn't be too hard on them. After all, they might need people's support when the time came. They couldn't get that by being too harsh on them. Soraya encouraged Oliver every chance she got to leave as soon as possible. He wondered about the reason behind her sudden interest. He knew she didn't like the idea of him being with Kate. She did feel insecure when it came to Kate, and that's what bothered him. She stayed down in her room most every night except for Thursday and Friday, using the excuse that school may close and that they had loaded them with work. The only way she could do it, she had said, was in her room where he would leave her alone. Oliver often took her to school in the morning and she didn't object, knowing Nader wasn't in a position to do that anymore. Oliver needed to discuss some things with her and used the opportunity one morning to talk to her.

"Once I get back from the U.S., we may have to push our plans up a little. I just wanted to give you some warning so you wouldn't be surprised if I come home and say let's pack;" "Is there something happening that I don't know about?" she asked with concern.

"No, nothing new. Just that my company may close if things don't settle down soon. As far as the embassy is concerned, I should leave if that happens."

"Are they concerned?"

"They are starting to be. You never know what may happen. We are always the first targets when things go wrong."

She knew only too well that they were going to be in danger if they didn't get the hell out of there soon, but she didn't know how to tell him that without getting him suspicious. She decided to talk to Nader and Mohammed that day and ask them for some advice. They arrived at school and decided to finish their conversation that night after they both got home. He kissed her good-bye and she watched him drive away, feeling so vulnerable. Her double life was getting out of her control, and she couldn't find a way to tell him the truth without taking the chance of losing him. There was so much to work out. As she went to her class, she brought her thoughts with her. She was unable to concentrate; all the upheaval was taking its toll on her. She looked at her professor but didn't hear a word he said. Almost in a daze, she felt like she could close her eyes and fall asleep right there behind her bench. A sudden sound almost gave her a heart attack. The door to their class flew open and army guards poured in with their machine guns. They took everyone by surprise and they all let out screams from the shock of the broken silence in the classroom. No one knew what was happening and they all tried to take refuge by hiding themselves behind their desks.

Soraya was horrified as the men took their places and pointed their guns at them.

Two men in suits walked closer to the students and looked at everyone trying to identify a face. Her heart was pounding, and she felt numb throughout her body.

The two men spotted Nader immediately and called out, "Arrest this son of a bitch!"

The guards flew over to where he was sitting and yanked him away from his desk. His face turned as white as the pages in front of him. They picked him up like a feather, and he didn't resist their arrest knowing it would be useless. Soraya was in shock. She didn't know what to say or do.

"Oh dear God, no, not Nader," she whispered. She just sat there trembling. They got what they wanted and ordered the whole university to close down until further notice. Everyone ran out into the hallways.

Soraya, sobbing, ran outside following the bastards. Nader was being dragged by two men. He turned and saw her standing there crying hysterically. He gave her a wink and a faded smile, and she crumbled.

"Oh my God, please let him free." she fell down to her knees crying out, knowing God was not hearing her.

There was so much commotion that no one noticed her sitting on the floor, holding her books, and already mourning for her friend. She saw his eyes saying good-bye to her, and she thought it was the last time she would ever look into those eyes that she trusted so much. They took him away from her. Her friend was gone and there was nothing she could do but cry and feel the empty world around her. Every time she remembered his eyes and the way he looked at her one last time it broke her heart. It hurt so badly that she wanted to take her heart out and live forever without one. Her professor came to her and lifted her to her feet.

"My child, you have to go home. You can't cry like this. There are still guards here and they might get suspicious of you. Wipe your face and go home," he whispered.

She began walking down the hall, not caring if anyone saw her cry, tears rolling down her face as she took each step. She never had a chance to say good-bye to him, never had a chance to tell him that she loved him so much, that he was her friend. There was nothing to feel any longer but hate. She hated the whole world and everything in it. Not knowing where to go or what to do, she walked outside and noticed his yellow car parked on the side of the road. Walking closer, she gently touched it.

"Oh, Nader, I love you and I am going to miss you so much, my friend. I wish they had taken me instead of you; it would be easier to bear. Life will stink without you, Nader, my friend, God be with you, wherever you are. I will never forget you."

Her heart ached so badly and her legs could hardly carry her. She remembered other days in her life when she had felt the same, so long ago. She could hardly carry her own body as she entered a phone booth. Her hands were shaking as she pushed the buttons on the phone and called Mohammed. She broke down again as she heard his voice on the other end, sobbing.

"He is gone, Mohammed. We were wrong; it wasn't safe for him, and we didn't protect him."

He was shocked to hear Soraya's voice like that, and for a moment didn't know what she was telling him.

"They took him away. He is gone. Nader is gone. Oh my God, I can't take it any longer. I want him back in my life. I want him back, Mohammed. Please give him back to me."

He quickly got the picture and asked, "where are you?" He was trembling and knew she needed him right then by her side.

"I am right outside of the university in a phone booth."

"Stay right there. I am coming for you."

He left immediately and was there in less than ten minutes. He got out of the car, ran to her, and held her fragile body. They both cried.

"Come on, Soraya. Get in the car with me. People are watching us."

She got in the car with him.

"Tell me exactly what happened."

"They just came in like an army, stormed in the room and looked at all of us, and then spotted Nader. They dragged him through the hallways. He looked at me and smiled. I will never see my friend again, I just know it. He is gone just like Reza."

She began to cry again. She looked like a wounded bird and Mohammed didn't know how to comfort her. His face looked hard and bitter. He too had lost a friend, someone he could never replace. He reached over and took her in his arms.

"They will pay for this." "I don't want them to pay for this; I just want him back, to see him get in that little yellow car across the street and drive away.

Mohammed looked over and saw Nader's car still parked there.

"There is nothing I can tell you that will ease your pain. I have known him since he was a little kid. I knew his uncle, and this will devastate his family."

She stared out the window.

how I am going to deal with this."

"You will do what we all did when we lost Reza, be strong and move forward. That's what he wants you to do, to keep his dreams alive."

Mohammed started the car and pulled away. "We have to find out why they have arrested him. We also have to change our meeting place and find out if there is anything that will jeopardize your safety." She didn't even care. No matter what she did, every so often tragedy, would find her and knock on her door. There was no avoiding it anymore; it would find her and hurt her again. "I should not care for anyone in my life, because in the end, they are all taken away from me. I would be much better off. God has cursed me to care for anyone. He takes them away from me, one-by-one. My whole family was taken away from me beyond my control. Then my father, who I loved so dearly, died. I had to let go of my only child. And now Nader. They are all gone. They left my life and me behind. I am sure Oliver is next," she whispered.

Mohammed let her talk and get it off her chest. He felt sorry for her, knowing she had been through a lot of heartaches.

"I want you to take a couple of days off, stay away from the group, and take care of yourself."

"I don't want to stay away," she said in anger. "Those sons of bitches are going to pay for what they did. I want to be involved in as many missions as you can give me and have a part in everything that would destroy their empire."

"You could be a danger to yourself and others, working in this state of mind. Believe me, I know. I have been there before."

She was upset and ignored his advice.

"Are we meeting today?"

"Yes, but not at the same place. I have to tell the group about Nader."

"I want to be there when you do."

He decided not to argue with her.

"Okay, I will call you in two hours and let you know where to meet."

"Can you please take me home?"

He just nodded and drove her home.

She got the call from him two hours later and left the house again. There were a lot of people at the meeting and Mohammed asked them to close the door if everyone was there.

"I don't see Nader," someone said and everyone else agreed.

Mohammed looked down for a moment.

"He won't be here today. Actually, this meeting is for him. Savak arrested him today."

Everyone looked sad and disturbed by the news, and Mohammed went into details of how it happened.

"He was one of the most valued members of our group. He has been around for a long time, and he wouldn't want anything to stop this mission. He would not want his arrest, or even his death, to slow us down. His family is already aware of the situation. The good news is that we are almost positive by our sources that Savak doesn't know anything about the group. He was spotted putting a flier up on a wall at the university, which tells us the arrest was not related to his involvement with the group. I believe the group is not in any danger, and we can meet again at the same location."

Mohammed cleared his throat and continued. "We all know Nader; he will spit in their face, and that will be the only thing they can get out of him. I, personally, have no fear of him speaking and telling anything about our group."

Everyone looked grim. They all had a hard time believing that he was gone. It was something that could happen to any of them and they all sympathized with him and what he was going through.

Soraya quietly left the meeting. She could feel his absence already and wondered what he was doing at that very moment. She walked out, not knowing where she was going.

Mohammed saw her leave the meeting and decided to go after her. He found her walking alone and deep in thought. He called out her name, and she turned around.

"Do you want a ride?"

She waited for a short moment and then got in the car.

"Would you like to go somewhere and get something to eat?"

She shook her head saying, "no thanks. I am not hungry."

"How about a cup of tea or coffee?"

She thought for a second, knowing how close he was with Nader, and realized for the first time how badly he must be hurting; and maybe he needed a friend, too, on this sad day.

"Sure, I could go for that."

They didn't say much in the car. He stopped near a cafe and parked. They got out of the car and walked in and picked a small table in the corner away from the crowd.

"How do you deal with all this time-after-time?" she asked him sadly.

"It gets harder each time, and I get a little more bitter and a little more angry; but it never goes away. It stays with me. Time is the healer of all wounds. In time, I will heal, but the memories will never go away. For now, I just keep up with my life and do what I am supposed to do, basically keep busy."

"What do you think they will do to him?"

"You can't think about that. It will destroy you quickly. It will drive you crazy. You have to do your best to not think about it. Most likely, he won't be coming back to us. He won't see the day we've all been waiting for. And I would give anything to change that; but the fact is, you can never change reality. For now, we have to accept what has happened and go on with our mission."

More than anything, Soraya was angry. For the first time, she felt the same pain that they had experienced in the past and had a hard time dealing with it. She looked away and noticed the crowd of people around her and wondered if any of them were hurting as much as she was?

She turned back and looked at Mohammed, and asked, "do you have a family?"

"I don't have a wife or any children, but I have a sister. Her kids are my family.

That's the closest I have ever come to having one. I never got married simply because of my involvement with the group. It wouldn't be fair to put anyone through this kind of life, so a long time ago I decided not to ever get married."

"You have sacrificed a lot being involved with the group."

"There were certain choices that I made, and I don't regret any of them. What about you, Soraya? Do you have a family?"

"Yes and no. I have my mother and a bunch of siblings, and they all live in the village. I was what you call an outcast, and just like you, I don't regret that part of it. The part I regret is not seeing my family and not being able to watch my siblings grow up."

"Can you ever go back and visit your family?"

"I went back once when my father passed away."

He could see the pain and sadness in her eyes.

"Were you close to your father?"

Tears filled her eyes, and she smiled.

"He is forever my hero. His death was more than I could ever bear."

"How long ago did you lose him?"

"Not long enough to be healed yet, and I truly don't believe that day will come for me. He had dreams that never came alive, and I have always tried to live those dreams for him. And now I have to live with the loss of Nader. To me, he was so much like my father, a unique individual, someone you don't meet every day, maybe once during your lifetime; and I was fortunate enough to have met two. And now, they are both gone. I feel so empty. When I look at other people, it makes me angry that they don't feel the same kind of pain. I want the whole world to stop until I can catch my breath, until I am done mourning for my loved ones; but no one seems to even notice that a good man is not among us anymore and soon he will be nothing but ashes."

Mohammed listened to this young woman who sat across the table from him, whom he barely knew, and felt a special bond with her. He had so many of the same feelings, yet no one had ever put them into words like she had. They shared the same pain. He reached over and held her hand.

"You are a very special woman, Soraya, and I wish there was something I could say or do to make you hurt a little less; but I know only too well what you are going through. I just want you to know that I am here for you if you need me."

"I want to continue with my work, that's what you can do for me. Keep me on, just the same as always, so I can finish what he started."

He listened to her carefully.

"I don't want you to lose your focus. You can't forget the purpose of our group and our goals. Our mission is our first priority. Revenge is not the foundation of our belief. Our goal is to have a free nation and having casualties is just a part of the game. We can't go after anyone in particular for what happened to Nader. We have to terminate the system that is responsible for our losses. And if the system is destroyed, we can say our point has been made; and at that point, we can go on with our lives and swallow our pride. It is easy to go after the guard who dragged him through school and shoot him one day as he leaves his house, but we would accomplish nothing, except some personal revenge which means nothing and the war continues." He stopped talking and looked at her. "Do I make any sense to you?"

She nodded.

"Yes, you do."

But deep inside she was after one thing and one thing only, and that was revenge for Nader. An eye for an eye. Wasn't that what Nader told her once?

It was getting late and she had to get back to the house before Oliver got home from work. Mohammed sensed her concern right away and told her he was ready to leave. He dropped her off and wondered if any of his advice had sunk in. He was beginning to get to know her and knew she was a lot harder than he thought. He just hoped she wouldn't do anything foolish to jeopardize her own safety.

She didn't want to see Oliver that night and decided to go to her own room and stay there by herself.

The knock on her door came sooner than she expected.

"Are you okay?"

"I don't feel too well tonight. Sorry I didn't make it upstairs, but I just needed to get some rest. I hope you don't mind."

He looked at her with concern.

"Can I get something for you?"

She just shook her head.

"I will be fine. I just need to get some sleep."

"I heard on the news about the university closing down until further notice and that they arrested a young man, but they didn't give any names. Do you know who he was?"

"No, just some kid. I had seen him before, but didn't know him personally."

She hated keeping the truth from him and not admitting the truth about Nader. Denying the fact that she knew him bothered her. She wished it could be different.

"In a way, I am glad that school is closed. With everything that is happening right now, it's not the safest place to be. It always worries me, knowing you are in the middle of it all." Soraya looked at him sadly and replied, "you don't have anything to worry about, for now it is closed."

He could see the stress in her face.

"Get some rest and I will check on you in the morning."

He pulled her close to him and held her tight for a moment. She felt safe in his arms, knowing it would be the safest place for her. All she had to do was listen to his words and do as he asked and everything would be okay. But she knew it was too late for all that now. She had gone too far and there was no way back. There was a war going on within her own mind and she had a hard time stopping even that.

The room was so quiet. She looked around and shook her head and wished no one would bother her anymore, so she could sleep for days. She wanted to sleep away her pain and sorrow and only wake up when she didn't hurt this badly. Looking at the ceiling of her room, she remembered the day she and Nader had gone shopping together and his silly smile each time she tried on a new outfit. Then she saw his eyes when they took him away, the last faded smile on his face. There was nothing silly about that smile. He was trying to comfort her so she wouldn't hurt so badly, but knew only too well that this path of pain and sadness had just begun for her.

"Oh dear God, give me strength to make it through this. Give him strength also. Please don't let him die."

She was past the point of tears and was unable to go on with her praying. Tonight was not the right time to ask God for anything. She felt too much anger and didn't want to be angry with God. It was not his doing.

She thought about the night they planted the bomb at Taimoor's mansion. A couple of guards had lost their lives, and she had never thought about them until now. How did their families feel? How did they deal with the loss of their loved ones? They were just a couple of soldiers that were doing what they were told to do by their master, nothing more. She then remembered her own words.

"If my best shot hits a couple of innocent people, I will live with that fact."

She knew the fact was that this war was going to get bloody. People would die and families would be destroyed and those were the facts.

"Why couldn't she be just happy with her life? she wondered. Why couldn't she have listened to her mother and not gone to the pond? Why couldn't she just let things be and live her life like all the other people? Was she so different from everyone else that she created her own miseries in life? Why did she get involved with a married man and destroy his marriage? Why was it that anything she touched would somehow be ruined? Was she paying for all her sins in this world? Was this hell on earth? Would she have a different life when she died? Would it be better then? What about Oliver? What was going to happen to him? Was he going to be destroyed some day because he was a part of her nasty life?

She had no answers. All she knew was that her destiny somehow always steered her in the wrong direction and she had no control over it. It took her with it and demolished everything that was dear to her.

"I will not rest until justice is done, my friend. They will pay dearly for what they are about to do to you, and that is my promise to you. There will be more deaths and more sacrifices, and I will deal with them."

She closed her eyes and hoped to sleep for a very long time. It was the only thing she could think of, to give her any kind of comfort at the time.

Mohammed left Soraya that day, knowing the only way he could go forward, was to keep busy, and put many plans that he had talked to Nader about into action. That was the way he was going to keep his mind free of what was happening at the time to his best friend. And so he did. And when everything was ready a couple of weeks later, he decided to let the rest of the group in on his thoughts.

"This mission is one of the most important missions we have ever done. It is very dangerous and the risks are high. I want you all to know what you are doing and to have no fear. We are planning to destroy the Savak building and everyone in it. The funds are now available to us from other sources. We want to paralyze the center of their human sacrifices, the center of their whole operation. Without that, they will not be whole; and that is what we need to make it difficult for them to operate. From there we will, with the help of other organizations, start our revolution. In a way, it has already started, but this mission will give us some advantages, because it will crush their spirit, and that is what we need."

Soraya sat and listened to Mohammed. She felt a new energy within her, wanting to be in every way, a part of this mission. She wanted them to feel pain, to die in agony. In her mind, she had given them all the death penalty and wasn't satisfied with anything less. A couple of weeks had gone by since Nader's arrest and no one had heard anything other than that he was in a maximum security prison in connection with Savak. The group's sources would most likely never get close to those areas. The security was tight and there wouldn't be any kind of news leaking out, even though Mohammed tried his best.

The plan was very dangerous. They all knew their chances of survival were not very high, but they were willing to risk their lives. This time they weren't going to do the bombing in the middle of the night. It was to be done during the day when it would take down as many enemies as possible. Soraya was assigned to the mission and was given training and instruction on how to use a machine gun. She had been going through the plan with Mohammed over and over again to make sure nothing was left out. There were four motorcycles, a car, and a van to carry the members to their destinations. She was to ride in the car and help protect the man who was to set the bomb and Mohammed, was to help with setting it and placing it in the right spot. She was to carry the machine gun and kill anyone or anything that came close to them.

Everything was worked out in detail and they were planning to execute the mission in two days. The meeting ended and Mohammed walked over to her.

"Are you nervous?"

"I am looking forward to it," she said with a smile. "After this, they will know who they are dealing with. For the first time, they will pay for their crimes in the right manner. I am proud to be a party to this revolution."

She talked without emotion and he didn't know what to say or think. He didn't know her well enough to try to understand what was going through her head. He had not noticed the change in her the last few weeks, just that she was angry and broken down because of Nader. Beyond that he couldn't tell what was happening with her.

"You know the danger involved with this?"

"Yes, I do, and I don't want you to worry about me. We all have our own private lives that we have to deal with, and so do you, Mohammed. I am not any different from anyone else in this operation. We have ones who love us and who need to deal with everything if we don't come back alive. I appreciate your concern, but please don't give me any special treatment because I am a woman."

He nodded.

"You go home and get plenty of rest and we will meet again tomorrow."

He walked away from her and admired her courage. He had never met a woman like her in his life.

She decided to stay close to home for the next day and spend as much time with Oliver as she could. She realized those might be the last days she would spend with him. That night she made dinner for him and cleaned the apartment and washed all his clothes. Then she sat down and wrote him a letter explaining everything and left it in her room in case she didn't make it back.

Oliver was getting ready to leave on his trip to the United States. He had already talked to a lawyer there about his divorce from Kate. He had called her and told her that he was coming home for a short visit. Soraya couldn't think of a better time for him to be gone. Her involvement with the group was taking most of her time, and she didn't know how she would handle it if school was to reopen.

"Hi, honey."

"Hello, my love. What's all this, dinner cooking, the house all clean, my laundry all done? Are you seeing someone behind my back and doing all this out of guilt?" he said jokingly.

She laughed. "No, I was just bored and realized that I have been neglecting you lately. So I decided to get busy and do something useful."

It had been a long time since he had seen her in such high spirits, and it made him feel good. He was happy to see her so alive again. Lately, he didn't know what was happening with her. She was distant and depressed, and he just figured it had to do with school being closed.

They had a quiet and romantic night together. It brought back a lot of memories from their trip to Paris. She lay in his arms and stared at him most of the night after he fell sleep. She held him tight and kissed him in his sleep.

"I hope you don't have to ever read that letter, my love."

She touched the ring he had given her. It was hard for her to imagine how Oliver would react if something happened to her. She hoped everything would go smoothly, for his sake.

"I would hate to disappoint you this way. I wish there was a way I could sit you down and tell you everything. This would be the worst possible way for you to find out."

The next morning, she got up early and made him breakfast and sat at the kitchen table watching him eat. She had a hard time taking her eyes away from him. Would this be their last meal together, she wondered. She felt a little knot in her stomach. The thought of never seeing him again, and him having to deal with the reality of her double life tore at her heart. She held on to him by the door before he left and looked him in the eyes.

"I love you, Oliver. Don't you ever forget that."

"I love you too, sweetheart. Are you okay? You have been acting funny lately.

I hate to bring it up after such a beautiful night, but I am concerned about you."

She just smiled. "I am fine."

She kissed him again and then watched him drive away until she couldn't see him anymore. It was getting late and she had to get ready as quickly as she could. She opened the small box that Mohammed had given her and put on a bullet proof vest. Then she wore a blazer over it to cover up the bulk.

She walked out and found Mohammed waiting. Everyone was dressed and ready, as she sat up front with the driver. Mohammed and the other man sat in the back, holding the equipment. There was a second van which she hadn't known about, but was told about at the last minute. Her heart was pounding and the tension was starting to have an effect on her. No one said much in the car. Everyone was trying to concentrate and keep all their energy for what was about to happen.

It seemed like hours before they finally arrived at their destination. Once the drivers of the vans got out, everything was to happen quickly. She couldn't believe it was all going to take place within the next few minutes. She turned to Mohammed and looked at him. He looked back at her and nodded, closing his eyes for a short second. She held on to her machine gun as tightly as she could and waited for the other drivers. The vans parked within two hundred feet of the building. She saw the two drivers get out and walk to the back end of the van and open the doors. They then pulled out special slides that created a bridge all the way to the ground. Mohammed reached over and touched her shoulder, squeezing it for a short moment.

"Here goes, my friend."

Two motorcycles flew out of each van and drove straight toward the building. Within seconds, the four men on the motorcycles jumped off and left their bikes on the side of the building. Machine guns went off and the loud sounds of shooting made everything a reality. They created chaos and soon the area turned into a war zone. The guards were taken by surprise, but it didn't take them long before they responded.

Mohammed looked at Soraya one more time and said, "It's show time!"

Everyone got out of the car except for the driver. She began shooting all around her, making a safe path for the two men she was protecting. The guards were busy with the bikers and they entered the building with no problem and went straight to work. There was no time to waste, because of all the shootings in every corner. They quickly went to the second floor and found the public bathroom, which was located directly under the chief's office. She held the door closed while the other two went to work. She could hear screams coming from every which way. People were running out of the building and finding refuge. For one short second it reminded her of the day Savak had poured into her class and how all the students had tried to find a place to hide.

Someone tried to push in the bathroom door but soon gave up. She looked over to see how her comrades were doing.

"Almost done," Mohammed said. "Just hang in there, babe."

There was another push on the door and this time the person on the other side was more forceful. She let go of the door, aimed at it with her machine gun and began shooting.

"One more minute, Soraya. Just one more minute."

She heard the sound of a body hitting the ground on the other side of the door and turned her face, not wanting to see who she had just shot.

Mohammed jumped to his feet and screamed, "let's go!"

This time they were not carrying a bomb in their hands; instead they were holding machine guns. The building was surrounded by the group members and not too many people could get out. They ran through a sliding glass door, the sound of the crash was obnoxiously loud. They jumped over the bodies on the ground and ran toward the vehicles shooting at anything that moved. Two cars pulled right in the front gate. Mohammed, Soraya and the other man jumped in, and the second car pulled away within seconds. They then heard the sound of the explosion as they drove away. Everyone turned around and saw flames coming from the building.

They drove for ten minutes, hearing the sounds of sirens heading toward the building. They finally stopped at an auto shop. The doors were wide open as they pulled in, and the second car pulled in right behind them. Everyone got out of the cars. They had started with eleven people, but only six got out. They were missing five members. They all entered the room on the other side of the body shop. There was to be one more car in case anyone got out at the last minute before the explosion, but it should have been here by now. No one said anything. They all sat and waited. Mohammed never left the window. He stood there looking out and finally let out a scream.

"Open the door! The last car is here!"

The garage door opened and the last car pulled in. As they all ran to the garage, two more men got out along with the driver. They cheered with joy, even though by now they knew that they had lost three of their members.

One of the men was really shook up. They helped him inside and gave him a glass of water to drink. He sat down trembling.

"I had to shoot Naser," he said, referring to his friend. "He was shot, but still alive, and I tried to lift him up, but there was no time left and he begged me to shoot him. He said he wouldn't make it. I closed my eyes and fired. I took his last breath."

The man broke down in a sob. They had lost three members, yet they all knew it could have been worse, and were all thankful for that at least. It could have happened to any of them, and they all realized that.

For now, it was their destiny to live, but there were other missions to come. The next time, it could be their turn.

They turned on the television and saw the burning building. There wasn't much left of it and what was remained of what was once called Savak was burning down. They didn't know the exact number of casualties. Once again it was described as an act of terrorism.

"So what else is new?" Soraya said.

She raised her glass of water and toasted. "Here is to all my terrorist friends. May God bless you all."

Mohammed looked at her for a moment and then looked away.

"Okay, we all go home now, back to work or whatever we have to do. This is not a time to celebrate. Today we lost three friends, and you should all go home and thank God for being alive. We will all meet again tomorrow."

And he once again thanked everyone.

He looked at Soraya.

"I will take you home."

She was especially cheerful, which didn't please Mohammed. Even though the operation was a success, he couldn't forget about the fact that he had lost three members that day.

"I don't want to go home yet," she said casually.

"Where do you want to go?"

"To get something to eat. I didn't eat breakfast this morning."

He looked at her in shock.

Are you celebrating something that I don't know about?"

"Of course I am. We got rid of a bunch of snakes today and I am thrilled about that."

"Well, I am not in the mood to celebrate. I hope you don't mind."

"Why is that Mohammed?"

"For your information, we lost three good men today. They are dead, Soraya."

"At least they chose their own death and didn't suffer a long agonizing death like what Nader is going through."

"This is it for you, isn't? This is nothing but revenge. Does our goal mean anything to you?"

"Of course it does, and we had both today. It could be you or me lying there dead, but it was our own choice. We all knew what we were doing. I left my house thinking I wouldn't be back; and I would be a liar if I told you that I am not glad for being one of those who made it out. But that doesn't mean I don't feel for those we lost today. I do, Mohammed; I really do. Today I felt a little more comfort than yesterday. I can't help the way I feel. It is like giving you the news that two of your children were in a car accident, one died and one lived. I will still thank God for the one who survived. I could have lost them both, and that's how I feel. My heart goes out to the ones we lost today; but at the same time, I don't forget the fact that this is like Russian roulette. It is a game of death. It wasn't my turn today, but who knows about tomorrow?"

He listened to her and wondered where all her anger came from. She was hurting so much, and he could see it in her face now; yet she played the game exactly as she was told to do. For the first time, Mohammed had a hard time playing the game he had created. He couldn't live up to what he preached.

"Keep your chin up and don't look back."

She on the other hand, did exactly as she was told, and it bothered him. He wondered if he'd created a monster who it was too late to change.

He turned and looked at her beautiful face.

"I am sorry. I know you probably hurt more than anyone else. You have the right attitude; I just hope it doesn't cost you in the long run."

She stood, staring at him without moving, and he came closer to her, not knowing how he really felt about this woman who stood before him. Suddenly he had a feeling that he had never had before. It was a new feeling, something that was foreign to him. He reached out and pulled her close to him and kissed her passionately. She didn't stop him, but let him take her. Her arms almost rose and then fell to her side. He stopped and parted from her, looking into her beautiful eyes, so mysterious, not knowing what she was thinking about, so motionless.

She stared back at him and said, "I could never belong to you. Don't allow your emotions to tell you otherwise. You and I could never be."

He reached over again and pulled her closer.

"But we are so much alike."

"That may be so, but we can't be."

"Soraya, your world is different from your American friend's. In the end, it will hurt you. We belong to the same world; we understand our culture; we share the same kind of God. We could be a lot more than you and he."

"My heart belongs to him forever. I have fought this forbidden love ever since the beginning, but it is not something I can control. I could never love you more than a friend."

He hated the way he felt. He didn't want to feel this way about her, knowing she belonged to someone else; but his feelings were not something he could contain. The first time he laid eyes on her, he knew this woman would steal his heart. He was a man of grace and character and there were many women who were after him. He was known to have many relationships, but he had never lost his heart to anyone before.

She looked him in the eyes, knowing this man could have anyone he wanted, but had picked the wrong woman. He was so strong and handsome, with deep black eyes. He wrapped his strong arms around her and pulled her close to him, feeling her long black hair, closing his eyes, and listening to the beat of their heart's against each other. Their eyes lock and their lips met again. It was a desire that they couldn't explain, and she knew it was wrong. It was losing control of the moment for her, and it was love being born in his heart. He kissed her with all his passion and she felt a rush throughout her body. He could have stayed that way for the rest of his life, but she knew it was a passing moment for her. She hated herself for that, but didn't have the strength to pull away, not until he was left breathless, and she knew it could get out of control. She was whom he had searched for all his life and never found. And now she appeared in his life, but he had no right to claim her; she belonged to someone whom he disapproved of.

"So, what happens now?" he asked.

"I think we should both forget what happened between us today."

"Are you telling me you didn't feel anything when I kissed you a few minutes ago?"

"It was a moment of passion for both of us. I don't regret it, but I know it could never be again."

"Is that what you want?"

"It is what my heart tells me, Mohammed. Maybe if I wasn't so in love with another man, but you see, it wouldn't be fair to you. I would hurt you in the end, and I don't want to do that. I respect you too much to do that to you and not tell you my true feelings."

"I don't need your respect. I need your love."

"My love belongs to another man. I am sorry. You could never love me; it would hurt us both."

"Why did you kiss me back and not stop me. What if I wouldn't stop and made love to you right here? How far would you let me go before you would put an end to it?"

She looked away.

"I don't know, but I am glad you stopped, and that's all that matters."

He looked away and then turned to her again.

"It is too late. I love you, and I will wait for you till the day I die, if that's what it takes. You can't stand there and tell me you didn't feel anything for me when I kissed you. I am not a child, Soraya, and you are not the first woman I have kissed; but you are the first woman that I have kissed and loved, and for that I will wait."

He took a step closer to her.

"I will never let my feelings get in the way, and I will respect your love for another man, but you can't stop how I feel for you."

Her heart went out to him. She remembered only too well the days when Kate was still in town and how she felt, knowing Oliver didn't belong to her and that she had no right to him. Those feelings were only too familiar to her. Now she was doing the same thing to Mohammed as was done to her.

"I am sorry, Mohammed. I don't know what to say to you. I shouldn't have played with your feelings this way. I guess I lost myself with today's events. It was all so emotional for me. I hope you can forgive me."

"Don't be sorry. This has been a very emotional day, but I don't want you to feel guilty for what happened between us. I promise that it will not happen again."

He grabbed her purse and handed it to her.

"I will drive you home if you promise to be a good girl and not attack me again."

And he laughed as he spoke, and it broke the mood and brought a smile to her face.

"Well, I don't know. You are kind of irresistible," she said, flirting with him; and he noticed her quick sense of humor.

They both walked out, and he looked over to her and smiled.

"Flirting is not banned, is it?"

She laughed out loud and replied, "hell no!"

The first thing she had to do was to destroy the letter she had written to Oliver. She still had a hard time believing that she was alive. It was almost an impossible mission, and they had done it. No one who knew her outside of the group could ever have believed that this beautiful young woman was behind the bombing that occurred that morning. She had no desire to listen to the news to find out any more details. She had done her job, and nothing else mattered. All she had to do was to sit back and wait for Oliver to return home and forget about everything else.

"Did you listen to the news today?"

"Yes, I heard about the bombing."

"I can't believe it. Savak headquarters, that's powerful stuff. Whoever is behind it must have some power and a lot of guts."

"Do you know how many people died?" she asked.

"No. They are still digging out bodies. The whole headquarters was destroyed with everyone inside of it, including the chief, himself. But that has not been reported yet. I found out through our own sources."

She was intrigued by his news.

"Are you sure?"

"Yes, I am. They could hardly recognize his body. I guess it was a bloody scene. How could anybody do this kind of thing? There were many innocent people there: secretaries, clerks with children, and mothers and fathers who were there to find out about their families who are kept in Savak prison. These people are destroying themselves. They are all bad signs. I think this country is going through a revolution, something that I never thought would happen here."

"Is the U.S. going to get involved if that happens?"

"I don't know. This is not our war. I don't see how we can get in the middle of it. The Shah appeared on television for a speech. They were showing the bloody scene of the bombing, bodies everywhere, the screams of families who rushed there to find their loved ones. Hardly anyone survived. The Shah announced that there will be a national mourning, and all offices and businesses are to close for two days. He sounded disgusted and promised to find the ones responsible for this gruesome crime that was done against innocent civilians. He said, it is time for our people to pull together and put a stop to this once and for all. As a nation, we owe it to our country and our land to see to it that justice is done. He went on saying that they already had some individuals in custody that could be from the responsible group."

Soraya immediately thought of Nader and wondered if he was one of them.

The phone rang and it was for Oliver. He talked for a few minutes and then hung up.

"I have to go to a meeting right now. I don't know when I will be done."

"Does it have anything to do with the bombing?"

"In a way, it does. Listen, sweetheart, I can't tell you anything. It is all for your own protection. Please understand that and don't be mad at me."

She nodded.

"I understand you have to do your job."

He kissed her and quickly left the house. Soraya often wondered what his involvement with the embassy was. Was he hiding something from her? Was he a spy for the U.S. government? She didn't know.

He never came home that night, which was very unusual for him. It made Soraya wonder even more.

The next morning, he rushed home and changed clothes, leaving in a hurry again. Soraya went to her own meeting and found everyone in a better state of mind.

Things were starting to happen fast, and people were beginning to be aware of the situation regarding the revolution. There were more talks about a man who lived in Paris and was challenging the Shah, and soon he appeared on B.B.C. sending a message to the Iranian nation. He got everyone fired up for a new Iran.

People were beginning to show signs of excitement, and that was about the time when demonstrations began in the streets of Tehran. It was something that that country had never seen before. They were peaceful demonstrations, but the government's reaction was harsh. The army would show up and begin shooting at the demonstrators and arresting many more.

People were starting to get fed up with the way the government handled the situation, and families were frustrated to have their young ones get shot at and arrested for something as small as a peaceful demonstration. Anger took over the country, and they fought back for the first time in decades.

The holy leader, who was known to everyone as the Ayatollah Khomaini, went on the radio station once again and sent another message to the Iranian people. This frustrated the Shah and his government to no limit. The radio was the only thing that he had no control over. Just about everyone had the kind of radio with a special antenna and could listen to the Ayatollah's messages. Whoever didn't own the right kind of radio went out and purchased one. There were daily demonstrations now, and everyone realized this was the beginning of an end for the Shah and his government.

Oliver was about to leave for the U.S. and was worried about Soraya.

"I don't want you to even leave the house unless you absolutely have to."

Soraya argued back, "I can't make a prisoner out of myself in my own country. I'll be fine. No one is going to do anything to me. Furthermore, I haven't done anything to cause you to worry like this."

"I know that, but you could be arrested for being at the wrong place at a wrong time."

"You have been hanging around with those embassy people for too long and are starting to get paranoid. Nothing is going to happen to me."

The Iranian revolution begun and no one could stop it any longer. Now the Freedom Fighters could sit back and watch it happen. They had done the impossible, and now the rest was up to the people.

The Ayatollah Khomaini was now sending daily messages to the people, encouraging them to speak out and not give up until they got the Shah out of Iran once and for all. Some people were confused. This was all so new and exciting to them. In a way, it was like a game, and they didn't know where it would take them. For the first time, they were obeying someone else besides the Shah, and it was a good feeling for them.

Before leaving, Oliver went through the details with Soraya of getting her a visa to the U.S. and putting enough money aside for her to purchase a ticket in case things got worse and he couldn't return. She packed the last of his things in his suitcase.

"Are you going to be okay when I am gone?" he asked her sadly.

"Yes, of course. It's only for two weeks. What do you think will happen in a short two weeks, a third world war?"

"I don't know, and that makes me nervous."

"Don't worry so much. I can take care of myself. You have to concentrate on your ordeal with Kate."

"To be honest with you, right now, that is the least of my worries."

"Give Ali my love and spend as much time as you can with him. Tell Kate I am sorry for everything. Tell her that she will always be loved in my heart, no matter how she feels about me from here on. Those are my true feelings for her, and they will never change."

The door bell rang. It was the driver to take Oliver to the airport. He held her close and Soraya looked at him with tearful eyes.

"I love you."

"I love you, too. Take care of yourself while I am gone, and don't go out."

She laughed with tears running down her face.

"Get out of here, you fool."

He kissed her one more time and closed the door.

The group was way too busy lately. She saw new faces every day, people she didn't know or recognize. But no one ever took the place of Nader in her heart. She thought about him often, almost every day. They hadn't heard anything, and there was a rumor that the government was letting some of their political prisoners go free. Everyone realized that it was just an act of desperation they were trying to pull at this late hour.

It was all too late, but she never gave up the hope of seeing him alive once again. Every day that went by, she thanked God for another day that he lived, even though she knew the kind of hell in which he was living.

She got dressed and left for another meeting. It was a beautiful day. The sun was so bright, it hurt her eyes to look at it. She felt sad in her heart, knowing Oliver was not there anymore, but Mohammed had such a full schedule for her that she couldn't possibly sit around and feel lonely. She entered the room. Mohammed glanced over and saw her right away. He left what he was doing and grabbed her arm.

"Come with me."

She followed him to his office.

"Have a seat."

She sat down and he walked over and closed the door. He knelt down by her and took her hand in his and looked her in the eyes.

"What's going on?" she asked nervously.

He looked down for a minute.

"I heard from Nader's family today. I am sorry, Soraya."

He closed his eyes so she wouldn't see his tears.

"Is he dead?"

"He's been dead for weeks now, and his family was never told. I didn't want you to hear it from anyone else."

She looked away.

"And I prayed for him everyday, hoping they would let him go."

She looked so broken down. He held her in his arms and they both cried for their friend.

"I am so sorry."

"I am sorry, too. He was your friend also," she told him with a sob. "Did his family get his body?"

"I am afraid not. There was an envelope delivered to his house with the news. Are you going to be okay?"

She got up and looked out the window.

"I don't know. Do you mind if I skip the meeting today?"

"No, not at all."

He waited a second and then added, "Would you like some company?"

"Don't you have to go back to the meeting?"

He just shook his head.

"They can handle it without me. I am entitled to a day of mourning for my friend. I'd like to take you to a place that may help you feel better."

She just nodded and never asked where they were going. All she wanted to do was to sit, keep quiet, and at times, shed a few tears, to look at the same streets that she once took with Nader and keep his memory alive. They drove for a while and neither one said a word, each in their own thoughts. Finally he stopped the car. He told her to get out. She just followed him and finally asked him where they were going.

"Is this where you live?"

He just shook his head. He rang the door bell and a few minutes later a middle aged woman, all dressed in black, opened the door. She looked like she had been through a lot, and as soon as she saw Mohammed, she flew to his arms and started crying.

Soraya stood back and watched. She didn't know whose house it was, or the identity of this woman.

"Come on in."

They walked into the living room. Soraya looked around, and for the first time realized where she was. There was a picture of Nader on the corner table. This must be his house, and this gentle woman was his mother.

Mohammed turned around and introduced Soraya.

"So you are Soraya. You are even prettier than Nader described."

"He talked about me?" she asked with a twinkle in her eyes.

She nodded.

"He talked about you often, and admired you. He said you'd been through a lot."

Soraya walked over closer to her.

"I want you to know how sorry I am. I know how hard this must be for you."

Nader's mother looked at both of them.

"And for you. I know you were all good friends, and this is a tragedy for all of us."

The maid brought tea for everyone. It was soothing for all of them to sit together and talk about the person they all loved so much.

"I knew he was involved, and I always prayed that he wouldn't get himself killed."

She shook her head.

"It is too late for that now. He died for what he believed, and I raised him that way.

I always told him to do what his heart told him, and he had a good heart. Nader was a good son.

"Mohammed, you were his hero. He admired you more than anyone else in his life, and he loved you so much."

Mohammed cleared his throat and said, "He was like a brother to me. I will never forget him."

They sat in the living room and talked for a long time. These were the people Nader was closest to.

"I am glad you two came by. Please don't make it the last time. Come visit me whenever you can. I am sure he would like that," his mother told them.

They talked about everything, happy times and sad times. They laughed and cried together and brought his memory back to life. Soraya thanked her for letting them come visit her and for helping her learn more about her friend. There was so much she didn't know about him, yet they were good friends.

"You two be careful. I don't want either one of you to go after revenge. We have the almighty God to take care of that sort of thing. And I don't want you to feel responsible and blame yourself for his death. If you do, forgive yourself and go on. He wouldn't want that for either one of you. He chose his own path, not you."

At the end of their visit, Soraya gave her a warm hug.

"Now I know where Nader got all of his wisdom. You are an incredible woman, and I am truly glad I got to meet you. I just wish this were under different circumstances. Thank you for sharing your time with us."

Mohammed held her for a long time.

"I want you to call me if there is anything you need. You haven't lost me yet."

They left her, both feeling so light and satisfied. They had needed to do that.

"Thank you for bringing me here. I feel so much better. She is a wonderful woman."

"I thought you might like to meet her. She is a rare woman," he said sadly.

They drove around for a long time, talking and getting to know each other. When he finally dropped her off at the apartment, there was a lot of uncertain feelings. He didn't want to feel this way about her, but it was too late. She had stolen his heart without even trying. She was on his mind all the time, and he never felt so helpless about anything in his life. He wanted to shake her and tell her that Oliver wasn't right for her, that it was a wrong kind of love. He wanted to protect her from a relationship that he believed would destroy her, but he wasn't sure his love for her was any better. He watched her walk away and take a part of him with her, a part that was forbidden for anyone to have; yet she walked into his life and took it, not even wanting it. It was a wasteful love and he knew that. She knew he loved her and wished somehow he could deal with it without getting hurt. What he wanted from her, she couldn't give. He was such a nice man, and she would probably have fallen in love with him if she wasn't so much in love with Oliver. Mohammed was the kind of a man you couldn't help but love; he was everyone's friend.

Every man in her life had turned out to be her life saver. She remembered how she wanted to hate every man on this earth, yet men had turned out to be her best friends; and that was amazing to her. She wanted him to be happy and not hurt, but didn't know how she could manage giving him that without offering herself to him. She knew all he wanted was her.

The apartment was so quiet as she walked in. The silence almost hurt her ears, and soon she found herself thinking of her lost friend. She wished she had had more time with him to communicate, to share, and to make more memories. Her memories with him were so limited.

Death was so cold and unknown. It brought out so many emotions that she didn't even realize she had. Every time she lost someone dear to death, it took a piece of her with it that would never be filled again. Death to her, was an emptiness. It emptied your body and soul. It ate your insides. Death was a disease for the living; there was no cure. There was no medication, and time could never heal your wounds. It would eat away your memories. You might never forget, but would let go of those precious moments. You would give up your right to your past with the ones you loved. So how could she go on living, knowing there were parts of her that were missing forever? She had to make do with what she had left, let go and move on to a new chapter of her life that didn't include the ones she lost.

"Don't shed a tear anymore. It won't bring them back. They will go down in the history of life as the dead. No existence, no life," she said to herself.

She didn't want to let go. She wanted to think about them every day of her life, bring their memories back to life somehow, tell the living of the memories with her lost ones, pretend they were still alive, talk to them and listen to her heart for the answers.

That's where she wanted to keep them, in her heart. As long as she lived, keep them there safe and sound, so no one would ever hurt them again, keep their memories alive in her heart. That's where they would be from now on, close to her body and soul, to fill the emptiness and to go on living. And she hoped someday, someone would give her a home in their heart after she died, so this circle of life could go on for eternity.

She let a faded smile take over her face and whispered, "you are home."

# CHAPTER ELEVEN

Kate stood by the airline gate waiting for him. It had been so long, and she didn't know what to expect anymore. He had a late flight, so she had left Ali with her mother. She wanted to be alone with him for the first night, due to the long separation.

There was so much she wanted with him that she didn't know where to begin. She knew of all the trouble back in Iran, and, in a selfish way, was glad of the timing, thinking she could now talk him into moving back home where he belonged.

She wanted Ali to grow up with his father close, and to give him everything she could.

He walked out of the gate area and she spotted him immediately, looking very tired. She flew to his arms and he held her tight. For some reason, he missed her, too; but not the same way she missed him. So much had happened and changed.

"I can't tell you how happy I am to see you," she said, wrapping her arms around him.

"It's good to be back home Kate. How are you doing? Are you feeling okay?"

"I feel great, especially now that you are home. We both missed you so much. "Welcome home."

Oliver didn't know where home was anymore, and it sounded kind of strange to him.

"Where is Ali?"

"I left him with my mother. He would have been miserable this late at night. You won't believe how much he has grown."

Oliver couldn't wait to see him, and he told Kate so.

"Are we going to pick him up now?"

"No, not until tomorrow. I knew you would be too tired, and I thought it would be a good chance for us to catch up."

He just nodded.

"How is Soraya?"

"She is fine. There is a lot of trouble out there right now."

"It's a shame. I have been listening to the news. Do you think the Shah may leave the country?"

"That may very well happen, but it will be one bloody day. They don't realize what may happen to their country in the future. I don't believe they are thinking straight. A revolution will take their country back a century."

Kate could hear the concern in his tone and wondered why he was so disturbed about a country that didn't belong to him. They picked up his bags and walked out to where she was parked. He smelled the air and couldn't believe he was home once again.

"It feels good to be back," he said.

"I am glad you feel that way, Oliver. I waited a long time to hear you say that."

He realized the situation with Kate was going to be a lot harder than he imagined from the moment he saw her. He didn't say much on the way home. She did most of the talking and knew he was too tired and blamed his silence on the long trip from Tehran. She finally pulled in front of a very nice looking house and stopped the car.

"This is a very nice house, Kate."

And he grinned, adding, "can I afford this house?"

"Wait till you see the inside."

He looked around as they walked in. It was beautiful, and he complimented her on the way she decorated it. He sat on the couch and stretched out.

"Can I get you something to eat or drink?"

He thought for a second.

"Do you have any beer?"

"Sure." She walked to the kitchen to get him a bottle and a couple minutes later she handed him an iced cold beer.

"Aren't you having one?"

"No, I think I'll pass."

She sat on the couch leaning against him.

"It sure feels good to have you home, sweetheart."

It tore at his heart, knowing soon he would hurt her badly by telling the truth and by disappointing her after all these years. He decided not to say anything that night, but to wait until the next day. They talked about different topics, and he almost fell asleep a couple of times, catching himself dosing off as she was talking. It was obvious to her that he was tired.

"Why don't we go to bed? I don't want you falling asleep out here. You need a good night's rest and will feel much better tomorrow."

They went to bed and lay next to each other. He was fast asleep before she had a chance to even say good-night to him.

She sensed something different about him, but couldn't put her finger on it.

Knowing how tired he was, remembering the last time she travelled all that way, and had practically slept for two days. She looked at him and knew this was the man she had always loved and nothing had changed for her. Though she was disappointed that he didn't make love to her that night.

The next morning, Oliver opened his eyes and saw Kate sleeping next to him. It felt so strange after all those years. He was so used to waking up next to Soraya. Not wanting to wake her, he got up quietly and left the room. It was a hard situation and he didn't know how to deal with it. He slowly closed the door so he wouldn't wake her up.

She slept with nothing on and for the first time in his life, he couldn't even look at her. The woman he had loved for so long was now a stranger to him, someone he cared for, but didn't love anymore.

It was a beautiful day. He quietly made some coffee and stepped out on the deck and sat there deep in his own thoughts. So much had changed, and he didn't know how to begin explaining to Kate that he didn't love her anymore and that he was willing to let go of everything they once had together. It felt so safe being there in a nice home with a loving wife and a child he loved for many more reasons. Was he ready to give all that up? Knowing he had no other choice, he knew what he had to do. He couldn't even think of a life without Soraya; she was so much a part of him and every breath he took. In the end, Kate would be the one with a broken heart, the one who gets hurt. The woman he protected from any harm for so long, he was now about to hurt; and he hated the thought of that.

"Good morning. What are you doing out of bed already?"

"Hi, I just couldn't sleep any longer. You were sleeping so peacefully I didn't want to wake you. I am sorry for last night. It was a long day, and I was totally exhausted."

"It's okay. Did you sleep well?"

He nodded.

"Just like a rock. Can I get you some coffee?"

"I'd love some. Thank you." She sat on a patio chair.

He walked over and kissed her on the forehead on the way to the kitchen. He hadn't shown her any sign of affection since he'd arrived, and she began noticing something was wrong.

It was time, and he felt nervous as he walked back outside and handed her the cup of coffee.

"When do we pick up Ali?"

"Whenever we want" she answered, waiting for something, but not knowing what.

He looked away and stared at the bright blue sky, not knowing where to begin?

She didn't like the feeling that had overwhelmed her knowing something was off.

"Are you okay, Oliver?"

"I'm fine." He smiled, and took a deep breath.

"Kate, you and I have to talk."

"I know that. It's been a long time, and we have to discuss a lot of things, Oliver. I want you to come back home. You need to think of our family now. It's not fair to any of us, especially with everything that is happening over there. It is not safe anymore, and I don't think you will lose your job. You have done your share and even more. Enough is enough, and they should understand that. And if they don't, then you should look for a different job."

Oliver cut her short.

"Kate, I want to talk about us and not my job."

Kate tried to avoid the issue.

"There is nothing to talk about, Oliver. We have a son who needs both of us, and we should put our problems aside and think about him first. I truly think if you come back, everything else will be solved. Things will go back to normal."

He grinded his teeth together.

"A lot has happened."

"I know that, but . . ."

He cut her off again saying, "please, let me finish. There have been a lot of changes in our lives that neither one of us had planned, and things will never be the same again."

Kate looked at him in disbelief.

"What do you mean?"

Oliver looked away for a moment.

"Kate, it's over for us and I don't know how else to tell you this. I am sorry."

"Why, Oliver? What is happening to us?"

And then she stopped for a second, thoughts racing thru her head.

"Is there someone else in your life?"

She was shaking as she said those words.

He looked away, not able to look her in the face.

"I am sorry, Kate."

"Is there?" she screamed.

"Yes there is."

Kate turned her back to him. She didn't want him to see her so broken.

"Who is she? Someone I know? Who is she? Tell me, I need to know."

Oliver closed his eyes clenched his teeth and whispered, "Soraya."

Her eyes widened. She couldn't believe her ears. Everything was spinning around her and she felt sick to her stomach.

"You should be ashamed of yourself, Oliver. She is twenty years younger than you. You could be her father!" And she broke into a sob.

"How could you, Oliver? Soraya? I don't blame her. She is just a screwed up little girl. But you, you should know better than to let something like this happen."

She was crying hysterically.

"I will never forgive you for this, ever."

He walked over to where she was standing and reached over to her.

"Kate."

"Don't touch me, you bastard. I don't want you near me."

"I am sorry, Kate. Please hear me out. I didn't plan it this way, and I wish you could believe that. I know you hate me, and I don't blame you for that. Sometimes, I hate myself. Please believe me, I didn't mean to hurt you. I tried to walk away from it, but I couldn't. I don't expect you to understand or forgive me. I can't forgive myself. It was time to tell you the truth; I just couldn't let it go on any longer. I am so sorry."

She looked at him in disgust.

"This is so unfair. I hope you can live with yourself after what you did to me. And as for Soraya, she gave me her child and then turned around and took my husband away. If you two think that was a fair exchange, I wish you both the best. Just remember, you two have a lot of guilt to live with. What are you going to tell Ali when he grows up?

Who are you going to tell him is his mother, me or Soraya? Have you thought of what this will do to him? Someday he will resent you both for what you did. He knows me as his mother."

Oliver cut her short. "Kate, no one will ever take that away from you. We want him to know you as his mother and no one else."

"Well, let me tell you something, Oliver. You look at him and tell me what you think. It's like looking at Soraya. He is a spitting image of her. Someday he will figure it out and resent her for giving him up. He will grow up being resentful toward everything. This will destroy him."

She was crying out of control, believing she had now lost her child, too. She was trapped in a situation that didn't leave her a way out. She stopped crying and wiped her face.

"Oliver, you have to do the right thing. I don't see a future for us anymore, but you need to think of Ali. He is an innocent child. You adopted him as your son and made a commitment to him, to protect him and be there for him; and now you must do what is best for him. Soraya can't be a part of his life. She gave him up and now has to stand by her commitment, and so do you."

"What do you want me to do, Kate?" he asked sadly, "Leave her? I have tried. We both tried, but we can't do that."

"You can't have it both ways, Oliver. It won't work. It will destroy our child. Think about that."

"I have," he said in a frustrated tone. "What if you and I broke up for other reasons? Are you telling me every child that goes through his parent's separation will not have a life? I don't believe that."

"Not every child would have his biological mother in his life," she said calmly, "and pretend that she doesn't exist."

"Kate, it could work. I am not planning on moving back any time soon. When all the trouble blows over, I will take a new assignment in Paris. He will visit me on some holidays and summers, or whenever you think it's best."

"Why even bother, Oliver? Why don't you just give him up altogether, like you did me? It's easier that way. Who are you doing this for anyway? For yourself or for Soraya? You won't be here to watch him grow up. You won't be here when he needs a daddy, or when he is sick. Oliver, you don't want him. You only want him for her sake, and I won't have my child being used like this. When you crawled in bed with her, you gave up all your rights, and that's a fact. I want full custody of Ali. I want you to give up all rights toward him."

"I can't do that, Kate."

He looked at her coldly.

"I love my son."

"No, Oliver. You love yourself first and then you want it all. I won't let you have him. I will do everything in my power to see to it that you are out of his life once and for all."

"Let me tell you something, and get it through your head. I am over there because my country wants me to be there. You and I both know the real reason, and the law will not take my child away from me for that. I am not asking you to give him up. All I am asking is to be a part of his life. That's all, and there will be no law that will take that right away from me, and we both know that."

It was the first time that Oliver hinted an admission to the real reason why he was in Iran. Even though Kate knew certain facts, they had never talked about it openly like this.

"I deserve to be hated by you, but don't do this to him out of revenge and bitterness toward me."

"You have done it all, Oliver, not me."

"Kate, I do love you, and that will never change. Can't we handle this in a good manner, for the sake of all the good years we spent together?"

"You destroyed those years by breaking your vows to me. It's over, Oliver, and I am not going to waste my time trying to save any of it. You are the one who walked away from it all. You chose her over me; and with that, you lost me and everything within me. I don't want you as a friend. I wanted you as a husband and a father for our son. There is nothing left for us."

"Kate, please don't do this. I know you are hurt and angry, and I don't blame you for that. Just don't close all doors on me."

"You chose your life, Oliver. I had nothing to do with it."

"I understand that, and now I am begging you to leave one door open so we can communicate for Ali's sake. I just want to be a part of his life. I don't believe that I am asking for much. I will be there whenever you need me concerning Ali. I promise you that. Please, let's not be enemies. What happens to you is important to me. Don't drag this through the court system and destroy whatever we have left. There is a part of me that will always be there for you. My involvement with Soraya has not taken away my sense of responsibility to you. I will support you financially and emotionally for the rest of my life. Please, at least think about it. That's all I am asking you."

"I need to think it over. At this point, I am not promising you anything."

He nodded and she left the room and closed the door, leaving him both relieved and concerned. He truly was worried about her and cared for her wellbeing. The whole situation had taken its toll on him and he felt drained and confused, not knowing how he felt any more. She had been more than just a wife to him, and for now he needed her friendship more than anything. It was hard for him to analyze everything that took place that day, but deep down, he wanted the best for her and was not willing to hurt her any more than he already had. There was so much that he wanted to tell her, but couldn't find a way to explain everything in the right manner. It had gone too far, and there was no way of turning back now.

He needed to call Soraya, but didn't want to call her from the house. He sat there for a while and finally decided to make a call to get a room in a nearby hotel.

Kate needed to sort out her thoughts. She buried her face in her pillow so he wouldn't hear her cry. She had lost so much and had a hard time accepting the fact that he loved someone else. Touching another woman's body and making love to someone else, it devastated her.

"How did all this ever happen? Was I so blind that I didn't see it coming?"

Soraya, who she cared for so much was the other woman. This was all more then she could handle.

"When did it all begin?" she wondered. Soraya was so much a part of her family. She had given Kate her child. At that moment, Kate wanted nothing more than to hate her, but found herself unable to do that.

She remembered Soraya's innocent face and all that she had been through. She felt controlled by her from a very far distance. Almost like a power that wouldn't let her hate the woman who took her husband away. Why couldn't she just hate her and hold her responsible for all her heartaches? Maybe because deep down in her heart, she knew that Soraya didn't mean to harm her.

"It must have been easy for her to fall in love with Oliver, as no one had ever shown her that kind of love before. She was raped and left to die and then cast out from her home, which left her pregnant with a child she couldn't care for. And I talked her into keeping him and caring for him and loving him and then turning him over to me. How can I hate her for never even questioning my motives? In the end, I ripped him away from her arms and took him where she could never see him again. Death would have been an easier choice for a mother. I left her with Oliver and let him pick up the pieces, and he did. dear God, what have I done?"

Then she stopped herself.

"I can't blame myself for this. I didn't do anything wrong, and I am not the one to be rebuked."

She knew Oliver wasn't the type of a man to go chasing after anyone, unless he felt there was no other choice. She couldn't let anger and hate destroy her life. She had Ali to think of, and no one was going to take him away from her. Down deep, she knew that. It was going to be so hard for her knowing Oliver was out of her life and she would never have his love. No one would ever take his place in her heart, and life would never be the same again. He was a good man who was confused. Maybe someday he would even see things differently and come back to her. In her eyes, he was worth waiting for.

"I am not willing to give him up, not yet."

She loved him so much, and knew in the end, no matter how hard she tried, she could never hate him or let go of him. She stayed in her room for a long time and finally decided to come out. She found Oliver sitting there waiting.

He sat up when he saw her.

"Are you okay?"

"I have to be," she answered, taking a deep breath. "Do you want to go to my parents and see Ali?"

He nodded, and walked toward her, taking her hand in his and pulling her close to him, wanting to hold and comfort her. She didn't fight back this time. He held her close and touched her soft hair. She felt so safe in his arms and wrapped her arms around him and suddenly began crying.

"What am I to do without you?"

He was choked up, too. He couldn't bear the thought of leaving her, knowing how hurt she was. He held her tighter, his tears falling on her face, mixing with hers.

Looking into her eyes, he kissed her on the cheek and said, "I never wanted to hurt you. I am so sorry for putting you through all this."

She stared into his eyes, hoping he would kiss her. It didn't take long before her wish came true and their lips met; and before they knew it, they were kissing each other passionately. Oliver wasn't thinking and let Kate take over. He closed his eyes and put everything out of his mind. Kate acted aggressively and soon unzipped his pants and began stroking him. He tore open her robe, lifted her up, and took her to the bedroom and laid her on the bed. Soon they were making love and couldn't stop. She had waited so long for this moment, and now she had him in her arms and in her bed. Nothing else mattered to her. It was a moment of passion for them and they never stopped and questioned themselves until it was too late.

He laid there, staring at the ceiling and wondering what it all meant. Was this just a passion that he couldn't control or was it that he still loved her in his heart?

"How can you make love to me this way and tell me you love another woman?"

He looked away.

"I don't know, Kate. I just don't know."

She got close to him again and held him. He held her too and gently stroked her arm, thinking of Soraya. Am I in love with both these women and unable to control my feelings?"

He looked at Kate lying in his arms and wondered if he could make love to her again. Was this out of guilt? He didn't ever want to feel that way about her. There was too much respect in his heart for her to let this go on, and he got up and sat on the bed, looking sad and confused. Not able to look at her, thinking she may read through him and find out what just went on in his mind.

He took a shower and got dressed. They were going to her parents to see Ali. She noticed how everything was neatly packed in his suitcase and knew that Soraya had packed for him. She got ready and saw him pack everything back in his bag.

"Aren't you going to unpack your things?"

"No, I think it is best if I stay in a hotel. I am sorry."

"You can stay in the guest room if that's what you want."

"Kate, what I want is to stay in a hotel," he said.

He didn't want to think about what happened earlier. He wanted to pretend it hadn't happened and that it would never be repeated, feeling ashamed.

"I don't want my parents to know anything yet. I will tell them after you leave."

This he didn't mind. He didn't want to have to explain everything to them.

They left the house a little later to go and see Ali.

"Hello, anyone home?"

He saw a small boy running toward them. He threw himself in Kate's arms. She picked him up and said, "Hi, my darling. Mommy missed you."

"Hello, Oliver. Welcome home."

Oliver walked over and hugged his mother-in-law.

"Hi, mom. How are you doing?"

"Keeping busy with your son. He is a handful, I tell you."

Kate was right. He looked so much like Soraya. Oliver looked at him and saw Soraya staring back at him. It brought tears to his eyes, knowing here was a part of Soraya so far away in a different country.

"Hi, sweetheart."

Ali raised his arms and in a child's way said, "Daddy."

Oliver took him from Kate and held him close and kissed his chubby face.

"I missed you so much. Look at how big you are. I love you."

"I love mommy," Ali said with a smile.

"Do you take good care of mommy?"

Ali tried to get down and Oliver followed him. Kate stood back and watched them together and wished things could be different. She wanted them to be a family again more than anything else. Oliver spent the whole day with Ali. He was such a cute little boy, and Oliver wished Soraya could see him, too. His eyes looked so much like hers, and his smile, it was like watching her smile through his lips, an incredible similarity. Oliver picked him up in his arms and went for a walk. Kate just watched them together. Was he thinking of her holding his son, she wondered. How could he not see the resemblance between the two. Looking at him was like Soraya looking back at you through his eyes and smiling through those lips.

Her mother broke her train of thought.

"Oliver is sure quiet. Is everything okay?"

"He has a lot on his mind with everything that is happening over there."

"Is he moving back home?"

"No, not for a while."

Her mother just shook her head and walked away.

"I didn't think so."

They left the house and Kate dropped him off at the hotel where he was planning on staying for the next couple of weeks. Her joy had lasted such a short time. She knew, for now, she had lost him and there was nothing she could do about it.

He walked into his hotel room and sat back on a chair, thinking of everything. He missed Soraya so much and wished he could just fly over there and hold her in his arms and tell her that he was sorry and ask for her forgiveness, not able to forgive himself for what happened that morning.

"How did it happen?" Was it just a moment of lust? I promised her that it wouldn't happen, and I didn't keep my promise to her. She can never find out. I could never tell her."

He knew it would never happen again and decided to lock it in his memories and never think about it again. With that he picked up the phone and asked the operator to assist him in making an overseas call. The phone rang a couple of times and then he heard her voice on the other end.

"Hi, sweetheart."

"Hello, Oliver. How are you?"

"Okay."

He sensed something was wrong.

"Is everything okay?"

She didn't want to tell him about Nader yet.

"Everything is fine. I just miss you so much. It's lonely here without you."

"I miss you, too, my love."

"How is Ali?"

"He is wonderful. I wish you could see him. He looks just like you."

"He does?" she asked with surprise.

"Your eyes and smile, and of course your beautiful black hair."

She liked listening to him talk about Ali. There was so much she wanted to know about him

"How is Kate?"

"I told her everything. At first she was angry, but she eventually calmed down. She is doing fine."

She didn't know what to say. In a way, she was relieved. There was so much happening in her mind at the time that she didn't know who to feel sorry for.

"You sound so sad. Are you sure everything is okay?"

"Everything is fine. You don't have to worry about me, not with what you had to do today."

She went on reassuring him that things were just fine. He told her to wait for his call in a couple of days and put the phone down.

There was something especially sad in her voice and he couldn't decide what it was. There was so much he still didn't know about her. She never brought home any friends, and he saw her as a loner and that made him sad knowing he was all she had in life. It was time for her to come out of her shell, and he was going to see to it once he got back. He wanted to be more involved with her life and get to know some of her friends, like Nader. Also, he'd take her out more and introduce her to some of his friends at work. They knew he had someone in his life, but didn't know who she was. He promised himself to change things once he got back to Tehran.

The next ten days, he spent as much time as he could with Ali. Kate was very supportive of that, but kept her distance, knowing there wouldn't be another close moment for them. Her pride stopped her from pursuing it.

Oliver talked to her some more about his plans for the future, and she told him to wait and give her some time to think about everything. She wasn't ready to rush to a lawyer and file for a divorce yet. He understood her position and decided not to push her yet. It was all so strange. The next time they would meet they would probably be divorced, something they never thought could happen to them. They were the kind of a couple that everyone envied and wished they could have what they had. Now there was nothing left of it, and soon Ali would be their only tie to each other.

He was leaving in a couple of days, and this time he really would miss his son. Ali called him daddy and was old enough to put a face to the name and hopefully remember him. Kate had made some decisions of her own. She was not going to take him away from Oliver, but knew he had to come to the States in order to see him. She would never allow him out of her sight; and she told Oliver that, one day when it came up. He understood and didn't argue with her. After all, why should she trust him and send her child to a different country? Kate was depressed as the time got closer to his departure. There was so much she didn't understand, and she couldn't get any answers from Oliver. He was very private when it came to his relationship with Soraya, and that's why she decided to wait and hope it would be a temporary relationship. Maybe he would eventually come to his senses. It broke her heart to know that soon he would leave, and she had no way of explaining it to Ali. He was still too little to understand anything like that.

They stood near the gate at the airport.

"Call me if you need anything. You know that I will always be there for you, no matter what."

She looked away, her eyes filled with tears knowing this time was the final good-bye. He hugged her one more time and walked out of her life, not knowing what might happen or what their destiny was. She gave up all her rights to him; and, for the first time, she felt the same kind of pain as Soraya had when she let go of her child.

Kate had never revealed the real reason why she wanted to leave the country, never told even Oliver that she had a fear that Soraya may change her mind one day and want her child back. Now that secret came back to haunt her. It was a risk that she wasn't willing to take, not even at the cost of losing the man she loved. The only thing that mattered to her was getting to the safe grounds of her own country where no one could take her son away from her. What if she had made different choices?

Would that have saved her marriage and future with Oliver? There were so many unanswered questions in her mind that she decided if she had to do it all over again, she would do anything to protect her son, and that was the bottom line. In the end, she had her son with her, safe and sound. No matter what happened, she would get to keep him and watch him grow up and forever have his love. That was all she needed, to go on and someday build a new life for herself, at home where she belonged.

Oliver sat in his seat, not knowing what would happen next. He was going back to a place that was called the trouble grounds of the Middle East now. If the revolution took place, it could change so many things that he had no control over.

This was a new chapter, leaving Kate behind and starting a new life with Soraya in a faraway country where their love was not accepted. He thought about his son and how hard it was to let go and leave him behind. That was something that Soraya had had to do without ever knowing if she would get to see him again. They had put her through the unthinkable, but it was expected of her to deal with it, to turn her feelings on and off and never question their motives. She was expected to love and then let go of the ones she loved and let it be nothing but memories. His heart ached for her, knowing how hard it was for her to hold her son one last time and then lose him to the unknown future.

# CHAPTER TWELVE

She was calm and in control. Everyone was quiet and anxious to hear her. They had never heard a woman give a speech before in their circle, and they found it odd to listen to her. She began and there was a special power in her voice that made the whole room go silent. They could hear themselves breathe as she began.

"His father was a military man. They were just middle class people like you and me, nothing more and nothing less." "Mohammed Reza Pahlavi, the Shah, is one of the top ten richest men in the world and also one of the most powerful men in the history of our world today. Where did it all come from? How did he acquire such wealth? Have you ever thought about that?

How did it all begin, and how did he buy so much power?" "Think about that. Iran is one of the biggest middle eastern countries. Size wise it is bigger than most European countries. He owns every inch of it, and everything within the land. He is the sole owner of our country, and it all belongs to him. As a matter of fact, he owns all of us and everything we have, no matter how big or small our possessions are, our home, our jewels, our cars, and even our children."

"He controls it all, and no one can question anything he does, or they will be destroyed. He owns our country's biggest resources, our oil; yet you and I have no right to it. We buy gas and heat our homes for the same price as other countries who buy our oil and then sell it to their people. We have no right to our oil."

"Half of our country lives in poverty and have no education. Of course we all know that he puts up a good front stating that he is educating our people and opening schools in the villages; but learning the alphabet won't feed a family of ten." "They need more than that, but it will not be available to them because it is too costly. A man who feeds his family nothing but broth and bread buys the oil to heat his broken down shack for the same price as you and I and the shah. He has to survive the bitter winters. His choices are limited." He eats less so that he and his family don't freeze to death. I am telling you all this from personal experience. Until just a few years ago, I was a child in a family like that. We are being used. Our nation suffers and our leader makes diplomatic relations with other western countries. He lives like a king and calls himself one, but in reality king of what? If you can imagine. It's as though we all stuck in a bottle, and if we breath too deeply he will put the top on and suffocate us. We have to get out of this bottle one-by-one and take a deep breath and look around us and decide for ourselves if we live in a world that is fair to us and our people."

"Don't be selfish. Don't look down and walk away. Stop! take a look around you and lift up someone next to you who needs help getting out of the bottle."

"This way of life is unjustified and heartbreaking to me and many more like me who lived their childhood never knowing what that was. Mine passed me by so fast that I chose not to keep any memories of it."

"This is an unfair war between them and us. We must hold each other's hand and break the bottle once and for all. We need to free ourselves and our nation from his evil. You need to go out there and break all the bottles and give everyone the freedom they deserve. We need to free our people, and we can't do it without your help. To be united and pull this together, we have to act as one. We have to do it for all the people who lost their lives and will not see the day this nation is finally on its own. Let them see it through your eyes. Let them rest in peace, knowing their lives were not wasted. God bless you all."

She stopped talking, and everyone was touched. Her speech had a strong impact on all of them; and they all liked and respected this quiet but strong young woman a little more. Mohammed was touched as was everyone else. He stood back and looked at her and knew why he was so madly in love with her.

She had kept very busy the last ten days and went on several missions. There was no doubt in her mind that there would be a revolution sooner than anyone thought. There was no way to stop it now.

Uprisings were happening everywhere. For the first time, people had no fear to shout out their emotions. The Shah was on television every other day urging people to stop and not let these radical groups get to them and ruin their country. No one was listening. It was too late. He was even beginning to get the picture himself.

Oliver was to come back that night and Soraya was ecstatic. She missed him so much. It couldn't have been a worse week, with him being gone and then Nader's death. She had to tell him about Nader, but hated the fact that she had to make a story about his death. She left the room after the meeting and as she got ready to leave the building, Mohammed stopped her.

"It was a very good speech, Soraya."

She smiled and looked down.

"I was a little nervous."

"It wasn't obvious to anyone. You seemed in control."

"I just hope everything I said sunk in. There are so many new members in our group; it's hard to tell."

"You seem to be in a good mood today. Is there a special reason for it?" Mohammed asked. He knew Oliver was coming back that evening, but wanted to give her a chance to tell him.

She smiled again and said, "in a way, I am."

But she didn't give a reason.

Mohammed liked to see her smile. It was something she didn't do very often, and he decided not to pursue it. In a way, it made him jealous of Oliver, wanting more than anything to be in his place.

"Would you like a ride home? I am going that way anyway."

She accepted his offer. After Nader's absence, she didn't have anyone to talk to, and Mohammed was always a reminder of her good friend. She didn't mind spending time with him every now and then.

They got in the car and drove away.

"So tell me, Soraya. Have you thought about what you are going to do after the revolution?"

"What do you mean?" she asked, surprised.

"You know, as far as your relationship with Oliver."

"We have talked about it, but it is too early to tell what may happen."

"Are you going to leave with him?"

She didn't know how to answer him that.

"I don't know. Maybe not right away."

"Is he planning on leaving anytime soon to go back home?"

"At some point he will. I just don't know when that would be."

"Do you want to leave with him at that point?"

"I guess so, but right now I want to stay right here and see what happens."

Mohammed wondered what she really wanted to do, but it was impossible to get it out of her.

"Why do you want to leave a country you are fighting so hard for?"

"I don't know. He means a lot to me, and I don't know if I can live here without him."

She knew where Mohammed was going with his line of questioning and decided not to beat around the bush.

"Mohammed, I know you have feelings for me, but that is not good for you. It will hurt you someday. I can't give you any promises or commitment, and I don't think you should give yourself any false hope. Most likely, I will leave with Oliver someday, but I don't know when that would be."

"Is he planning to marry you?"

Soraya didn't want to talk about all that with him, but didn't see a way out.

"Yes, he is."

"I just hope you know what you are doing."

She knew there were too many things to work out, and he was asking her things that she didn't have answers to yet.

"I don't. I am not looking for the easy way out. It could be much easier for to cut my involvement with the group and just leave with him, but that is not what I have chosen to do. I understand my obligation and want to do the right thing, but at some point in my life, I am going to do the right thing for me. I will go with my heart and do as it tells me.

"I don't know how he would react knowing I was involved in the Savak massacre or many more missions. In his eyes, the ones responsible for the bombing are nothing but a bunch of terrorists. He doesn't realize that he is in love with one of those so-called terrorist. Who knows what he may say to that? He will probably walk away from me, and I'll have to deal with that then. If he still wants me, I guess I will go with him to wherever he takes me."

It tore at Mohammed's heart knowing someday she would be gone but he didn't want to think about it right then. It pained him too much. He was now in front of her apartment.

She turned to him, wanting to talk to him once again about the way he felt about her.

"Mohammed, I know how you feel. It is obvious to me and even others in the group. I don't want you hurt. You are my friend like Nader was, and my friendship is all I can give you. Please don't try to make anything else out of it."

He looked away.

"Don't you understand? I want the same thing for you, and I know someday you will be hurt. You don't belong to his world."

"Maybe not, but I have to do my best to make it work, simply because I want it that way."

She stopped talking for a while and then leaned over and kissed him on the cheek.

"I want you to be happy, and I will only hurt you. Go on with your life and forget about me. You deserve someone who could return your love, and I can't be that someone."

There was so much he wanted to tell her but couldn't. He didn't want to lose her, not yet. He had to just wait and be there when she needed him, and he believed in his heart, that the day would come. It made her sad knowing he was trapped within his own mind and emotions and couldn't get out. She knew being honest with him might hurt him at first, but it was the only way for her to let him go.

Oliver got in a taxi and sat in the back seat, looking at the city that was about to go through a lot of changes and didn't know how they would affect his life. There were so many things floating through his mind. It had been so final with Kate. He had said good-bye to the woman he had loved and known half of his life, not to ever love her again or share his life with her. He forced her out of his life and now he felt that he had lost his best friend of many years. It was a sad day for him, and he knew exactly what he had put her through. He felt so empty and wondered if that emptiness would ever be filled again. The reality had finally hit him, and he experienced a pain that he didn't think would leave anytime soon. The taxi stopped and he got out. Standing in front of his apartment, looking at the door, he thought of the other woman who was sitting on the other side, waiting for him. She was someone who had changed his life from the moment he first met her, and now he couldn't exist without her. She had become so much a part of him that he had a hard time understanding it. He quietly opened the door and found her sleeping on the couch, waiting for his arrival. He put his bags down and slowly walked toward her. He had missed her so much. She looked like a child, sleeping there so peacefully, so innocent. Never in a million years could he dream what this innocent child had done or become.

To him, she was just a young woman who needed more than anything to be loved and feel safe, and he had provided that safety for her. He leaned over and gently kissed her. She moved her head and slowly opened her eyes. Looking at her, he still couldn't believe how much Ali resembled her.

"Hi pretty lady."

And for a moment, she thought it was a dream. She had almost been thinking in the back of her mind that he may never return to her. She smiled.

"You are back."

He knelt down by the couch and held her in his arms.

"I never want to be apart from you again."

He kissed her passionately.

"Neither do I," she said, responding to his kiss with even more passion.

They sat right there holding each other, neither one wanting to break the silence, enjoying each other's company, and wanting it to last forever.

She knew how tired he was, but there was so much that she needed to know about his trip.

"Did everything go as you planned?"

He nodded, not wanting to discuss with her all his feelings that were tearing him apart. Suddenly he noticed how pale and thin she looked.

"Are you losing weight?"

"I don't know. Why do you ask?"

"You look so thin and drained. Have you been eating much lately?"

She shook her head. "No, not really."

"Is there something you want to tell me?"

Soraya looked away.

"I didn't want to tell you when you were away. I lost my friend Nader the day you left for the U.S."

"What do you mean, you lost your friend?"

"He died," she replied, and she looked down with tears in her eyes.

"How did it happen?"

"He was shot during a demonstration and didn't make it."

Oliver was disturbed by the news.

"Who shot him?"

"I don't exactly know, either the police or the guards."

"Was he involved in anything?"

"I guess he was. I don't know much about it. I heard it from a friend. I called his house and talked to his mother, and she told me it was true. He was a good man and my only friend." Oliver shook his head.

"I am sorry. It must have been awful and I wasn't here for you. Did you know about it the first time I called you?"

She nodded. "Yes, I did."

"I knew there was something wrong. Why didn't you tell me?"

"You had so much on your mind, and I didn't want to worry you."

"Is there anything I can do?"

"No, he is gone now and nothing will bring him back."

She sounded disturbed. Oliver looked at her, doubtful.

"Did you know anything at all about his involvement?"

"No. All I knew was that he didn't like the government. I just gathered that information from the way he talked at times. He kept to himself most of the time."

Oliver felt sorry for her, knowing she had lost yet another person in her life.

"I am sorry about your friend. That's what I've been trying to tell you; it's crazy out there and you can't trust anybody. The government still has a lot of power, and they will get to whoever is against them, sooner or later."

She pulled away from him.

"I think their time is up. It's over for them; and sooner or later, they are the ones who have to hide and be afraid of their own shadows. This game is definitely over, and they lost."

He was too tired and she didn't seem to get it through her head that it wasn't over yet.

"Listen, Soraya. I know you've been hurt by your friend's death, but remember, they are still running this country; and right now things are a lot tighter than you think."

She smiled sarcastically. "Not for long, Oliver, not for long."

There was no way that he was going to keep quiet anymore, he had to know where she stood.

"I want you to tell me the truth. Are you involved in any way with this revolution? I need to know, because it could cause a lot of problems for us."

"Just because I have an opinion doesn't mean I am involved. But as long as you asked, let me tell you something. I hate them with all my heart. I hope to God this revolution takes place and destroys their filthy empire once and for all."

"That's fine. All I am telling you is to keep your mouth shut. You are to trust no one. Do you understand me?" She nodded.

"Yes, Oliver, I do."

This time she didn't care anymore. He had to at least know how she felt; and for the first time, she didn't feel bad for saying too much.

She went to the meeting the next day after Oliver left for work and found everyone in a state of shock.

"What's going on?"

"Haven't you heard the news?"

"No. What news?"

"Some people started a fire in a movie theater with many children inside. They locked the doors to the theater and set the whole damn thing on fire. All the children inside died."

"When did this happen?"

"We heard about it last night. The government is blaming the Ayatollah's group, and they are pointing fingers at the government, saying they did it to make them look bad in front of the people so that everyone would lose faith in them."

"Do you know who really did it?"

"No, but I know what our government is capable of doing."

Soraya was shocked.

"But little children. Oh my God, how could anybody burn down a theater knowing there were small children inside?"

She wondered what all this meant.

"If anything will set off this revolution, I guarantee you that this will. We have to use it and cause as many disturbances as we can among the people," Mohammed said.

"Tell me, Mohammed. Do you honestly believe the government has done this?"

"I hope they did. It would devastate me knowing the people we have trusted are capable of performing such a heartless act. Whoever is responsible has given us what we need. And I hate to tell you that, but it just worked out that we can use this tragic event to our benefit. No one would ever claim this. We are talking about children burning alive in a movie theater."

This tragic event was a true beginning for the Iranian revolution. People went crazy. It was easier for the people to blame the government than anyone else, and so it began. It took a few months and one hundred thousand deaths to complete the Iranian revolution. The day the Shah left Iran for Egypt, people shouted and screamed with joy. They took many more lives before it ended; the government troops fired at people with no guns in Shahyad circle near the airport and created a river of blood. After the Shah's departure, they renamed the circle Freedom Circle.

Soraya stayed active all through the process until it was completed. She was there in the middle of the whole mess. The final day was one that no one would ever forget. It left half the city of Tehran in mourning. Everyone knew of someone who had lost their lives, and it was a day that will be written about in the history of that country for many years to come. She cried for weeks after, unable to forget what she had witnessed on that bloody day.

Oliver kept very busy at work. All Americans were ordered to leave Iran by the President of the United States because of the hatred that was spreading throughout the country. Demonstrators walked around for miles and shouted, "Death to the Shah! Death to America! and Death to Carter!"

Many of them didn't even know why they were saying it. It was something that their new government had preached to them. Anyone who was a friend of the Shah was considered an enemy of theirs, and that's how they saw it.

The American embassy was under tight security. There were guards everywhere. Most American companies were beginning to close shop and go back home. That's what Soraya hoped Oliver would do, but he was not willing to do that, giving the excuse that they had a lot invested in their company there, and at least one person from the company should stay behind and protect their investment. Plus, he told her that he had a lot of friends at the embassy who would support him in case of any problem. Not for one moment did it cross his mind that anyone might have enough guts to attack the embassy of the most powerful country in the world. There were bomb threats every day, but that was to be expected. Oliver had too much faith in his government and their power. And he thought, in the end, things would work out.

The Ayatollah Khomaini arrived in Iran after decades of being exiled and people were all in favor of him, thinking he would change things. His religious background gave them the trust they needed to have him run their country and put a stop to all the unjust events that had taken place in the last decades. The new government and the Carter administration didn't see eye- to-eye on many issues. What had been called friendly relations between the two countries for years turned to hate and distrust.

Soraya didn't like the sound of what she was hearing and kept on telling Oliver it was time to leave, but Oliver was not willing to leave yet. She kept up her involvement with the group for Oliver's sake now. She had finished her mission; the Shah was gone and there was no reason for her to keep up her involvement with the group except for Oliver. Mohammed told her many times to talk Oliver into leaving.

"I am telling you, Soraya. His life is in danger. I don't care about any of those sons of a bitches at the embassy, but I know what it will do to you. Tell him to pack and leave as long as there is still time left."

"He doesn't think that it is up to him any longer. He said that if he tries to leave now, they would get suspicious of his reasoning for staying behind this late."

"Is everyone in his company gone now?"

"Yes. They are all gone except for him."

"Have you ever asked him why he didn't leave with them?"

She nodded.

"He tells me that he stayed to protect the interest of his company, and now he believes it is too late for him to leave simply because of his involvement with the embassy. He has been questioned by our authorities a couple of times regarding his position."

They wondered the same thing, wanting to know why he didn't leave when his company shut down. Mohammed was truly worried.

"The Americans at the embassy are going to be next. This revolution hasn't gone exactly the way I anticipated. They are slowly taking over and forgetting everyone who helped them along the way. Soraya, you have to tell him the truth. That's the only way you can protect him. He has to realize that you are not just making these things up and understand that it is coming from a reliable source. He should try to leave legally, and if he gets stopped, then at least we know, and I can get him out through the borders. But he has to know first where he stands. Don't tell me that I didn't warn you. They are going to go after every American in this country, sooner than you think. Go home and talk to him and convince him to leave. It is the only way to save him."

Soraya left Mohammed with a heavy heart, knowing what she had to do. She would have a hard time telling him the truth after all this time. The longer it took, the harder it got, and now it seemed so hard to go back and explain everything. She had wished it would be different and that it wouldn't come to this. There was so much doubt in her mind about the new government already. That made things so much harder, not wanting to hear him tell her, "I told you so." She had a feeling that Mohammed had the same feeling toward the new government. They had chosen the wrong path already, and it was obvious to many people. That night, she waited anxiously for Oliver to get home. He was coming home later and later each night. She never knew where to find him if she needed him for anything. He looked very tired as he walked in the apartment that night, and she wondered if it was the right time to talk to him.

"Oliver, we need to talk," she said with a concerned look.

He leaned back on the couch and looked at her with tired eyes.

"What's on your mind?"

She looked down for a moment. "I need you to listen to me, first. Let me finish what I need to tell you, and then decide for yourself. I don't even know where to begin. I wanted to tell you all this, but not this way. Now I am forced to involve you simply for your safety."

She took a deep breath.

"I have been involved in this revolution from the beginning. I have been a part of it all along. We were one of the first groups to start the whole thing. We did the bombing at Taimoor's house, the Savak headquarter explosion, and much more. We never thought it would come to this. All we tried to do was to free our nation and nothing more. Somehow things got out of hand and other groups got involved and it eventually turned into this mess. This is not what we fought so hard for. Our mission was far from that and has been destroyed right before our eyes. We lost control soon after Khomaini's group took over. What is happening today is not our doing anymore; but like I said, we lost control at that point. Oliver please, believe me, I am telling you all this because I am concerned about your safety. Things are happening as we speak that could jeopardize your life. Please sweetheart, listen to me and take yourself and get out of here. If you decide you can forgive me for keeping this a secret, then I will join you at a later date. I would understand if you couldn't find it in your heart to forgive me, but at least I will know that you are alive and unharmed. I beg you to leave as soon as you can. You are not a soldier, and this is not a battlefield. As a matter of fact, this revolution shouldn't concern you. It was our war and ours only. I am so sorry for not telling you this earlier, but I thought things would work out differently and I could tell you when I knew it wouldn't matter anymore."

Oliver was shocked. He couldn't believe what she had told him. He got up and walked over to the window, looking out for a couple of minutes, unable to even talk. She had done everything that was against his beliefs.

"I gave you many chances to tell me the truth and free yourself of this burden. Why didn't you trust me and tell me then?"

"The timing was not right. I did it for your own protection and also because of my commitment to my country. Listen to me, Oliver. I am not sorry for what I did, because I had nothing but the best interest of my people at heart. Our mission was done when the Shah left the country. I have to still believe that in time things will work out, but if you wait too long, you may never see that day."

"Tell me something. How about the theater incident; did you have anything to do with that?"

"No. Please believe me. We had nothing to do with that, and we were as shocked as everyone else at the time."

"What about your friend, Nader? Did you work with him at any time?"

She looked down and nodded.

"Yes. He was the one who first introduced me to the group."

"Are you willing to tell your story to a friend of mine and give us some information that may help us get our people out the right way?"

"You want me to spy on my own country. Is that what you are asking me? I could never do that to my people. Oliver, you are all I care about, and I will not use my friends and my people to spy for your government, who in reality has done a lot of damage in this land."

"And how do you figure that, Soraya?"

"Your country supported a dictator who killed and tortured his people. They knew what was happening here, but they turned their faces the other way. Hitler and the Shah had one thing in mind, Power. They destroyed anyone who was in their way. The sad part is, the Shah killed his own kind. Oliver, people shouldn't die for the color of their skin or their religious or political beliefs. It is all wrong. He was fully supported by your government. They supported who he was and what he stood for."

"I am not blaming the U.S. for what the Shah did; but at the same time, it makes me wonder about their integrity and love for other nations. Does it all have to do with their own financial interest, and the fact that people like us do not count?" Oliver thought about everything she said and decided not to respond, obviously their views were so different.

"I still have a hard time believing you couldn't come to me and tell me the truth."

"I knew you would try to stop me. My choices were limited."

"We know what may happen in the near future, and we are ready for the worst. They won't harm us. That we are sure of. Let's not forget that they are dealing with the most powerful country in the world. But as far as me leaving right now, I truly believe it is too late. I have to wait with the rest and see what happens."

Soraya looked at him with curiosity.

"So where do we stand? Do you hate me for what I did?"

"I can't hate you for this. After all, this is your fight and this is your war. I am just sorry to say that this revolution hasn't changed anything for your people. You got rid of one dictator and replaced him with another one. In this case, history has repeated itself again. You all trusted the wrong man. He is in, and in time, you will all be out."

In a way she knew he was right. They had accomplished nothing. People lost their lives for no purpose. The whole country turned inside out and the outside was much darker than expected. She knew that only too well. Their meetings were meaningless now, and she found no purpose to it anymore. They had lost control and there was no one to blame but themselves.

Oliver felt sorry for her, knowing their revolution had done nothing but create a monster who in the end would swallow them all. All his dreams were so out of reach. They were trapped in a hole, and it was too deep to get out. He was still hoping for the day that he could take her away from it all. The question was, would she let him help her out? She was a revolutionary who tried to save her nation and do the right thing, but so much had gone wrong that the scars from it would never leave her alone. He had never known anyone like her. She had no fear, and nothing could stop her from doing what she thought was the right thing. It would be almost impossible to control the side of her that fought back the system. No matter what system it was, if she found fault with it, then it was okay, in her eyes, to fight it even at the cost of her life. He could never protect her from herself. He believed that she was her own number one enemy. So many things began making sense to him concerning Soraya. He began understanding the true her. It had taken him a long time to get to this point, and now he had to decide if he wanted to spend the rest of his life with her, the new Soraya. To her people, she was a revolutionary and that frightened him more than anything. They knew who she was and what she was capable of, and people like her were a threat to their kind of society. In the end, people like her were eliminated, and that was what the Shah did. He knew that he still loved her. Nothing had changed in his heart, and he was going to fulfill his destiny with her and go wherever it took them.

It had been a long day for both of them. It was one full of emotions and new discoveries that were not so pleasant. She felt ashamed for keeping that part of her life a secret from him and had a hard time looking him in the eyes, knowing he was still loving and understanding toward her. In her eyes, she didn't deserve his love; but, at the same time, wished some day they could put it behind them and start all over again. Her mission was done and there was nothing left to do except to sit back and wait for whatever came their way. The thought of that gave her a chill.

Oliver wanted to show her his love, and to make her understand that no matter what had gone wrong in the past, he was willing to forget and move on. He went to bed with her that night and made love to her more passionately than he had in months.

"I couldn't love you this way if I hadn't forgiven you, so you can put your mind to rest, my love, with the thought that I love you for life. I need you now more than ever."

Tears filled her eyes, and she hid in his arms protected from the rest of the world for the moment. She was glad that she had finally opened up to him and told him the truth. That night she slept more peacefully, and she had Mohammed to thank for that. He was the one who finally talked her into telling Oliver the truth.

A few days later, she called Mohammed and asked him to meet with her. She needed to find out what was going on concerning the American embassy.

She sat at the cafe waiting for Mohammed. She was a few minutes early. It felt good to get out of the house. She couldn't stand sitting there day-after day and listening to the disturbing news on television. The silence in the apartment was driving her crazy. It had been a week since she had seen Mohammed last.

He walked in and spotted her right away.

"Am I late?"

"No, I am early. How are you?"

"I am fine. How about yourself?"

"Hanging in there, I guess."

He looked at her and realized how much he missed her.

"What is going on with you these days?"

"Not much, just sitting there in the apartment and waiting for something awful to happen. I don't know how much longer I can take this."

"Did you have a chance to talk to Oliver?"

"Yes I did, right after I saw you last. He won't leave. He says that it is too late for that. I don't know, Mohammed. He has his own reasons for why he is staying here. Nothing makes any sense to me. I asked you out here today because there are certain things that I need to know. There are so many mixed feelings floating around in my head that I don't know what to think anymore. What do you think of this whole mess with the government? Did we do the right thing?"

Mohammed looked deep into her eyes. He knew she was smart enough to see the changes and not accept them, but didn't want to destroy all her hopes.

"It is too early to say. I hope and pray every day that we did the right thing. I hate to think we handed over our country to another dictator. All I can do at this point is hope that they will do the right things in time. When I listen to them talk, it sounds like they will; but who knows? What they say and what they do could be two different things. It would be a shame if we look back five years from now and see nothing has changed. That would make this all a lost cause. A lot of people sacrificed their lives for this; and in the end, I just hope everything works out. Time will tell if we did the right thing."

"So, where do we go from here?" she asked doubtfully.

"I am not quite sure yet. They have offered me several different positions within the government. It would be the right thing for me to do to keep an eye on them; but then again, it would be hard to be employed by them and not believe in what they are doing. I haven't figured it out yet, but I will let you know as soon as I do."

Soraya still didn't feel that she had any of her questions answered.

"It seems to me that they just took over power and no one can question anything they are doing."

"It seems that way right now, but it is too soon to make any judgments. They are not organized yet."

She interrupted him. "They surely have the people under control. These people are doing exactly as they are told."

"But you see, Soraya, the people who they control are very confused. The thought of actually demonstrating and chanting death to the Shah or death to America is very exciting to them. They didn't do what we did for this revolution. You won't find people like you and me out there to give support to what they are saying. Death to Carter, Death to the Shah, or Death to America. Americans most certainly won't die and neither will their president. It just shows you what kind of people they are controlling. The sad part is that they are the majority of our people and the government has the upper hand."

"Remember Soraya, these are the forgotten people. The Shah didn't do what he should have for them and for now they are just letting off some steam and frustration. They have been given promises like more money, more work. Take away from the rich and give to the poor; and these people are buying it. You and I know that it's not right. For now, we have no control. We have to give these people some time to let out all the frustration and hope they will eventually get tired of it and stop this circus."

Mohammed was right, people like her and Nader would never go out there and follow a group of people who accomplished nothing by demonstrating except waste their time and create a lot of traffic. She knew this must eat him inside, knowing all their hard work had come to this.

"What is happening with the American embassy?" she asked, knowing that's where most of the demonstrations were being held.

"I don't know exactly. All I know is that something will happen soon, either a bomb or some kind of temporary take over. If the Americans choose to stay, it means they have more trust in our new government than I do. They should know that religion and politics don't mix. It's like oil and water, and one will sink the other."

"It makes me sick to my stomach. They think their prayers will destroy America. Well, it is not so. Our government should start negotiating with them; and for once, use them the right way. They need us just as much as we need them, Persian Gulf, being neighbors in the north with Russia and most of all, with our oil resources. It is all very important to them. We should use our heads so we don't screw ourselves in the end, over revenge and hateful behavior. The Shah was one of the most powerful men in the Middle East and with him gone, Israelis have gotten us where they want us. They want to be the power, and in a way, they are, thanks to the U.S. But you see, we should play the same game. Cutting our ties with the Americans will only hurt us in the end.

"Sadam Hussain of Iraq is the next one to worry about. Iraq will use our revolution and our government's hate for the U.S., and kiss up to them as we speak. Eventually, they will be provoked by Americans and Israelis into attacking Iran."

"Why would they do that?" she asked with curiosity.

"It will weaken our military power. It will destroy our economy and keep us busy so we can't start any disturbances in any other Middle Eastern countries. It is all to the benefit of the U.S. and Israel at this time; and of course these two countries would help Sadam to accomplish this goal. What they don't know is that they are shacking up with a snake. In the end, he will turn around and bite them and give them his poison." "So what you are telling me is that our government has every right to be anti-American."

"Soraya, we have the right to be anti-anything we choose, but we don't want to get fucked by them as a result. We need to keep peaceful relations. They are not going to get their hands dirty; they have Sadam Hussain to do that for them. They will support him all the way. They will sit back and be the good guys, in a civilized manner. At the same time, they'd like to teach us a lesson because our people are burning their flags every day, and their reporters are here showing it on national television. They don't take that sort of things well, and we shouldn't forget for one minute that we are dealing with a super power."

"Do you think Oliver is aware of all this? she asked him sadly.

Mohammed smiled.

"Of course he is, but you shouldn't question his loyalty to his country, not even for one second. The love of roots and country comes way before the love of life. He will never choose you over his country, and don't be stupid enough to put him in that position. Stand your ground and let him do the same. That's only fair."

She enjoyed listening to him. He was such a smart individual, well-read and so realistic. At times, she wished they would give him a chance to take over power and show them how it should be done. He told her what she needed to know and never gave her false hopes. She appreciated his words of wisdom and was glad to have him for a friend. He filled so many empty spots in her life like Nader.

They sat and talked for a long time. She didn't find out anything that would make her worry less, but it somehow made her feel so much better. It gave her peace, and she knew if the time came, she would deal with the challenges with him by her side.

Mohammed knew the time was near, and he wished Oliver would just leave and take her with him. By now, he realized how committed she was to him; and if anything happened to Oliver, she would never get over it. He wanted Oliver safe for her sake. He had put all his feelings aside and accepted the fact that it would not be. His love for her had gotten deeper, yet he loved her enough to let her go when the time came. He wanted nothing less than happiness for her and knew Oliver would be the one who could give her that. She left him that day and decided to go for a walk in the park. It had been so long since she had done that. She remembered the days she used to go there and study for her school exams. It seemed so long ago. Everything had begun when she started at the university. So much had happened since those days. She found an empty bench and sat there looking at the people. There were families who were trying to forget what was happening in their country and who had brought their children there to prove that life went on. Her mind drifted off to her own family. It had been so long since she had heard anything from them. She wondered if they even realized that they had a new government. They had such sheltered lives, so secluded from anything in the world. There wouldn't be any demonstrations or bloodshed there, just the peaceful sound of the mountains that she dreamed of often. She knew her mother had kept her promise and let the kids go to school if they chose to do so. At that moment, she would have given anything to see their faces and hear them laugh. But things had changed so much. She could never be a part of them again. Thinking of her father, his kind face and wrinkled hard working hands, she wished so much for his loving touch and his presence in her life.

Her train of thought was broken by a gentle touch. She looked down and saw a little boy standing next to her and touching her knees, trying to get her attention. He handed her a soft little gray rock. She raised her hand and took it from him.

"Thank you," she said with a smile.

The little boy stared in her eyes for a short moment and then ran toward his mother. She looked at the rock and followed him with her eyes.

She had a little boy, too, once. He was the only part of her life that she couldn't think about without having tears just roll down her face. How did she ever let go of him? How did she lose him so quickly? It was so hard to think about him knowing he was so far away and so out of reach. Now she had to face losing Oliver. She had never let go of her loved ones by choice. She looked up in the sky.

"Dear God, you have given me one last person to love. Please, spare me his life. Don't take him from me. The world would be a dark place to live. The sun would never shine upon me again. Help him out of this mess that I helped create."

She got up and kept on walking, holding the little rock in her hand, feeling it with her fingers. She knew that if something happened to Oliver, this rock would have more life in it than her. Deep in her own thoughts, she slowly walked home. She couldn't remember how she got there, standing in front of the door, not knowing how long she had been walking. She turned the key in the lock and heard the phone. It broke her train of thoughts, like waking up from a deep sleep.

"Hi Soraya, it's Mohammed. I thought you told me you were going straight home. I have been calling for a couple of hours now."

"I walked home. What's going on?"

He waited for a moment.

"I assume you haven't heard yet. I wanted to be the one who broke the news to you."

Soraya waited quietly, waiting for him to finish.

"They just took over the American embassy and took all the employees as hostages. No one is hurt, so don't panic; but do you know where Oliver is?"

She began crying.

"No, I don't know where he is. By whom were they taken?" she asked, sobbing.

The government is claiming that it's the students, but I have a hard time believing that. Soraya, listen to me carefully. You should take everything you think he might want out of there and hide it in a safe place. As of today, do not stay in his place anymore. I am sure it will be searched for documents. That is, if he's been taken among the others. They are accusing all of them of spying for the U.S. It's best if you are not there."

"What am I going to do?"

"Whatever you do, just don't panic. Do as I told you and I will get as much information as I can and will stop by later. Don't worry, he may be out and on his way home right now; but I am just thinking of the worse."

"Please let me know if you hear anything," she said still crying.

"I will, just as soon as I find out what the hell is going on. I am sorry, Soraya. I hope it all works out for both of you."

She swallowed her choking tears, "I know you do."

There was no time to waste. She had to act quickly and do as Mohammed asked her. She put all of her belongings and some of Oliver's documents in a box and quickly ran to her room. There she sat on her bed, feeling disgusted with everything that had taken place. She was angry with herself. She was angry at the whole world. It seemed like hours before she finally heard a knock on her door. With a jump, she opened the door and saw Mohammed standing there. He walked in and looked around.

"What is going on?" she asked, not able to wait any longer.

"Oliver is among the hostages. He was there during the take over, and from what I gathered, students are the ones responsible at this time."

Mohammed was concerned.

"Let me give you some advice. You are not to admit to anyone your relationship with Oliver. You have to remember that these are Muslim fundamentalists. They don't believe in a relationship such as yours. At some point, they will be suspicious of your involvement with him. Take my advice and stay away for now. Let me do all the work. It is very dangerous out there. They are afraid of their own shadows. As far as I know, all the hostages are doing fine and no one has been harmed."

"Do you think it is possible for you to see him?" "I don't know. I might be able to see him, but only as one of the authorities, in search of the truth."

"Do you have any clue how long they are planning on keeping them there?"

"No one knows that. I don't think they even know the answer to that."

"Would they harm them or even kill them?" she asked.

He shook his head.

"They may keep them hostage for a long time, but I truly don't believe they would hurt them in any way. They know better. If any of those hostages die, I guarantee you that the U.S. will attack us, and I don't think they are that dumb."

He took her hand and pulled her close to him.

"Soraya, we knew something was about to happen; and to be honest with you, I was afraid of some kind of bomb. This way they are all safe and no one is going to harm them. They will eventually let them go. The question is how long are they going to keep them as hostages? I know this is hard for you, but at least you know he is ok.

The students will never do anything to those people without the government's permission. They are going to make sure that they are all alive."

Mohammed hated to change the subject and steer her mind in a different direction, but he needed to find out some things from her.

"Do you have a passport?"

She looked up. "Yes, I do, and also a visa for the U.S. Oliver also left me enough money to buy a ticket if I needed it. He took care of everything except himself," she said sadly.

It was so hard for Mohammed not to pull her in his arms and comfort her. He hated to see her so broken down. The time had come and what he feared the most was near. He had to make sure she was protected, as long as nothing could be done for Oliver at this point.

"I want you to keep yourself busy and to not think about this all the time. I know it's hard, but you have to try."

She knew he was right, but it was easier said than done. She was so dependent on Oliver's love that it was hard for her to even imagine life without him.

"Is there anything I can do for you?"

Soraya looked up, tearfully, "just don't forget about me."

He couldn't take it any longer and pulled her into his strong arms.

"I won't. You can always count on me."

She let him hold her and comfort her. There was no one left in her life that could do that for her, and she felt sorry for herself.

That night she stayed in her room all night and never turned a light on. She just sat there in the dark wishing Oliver could be with her, missing his tender touch, the warmth of his arms, and most of all, his love.

"I need you, sweetheart. Please, come back to me. I don't think I am strong enough to make it without you."

She held one of his shirts in her arms and smelled his cologne. She held it near her face, kissing it gently wondering what he was doing at that very moment.

"I hope they are treating you well. I know you are sitting there and worrying about me, so unselfish you are, my love."

She remembered their trip to Paris and it brought a smile to her face. She thought of them sitting on that bench and making future plans, looking at the small pond in the park which reminded her of the pond which she once called her hiding place.

"I will forever wait for you, my love; and I promise you that someday, we will be together again."

She covered her face in her hands and cried for her lost love.

It was a very hard week for her. It didn't look like those responsible were going to release the hostages anytime soon. She cut herself off from the outside world, except for Mohammed. He gave her all the news she needed to know. Besides that, she didn't want to have anything to do with anyone else. It broke her heart to see how everything was being demolished in her country. Dreams had fallen apart and all the bloodshed was washed away and out of everyone's memory. Hate and distrust had taken over the country, and people found themselves whispering once again. She didn't want to have anything to do with the outside world. Nothing mattered to her any longer. She never listened to or watched the news. She preferred not to look at the faces of those hostages. It was not fair. They were taking years of frustration with the government out on innocent people who had done nothing but their jobs. She hated the system for what it had become once again. It was not working and they knew that already, and so did Mohammed; but their hands were tied.

It was happening all over again. If the Shah killed and tortured people behind closed doors, these people were doing it in the open and bragging about it. Their revolution did nothing but take the country half a century backwards. The hard thing for her to take was the fact that she helped them achieve that. So for now, she removed herself from society by locking herself in her small room. She only went out when she absolutely had to, and Mohammed was her only contact with the outside world. He was worried about her, but knew it was her way of mourning for her tragic life.

"I heard the university will soon be open again. Are you planning on going back?" he asked.

"I don't know," she answered, not caring anymore about anything that was once important to her.

"Don't you think you have worked way too hard to give up on that now? Oliver would want you to go back. You know that. I know it is hard for you, but you have to go on. You can't lock yourself up in your room like this. If not the lack of food, the depression will kill you."

She looked up with anger.

"I didn't say that I was quitting. All I said was that I didn't know."

"And why is that, Soraya?"

"I don't know, Mohammed. Sometimes I think, what for?"

"For yourself. You are alive, and you can't stop living because things have turned out this way."

"Life has offered me nothing but pain and suffering. It has given me people to love and then taken them away. Life has not been too kind to me. It started when I was a child, being born to a mother who was so hard on all of us kids. I never knew what playing was until I left my village. My only joy in life was taking a hike in the mountains and reaching this little pond. To me, if there is a heaven on earth, that place was it. Until one day, that beautiful, special place turned into hell on earth when I got raped by two men. I got kicked out of my village and had to leave without ever saying good-bye to my loved ones. I met Kate and Oliver when I came to the city and worked in their home as a maid and came to find out that I was pregnant. Kate talked me into keeping the child until we found him a place to live, and so I did. I was going to give him up without seeing him, because I knew how hard it would be to give him up if I got too attached to him."

"But then, they decided to adopt him. I had no other choice but to agree. And I watched my child grow before my eyes. Then one day, she just took him right out of my life. Losing my son was an experience that I will never forget."

"Meanwhile, my father died. He was so special to me. I went to pick him up at the bus station and he never showed up. I found out later that he had had a heart attack and died before I could tell him that I was okay now and things had changed for me, for the better."

"I put all my effort into my school work and got involved with Oliver at the same time. And then I met my dear friend, Nader. The rest is history. When I was being raped, I closed my eyes and I woke up years later hoping it all was just a bad dream. The bad dream began by the pond and it never ended. My whole life is a bad dream, Mohammed. It is all bad."

He looked down at his feet the whole time she was talking. Once she was done, he had a hard time looking at her. He had had no idea what she had been through and so was speechless for a long time. His eyes were filled with tears at the thought of her being raped by two men, her frail body being violated and beaten. He wanted to hold her in his arms and never let her go, just like Oliver did. He wanted to tell her that things would be okay someday. And most of all, he wanted to tell her again that he loved her with all his heart. Looking up after a long time, he found her crying

"Words cannot explain what I feel right now. I don't know what to say to ease your pain; but one day these gloomy pages of your life will turn. The future will be brighter and better. I promise you that. You do have a pure white page in your life hidden somewhere, and it will come your way in time. The past will be nothing but some sad memories, and it should give you even more reason to want to claim it. Your life has been such a sad story from the beginning, that right now you are only looking to the end. That's when you should stop and pick up the pieces that are left and move on to a new chapter of your life. You should do it for your son, because some day he will learn about you, and you should give him all the good reasons to want to know the real you."

Mohammed left her house that day, shocked at what he had found out. Rape wasn't a very common act in his country. He had no idea what she'd been through.

No matter how many things happened to her, it seemed like she kept on going and made good out of every bad situation. For the first time, she was trapped, and he didn't know how to help her. He wanted to do something nice for her, something that would make her feel alive, and the only thing that entered his mind was to arrange a visit for her and Oliver. There were not too many people he could trust within the system, but he was going to do his best to arrange for a meeting. He decided not to tell her anything unless it could be done, knowing it might take a long time. He began his work without raising any questions.

The Americans were being watched every moment of the day, and the security was so tight that it made his mission almost impossible. It had to be done within the system and with the use of all his sources.

The hostages were being questioned daily. Mohammed knew that the government had accused many of these people of spying. His plan was to get in as one of the investigating officers, and he began working on it immediately. After several meetings and due to the fact that he was one of the very first leaders to start the Iranian revolution, he finally got his first break. It took a long time for him to reach that point, but he had all the paper work clear for Soraya to act as a translator for him. Those in charge gave him a list of names to choose, and he casually slipped Oliver's name among the ones to be investigated by him.

It was just a matter of time before he was called to start his work, and the news came one afternoon when he was working in his office. After reviewing his record, they were impressed with all his achievements during the revolution and knew of his interest in the matter. They gave him permission to begin his investigation with the hostages. He had used all of his sources to arrange the meetings, and now it was time. They told him to be there the next morning.

Putting the phone down, he couldn't believe that it was done. He grabbed his jacket and left work immediately. It felt good to give Soraya some good news for a change, and he drove straight to her place. He knocked on her door and a few minutes later she answered and smiled to see her friend waiting in the other side.

"Hi, Mohammed. Come in. I was beginning to think you had forgotten about me."

She looked so thin and pale.

"I have been very busy. I am sorry."

"Don't apologize," she said.

"Are you eating at all?" He was disturbed by how thin she looked.

"I don't eat much, but I do my best."

"You look thinner every time I see you."

She shrugged it off.

"Don't worry, I am fine. Any news?"

He had kept it a secret all this time, not wanting to get her hopes up in case things didn't work out.

"Well, I do have some news for you."

Immediately, she looked worried.

"Is he okay?"

"Yes, he is; and as of tomorrow, I will be one of his investigating officers."

She screamed with joy.

"You are going to see him?"

"Slow down, babe. You are going with me as my translator."

It was hard for her to believe him.

"You must be joking."

He just smiled and shook his head.

"No, I am not."

"How long have you been working on this?"

"Long enough. I didn't want to say anything to you unless I was sure."

She jumped to her feet and ran toward him and gave him a warm hug.

"Oh, my friend, I will never forget this, not ever. Thank you. This means more to me than you could ever know."

He smiled again.

"I know that, and that's why I did it."

"So what do we do next?"

"We will sit across a table from him and ask him questions. You will get to see him and maybe say a few words to him. I am not sure of all the details. All I know is that you and I have permission to see him."

"How do I ever repay you for this?"

"Well, there is something you can do for me. Get up and get dressed and have dinner with me. You have to eat a good meal before tomorrow. Look at yourself; your skin has turned yellow. And also, eat some breakfast before I pick you up tomorrow. You don't want him to see you like this. It will only worry him."

"It's a deal. Actually, my appetite just came back."

They went to a quiet restaurant and he filled her in on all the details he had. She listened carefully to him, still not believing she would see Oliver the next day.

She finished all her food and said, "This was a great idea Mohammed. Thank you."

She couldn't stop smiling, and he could see the excitement in her face.

"Listen to me. I want you to know that you may see him once or twice at best. We don't know how long this whole matter is going to be dragged out, but you have to promise me that you will start living again. This is not a life that you have made for yourself, and I can't always be there for you to make sure you eat and take care of yourself. I want you to go on. You may have to do it alone, but you have to create a new world for yourself. Think of the many wives and mothers whose sons or husbands go out on a battlefield; they have no idea if they will see them again. They don't give up on life. They go on and wait. The time will come for you, and you have to be patient and take care of yourself. At least do it for the man you love and for me, your friend, if not for yourself."

She listened to him and promised him she would do better from then on.

"You have proven to me the kind of friend you are. I am sorry for acting this way. Tragedies should make people stronger, but this time it broke me to pieces. I've been unable to function and go on. Things will be different from here on out. You will see. I can't be a help to anyone sitting in my room feeling sorry for myself, and you made me see that."

They sat in the restaurant and talked for hours. She also told him that she was going to start school the following week which made him feel better.

"Okay, we have to go and get some sleep. We are going to have a full day tomorrow," Mohammed said.

He drove her home and stopped the car in front of her room.

"Thank you, Mohammed. I don't know what I would do without you."

She leaned over and kissed him on the lips, but parted quickly and got out of the car. He sat there and watched her go to her room before leaving. His heart pounded faster than any time he had gone on a mission, and he wondered how it was possible for a woman to make him feel the way she did.

She closed the door behind her and just stood there leaning on it.

"Well, my love, my prayers were answered for once and tomorrow is our day. We will get to see each other even though it won't be for long. Maybe this time we could say good-bye to each other, knowing it will be awhile before we can be together again, whenever that may be."

She woke up the next morning and quickly took a shower. She ate a small breakfast, as she had promised Mohammed. It was hard for her to imagine what he had gone through to get this arrangement set up. She sat there thinking of what she wanted to tell Oliver and finally gave up on the idea.

"I know once I see him, it will automatically come to me."

She grabbed her purse and walked out of the room. It was early yet, but it felt good stepping out and smelling the morning air. Like Oliver, she too had been locked up. Mohammed pulled up and saw her waiting. She still had a smile on her face, and he knew that's how she had gone to sleep the night before.

"Good morning, smiley."

And she smiled even broader as she sat next to him.

"Are you nervous?"

He glanced over and looked at her.

"Yes, I am. What about you?"

Mohammed laughed.

"Seeing another man doesn't make me nervous."

"You are not very funny," she said laughing, too.

It was nice to see her laugh again. He drove straight to the embassy and showed a card by the gate and they went in. He parked the car and they began walking toward the building.

"Well, my dear, it's show time."

She remembered him saying those words another time, when they were on a mission together. In a way, this would be one last mission they would do together.

Soraya stood back and let Mohammed take care of everything, and he was received very nicely. They showed them to a room and told them to wait until they brought in the hostages, one by one. Mohammed took all his paperwork out and laid it on the table.

The first hostage was shown in, and he took a seat across from Mohammed, looking nervous. Mohammed told him to relax and began asking him questions. The man answered calmly. Mohammed didn't want to cause him any discomfort, and the man looked appreciative. That gave Mohammed the indication that he had been through some tough interrogations before. Mohammed soon finished with him and called the guard. He couldn't quite understand the purpose of Mohammed's investigation, but was glad that it was fairly easy.

They sat back waiting. Soraya's heart was pounding. She purposely sat on a chair writing things down and kept busy, with her back toward the door. They didn't want Oliver to walk in and show any sudden reactions to cause any suspicion. A few minutes later, the door opened and the guard gave Mohammed a file with the next hostage's name on it. He looked at it and saw the name Oliver Reed. It was the first time he would see him. Oliver entered the room; he looked over to Soraya, but didn't recognize her from the back. The guard left the room and closed the door behind him. Mohammed walked over to him and raised his hand to Oliver.

"I am Mohammed Nasri."

Oliver hesitantly raised his hand and shook Mohammed's. Mohammed looked him in the face and said, "I don't want you to show any surprise, but I have someone here to see you."

Mohammed didn't actually need a translator, after all. He spoke fluent English.

Oliver looked at him with curiosity as Soraya got up and turned around. He slowly turned to look at the other person in the room and their eyes locked.

He whispered, "Soraya."

"Oliver."

Mohammed took a few steps away to give them a little privacy. They all knew not to do anything unusual at that moment. She controlled her tears as much as she could, but they poured down her face at last.

"I've missed you so much."

Oliver was still in shock, but came around quickly. Soraya sat across the table from him with her pen and the pad of papers.

She whispered, "I love you, sweetheart."

He still couldn't believe she was there in his presence. He knew she had taken a big risk by being there.

"I love you, too, darling. You look so thin. I am sorry for all this. You tried to warn me, but I had no other choice."

"I know that. Are they treating you okay?"

"Everything is fine. There is more mental abuse than anything else, and I can handle that. How did you arrange all this?"

Soraya looked over at Mohammed.

"It would have been impossible without his help. He is a good friend."

Oliver nodded.

"Are you staying in the apartment?"

"No, I moved to my room, just in case they show up for a search."

"That's a good idea."

He wanted so much to pull her into his arms and hold her, but knew it wasn't safe.

"What do you think will happen, Oliver?"

"We don't know anything. We are cut off from the outside world. They keep telling us that they are going to kill us, but that doesn't worry anyone. Just so you know, they will soon move me out of here because I am not considered one of the embassy employees."

Soraya nodded.

He slowly reached over and held her hands.

"I want you to just hang in there. This won't last forever, and then I will take you away from here. Just take care of yourself, and don't worry about me."

She smiled and wiped her eyes.

"I will."

"That's my girl."

"They think the company was just a front for cover up. They think I am a spy for the U.S."

She closed her eyes. That feared her the most, for them to think that about him; but for now, there was no time to discuss it any further. She looked over to Mohammed and called him over. "Oliver, I want you to meet Mohammed, as my friend, not the way you were introduced here before. Without him I couldn't have even gotten close to this place."

"Thank you. I truly appreciate that, and also for being a friend to Soraya. I understand that this was a big risk and you put your neck on the line here."

Mohammed nodded.

"It's okay. Is there anything we can do?"

"I need to get a hold of my supervisor. He needs to send me the right information so these people realize that I don't work for the embassy."

"Why were you here when they got the hostages?"

"I do all their computer programming, and it often changes for security reasons. Plus, I have known these people for a long time. We are all friends."

"So that explains why your name is not on the list of hostages. It shouldn't be too hard to prove that you are just a business man and don't belong here. Once we have the right information, you should be able to get out."

Oliver gave him the phone number.

"I have told them everything, but they don't believe me or even allow me to contact my people and prove it. Without the right documents, it is my word against theirs."

Mohammed looked at Oliver for a moment.

"You have to realize that the documents don't mean much to them at this point. There is no way for them to verify any information on those papers. The most important thing is to make them understand that they have gotten the wrong man. I am going to give you my phone number. Just memorize it and don't forget it, in case you are ever allowed to call me. And please don't tell anyone about our meeting. It could cause us problems. I hate to cut this short, but we have to end our meeting before they get suspicious."

Soraya looked at him and it took everything she had not to fly into his arms.

"Take care of yourself."

He smiled.

"You do the same, darling. I love you."

"I love you, too," she whispered.

Mohammed called the guard and they took Oliver away. They left the embassy after a couple of hours and she found Mohammed deep in thought.

"What are you thinking so hard about?"

"Nothing important. Don't worry."

Soraya was not convinced.

"You can tell me."

Somehow she knew what was bothering him. He thought for a moment more and then said, "I will try to help Oliver because of you, but at the same time, it is easy to come to the conclusion that he may be a spy. I can see why they are questioning him in a different manner and plan to separate him from the others. His job gave him the perfect opportunity to transfer information to the U.S. Of all the people they are holding, he is the only one who legitimately could be a spy."

She looked at him for a moment. It was hard for her to hear him say those words.

"Why do you want to help him if that's what you think of him?"

"Let me be honest with you. Whatever his position is, I don't really care, because at this point I am not in favor of either the past or present governments. It would bother me if he did it against my choice of government. Our current government is not organized enough to be damaged by anything he could have said. We don't know our head from our ass yet and there are so many things getting leaked out by our own people, which makes Oliver's position insignificant.

"No one has even admitted or taken responsibility for holding these hostages after two months. They haven't even come to an agreement on that yet. So, I am just going to take his word that he is just a businessman who was in the wrong place at the wrong time."

Soraya listened to him and didn't say anything. All she knew was that she wanted Oliver out of there no matter what it took.

The following week, Mohammed got in touch with Oliver's supervisor in the U.S. He, of course, verified his position in his company and sent Mohammed the documents to prove that. Mohammed showed the authorities the documents which he told them was the result of his investigation with Oliver. He hoped they would release him at that point; but to his dismay, the authorities were not willing to let him go yet. He decided not to pursue it further because it could have raised curiosity about his position or even Soraya's.

They saw Oliver once again and Mohammed discussed the matter with him. He told him to just hang in there and not to make any more statements regarding his position, thinking it may cause him more damage.

The next time Mohammed went there, he found out that they had transferred Oliver to a new place, and he was no longer with the other hostages. It was done, and Soraya knew seeing him would be impossible now. They had their own translators and Mohammed got to see him only one more time. He passed on any messages they had for each other.

There were talks of freeing some of the hostages, but Oliver was not among them. Eventually, they did release some of the women and also black members, but the rest remained in captivity. Soraya had started school again, but this time her heart wasn't in it. She saw Mohammed almost every day and worked with him in order to free Oliver, but that didn't seem like it was going anywhere. They had no solid evidence against Oliver, but were dragging their feet. Months had gone by since his arrest, and she knew by now that he had lost hope of ever getting out. She didn't give up and made sure Mohammed didn't either. She wrote everything down that came to her mind and discussed it with him the next day. Soon her room was full of boxes regarding Oliver's case. They had searched Oliver's apartment, and she was satisfied that the danger of them ever questioning her was over. She sat in her room day after day and worked on his case, contacting anyone she could and getting any information that was of benefit to him. All she knew was that no matter who Oliver Reed really was, it didn't matter to her anymore. She was not going to give up on him. She just got more determined each day that went by.

Mohammed was sitting behind his desk making notes when he saw the door open without a knock. Several men walked in with their guns pointed at him. He immediately raised his arms.

"What is going on?"

"We have orders to take you in for questioning," one of the men told him.

He knew better than to argue with them and got up and walked out of the room. He got in one of their cars and they drove him to a place which was the new Savak with a different title. They left him in a room and told him to sit and wait. He sat there, not knowing what exactly they had on him. It seemed like forever before the door opened up and two men walked in and introduced themselves as the head of the new Islamic Savak.

"We are going to get right to the point. If you cooperate with us and tell us what we need to know, we will let you go."

Mohammed just nodded. One of the two men sat exactly across the table from him and looked him straight in the eye.

"First, we need to know about your relationship with Soraya Noor."

"She is a friend of mine."

"What kind of a friend is she?"

"Just a friend. She was also a group member before and during the revolution."

"What did she do exactly?"

"Same as everybody else. Like I said, she was a group member."

He stopped for a moment gathering his thoughts.

"She was involved in the bombing of Taimoor's mansion, the bombing of the Savak headquarters, and also had a meeting with Ayatollah Khomaini's men in Paris before the revolution. She also participated in many smaller missions that were related to our cause."

The man touched his beard for a second.

"How did you first meet her?"

"I met her through a good friend of mine and group member who lost his life by the Savak before the revolution.

"How did he die?"

"He was tortured to death. I am not exactly sure."

"What do you know about her background?"

"Not too much. I trusted and took my friend Nader's word. He was like a brother to me. He met her at the University of Tehran."

"And what do you know about her personal life?"

Mohammed tried to stay within the lines and hoped Soraya would do the same. They had talked about this in case it should ever happen.

"I just know she worked for an American couple and lived in a room downstairs from them and helped the lady with the housework."

Mohammed was starting to get tired of their questions.

"Listen to me. She is a good woman. She acted more like a man than many others during our revolution. Why are you asking all these questions? Neither one of us deserves to be interrogated like this."

The man looked untouched by what Mohammed had just said.

"We have good reasons to believe that she may be a spy for the Americans, and we want to know what your role is in all of this?"

Mohammed looked disturbed.

"She would never spy on her country. She put her life on the line many times to complete our revolution. She went out there and fought like a soldier, which is more than I can say for many others who sat at the safe grounds of their homes or in other countries while people like Soraya fought their battles. You are wrong in accusing her of something of that magnitude. Just take a look at her records."

"We happen to think differently. For example, she could have used you in many ways without you even knowing it."

Mohammed looked at the men in disgust and they could clearly see it in his face.

"You don't have a clue who you are talking about. She is one of the most decent people I have ever met in my life. Where are you getting your information anyway?"

He ignored Mohammed's question and went on.

"What kind of relationship does she have with Oliver Reed?"

"I think you should ask her that question. We never got involved in our member's personal lives."

"We have information that tells us they are lovers."

"Like I said, that was never my concern."

"Of course you are aware of Oliver Reed being in our custody with the charges of possible espionage. After all, you were one of the agents who interrogated him. Tell us what that was all about?"

"I interviewed many of them. Oliver Reed just happened to be among them."

The man smiled.

"And ironically, Soraya was your translator. Isn't that true?"

"I asked her to help me out in that matter. At the time, we didn't even know that Oliver Reed was among the hostages. To our knowledge, only the embassy employees were taken as hostages. His name, to this day, is not on that list."

"Did they speak to each other?"

"Yes, they did."

"What did they say?"

"The usual things: How are you doing? Are you being treated right? And I hope it all works out. The same things she would tell me if I were in his shoes."

"Did she know he was one of the Americans to be questioned by you?"

"No, she didn't. I never said anything to her."

"What was her reaction when she saw him?"

"She was happy to see him."

"Just happy to see him?"

"That's what my understanding was."

"By the way, Mohammed, where is she from exactly?"

"I am not exactly sure. Some small village by the Damavand Mountains."

"Have you tried to help Oliver Reed in any way?"

"I only tried to find out facts. I called a number he gave me to verify his statement as far as his position in his company."

"And?"

"They seemed very concerned about his whereabouts, knowing his name was not on the list of hostages."

"Did you tell them where he was?"

"Yes, I did. I didn't see anything wrong with that."

"Did his supervisor send you any information?"

He nodded.

"What did you do with it?"

"I turned it over to the authorities."

"Are you willing to swear on the holy book of Koran that everything you said is true?"

"Yes," he said without hesitation.

The man leaned over and got closer to Mohammed. S "Let me tell you a few things. Soraya is being arrested as we speak. She has a lot of questions to answer. At this point, we will let you go, mainly because of all your positive efforts in our Islamic revolution. Please don't leave town. We know where your family lives. I hope you get the picture. If her statement matches yours, and we believe it, you will be off the hook for now. But like I said, she has a lot of questions to answer."

Mohammed looked at the guy with hatred.

"She hasn't done anything wrong. She is not a spy like you think she is."

"Even if everything you say is right, she has broken the Islamic law and slept with a man who is not her husband. For that alone, she could be stoned to death. But there are other things that I prefer not to discuss at this point."

Mohammed got up.

"Am I free to go?"

"Yes, you are, but I wouldn't try to run over to her house. She has been taken into custody already."

Mohammed stopped and leaned over the table and looked the man in the eyes, only inches away from his face.

"You are making a big mistake. She doesn't deserve to get treated like a criminal. She has done more for her country and for this revolution than any of you who are sitting on your comfortable chairs and who have no clue what goes on out there. And let me tell you something, and take it however you want, if anything happens to her, I will be back. And I guarantee you, if you take a look at my file you will learn what I am capable of."

He walked out feeling so helpless. He didn't know where to go or what to do. He was so angry for ever trusting the system, the system that he helped build. Now it was destroying him and others like him. He was losing friends he cared about to the new power. It had started all over again. This time there was no shame; they laughed in your face and did whatever the hell they wanted.

He felt responsible for many things. She wasn't just another member in his group. She was the woman he loved more than anything in the world. He remembered all the promises he had made to her, that everything would work out and she would some day look back and it would just be some sad memories. It wasn't fair. He had to sit back and wait, just like he always had. The system had failed him and her all over again, but it was a lot harder to take this time.

# CHAPTER THIRTEEN

Soraya opened the door and stepped in. She stopped cold in her tracks.

"Hello, Soraya." It frightened her and she got tense. Many bad memories rushed through her head. She didn't let go of the door handle, leaving the door half open so she could run.

"Who are you?"

"We are with Islamic Savak."

She quickly got the picture and calmed down a little. "What do you want from me?" She looked around her room. It looked bare without all the boxes and the paper work that she had been working on for months.

"We need you to come with us and answer some questions."

"Why can't you ask me here?"

One of the men got up.

"You don't get to ask the questions. Remember, we ask you the questions."

She stayed calm.

"Can I make a call before you take me in?"

"You don't have anyone who would even notice your absence."

"I have friends who might be worried."

"He already knows and has cooperated with us fully, so why don't you just walk out of here without causing any problems?"

She took a deep breath, and for the first time realized what Nader had felt when they took him away. There was no one there for her to smile or wink at, and she obeyed their orders and walked out with them. Not knowing what would happen next, she sat in the back seat looking out. People were going places, shopping, picking up their children after school, living their lives. They all had someone to go to and someone to love. She had no one anymore who would worry about her if she were late, or to just simply love her for who she was. Oliver was in prison, and, as far as she was concerned, that's where Mohammed was now too.

Soraya, feeling sad for herself, sitting almost lifeless in the back seat of a car being driven to an unknown place with some unknown people. Mohammed would never say a word that would jeopardize her situation. They had talked about this and she knew exactly what he had told them. The question was, did they buy it?

She reached in her coat pocket and felt the softness of the rock and remembered the little boy's face who had given it to her. She took it out and looked at it and smiled, giving it a small wink. Looking back at her were two big brown eyes.

"You are forever safe, my son. The one and the last thing I did for you was to make sure you are loved and away from all of this. You don't ever have to go through anything like I have; and that, my boy, was my only gift to you. So someday you can grow up and love whoever you want and not be afraid to speak your mind. you can play your childhood away, something I was never allowed to do. I want you to play and play all you want, my baby. Do it for me, because that was something I was denied of as a child."

She looked at the two men in the car with her.

"They are taking over my life. I have lost control once again, sitting here and letting them take me away. Maybe the end is finally near for me. I don't know. But if it is, I will no longer fight it. I trust you God with all my heart. All I am asking you is to make me suffer the pain in this world, and if it is time for me to go, give me bright sunny days and lots of laughter once I finally reach you and your heavenly home. I need to pay for all my sins in this world, and I want to be yours and yours only when my soul flies out of my body."

The car came to a stop, and she was ready to face whatever came her way. A strange power took over her that gave her the strength she needed. They opened the door for her and she got out. Like Mohammed, they took her to a room and told her to sit and wait. She sat there and waited, knowing her relationship with Oliver was the only thing that they could punish her for. In her eyes, it was the only act she had ever done that was pure. There was no violence, no lies. It was consist of nothing but love. And for love, she was to be punished. It was a sin, an unforgivable sin. If that was wrong in their eyes, then she was ready to fight them and tell them to go to hell, where there is no sign of love, affection, or forgiveness. That's where they belonged. In their eyes, she was considered a sinner by the new laws. She could be punished to death for that.

The door opened and broke her train of thought. Two men walked in. She didn't move from her seat. Cold and lifeless, she just looked at them as if to tell them, "You can't hurt me. There is no more life left inside of me." And if someone looked closely enough or deeply enough, they could have seen a smile on her face. Someone inside of that body was laughing at them. She didn't take her eyes off of them, and it made them uncomfortable to start. They knew just then that they had their hands full. This woman seemed almost glad to be there.

One of them whispered, "hello," but she didn't answer.

"Do you have any idea why you are here?"

She never took her eyes off of him.

"Yes, I do."

"Then could you help me a little and fill me in?"

"She smiled, and replied. "No. I have done enough for you and your system. I can't help you in any way."

"Don't try to make a game out of this. You will only cause more trouble for yourself."

"And for you," she answered back.

"Is this how you would like to start, Soraya?"

"I would like to walk out of here is what I would like to do."

"You cooperate with us, and that may happen. It is all up to you."

She didn't answer back and kept staring at him.

"Could you tell us about your relationship with Oliver Reed?"

"He is the man I love and plan on marrying him someday. That is, if we both get out of this place."

"Have you ever slept with him?"

"Don't ask me questions to which you already know the answers. It is only a waste of our time."

"Mine maybe, Soraya; but it looks like you are going to have nothing but time on your hands," he said with a small laugh.

"Do you have any other relations besides sex with him?"

"Like what?" she asked.

"Oh, maybe giving him information that is top secret?"

"I don't need to do that; your own people leak it all out."

The man turned and suddenly slapped her so hard in the face that it threw her off her chair. She turned and touched her burning face and felt a wetness pouring down her nose. She took a deep breath and took a tissue out of her pocket.

"We are starting on the wrong foot, Soraya, and you chose that, not me."

"What is it that you want to know?"

"Are you and Oliver both spying on our government?"

"No, we are not."

She wiped her nose again; the bleeding wouldn't stop.

"You two share a bank account. Where did you get all that money sitting in the bank?"

"It doesn't belong to me. He had my name on it in case something happened to him."

"Something like, if he got caught spying?"

"He is not a spy."

"Do you expect us to believe that?"

"It's the truth, Mister! And furthermore, let me tell you something, you will never, ever, not in a million years, get a confession out of me. That will never happen. I am only too familiar with the system. I know

355

what happens behind these closed doors. I have lost friends who didn't live through it before; so remember one thing, I was trained in this country by the good men of our soil how to fight back against injustice. One thing I learned well, there is nothing in this world above death. Go ahead and torture me. Do whatever you want. It will only bring me one step closer to the top, and when I reach the top, you can go to hell with me. No confession, remember that. I have too much love for this land and for our people, the real people who hate what is happening to their land. For them I fought and for them I may die; but you will never put a spy label on me, because the ones who count will never believe you."

"Good speech, Soraya. Let me ask you this. What if I told you, we will free your friend and let him go back to the hell he came from if you tell us the truth?"

She smiled.

"Hell belongs to us, Sir; and I have no trust in our system. I will never confess to the kind of filth you are asking me to. He will understand my position and even rot in your prisons until the day he dies; but he wouldn't want me to do anything that will give you satisfaction. Go ahead, kill Oliver. Kill me. Have us witness each other's torture and death. It will still not change a thing. The sun will shine the next day; but remember, it will never shine upon you. You are lost in the shadows of darkness and will die in it someday; I promise you that."

She had truly exhausted and frustrated both of them. They decided to end the session and start the next day. They needed to learn some other techniques in order to deal with her.

"I think we've had enough for one day. Don't you think, Soraya?"

With a sarcastic smile on her face, she asked, "Am I free to go?"

The two men looked at each other.

"I didn't think so," she said and smiled again.

They left the room and a few minutes later two guards came in and took her to a cell and locked her up. She couldn't believe they were labeling her as a spy.

She stood looking out through the bars and thought, "this is what it has all come to."

Soon two women came in, and they searched her and took away everything she had.

"Can I keep this small rock?"

The woman looked at it closely and gave it back to her, and they both left the room a few minutes later.

Mohammed was fuming when he got to Soraya's room. He didn't care what they told him; he needed to see it with his own eyes. The room was all torn and taken a part. He knew they had been there. He sat on the edge of the bed, feeling totally lost. He didn't know what to do. This time there was no secret meeting or any mission to keep his mind off of what was happening. He sat there looking at her room, finding stacks of books piled everywhere. He knew those were with what she filled her long lonely nights. These books were her companions day after day and night after night. He wanted to be close to her somehow and learned the only way that was possible was for him to be in her room near her personal things, to smell her pillow, and to lay on her bed, searching for comfort. The room looked cold and he knew it meant she was gone. He had no idea when he would see her again, and the thought of not ever having her in his life was more than he could bear.

Oliver spent his days reading and thinking, not knowing what would happen to him, isolated from the outside world. He found himself thinking of Soraya often. What was she doing? How was she getting by? He often wondered if they would ever have a life together and be left alone, so for once they could live their lives without ever wondering what others thought. He often thought about their trip to Paris and remembered the small park across the street from the hotel where he gave her the ring and promised her his love for eternity. It was hard to believe it had come to this, a small cell in a prison where they kept him and questioned him almost daily.

Prison was such a lonely place. There was no existence of time. His days and nights and even weeks were all mixed together. There was nothing to separate them. The reality that there was an outside world was so out of reach. The longer he stayed locked up, the harder it became to think of anything else, but a life of darkness.

He was deep in his own thoughts when he heard the door.

"Another interrogation," he told himself.

But this time they came to him and he wasn't taken out of his cell.

"Hello, Mr. Reed."

Oliver quietly answered back.

"We thought to stop over and see you in your room this time. Is everything okay here for you?"

"This is a prison, in case you have forgotten," he answered.

"We had a little problem and thought maybe you could help us. Just a few minutes ago, we had a little visit with a woman named Soraya Noor. Does that name sound familiar to you?"

His heart dropped at the sound of her name, and he squeezed his teeth together.

"Yes, it is. Why?"

"Well, during our conversation, she told us things that we need to verify with you, things that don't match what you told us."

Oliver looked up. "Like what?"

"Let's see. For one thing, she confessed to espionage." Oliver just froze for a moment.

"I don't believe she would ever say a thing like that. She loves this country."

"Were you aware of her activities during our revolution?"

"No. She kept them from me."

"You see; she lied to you, too. She was dishonest to everyone and also to her country. Why would you want to protect someone who lied to you?"

"She didn't tell me because I would have stopped her."

"Why is that? Are you in any way opposed to our new government?"

"Only because her involvement was dangerous."

"She also told us that you two were lovers. Is that correct?"

He decided not to answer that question.

"I won't answer that because it is personal."

"Yes, and it is also against Islamic law. Now, why would she admit to something like that? She knows it may cause her a lot of problems."

"I don't know. You have to ask her that. He looked at the man. Are you holding her?"

"Yes we are. But before we leave, just a few things for you to think about: if you don't cooperate with us and tell us what we need to know, she may be killed. It is up to you."

His heart sank at the sound of those words. He hated these men, so heartless and twisted. He was left with a lot of questions; but, at the same time, he knew she would never admit to espionage. It was not true. Her relationship with him was the only thing that he thought she might have admitted to, and they made up the rest to confuse him and make him doubt her. He decided not to say anything to them anymore. He had already said everything that was necessary, and it was all on record.

That night he lay in his bed, thinking of a life without her. There was no law to protect either one of them. These people had total control over both of their lives, and there was nothing he could do to change that. They had taken her into custody and there was no one they had to answer to for their actions. Those were the bitter facts. The thought of them ever hurting her left him without breath. He wondered if they had already hurt her in any way.

She lay in her bed, just like Oliver, and stared at the ceiling. She decided not to tell them anything from that moment on. Somehow, it was like she and Oliver had communicated and decided to stay silent, forever Silent. It was out of her control. There were no more decisions to be made, no more sneaking around or fact findings, no more missions, and no more fear. Nothing mattered to her anymore. In a way, she gave up and decided to just let things be and take their course. It was a life from hell; and, for the first time, she decided not to fight it anymore. She just laid in her bed and finally closed her eyes, and there was one tear that rolled down from the corner of her eye. For the first time, that tear belonged to her, not to her father or Ali, Nader, or even Oliver. It belonged to her and no one else.

The next morning, she opened her eyes and found herself in exactly the same position. It was as though she was drugged and had not moved all night. Soon the door opened and a woman brought a tray for her. She couldn't remember when she ate last, but still she didn't have an appetite. The woman left her tray on the floor and only glanced at her once. She looked back at the woman, who was about fifty years old, and wondered what was going on in her head. Those were the people she cared about, just the simple, hardworking people, who never got a break in their lives. The fatigue showed in her tired face. Soraya poured herself a cup of tea and she took a few bites of her bread, but couldn't eat much more than that. The door opened once again and this time it was a female guard with no expression of any kind.

"Come with me," she told her.

Soraya followed the woman to the same room she had been questioned the day before. She sat in the same chair and waited. This time it didn't take long before three men and a woman entered the room. One of them who had questioned her the day before sat across the table from her with a sarcastic grin on his face.

"Did you sleep well last night?"

Soraya didn't answer him and just stared.

The woman moved from where she was standing and walked closer to her and grabbed her hair and yanked it with force.

"You answer him, bitch! Do you hear me?"

This caught Soraya by surprise, and she let out a scream and quickly got the picture. She decided not to give them the satisfaction of hearing her in pain.

"We talked to Oliver last night, and once he found out you were in our custody, he changed some of his statements. I was wondering if you would like to do the same. I will only give you one chance and no more. Would you like to change anything at this point?"

She just shook her head.

The woman yanked her hair even harder this time.

"You answer him loud and clear. Do you understand?"

This time she made no sound. As the man went on asking her more questions, she sat silently and just stared at him.

The interrogators moved to the corner of the room, whispering and making decisions concerning her, but Soraya couldn't hear them. A few minutes later, the woman told Soraya to lay on her stomach. She followed the instructions as the men kept on talking.

She lay on the table with her face toward them. It was obvious to her what was about to happen. The woman showed her a whip.

"This will make you talk soon," she said and whipped it on her back with extreme force, wanting to hurt her as hard as she could.

The pain took Soraya's breath away, and she began to count, "One, two, three, four, five . . . ."

Each time hurt more than the last, and Soraya never took her eyes away from the men who pretended they hadn't seen anything unusual. It was a game they were playing, and she knew the game only too well. The woman stopped, almost out of breath.

"Are you ready to talk?"

Soraya closed her eyes and whispered, "go to hell."

The woman started again. As Soraya lost count of the whipping, her body became numb and she felt her shirt sticking to her back. Finally, she passed out in silence. The woman stopped, even more aggravated having lost the battle to this stubborn woman.

"She is out, but don't worry; it will hurt even more tomorrow when her back swells up. She will talk then."

They carried her body to her room and left her on the floor. Hours went by. Soraya drifted in and out of consciousness, not aware of what was happening. Later, they came back to check on her, but found her the same way and left the room.

She opened her eyes and noticed it was dark. The pain was incredible. She felt as though every bone in her body was broken. Not able to get herself off of the cold floor, she closed her eyes once again.

The same woman who brought her food the day before walked in her cell and found her on the floor. Her shirt was sticking to the dried blood on her back. This woman hated her job. She looked around for a moment and then decided to help Soraya. She was a mother herself, and felt sorry for this young woman.

"Come on, girl. Get up. I can't carry you to your bed."

Soraya opened her eyes. Everything was spinning around and the pain was the next thing that struck her.

"I can't move," she said with a whine.

"Yes, you can. Come on, get up."

She helped Soraya to her feet. Then she reached in her pocket and took out some pills.

"Here, take these, but don't tell anyone I gave them to you."

She gave her a glass of water to swallow them.

"Save some for later," she said and handed her some more pills.

"What are they?"

"Pain killers."

Soraya quickly took them.

"Eat your food and drink your tea; otherwise, you won't last long."

The woman handed her a cup of tea, and quickly slipped out of the room.

Soraya hid the pills and ate some food, not remembering how she got there. The last thing she remembered was the faces of the three men. There was a fear in their eyes and she knew it was fear of God and nothing more. They had to go home that night and look their wives and daughters in the eyes and be able to sleep knowing what they had done to a young woman caught, helpless within their system.

Soon they would be coming for her, and it would begin all over again, but she had to stay quiet for Oliver's sake. Anything she told them could jeopardize his life. He didn't belong there; this was her fight. If there was someone to be sacrificed, it should be her. He had to get back to his own country and help Kate to raise Ali. For now, that was the only thing that mattered to her. All her dreams were just that. The future didn't exist for her; and if Oliver escaped this nightmare, it would all be worthwhile.

The pills were taking effect and the pain was slightly better. She decided to just rest her body before they came back for her. She thought of Oliver and wished he could wrap his arms round her just one more time and make all her wounds go away. She hoped no one would tell him of what they had done to her. The guard brought her some clean clothes to wear; and as she took her shirt off, she could feel her skin separating from her body with the shirt. It was obvious that the open wounds would soon get infected if she didn't get treated; but, she didn't think they were concerned about that at all.

The guard came back for her a few minutes later and told her to follow him. She got up, barely able to walk, and pulled her weak body out of the room.

She sat at the same chair and was glad they weren't there to see how much pain they had caused her and that she was able to catch her breath. They walked in and one of the men looked at her.

"Good morning. How do you feel this morning?"

She looked up and replied, "I feel just fine."

"Good. Can we then begin our work? Are you ready to talk to us and tell us what you know about Mr. Reed's involvement within the embassy and also of his activities? You were with him more than anyone else. If there is anyone who knows, it should be you. If you tell us what we need to know, you might save your own neck. I promise you that. We will consider everything you have done in the past for our revolution and make sure you get a fair chance."

Soraya looked him in the eyes and smiled.

"Your promise means nothing to me. I trusted your kind once before when I met with your superiors in Paris. Those were the days you needed me and my group, but as soon as you got what you wanted, you forgot all about your promises. We didn't count anymore. Shacking up with a snake is better than shacking up with you, and I will take my chances."

"This is going to cost you more than you think. Not cooperating with your government and helping someone who, according to our records is nothing but a spy, will cost you your life in the end."

"This government will kill me anyway. You know that, and I know that. So, what's the use?"

"Who does your loyalty belong to?"

"My loyalty is to my country, not to you and your kind. I did everything in my power to free my land, and this is how I am getting treated, like a criminal, a traitor, someone who sells her country for a price. I am none of the above; and if you feel good in your heart to treat me this way, then go on and do what you have to do. But don't expect me to play your filthy game. There are many people out there, like me, who did everything within their power to make you what you are today. Not for a minute are they satisfied with the outcome of our country. In the end, we are the ones to pay the price for your mistakes and poor judgment. I haven't done anything to be ashamed of. Everything I did was to better our country. Yes, we made mistakes, trusting people like you. It wasn't done to hurt our people or our country. You have the wrong man. Mr. Reed is nothing but a business man. You will never get a confession out of me or an admission from him of espionage, never; because it is just not so.

Furthermore, this is the last statement you will get from me. I have nothing more to say or to add from this moment forward."

The man sat on his chair looking at her. It was obvious that she was not afraid to die; but the only thing he wasn't sure of was the measure of her tolerance of pain. He knew that was his last choice.

"You leave me no choice but to use more force. I want you to know that it is your choice and not mine."

He got up and told the guard to take her back to the cell until further notice.

She sat in her room wondering what was next. What were they going to do to her now? She just wished it would all end soon.

Oliver was getting used to the routine interrogation by now. They had never physically punished him, yet; but he didn't put it out of his mind completely. He just hoped Soraya was not in any danger physically. He tried not to think about it. A week had passed since he first found out that they had arrested her. They played many mind games with him, but they had not succeeded at breaking him yet.

There was so much he wanted to know. The silence was driving him crazy. He spent his days just looking at the four walls of his cell. It had been months since his arrest and there was no one to help him. With Soraya being taken in, he had lost all hopes of ever freeing himself of this hell. He heard a noise and a footstep and soon saw a guard by his door.

"Come with me," he ordered Oliver.

It was another day of questioning. He followed the man wondering where he was taking him; it wasn't the usual time he got questioned every day. They walked through a long hallway and finally stopped in front of a room. The guard knocked on the door and then opened it without waiting for any response. He pointed to a chair for Oliver to sit. There were others in the room. Oliver looked around, not knowing what to expect, and sat.

"Mr. Reed. We are giving you one last chance to talk, and then it will be out of our hands."

Oliver looked at the man.

"I have told you everything I know. There is nothing more for me to add. I wish you could believe me and stop all this. Do you wish for me to lie to you and make up a story that isn't true?"

"I wish for you to speak the truth, Mr. Reed. That's what I wish; and it's a shame. I wish it wouldn't have to come to this."

Oliver's heart was pounding. The man nodded his head and Oliver turned in that direction and saw a man open a window size curtain. His heart sank at what he saw. It was the body of a fragile woman hanging from a rope from the ceiling. Her back was toward him and she was covered in blood. The man nodded again, and the woman standing next to her began hitting her with something like a heavy leather belt that ripped into her back. Tears rolled down Oliver's face. It didn't take him long to recognize his beloved Soraya, the body he had held so many times and loved. It was his precious Soraya, all torn and beaten. He turned his head and covered his ears so he wouldn't hear the sound of the slashes on her body which moved her from side to side with each stroke. It didn't look like there was much life left within her.

"Jesus Christ, you sons of a bitches!"

He cried like a baby, "Please stop. She hasn't done anything wrong. She is just a child. Please stop!"

"Mr. Reed, like I said, it is all up to you."

Oliver looked at the man in disgust and hate. He couldn't take it anymore and ran toward him. He caught everyone by surprise by grabbing the man by his neck and starting to squeeze as hard as he could. The man tried to free himself as the others ran toward Oliver and tried to pull him away. He suddenly had an incredible power and no one could pull him away. His hands were stuck to the man's neck like glue, and he squeezed so he would take his last breath out of him. The man was choking to death, and Oliver was almost successful until a man hit him over the head with something that felt like a heavy rock. Oliver fell to his knees and passed out.

He opened his eyes and felt dizzy. The whole room was turning in circles, and he felt sick to his stomach. The headache was the worst. As he touched the back of his head, it hurt, even with the gentle touch. He looked around and noticed that he wasn't in his cell.

"Where am I?"

The pain was unbearable, and he noticed dried blood on his shirt as he looked down. Soon, everything came back to him. The blood was a reminder of what he had seen earlier.

"Oh, my dear God!"

He covered his face with his hands and remembered only too well Soraya, hanging in the room, her clothes covered in blood and her eyes closed, not even knowing what they were doing to her anymore. She looked like a small child, so thin and frail. He realized why he hadn't recognized her at first; that body was so unlike the woman he loved. A woman once full of life and so beautiful now looked like nothing but a lifeless body, hanging in there, almost taking the last breath that her nasty life had to offer her. He broke into a sob remembering in detail how she looked. Her shirt was all ripped in the back from the beatings, and in parts, it was mixed with her flesh.

It had looked like the beatings had been going on for a long time; otherwise, she wouldn't be the way she was. Wishing it was he who took all the beatings and the torture, not his precious love, he wondered why this was all happening. How did it all begin? Why didn't he listen to her and leave, taking her with him and forgetting about this hell that had ruined his entire life? It had destroyed his every dream. His heart was filled with hate for everyone responsible for her pain, including himself, for not taking her away and giving her what he had promised her: bright sunny days with lots of love and laughter. Instead, she was given a dark cell with nothing but pain and suffering. He wanted to blame someone for everything that went wrong. Oliver just sat in his chair, rocking back and forth and crying for a woman whom he loved so much, he couldn't even begin to think of a life without her. As far as he was concerned, this earth could go to hell with everything inside if he couldn't be with the woman who had given him so much happiness. Nothing mattered to him anymore. He had no desire to live. It was all over for him. All there was left to do was to sit and wait for nothing; because that's how he looked at life without Soraya, nothingness and emptiness.

Mohammed was beside himself. Every plan he had made to free Soraya had met a road block. He was being watched closely. It was hard to make a move without them knowing it. He used all of his sources to find out what was happening with her, and finally he was told of the incident with Oliver. He had to get her out of there, but didn't know how. Everyone had let her down, and now he felt he was doing the same thing. He was not able to help her or save her life, whatever was left of it.

It was hard for him to do anything and not think of her. She was forever on his mind, which made it almost impossible for him to function. Knowing she was being held and beaten everyday so she'd confess to something she was no part of broke his heart. He often thought of his friend, Nader and wished he had him back in his life, to comfort him and listen to him. He wanted to tell someone how he felt about Soraya and how badly he was hurt; but there was no one left. Everyone who was a part of a group he once created was gone. Now, he was trying so hard to hang on to the one who stole his heart.

Soraya had not said a word in days. She just stared into space. Her body was beaten and tortured. They had tried everything to make her talk, but she never said a word. They wondered if she felt the pain anymore. It seemed that her soul had flown away long before, but there sat this body that functioned and was still considered alive. Oliver's name didn't even change the expression on her face. Nothing did.

Her fight to live had ended, and she knew the end was near. In a way, she gave up and let nature take its course, once and for all. There was nothing left of her except a bag of bones. Her beautiful eyes had no sparks anymore. The guards in the prison often wondered if she could even see through those eyes. The story of her life had touched everyone's heart. It was hard for many of them to let go of someone who they believed had tried to change things for them. Secretly, they admired this woman. They also knew the end was near for her. Nothing moved her, not Oliver, or Ali, or even her father. She didn't think about anything anymore and just stared at something that didn't exist. People often wondered what went on in her head. Maybe there wasn't anything there anymore. Maybe she was just a ghost of a woman named Soraya. The rest of her had flown away and was far from this place called hell.

Little by little, she had lost herself within a system she once helped to power. Now she was so lost that she couldn't find a way back, even if she tried. This woman didn't know if she even wanted to find her way back. It was so much easier to let go and to finally accept that this earth and she didn't see eye to eye, that her presence on this earth only hurt the ones she loved. She wanted to be forever lost and never found again. It was so peaceful where she was. There was no sound, no life, and no pain. It was free. It was her world and there was no one there but her. It was her way of protecting the rest who were close to her. They would all do just fine. They would go on with their lives and her being would not bring them bad luck. She wished they would all let go of her and let her fly away. There was no reason to hang on and make this suffering last longer. They had to let go of her and let her be. This woman was ready, was willing, and she looked forward to the day that they were all free once again. She wouldn't be able to see that day come until they were all willing to let her go.

So, she went on staring at one spot where she could see a light waiting for her. She wanted so badly to reach that light. It was where she belonged, and it was where she wanted to be. If she just stared and never took her eyes off it, maybe she would one day get there and not lose it. She kept on staring and held on to the only thing she had left, a small bright spot deep down in the back of her mind, in the tunnels of human thoughts, where Soraya was lost.

# CHAPTER FOURTEEN

A look of pained yearning crossed Oliver's face as if he wanted badly to speak to Mohammed, knowing he was his only way out. All his efforts to make a phone call, however, had failed. They had moved him to a new prison after the last incident; and they had finally stopped questioning him, knowing nothing would change. For now, they just let him be. The new prison was much bigger than that where he was kept earlier.

He ultimately decided to come out of his depressed mood and try to help himself and Soraya somehow. He never gave up on the thought of eventually getting out of there, but knew it was only possible through Mohammed. If only he could get in touch with him.

It was much easier for him being where he was. Everything was more restrained, and it wasn't a moment that went by that he didn't think of Soraya and wonder how she was. One guard had told him that she was still alive, but didn't tell him anymore. That was all he needed to hear to not give up hope. It was all he had to go on, wishing maybe someday it would all be put behind him.

At times, he felt like a forgotten soul. No one was there to visit him, and no one gave him any news of what was happening beyond his cell. He knew all his friends at the embassy were still in captivity, and the hostage crisis was still going strong.

He was lost deep in his thoughts when he heard noises that were not the usual sounds but couldn't figure out what it was. There was some sort of commotion, but he didn't know from what part of prison it was coming. It was getting louder and closer, as he stood by the door looking out. He called out for the guard, but there was no answer. He became anxious and soon he heard gun shots and more racket coming his way. His heart was pounding, wondering if the guards were shooting at the prisoners. The noise got closer by the second. It was almost like hundreds of people running all at once and there were more gun shots. He felt like a caged animal.

Shaking the bars to his cell, he demanded to be told what was happening. But found the rest of the prisoners standing by their doors and wondering the same thing.

Suddenly, the doors at the end of the hallway flew open. Inmates came pouring in,

Screaming with joy.

"What the hell is going on?" He asked himself.

He witnessed the prisoners running with key chains in hand and opening doors for the rest of the prisoners to run free.

"Over here! Please this one, too! "Get this one! He shouted at anyone who ran by his cell, begging them to let him free, not even knowing if there was a way out, or if this was false hope.

"Hey man, please open this door."

The man paused for a split second and then quickly went to work opening his cell.

Oliver flew out, running in the same direction as everyone else. He had no clue what was happening. All he knew was that maybe this was his only chance to freedom.

Running as fast as he could, pushing anyone on his way. Soon he reached the big gate to the street and couldn't believe that in less than thirty seconds he would be running as a free man.

Prisoners were running out from every direction. Shots were being fired every now and then, and Oliver just ran among them and never looked back. At the time, nothing mattered to him. All he knew was that he was running toward freedom, something he was deprived of for a very long time. Feeling a new power, he ran like he had never ran before.

Once he reached the main street, he stood for one short moment inspecting the scene. People were gawking at the horrific sight. It didn't take him long to choose a route, and kept on going until he was out of breath. He didn't know where he was going, as long as he was far away from the prison.

He slowed his pace not wanting to get anyone's attention, thinking where to go next. Knowing the only person he could call was Mohamed. All he had to do was to find a phone in a local shop that would allow him to use it. He entered a small grocery store and asked the man behind the counter if he could use his phone. The man looked at him for a moment and without answering , he picked up the phone and sat it on top of the counter. Oliver tried to slow down his emotions so the man wouldn't notice his shaking hands. Seconds later the phone rang on the other end. Not knowing if it was Muhammed, he went ahead and asked.

"Is this Mr. Ferdosi?"

"No, you have the wrong number."

Muhammed had already heard about the prison break and knew Ferdosi was the most popular café in Tehran and where Soraya went often. Without a doubt, it was Oliver letting him know where he was. Oliver had a good mile to walk before reaching his destination and praying Muhammed recognized his voice. It was a risk he had to take in order to reach Muhammed.

Standing in the corner watching the crowed go by, Oliver eyed everyone with great interest and wondering if Muhammed was going to be disguised as someone else.

"Follow me." Is what Oliver heard over his shoulders and stunned him momentarily.

Oliver followed him without hesitation almost in a state of disbelief that he was going to safety.

"Get in the car and lay down. Still looking around making sure they weren't followed.

Neither spoke a word for a while.

"How are you holding up? He was still so excited from the whole event, he couldn't believe he was free and in the car with Muhammed driving through streets of Tehran.

"I am alright. Where are we going"

"Someplace safe, so we can talk. I heard about the break-out from the prison shortly before you called. In a way, I was waiting for your call."

I appreciate your help. I hope you know that."

"I do." Muhammed replied.

They drove for what seemed like a long time to Oliver before he stopped the car.

Shortly after Oliver followed him and they walked into a house and Muhammed quickly closed the door.

"where are we?" Oliver asked nervously.

"A friend's house. Don't worry. It is safe here, for now. Can I get you a drink?"

His mouth was so dry from all the running and the excitement. "Yes, water would be great."

Muhammed gave him a glass of water and let him have a chance to catch his breath.

"Can you talk now? Tell me what happened."

"I still don't know. Suddenly, I heard noises, some gun shots, and then, inmates running in every direction and opening all the cells. It looked to me like half of the inmates in that prison got free tonight. I just ran out and never looked back. I didn't know who else to call but you." If Soraya trust you, so can I."

You did the right thing. I will do everything I can to help you; but first, tell me everything that happened since our last visit."

Oliver was so filled with emotions that momentarily he was unable to focus and then began telling him everything that had taken place, and he finally told him about Soraya and all the details.

"She looked like a child, so thin and frail almost tortured to death; but this was a while ago and I haven't heard anything since." When he was talking about the last time he saw her, Oliver was doing his best to keep his emotions in check. "To be frank I was hoping you would have some news from her."

"All I know is that she is still alive, but not in very good shape. None of my efforts in order to get her out have paid off the last few weeks."

"Now that I am out I can arrange for as much money as you need to get her out of there."

Muhammed shook his head in defeat.

"I don't know if money can buy her freedom. I have been trying for a long time to find a way to get her out of there; but keep running into dead ends."

"If she stays there any longer, the captivity will kill her before they do."

"I know that, but my hands are tied. They have a spy label on her. I have done everything in my power to make them understand that they are wrong and I think they do know that now; but at this point, they will not admit to their mistake."

Oliver could see the same kind of rage on Muhammed's face as he felt in his own heart and wondered if his feeling for Soraya was more than just friendship.

"Were you two good friends?"

He nodded. "I'd like to believe that. She has a way of touching people's lives. I always thought that you two would someday leave this place forever; but it always made me sad to think that if she leaves, I may never see her again. I have seen a side of her that you may never know exists, the side that has no fear. That's how she handled all her missions. Nothing got her excited, in total control, and it almost made you feel the same way when you worked with her. It was as though it was two people."

"Tell me about Nader. What was he like?"

"He was a very different individual with a very weird sense of humor. He was a good man. Soraya loved him so much, and so did I. They became good friends fast. She trusted him because he wasn't after her, and that's how it all began. They enjoyed each other's company, and they trusted each other. In a lot of ways, there were alike. It was safe for both of them to let their hair down and act silly at times, because neither one would ever take advantage of the other. They were pals, good friends. I knew Nader most of his life, and they don't come any better than him. Soraya discovered that quality about him immediately. She understood him and got to know him, and he opened up to her more than anyone else in his life. They had a very special relationship. No one quite understood it except them."

Oliver listening intently, almost jealous of that trust and bond one had with others when it came to matters of life and death. "How did you meet her?"

"I met her through Nader, of course. First, I was struck by her beauty, but soon I realized there were so much more to her. I have great deal of respect for her. I am grateful to have known her."

Oliver could clearly see the pain in his face, talking about her.

"Do you love her?"

"Yes, I do. I don't know when or how it happened, but one day I found myself in love with her. She never wanted that for us and was only interested in you. She never hid that from anyone who got to know her. All I could have with her was friendship; so I cherished that."

They both sat and talked for a while and Mohammed finally decided to discuss the future with him and find out where he stood.

"So tell me, Oliver. Where do you go from here?"

"I don't know. It all depends on Soraya and what happens to her."

"Just so you know, I can get you over the border into Turkey or Pakistan. The question is when do you want to leave?"

"I can't leave until I find out about Soraya."

"That could take longer than you think."

"I know that. I also know that I am asking a lot of you, but we have to find a way for me to stay hidden. They may free her just to get to me."

"Your best shot is to leave and wait for her outside of the country where it's safe. There is nothing you can do for her by staying here. I tried to tell her that eve before they got the hostages."

"let's just wait a couple of weeks and see what happens. If they don't let her go in that time, then I will make a decision."

"You can stay here for now. It's safe and there are not too many nosey neighbors around here; but you have to be careful to not let anyone see you. Keep the drapes closed at all times. Don't answer the phone unless you know it's from me. I will let it ring three times, hang up and dial again. There is food in the fridge and I will get you some clean clothes. Don't call me at home or work. I will be in touch with you every day; and please don't leave this house."

He went on explaining everything Oliver should do before he left.

Oliver listened to this man he hardly knew, who from that moment, had taken his life in his hands, but he trusted him.

"Thank you. I appreciate everything you are doing for me and hope to repay you some day."

"Don't thank me yet. We have a long journey ahead of us; but for now I have to leave. As soon as they do a count and realize you are missing, they will come after me for questioning. I may have to send someone else to check on you; but remember he will have a key."

Oliver sat there for a while, still numb from the whole day's events. He couldn't believe that he was out of prison and, for now, safe. No more interrogations. At the same time his heart ached for Soraya. He couldn't find it in his heart to leave this country to safety, without her, no matter what Mohammed said. For the first time, he understood what Soraya fought so hard for. He wanted nothing more than to get a machine gun and go to the place they held her and shoot anyone who dared to stop him. It wasn't right what happened to these people before and after the revolution. They were fed up with a system that ruled them unfairly and under dictatorship. In his eyes, Soraya was not a terrorist, she was simply a freedom fighter who wanted to see her people free of the chains that kept them tied. After all isn't that what she had done from the time she was a child? Fight to free herself from the village and the blindness that demanded to keep her in the dark.

Nothing had changed for these people. Both system abused them and used them to their own benefits. And his country, and most of the westerners, supported one system, but were not willing to crawl in bed with the other, simply because they didn't have the same kind of agreement. The Ayatollah's didn't like what the west had done to them for centuries. Control their oil, to benefit their own, and wealth, while most\Iranian's lived in poverty. These were the forgotten people who suffered, and no one ever heard their voices. Oliver felt a pain in his heart for Soraya, Mohammed, Nader, and all the ones who had been lied to, used, and in the end, killed for no reason at all.

The next morning, Mohammed walked into his office and found two men waiting for him. He recognized one of them as the one Oliver had almost chocked to death.

"I am sure, by now, you have heard of the prison break last night. Do you have any idea who was behind it?"

Muhammed looked at him without any reaction.

"I had nothing to do with it, if that's what you are implying. Sounds like it was from the American company who's employees were being held or that's what I heard on BBC this morning. They are the ones who claimed responsibility for it.

"We hope not. You see, we now know that Mr. Reed was involved in some kind of espionage. The break in the prison was done by Americans, and we believe it couldn't have been done by anyone else except the U.S. government. We had several Americans in our custody who insisted they were just business people, and they were also freed."

The man saw no change in Mohmmed's face as he spoke.

"Have you heard from our friend, Mr. Reed?"

Mohammed gave him a sarcastic smile.

"Why would I hear from him? I could care less what happens to him. I have no idea what Oliver Reed was up to, and I don't care to know either; however, I do care about Soraya. I know her well. I worked with her and did many missions with her. You shouldn't punish her for what you think Reed did. She helped you to power. Does that not count for anything?"

"Yes, but we believe she later switched and turned on us."

"She would never do anything against her country and her people. I wish somehow you could believe that and let her go."

The man ignored everything Mohammed said.

"We'd like to have your full cooperation, in case you hear from Reed. My people are looking for him everywhere and he won't be able to escape. He is playing with his own life. They have orders to kill him, and I won't rest until he is in our custody again. Sooner or later, it will happen. It is both to your and Soraya's benefit if he turns himself in."

"What he does is out of my control. You are looking for him in the wrong place. As far as I am concerned, he is out of this country by now, if he has an ounce of brain in his

head."

"I somehow have a hard time believing that. We will be in touch."

Muhammed took a deep breath and knew he was going to be watched closely. He had to be very cautious and convince Oliver to leave as soon as possible; it was best for all them. He knew he couldn't keep him in hiding for very long. At some point, a mistake on someone's part would cost all of them their lives. He couldn't take that chance. Too many people were dead already, and he couldn't do it anymore. Oliver had to listen to him and leave the first chance he got. He soon left the office to make arrangements, not even trying to find out if he were being followed. He already knew the answer to that.

Oliver woke up the next day and looked around for a minute, trying to find out where he was. He rubbed his eyes and realized it wasn't a dream. He was out of prison.

It was a miracle, and he knew that; but he somehow had a hard time being thankful. He was still filled with anger for what was happening to Soraya. He couldn't rest until she was back in his arms.

The sound of the phone ringing startled him and woke him up quickly. It rang three times and then stopped. He walked toward the phone; and picked up on the first ring.

"Hi, it's me. I had a visit from them this morning. They are searching for you everywhere. I won't be able to come see you for a couple days. It's not safe at this point, but someone will come over and bring you some things."

"Did they say anything about Soraya?"

Muhammed didn't want to tell him about the threat that they made; it was best that he didn't know.

"Nothing that we don't already know. Listen, you have to sit tight for a couple days until things settle down a little. I will call you, in the meanwhile you should think of nothing but leaving as soon as possible. I can't talk anymore right now, but will call soon."

Standing in the livingroom, he looked around the house for the first time. Not knowing what part of the city it was and was told not to look out the window. It reminded him of his own apartment and wondered what they did to all his belonging not that it mattered to him anymore. But what else did he have to do but sit there and think about what it used to be and the direction his life had taken. The thought of not seeing Soraya maybe ever again filled his eyes with tears. Why was he so blind to what was going on around him? Tears rolled down his face, feeling so alone without her in a country that was now punishing them for their forbidden love.

Mohammed made all the arrangement for Oliver to leave without telling him. He didn't want to talk to him on the phone and looked for an opportunity to visit but knew Oliver was beginning to get impatient; but, at the time, there was nothing he could do to change anything. He knew he was still being watched and followed daily. Another visit from the authorities told him they were getting annoyed, and refused to even discuss Soraya with him. All he knew was that something was about to happen, but didn't know what it was they were covering.

Mohammed's sister lived near the house in which Oliver was staying. He decided to pay her a visit and use the opportunity to see Oliver. When he got to her house he made a point of knocking on the door and having his sister answer the door. It wasn't the first time someone was being kept in that house and she knew the routine. He gave her a kiss on the cheek and entered. If they were watching him, it was obvious that he was there for a casual visit.

He quickly thanked her and took the back stairs to the roof and climbed over a few short tops until he was a few houses down. Walking quickly he went down in the back side of a house and jumped into a back alley. Few more block and he finally entered the house where Oliver was. He quickly opened the door and walked in.

"Hey Oliver. How are you doing? Sorry I haven't been here sooner. Things are pretty tight out there and I am being watched around the clock."

He took a few minutes and gave him as much news as he could about the outside world before filling him in on all the arrangements he had made to get him out of the country. He could see Oliver was not pleased with what he was telling him.

"Hear me out. There is absolutely nothing you can do for her right now. This situation will get all of us killed. And, if by any chance, they let her go, it is just to get to you. It will be impossible for you to even see her. There is no reason for you to be locked up here waiting for something that is uncertain to all of us. I promise you that if they let her out, I will find a way for her to get her out of the country the same way as you. Keep in mind that if they free her it will be the next few day if not sooner."

"What if they let her out and then turn around and take her back?"

"I won't let that happen this time. Once she gets out, I will keep her hidden until it is safe to leave. You have to trust my judgement. There are no other obtions."

"What if they don't let her go?"

"In that case, there is for sure no reason for you to sit here and wait. You might as well get out of the country. Oliver, you are no help to her being locked up here. Believe me, this is what she would want for you."

He knew Mohammed was right, but giving up and leaving gave him an uneasy feeling. It would be as if he gave up on her, and saved his own life. It would make it all so final.

"How soon do you want me to leave?"

Mohammed took a deep breath. "Within one week. Once I get the okay from my sources, you won't have much time. We have to wait until I hear from them, and then it would be a matter of packing up and leaving within a few hours."

Mohammed gave him all the details on how it was going down. It sounded dangerous, but Mohammed assured him it would all work out and he should not worry. The days were long and stressful. Oliver had so many uncertain feelings about leaving. How could he just leave her behind, not knowing if she were dead or alive? Mohammed wasn't able to come to see him for another three days. He was Oliver's only source to the outside world, but he understood how dangerous it was for him to come each time. Each day went by so slow and he had a lot of time to think about the future and the possibility of not having Soraya with whom to share it with. It was all so dark and gloomy, but he knew there weren't any other choices for him to make. He got calls from Mohammed daily, and they discussed what needed to be done before his departure. News of hostages and their situation made him sad also, having so many of them such good friends. Soraya was the only one he never had any news of, and Oliver began losing hope with each passing day. At times, he thought he would choke if he didn't break down crying. So much had changed in such a short time. He didn't know how he would deal with life without Soraya at his side.

Mohammed finally got the news early one morning. Oliver was to leave in two days. The way it worked out, they had more notice than he originally thought. Oliver was glad to have the next couple of days to finalize everything in his mind. All was set to go, he told him and he even got Oliver some cash so he could get to the American embassy once he reached Pakistan.

Oliver wasn't worried about it anymore. Nothing phased him, not after everything that he had gone through. His only fear was not to ever see Soraya again. He sat on the couch and pictured her beautiful face.

"I don't know how to reach you, my love, to look at your beautiful face and tell you that it is all out of my hands and for now I have to go; but I will search for you to the day I die and will never give up on having you back in my arms where you belong.'

# CHAPTER FIFTEEN

They opened the door to her cell and slowly walked over to where she was sitting.

"You have to come with us."

She was so weak, unable to even stand on her own. The guards realized how fragile she was and held her under her arms. They lingered slowly, giving her a chance to walk mostly on her own. It was a long hallway, and they stopped in front of a door. One guard opened it and they helped her inside.

"have a seat here." They left her sitting there.

Moments later two other guards came in with a glass of water in hand.

"Take this pill. It will help you."

She looked at them and reluctantly took the pill and placed it in her mouth, and washed it down with the water they offered her. It didn't make a difference any longer. They helped her up to her feet again and began another walk through the hall. They stopped at yet another door, and to her amazement, this door opened to an outdoor area. She immediately felt the warmth of the sunshine on her face. She looked around and the bright of the day bothered her eyes, but she didn't care; it was sunshine, something she had been deprived of for a very long time. It was clear to her what was about to happen. This was her execution place. This was where it would all end for her, and the thought of it brought a smile to her face. She was glad no one could hurt her anymore.

She could cry of pain if she chose to, no more pretending that it didn't hurt. The game was finally over.

She was so close to freedom, and now she could go and find Oliver and forever be his guardian angel. No one could stop her anymore. A new life would begin for her, and maybe Ali would live her life and bring her dreams to reality. That was when she saw the armed man standing only a few feet away from her. One man walked over to her and tried to put a blindfold over her eyes. Soraya looked him in the eyes.

"Please don't." It was the only thing she had said in weeks. The man dropped it by her feet and walked away.

Looking directly into the eyes of the man who were about to take her life, she had a dead smile on her lips. One tear rolled down from the corner of her eye, one last tear and one final smile. This was the end for her. She never thought it could all end in such a serene moment. There was so much she had done in her short life, and there was no remorse. Soraya was thankful for her time on this earth, and also for knowing the essence of a true love story.

The man aimed.

Her knees began to collapse and not able to hold her, before the man fired.

"Good -bye, my love," she whispered.

She heard the shots, and her fragile body fell to the ground immediately. Life came to a stop for this courageous woman as others witnessed it. Her death brought tears to their eyes and haunted the men who witnessed it forever.

"She was no spy, just a worrier." One guard said angrily.

The same two men who walked her to this place, carried her lifeless body out of the courtyard. They were gentle with her remains and left drops of blood as they took her. She dropped the gray rock where her body laid minutes earlier. One of the soldiers picked it up and held it in his fist. It was a sad day even for her captors. They would never forget this young woman.

What happened? What went wrong? Was it all over for her, or would there be the ones determined to keep her memories and actions alive?

It was an unusually bright day, too bright to look at, way too bright.

Mohammed finished the last minute details before Oliver's departure that night and was, about to leave his office, when he heard a knock on the door. The door opened and a soldier walked in. It didn't take Mohammed long to recognize him; he was one of his sources.

"I have some bad news for you."

He was chocked up as he spoke. Mohammed looked at him and took a seat without a word.

"She is gone. They shot her early this morning. I wanted to be the one to tell you. I volunteered."

He closed his eyes as tears rolled down his face. The soldier then gave him the gray rock. "She dropped this after they shot her. I thought you may want to have it."

There was nothing more to say. He turned around and walked out, leaving Mohammed to mourn. He took an hour behind closed doors before he was able to find enough strength to go and see Oliver and tell him that she had passed. Oliver had no reason to wait any longer, he could leave and never look back. Something inside of Mohamed died that day. So many missions, planning, deceiving and so many lost their lives who he loved. Everything had ended now. He had to pull himself together before seeing Oliver that day.

Oliver took a shower, knowing he wouldn't be taking another one anytime soon and paced the floors waiting for Mohammed. He was late. Looking at the clock and

wondering if anything had gone wrong, feeling uneasy. The sound of the lock turning in the door made his heart skip a beat. Second later, Mohammed appeared, looking as though he's been through hell, but forcing a smile.

"All set to go?"

"I guess so."

Oliver smiled back, but recognized something was wrong.

"Is everything ok?"

Mohammed looked down, not able to look at him, while Oliver took a step closer to him.

"What?"

"She is gone. I am so sorry. I've been trying to find a way to tell you this all day and couldn't find the right words, brother."

"She is gone?" he whispered and slowly walked to the window. He stared out through the small crack of the shades and trying to refuse the news of her death.

The little girl who walked into his life one day, looking for a job, and capturing his heart was gone forever. But she had taken his heart with her. He turned around and saw Mohammed standing there, but there were no words to console him. He knew it only too well.

He swallowed his rage and sadness, knowing how much Mohamed was hurting also.

"I am sorry too. I know how much you cared for her also."

"I wish I were in your shoes, Oliver. I wish I could just leave this place and never look back."

"I can help you, Mohammed. I can get you a visa to come to U.S. if you wish."

"I know that, but no matter how bad things get, this is where I belong. We started this so-called revolution, and I don't feel right leaving it now. What I need to do is to stay behind and finish my mission once and for all. Someday they will realize what she had done and I just hope to be around to see that day."

Oliver wrote down a number and gave it to him.

"call this number if you ever change your mind."

Taking the small piece of paper and putting it in his pocket, he felt the small rock and pulled it out.

"She was holding on to this rock when they killed her. In a way, this belongs to you."

Oliver took it and looked at it. He brought it to his lips and gently kissed it.

"you keep it. She has left me someone that will be a reminder of her every time I looked at him. He is all I need now."

The two men stood looking at each other for a moment, and soon they both opened their arms. There were tears in their eyes. Soraya's love had brought these two men together. She had changed both their lives forever, and they both realized that.

"Good luck with your journey," Mohammed said sadly.

"Good luck with your mission."

They shook hands and looked at each other, knowing they would never see each other again, but that they would forever remember that part of their lives. They would never forget their connection.

Oliver left Tehran that night for the eastern borders. It was a hard and long journey, but just like how Mohammed promised, he found himself on the other side of the border soon.

He left a part of him behind that would never leave his mind or his heart. At times he thought it was all a dream and soon he would open his eyes and it would all be a figment of his imagination. He only wished the dream could have continued with her back in his life. That was how he wanted the dream to end. He never had time to mourn for Soraya. Everything happened so fast once he reached Pakistan. He walked in the

American embassy and told them who he was and was soon recognized by the authorities. The news spread and they told him that his hometown was awaiting his arrival for a big celebration; but he turned it down for the time being. He bought a ticket a few days later and left for Paris. Oliver checked into the same hotel and requested the same room he shared with her. Nothing had changed. Her memory was so alive there. He sat down on a chair looking out. For the first time in weeks, he had the chance to sit alone and think about his life without the woman he loved so desperately. Sitting on the same chair in which she once sat and looking at the same stars as she, he remembered when he woke up one morning and saw her looking out, deep in thoughts. He had wondered what went on in her mind. Now, there he was, sitting on that same chair and looking out, and seeing the same stars. There was no doubt in his mind that she was thinking of the ones she had left behind. That was what he thought when he looked at those stars. He thought

Of the ones he had left behind, the people who were now known throughout the world as the American hostages, his friend Mohammed, and most of all a free spirit named Soraya.

It was so peaceful there. He picked up a pen and began writing.

The next morning he walked through the same park and sat on the bench where he had given her the ring. He stared at the pond in front of him where it had all begun for her. At times, he cried and then laughed. People walked by and saw him talking to himself. Some thought he was crazy, but he didn't care. Reaching in his pocket he took out the letter he had written the night before and began to read.

My dearest Soraya,

"Words can never express how I feel right now. A part of me wants to live forever for you and also for our son Ali. The other part wants me to join you forever, wherever that may be. Life without you will never be the same, my darling. Emptiness and dark nights are what awaits me. I left my heart in your land, and in your honor. All my dreams relinquished with your untimely death. You will forever be on my mind and in my heart. I love you for eternity, as long as I live, and maybe even after I am gone from this earth.

I leave you this letter her on this bench, hoping you will find it through the wind and sounds of human melodies. This is where I wanted to start my life with you, and this is where I will finally say good-bye to you, my love. I am hoping wherever you are, you have found peace and freedom, once and for all, so you can fly around and do whatever our heart desires."

Rest in peace, my love. Rest in peace.

Oliver

He left the letter on the bench and walked away. The wind picked up the letter and took it flying up in the sky. Oliver turned around and looked at the empty bench. The letter and was gone, and for some unknown reason, he believed she was there picking up what was hers. He kept on walking, knowing she had come, and he smiled.

Soraya was a victim of her society, her faith, and her beliefs. There are many more like her who fought both systems in the name of a movement in which they believed in and who lost their lives or who became forever silent.

www.ingramcontent.com/pod-product-compliance
Lightning Source LLC
Chambersburg PA
CBHW031420240626

47154CB00001B/131